D0952359

THE MIDSUMMER CROWN

THE MIDSUMMER CROWN

A Roger the Chapman Mystery

Kate Sedley

This first world edition published 2011
in Great Britain and the USA by
SEVERN HOUSE PUBLISHERS LTD of
9–15 High Street, Sutton, Surrey, England, SM1 1DF.
Trade paperback edition first published
in Great Britain and the USA 2011 by
SEVERN HOUSE PUBLISHERS LTD.

Copyright © 2011 by Kate Sedley.

All rights reserved.
The moral right of the author has been asserted.

British Library Cataloguing in Publication Data

Sedley, Kate.
   The midsummer crown. – (Roger the Chapman mysteries)
   1. Roger the Chapman (Fictitious character)–Fiction.
   2. Peddlers and peddling–England–Fiction. 3. Great
   Britain–History–Edward IV, 1461–1483–Fiction.
   4. Detective and mystery stories.
   I. Title II. Series
   823.9'14-dc22

ISBN-13: 978-0-7278-8019-2 (cased)
ISBN-13: 978-1-84751-342-7 (trade paper)

Except where actual historical events and characters are being
described for the storyline of this novel, all situations in this
publication are fictitious and any resemblance to living persons
is purely coincidental.

All Severn House titles are printed on acid-free paper.

Severn House Publishers support The Forest Stewardship Council [FSC],
the leading international forest certification organisation. All our titles that
are printed on Greenpeace-approved FSC-certified paper carry the FSC logo.

MIX
Paper from
responsible sources
FSC
www.fsc.org FSC® C018575

Typeset by Palimpsest Book Production Ltd.,
Falkirk, Stirlingshire, Scotland.
Printed and bound in Great Britain by
MPG Books Ltd., Bodmin, Cornwall.

ONE

Everything was very hot and very still. Sunlight splashed across the walls of the farmhouse making them tremble in the afternoon heat. The courtyard was an empty, glimmering shell, and the tantalizing smell of early honeysuckle mingled with the more elusive scent of newly scythed grass. May, that most capricious of months, had today decided she would play at being August. Tomorrow, doubtless, she would again be as tearful as Niobe, alternating sunshine and showers with a chilly wind better suited to April weather.

I was five or six miles distant from London which I had quit early that morning, just after sun-up, passing through the New Gate and the fields around Holborn to join the Bristol road. I had left behind me a city fretful and uneasy, searching for the answers to questions, but uncertain exactly what those questions were.

It was just over five weeks since the sudden death of King Edward IV and the accession of his twelve-year-old son as Edward V, provoking a general sense of misgiving at the prospect of another minority reign. More than once recently I had heard Ecclesiastes quoted: 'Woe unto thee, O land, when thy ruler is a child.' Older people remembered, and younger people knew of, the chaos that had prevailed for so many years after Henry VI had been proclaimed king at nine months old; the jockeying for position by his various uncles, the barons' struggle for power. And today, everyone was fully aware of the enmity between Queen Elizabeth – Dowager Queen as she now was – and her vast family of brothers, sisters and first-marriage sons and the rest of the nobility. Particularly keen was the dislike between the Woodvilles and the man who was at present the most important personage in the kingdom after the king: Richard, Duke of Gloucester.

If the duke were to be believed – and most people would choose to believe him rather that the queen and her kin – there had already been one attempt on either his liberty or life at Northampton, during the journey south from his Yorkshire estates. It was there that Richard had arranged to rendezvous with the cavalcade travelling across the country from Ludlow Castle, where the young king had been raised for most of his life as Prince of Wales. It seemed that only the timely intervention of another of the royal Plantagenet cousins, Henry, Duke of Buckingham, had revealed the plot to Richard in time for him to arrest the ringleaders – the queen's brother, Anthony, Earl Rivers, her kinsman, Sir Thomas Vaughan and her younger first-marriage son, Sir Richard Grey – and have all three escorted to separate prisons in the north. The Dukes of Gloucester and Buckingham had then taken charge of the young king, escorting him into his capital, while the Queen Dowager had fled into Westminster sanctuary accompanied by the little Duke of York and her bevy of daughters, where they still remained today.

Five days previously, I had been a witness to that entry into London, being just one of the cheering throng who had greeted the arrival of that blond, blue-eyed child as he rode towards St Paul's and the service of thanksgiving for his safe deliverance. The crowd had been mainly made up of women, all of them ecstatic at the sight of such an angelic countenance, their maternal instincts leaving them almost breathless with the desire to mother the sweet little soul. The men had been nearly as bad, and I had wondered at the time if I were the only person to note the sour expression in the boy's eyes and the bitter twist to his rosebud lips.

But, after all, who could blame him for being bitter? All his life he had been surrounded by members of his mother's family; he was himself entirely a Woodville in looks, with Elizabeth's famous silver-gilt hair. And suddenly, without warning, he had found himself bereft of everyone he trusted most and taken into the custody of two uncles whom he barely knew: his father's youngest brother, Richard, Duke of Gloucester, who had lived mostly away from court in his northern fastnesses, and Henry of Buckingham, the reluctant and resentful husband of his mother's sister, Katherine.

And the king had not been the only disgruntled member of that procession. I had also noted the equally sour face of the Lord Chamberlain, William Hastings, the late king's greatest friend who had expected to find himself the Duke of Gloucester's right-hand man, but who had been pushed into a secondary place by Henry of Buckingham, now basking in his cousin's gratitude and elevated to the position of saviour, confidante and friend which Hastings had assumed he would occupy. The Lord Chamberlain's resentment and anger had not surprised me, but the speed of his reaction had. It was only the following day that, quite by chance, I had stumbled on a conspiracy between him and his former enemies, the Queen Dowager and some of her adherents, with the late king's favourite mistress, now living under Hastings's protection, acting as go-between.

It had, of course, been my duty as a good citizen – and more particularly as a loyal servant of Prince Richard – to report what I had discovered to the duke's Spymaster General and my old friend, Timothy Plummer. But for reasons of my own I had not done so.

It had never been my intention to go to London at such a difficult and transitional time in civic affairs, but fate, in the person of one, Juliette Gerrish, had forced my hand. A month or so ago, while I was away from home, virtuously plying my trade in order to keep my loved ones in food, clothing and those little luxuries they had come to take for granted, the aforesaid Juliette had arrived in Bristol and, for reasons I had not yet fathomed, persuaded my wife that the baby in her arms was also mine. Adela foolishly believed her – although I have to concede that there were grounds for her credulity – and went to stay with distant relatives in the capital, taking Nicholas, her son by her first husband, and Adam, our son, with her. She left Elizabeth, my first-marriage daughter, with her grandmother.

To cut a long story short, I went after her, having an unshakeable alibi for the time I was supposed to have been fathering this bastard child. (I hadn't even been in the country!) Adela realized she had made a fool of herself – of course I failed to mention the fact that there had been a time, long before, when I had allowed Juliette Gerrish to seduce me – and welcomed me with open arms. Unfortunately, the rapid return to Bristol that I had planned for us all was delayed by the fact that her cousins, a large family by the name of Godslove, had been in need of my assistance: an old enemy had been intent on killing them all off, one by one. I had eventually managed to expose the culprit, but in doing so, I had, as previously noted, stumbled across the fact that Lord Chamberlain Hastings was plotting treason against the Duke of Gloucester.

I knew very well that I should have informed Timothy Plummer, of my discovery straight away. But fear of being once again sucked into his and the duke's affairs – which invariably proved life-threatening – and being trapped in London when I wanted to be at home, stayed my hand. Finally, I salved my conscience by writing Timothy a letter which I had arranged to be delivered to him that very day, but not until noon at the earliest, by which hour I hoped to be well clear of London.

As indeed I was, although not as far on as I could have been had I remained on the main Bristol road, where I might easily have got a lift on a cart travelling in my direction. But having, three days ago, sent Adela and the children home ahead of me in the care of our good friend, the Bristol carter, Jack Nym, I had prudently abandoned the highway for the byways, taking the unused tracks and half-hidden paths known only to those who, like myself, use Shanks's mare rather than the four-legged kind. I had no intention of finding myself overtaken by stalwart young men in the Gloucester livery with instructions to hale me straight back to the capital, not just to explain my conduct, but doubtless to be embroiled in further work for Master Plummer. In the past year, I had been first to Scotland and then to France on the duke's business. And I wasn't even officially in his employ. I was a simple, honest – well, perhaps not so simple and not always, I regret to say, entirely honest – pedlar who, twelve years previously, had accidentally stumbled into Richard of Gloucester's life, rendering him a signal service, and never completely left it since.

But enough was enough, and it seemed to me that London at the present moment was a particularly dark and dangerous place to be. I was not going back there if I could possibly help it.

*   *   *

Which was how, on this sunny May afternoon I came to be lying on my back on a wooded ridge, staring down into a secluded dell housing a small daub-and-wattle homestead with a roof thatched with twigs and brushwood. A few scrawny hens scratched for food in the courtyard and a black pig dozed in its sty, overcome by the sudden heat. Of human life there was at present no sign and I presumed the goodwife of the house to be indoors, also keeping cool. The homesteader himself could well be with her or, if he had sheep, out somewhere on the neighbouring hills. (Although this was not good sheep country, as even I could tell. But judging by the size of his other animals and the state of the property in general, the owner was not, in any case, much of a husbandman.)

I stared into the interlacing branches overhead where leaves clustered in pendants of lime and jade-green, stirred gently by the faintest of breezes as it went whispering among the trees. A ladybird, emerging from its hideaway, crawled down my arm like a drop of blood oozing from an unseen wound, and a chorus of insects chattered among the grass on which I sprawled. Silence and sunlight were both golden and a bee droned past my ear, searching for clover. I was where I liked to be best on my own, out of the world, where no one could find me.

Don't mistake me. Anyone who has done me the honour of reading these chronicles thus far will know that I am a devoted family man. We-ell . . . all right! Devoted may be too strong a word, but I love my wife and children. The trouble is, I love my freedom more. It was why, after I left Glastonbury Abbey and my life as a novice there, I became a pedlar. Not the life my mother had intended for me, nor one really suitable for an educated man (and my education at the abbey had been of the best: it was noted for its learning). But the open road, the happy encounters with fellow travellers, the protracted silences of early summer mornings or winter afternoons, the decisions when to eat and when to sleep that were mine alone, above all, the luxury of enjoying my own company undisturbed, these were the things that bolstered my determination never to renounce the calling I had chosen for myself.

Naturally, there was a reverse side to the coin. After weeks, even months, of tramping the roads in all weathers, there was nothing pleasanter than returning to a warm house, a loving wife, adoring children and a dog who regarded me as the hero of his canine dreams. (And if you believe that about the children and the dog, you're more credulous than I gave you credit for being.) For a while at least I enjoyed the domesticity, the comfort of a settled life, the petty trivialities of day-to-day existence, the drinking sessions and meetings with friends in my favourite among Bristol's numerous alehouses, the Green Lattis (alias the New Inn, alias Abingdon's; it has had many names in its time). But in the end, the desire for solitude, for freedom continued to assert itself, making me increasingly short-tempered and restless until my understanding wife, God bless her, handed me my pack and my cudgel and told me to get out from under her feet, to go and earn some money further afield than the local villages and hamlets around the city. (It's different nowadays, of course. Old age and the infirmities of the body make you a prisoner more surely than stone walls or iron bars because there's no reprieve.)

So, as I said, I lay on my back that sunny afternoon in late spring, basking in the unexpected warmth and sunshine, grateful to be on my own again, particularly as the past week or so had been crowded with too much activity and too many people. I congratulated myself that I had successfully eluded Timothy Plummer should he come chasing after me when he had read my letter, and planning the long, slow route home to Bristol. I would go, I decided, through Avebury and see again the weird and ancient hump of Silbury Hill and the remains of the stone circles raised by our Celtic forebears hundreds upon hundreds of years ago. I had only seen them once before, whereas I had visited the great Giant's Dance on Salisbury Plain on more than one occasion.

My belly rumbled and I realized that it must be getting on for four o'clock and supper time. I reckoned it was all of six hours since I had stopped at a wayside cottage to buy bread and cheese and home-made ale which I had swallowed sitting on a stone bench in the cottage garden. I also needed to find shelter for the night, although dusk was still some hours distant. But it was always well to be prepared, to have somewhere in mind unless the night was fine and dry enough to spend it under a hedge or in the lee of a barn. Tonight might well be such a night, but May, as I said at the beginning, is a notoriously fickle month and rain could easily arrive with darkness. Besides, I had a fancy for the comfort of a bed such as I had occupied at the Godsloves' house. I was not yet ready to sleep rough.

I rolled on to my left side, propping myself on one elbow, and looked down again into the farmhouse courtyard. It was still as quiet as the grave, devoid of life, almost eerie in its silence, and I was just wondering if perhaps it really was uninhabited when the door burst open and a child, a young girl, her skirts bunched awkwardly in one hand, went laughing and screaming across the compacted earth towards the gate, scattering the indignant hens as she ran. She was plainly escaping from someone, hell-bent on mischief, and a moment later that someone appeared. A middle-aged woman, the girl's mother I guessed, also laughing and shouting, emerged from the house in pursuit of her errant daughter, catching her just as she was about to make her bid for freedom. For a moment or two, the girl fought her captor, wriggling and squirming. The woman continued to laugh, at the same time giving the child what seemed to be an affectionate scold, holding her gently but firmly in one arm while wagging a finger of her other hand in mock severity. Eventually, tiring of a game she knew she couldn't win, the girl collapsed against the woman's side and allowed herself to be taken back indoors.

As they were about to vanish inside, I got to my feet, stretching my arms above my head to ease the cramp in my shoulders. The woman must have glimpsed the movement out of the corner of one eye for she stopped and stared up at the ridge on which I was standing. I raised a hand in greeting, but she gave no answering wave, merely pushing the girl ahead of her through the open doorway and following herself with all speed. I felt somewhat aggrieved by this unfriendly treatment but decided that there was probably a good reason for it. Perhaps the lass, although she looked young, had an eye for the men; perhaps that was why she had been attempting to escape, to keep a tryst with some youth of the district. In which case, my request for a bed for the night might not be well received, but there was no harm in trying. I therefore shouldered the canvas sack containing the clothes I had taken with me to London, picked up my cudgel and descended the path to the farmhouse gate.

All was now peaceful, so I crossed the courtyard and rapped loudly on the door. Nothing happened, and I had raised my hand to knock again when a snarling sound made me whirl about just in time to see a man and dog appear around the corner of the building. The latter was one of the largest dogs I had ever encountered, with small, malicious eyes and excellent teeth. Heaven alone knew what mixed parentage had gone towards its making. With mounting horror I saw it crouch, ready to spring, and clutched my cudgel horizontally in both hands. My one hope was to thrust it between the animal's jaws as it launched itself at me, and I braced myself for the attack.

It did not come. Instead, there was a thunderous roar of 'Stay!' and the dog, almost in mid-jump, lay down obediently at his master's feet, although his beady eyes never left my face and he slobbered in frustration. The man himself was hardly more prepossessing than the beast; a big fellow both tall and heavily built with a bull neck and powerful thighs. His hair was grizzled and there were wrinkles around the slightly protuberant brown eyes. I judged him to be somewhere in his late fifties.

'What do you want?' His voice was harsh, suspicious.

'I was hoping to beg supper and a bed for the night,' I said, adding, 'I'm an honest pedlar on his way home to Bristol.'

His gaze sharpened. 'A pedlar, are you? Then where's your pack?'

I cursed silently. For the moment I had forgotten that I didn't have my pack with me. There had seemed no reason to take it to London when I had set out in pursuit of Adela, and indeed I had not needed it these past few weeks.

'I – er . . .' I was beginning lamely, but the man gave me no chance to explain.

'Be off with you!' he shouted (or words to that effect), and indicated his inability to control the dog for much longer.

I held up my hands placatingly. 'All right, all right! I'm going,' I said and turned away just as the door of the farmhouse opened yet again and the woman I had seen earlier reappeared.

'What's the trouble?' she asked. 'Lower your voice, John. You're disturbing the child.'

Close to, I could see that she was much younger than the man, perhaps by about as much as twenty years, but she wore a wedding ring and spoke in that proprietary way wives do when taking husbands to task; a way that is easily recognizable but difficult to describe. She was a pleasant enough looking woman with a pair of fine hazel eyes but a nose that was, unfortunately, somewhat too large for her face. Her apron, over a gown of grey homespun, was scrupulously clean, as was her coif, and she had pinned a sprig of greenery to one shoulder with a small, round pewter brooch in a seeming celebration of the newly burgeoning spring.

'I'm afraid it's my fault, mistress,' I interposed before the man could speak. 'I was hoping to find a meal and shelter here for the night, but my request seems to have given offence.'

The woman shot her husband – if I was correct and such he was – a venomous look from beneath lowered lids before she turned a smiling face towards me.

'I'm sorry, master, if my husband was rude, but our daughter is sick and we are both very worried about her.'

'That would be the young girl I saw running across the yard just now, would it?' I enquired caustically. 'She didn't look very ill to me.'

'No,' the woman answered reproachfully, 'that was our younger daughter. She's been set to look after her sister while I do some of the household chores, but she's only thirteen and resents the enforced inactivity. She tries to sneak out every now and then when she thinks I'm not watching. Indeed, sir, our older child is very sick and we don't know what ails her. We wouldn't want a stranger to take anything from her. No doubt if my good man here –' she gave him another searing glance – 'had explained the circumstances, instead of shouting and threatening you with the dog you would have understood immediately.'

'Of course,' I said with a smile, 'and I'm sorry for having bothered you. I'll be on my way at once.' I turned to leave, then turned back. 'I seem to have wandered well off the beaten track. Do you happen to know of anywhere hereabouts where I might find a bed and supper for the night?'

It was the man who answered. 'There's an alehouse about a mile or so along on the opposite side of the ridge,' he offered grudgingly, but then gave me a gap-toothed grin as though to apologize for his former incivility. 'It's not much used except by a few locals. We don't get many strangers this far off the main roads to Bristol and Oxford and the like, but I daresay the landlord could find you food and a place to sleep if you're not too fussy.'

I thanked him and retraced my steps to the top of the ridge. Halfway up the slope, I glanced over my shoulder and saw the couple still arguing or having an altercation of some sort, but by the time I had regained the summit, the courtyard was once again silent and empty, the pair having obviously retreated indoors.

An hour or so later – or so I judged from the position of the sun, still glimmering between the overhanging branches – I was beginning to wonder if the farmer had been deliberately lying concerning the distance involved, or if his notion of a mile was a country one. I had still seen nothing resembling an alehouse; indeed, when I came to think of it I had seen no dwelling of any kind. The track along the crest of the ridge had dwindled to a mere footpath, and on occasions not even that. Underfoot, cuckoo-pint gleamed palely from beds of glossy, opulent leaves, and tattered spikes of purple orchis stood sentinel in a matted carpet of ground ivy and wood sorrel, whose tiny, white-starred flowers were starting to close against the dusk.

I paused in a clearing to rest my back against a tree trunk, listening to a silence broken only by the singing of the birds. Then, from somewhere behind me, I suddenly heard the snapping of a twig as though it had been stepped on by too heavy a foot. For some reason I felt the hairs rise on the nape of my neck, but told my self not to be so foolish. Even if someone else was walking the ridge, there was absolutely no reason

why I should feel threatened. This was a common right of way
used by the local inhabitants. How else would they reach the
alehouse mentioned by the farmer? If I waited for the man
to catch me up, perhaps he would be able to direct me to
the elusive hostelry.

But then I heard the faint whine and snuffle of a dog and
immediately, against all rhyme and reason, felt convinced
that it was the same brute I had met earlier. And if it were?
the more rational half of my mind enquired. Why should the
farmer not be exercising the animal before shutting it up for
the night? But an hour or more distant from the homestead?
No; it didn't make sense.

I glanced hastily about me. The undergrowth had thickened hereabouts and an all-concealing brake of gorse and
brambles offered cover. I scrambled behind it at the cost of
no more than a scratched hand and a rent in my hose which
Adela could easily repair, and crouched down, calling myself
all sorts of an idiot, to wait.

The dog appeared first, followed by the man who paused
in the middle of the clearing and stared around. I raised my
head very slightly and noted a wicked-looking hunting-knife
stuck in his belt, so I hastily hunched down again in my
prickly hideaway and hoped that I had not been seen. But
the movement, stealthy as it was, had attracted the attention
of the dog who came bounding across, snuffling excitedly
at the other side of the brake. I held my breath, certain of
discovery, and found that the hand holding my cudgel was
slimy with sweat.

'Heel!' his master snapped. And then again, more viciously,
'*Heel!*'

I was sure the dog could smell me by the way he whined
and scrabbled at the earth, but to my astonishment, he backed
away and lay down, whimpering. The man kicked him into
silence. This was no friendly master and dog relationship,
just fear on one side and brute force on the other. In some
dim corner of his brain, the dog knew that I was there, just
a few feet from them, but in the long run his mother-wit was
only as great as his master's, and I had no very high opinion
of the homesteader's.

After more agonizing seconds had ticked by, my pursuer

– for I felt sure he was that – suddenly swung on his heel and grunted, 'Back!' He continued, talking more to himself than the dog, 'I'm damned if I'm going any further. He's gone. I said it was a fool's errand at the start. Women! They get these crotchets in their stupid heads. That oaf was no robber.' He stamped one foot, obviously in a rage. 'Got a fucking blister on my big toe now, God damn her!'

He stomped out of the clearing, returning the way he had come. I stayed where I was until all sounds of his departure had ceased and blessed silence once more enfolded me, and until cramp in both my legs forced me to my feet. I extricated myself from my hiding place, not without some difficulty and further damage to my clothes, and resumed my journey with more speed than dignity. Just before sundown, I found the alehouse, clean and welcoming, and breathed a sigh of relief.

TWO

There are people who maintain that the thirty-three Daughters of Albion were the children of that scourge of the Christian Church, the Emperor Diocletian. But that's arrant nonsense, of course. The story is obviously set in the dawn of history, long, long before the rise of the Roman Empire. And surely even legends must have their logic. So I favour the version that the sisters were the offspring of some ancient Grecian king who, when his daughters rose as one woman and slaughtered their husbands, was so appalled by the deed that he was unable to tolerate their presence at his court. But neither could he bring himself to kill his own flesh and blood. Instead, he provisioned a ship with six months' supply of food and water and set the women afloat upon the open sea, at the mercy of wind and tide.

When half a year had passed and the provisions were about to run out, the ship fetched up on the shores of an island rising out of the mists on the edge of the world; an island without a name. Albia, the eldest of the thirty-three sisters therefore decreed that it should be called after her: Albion. The island was peopled only by demons, horned and tailed, with whom the sisters mated to produce a race of giants, and these giants ruled Albion for the next seven hundred years. (The great gorge, just outside Bristol, is said to have been hewn from the rock by two of the giants, two brothers, Vincent and Goram, and you can still see the latter's chair carved into the rock face, rising sheer from the bed of the River Avon to the heights above.)

But then came Brutus – son of Silvius, grandson of Ascanius, great-grandson of Aeneas – and his band of Trojans, landing, so it is said, at Totnes in south Devon. He renamed the island Britain and finally, after many hard-fought battles, overcame the giants, carrying their leaders, Gog and Magog, in chains to the Trojans' new settlement on the banks of the River Thames. There the pair were forced to serve as doorkeepers until they were too old to be of any further use, when they were turned, by magic, into two painted effigies of themselves, and where they can still be seen, one on either side of the Guildhall entrance. Mind you, older folk will tell you that, in reality, these effigies formed a part of the street decorations when King Henry V entered his capital in triumph after the battle of Agincourt. (Of course, older people always like to air their superior knowledge in order to disillusion the young. They gain great enjoyment from it. I know because I do the same myself nowadays.)

So how, you may ask, did I become acquainted with these myths and legends? Well, the history of Brutus and his Trojans is told in Geoffrey of Monmouth's *Historia Britonum* which Brother Hilarion, our Novice Master at Glastonbury, permitted his charges to borrow now and then from the abbey library. But this interesting room also contained other delights in the shape of a locked cupboard whose contents we novices were forbidden even to touch, let alone to read. So, naturally, we were desperate to get our hands on them. Now, I think I have mentioned on more than one occasion in these chronicles my friend and fellow novice, Nicholas Fletcher, whose talent for lock-picking was unrivaled by anyone else whom I have ever met. I don't believe the lock was invented that he was unable to open. It was therefore inevitable that, sooner or later, he would break into the forbidden cupboard and allow the rest of us a glimpse of the banned folios – which is how I first learned of the legend of the Daughters of Albion. This particular tale was lavishly illustrated with graphic depictions of the thirty-three sisters mating with the demons; drawings which made our hair stand on end. (And not just our hair, I can tell you. I believe it was that book, as much as anything else, which made me realize that the celibate life was not for me.) Of course, in the end, Brother Hilarion discovered what we were up to and we were all thoroughly whipped and set penances that seemed to last for an eternity. But it was worth it, for me at least.

These legends came crowding back into my mind one showery morning seated on the lower slopes of Silbury Hill, that strange and eerie mound built thousands of years ago by the Celtic tribes who originally inhabited this island, although for what purpose no one has ever discovered. I have even heard it suggested that it was raised by a race of beings who came from a land beyond the stars. But that is blasphemy. Beyond the stars is Heaven, God's paradise, which we all hope to attain some day.

Ten days had passed since I left London; ten days of steady walking, still keeping to the side roads and woodland tracks, following the path I had mapped out for myself in my head. It brought me, eventually, to Silbury Hill and, later that same day, to Avebury village where I managed to obtain a supper of freshly-baked bread, goat's-milk cheese and some of those little leeks which grow so profusely in spring and are eaten raw. 'Stink-breaths' we called them as children, not without good reason. After my meal, and in order to disperse some of the flatulence it was causing, I walked around the remains of the ancient stone circles which echoed the great Giant's Dance to the south, on Salisbury Plain. The stones at Avebury have worn less well and are mere stumps in many places, but they are spread over a far greater area than those at Stonehenge. As far as I could tell after walking around for an hour or so – and it was not easy to discern anything with certainty – I thought I could make out two smaller henges within a larger one, and reflected how the circle, without beginning and without end, had always been a source of fascination; the serpent biting its tail, the ring that signifies fidelity.

A butterfly hovered and settled near me on one of the stones, the pale transparency of its wings opalescent in the watery sunlight. Then, just as suddenly as it had arrived, it was gone in a shimmer of coruscating amber and pearl. Indeed, so brief had been the time between its appearance and disappearance that, for a moment, I wondered if I had really seen it or if it was simply a figment of my imagination or the incarnation of a visitor from another world . . .

I gave myself a mental shake and also, literally, shook my head in order to clear my mind of such dangerous fancies. But there was something about this tract of country that gave one fantastical thoughts; visions almost. As I have said, the Giant's Dance lay some miles to the south of Avebury, while roughly an equal number of miles to the north, as I knew from my travels among the lower slopes of the Cotswold hills, was Wayland's smithy and the strange white horse, carved into a hillside near Uffington. The latter is thousands of years old and nothing but a series of sweeping curves cut into the chalk beneath the downs, not at all as our artists today would portray the beast and yet, from a distance, instantly recognizable as a horse. Locals secretly worship it as the depiction of an ancient goddess and for century after century, in defiance of the Church's ruling, have kept the outline clear of encroaching grass. As for Wayland the Smith, he belongs to Norse mythology and perhaps came to these shores with the Viking invaders; a magical being who would shoe travellers' horses in return for a silver coin. I once knew a man who had tried it, leaving his offering at the mouth of the long barrow where the smith is said to have his forge, but nothing, he informed me sadly, had happened. When he awoke in the morning, his horse still had the same old shoes. He really wasn't surprised, but disappointed nonetheless.

And as I stood there among the Avebury circles, I could feel the strangeness of the place seeping into my bones, could feel the prickling of the hairs along my arms and was aware of an inability to control my thoughts. Visions of Druids and blood sacrifice filled my mind and I found that I was sweating profusely in spite of the evening chill. For a moment or two I felt unable to move, as if some unseen force had me in its thrall; as though if I fell sideways I might find myself in some fairy world peopled by elves and demons . . .

I fought back, struggling to recite the words of St Patrick's Breastplate. 'I bind unto myself today the strong name of the Trinity, the power of Heaven, the light of the sun, the whiteness of snow, the force of fire, the power of the Resurrection with the Ascension, the power of the coming to the sentence of judgement. I have set around me all these powers against the incantations of false prophets, against all knowledge which blinds the soul of man.' And suddenly I was free of the miasma of weird fears which had beset me, whole and sane once more.

But I decided not to linger amongst the stones but to return to the village to see if I could beg a bed for the night.

I arrived home some eleven days later, three weeks by my reckoning since leaving London. I had deliberately taken my time, even, on one occasion, refusing a lift from a carter who was heading towards Bath with a load of peat, preferring my own company to the trial of making small talk. Besides, the man had only come from Chippenham and would have had no knowledge of what might be going on in the wider world, beyond the boundary between Wiltshire and Somerset. So I made up my mind to let Adela think that her cousins' business had taken longer to solve than was actually the case, and that I had subsequently made all speed back to Bristol.

Fortunately, she was so pleased to see me, and so anxious to be told the outcome of my investigation into the Godsloves' affairs, that her enquiries concerning my journey were perfunctory and easily satisfied. The children, as usual, wanted only to know what I had brought them and were perfectly happy with the sweetmeats and stuffed figs I had managed to buy in Bath market; although Elizabeth did give me a hug and Adam punched me in the belly, which recently had become his chosen method of greeting. All the same, I sensed that everyone was happy to have me at home once more, and reconciled myself to a prolonged period of domesticity, peddling my wares amongst the town's citizens and the surrounding countryside. And, of course, drinking with my friends in the Green Lattis.

'You're back, then,' Jack Nym observed when I sought him out to thank him for his care of Adela and the children during their journey from London to Bristol.

'No, I'm still on my way,' I replied with a grin. 'This is my ghost you're talking to.'

'There's no need for sarcasm,' he grumbled, but waved aside all my attempts to express my gratitude. 'It were business,' he disclaimed. 'You paid me and they weren't 'ny trouble. Leastways, not the humans, but that dog o' yours, he's another matter. He'll chase anything what moves. There weren't a sheep between here and Lunnon what were safe

from him. On and off the cart he was until I came very near
to strangling him with me bare hands.'

'I'm sorry,' I said. 'He usually does what he's told.'

'By you, yes. But you weren't there, were you?' He sniffed.
'So, how did things go in Lunnon then, after we left? Solved
the problem, did you?'

'Yes.' I answered briefly, but I wasn't really interested in
going over events yet again. I had spent my entire first two
evenings at home satisfying Adela's curiosity and was tired
of the subject. Besides, I had questions of my own that
wanted answering. 'Is there anyone here,' I went on, glancing
around the usual throng that packed the ale-room, 'who has
recently returned from London? Within the last two or three
days?'

'What are you up to now?' Jack asked with a leery look,
but being the obliging chap that he was, peered around at
our fellow drinkers until suddenly he nodded and pointed a
bony finger at a man sitting alone in a corner. 'Over there.
Joshua Bullman. A carter like meself, but transports animals
mainly. I know he was taking some sheep up near Lunnon
. . . oh . . . week afore last, maybe.' He raised his voice above
the general hubbub and called, 'Josh! Josh Bullman!' And
when, finally, the man looked our way indicated that the
carter should join us.

I ordered fresh cups of ale all round as Master Bullman
wedged himself alongside me on the bench.

'You've not long returned from London Jack tells me.'

'Yesterday as it happens.' He finished the ale that remained
in his beaker as the pot-boy scurried off to execute my order.
'Left there a week ago. Why d'you want to know?'

'I was there three weeks back myself. I wondered what's
been happening in the meantime.'

Joshua Bullman shrugged his powerful shoulders. 'Nothing
much. They're beginning to put up the street decorations for
the young king's coronation. He – the king that is – is in the
royal apartments in the Tower, but the queen – well her that
was queen – and the rest of the children, they're still in sanctuary at Westminster and refusing to come out.' He shrugged
again. 'That's about all there is to tell.'

'And the Duke of Gloucester?' I queried.

'Governing the country, I suppose.' The man laughed. 'How should I know? I'm only a poor carter.' He added with heavy humour, 'No doubt His Grace would like to consult me, but I'm a busy man. He'll just have to manage without my advice as best he can.'

I forced a smile, but Jack, a more appreciative audience, roared with laughter and continued chuckling to himself long after the time warranted by such a feeble joke. I kicked him hard on the ankle, but it didn't stop him.

I turned back to my informant. 'There hasn't been any . . . any trouble then in the capital?'

Our ale arrived, plonked down in front of us by the harassed pot-boy with more haste than ceremony. He held out a grubby hand for the money before hurrying away in response to a shout from the landlord.

'What do you mean by trouble?' Joshua Bullman asked, his small, round eyes peering at me enquiringly over the rim of his beaker.

'Roger knows something,' Jack said with conviction. 'I never met such a man for gettin' tangled up in things he shouldn't. Go on, then, lad! Tell us what trouble you're expecting.'

'I'm not expecting anything,' I retorted irritably. 'But the Queen Dowager's family aren't any friends of the duke, and there was that plot by the Woodvilles to either arrest or quietly despatch him at Northampton. And if it hadn't been for the Duke of Buckingham it might well have succeeded. And also Sir Edward Woodville has put to sea with half the royal treasure.'

Joshua Bullman nodded. 'Oh ay! I heard men'd been sent to waylay him before he reached Calais. But that's all. What the outcome was, or is, I've no more notion than you.'

'And Lord Chamberlain Hastings?' I persisted. 'He hasn't been stirring things up?'

'Not that I heard. Why should he?'

I hesitated, picking my words carefully. 'Oh . . . I just thought . . . I thought he might resent Buckingham's growing influence with my lord Gloucester. After all, right-hand man to the Protector is the position he'd probably decided upon for himself. Indeed, the position he had every reason to expect would be his. To be usurped in such a fashion could make him discontented, to say the least.'

Again came the shrug. 'I know nothing of that. There were no rumours in any of the alehouses and taverns that I heard tell. London seemed peaceful enough when I left it. Everything going forward for the king's coronation as it should. The place'll be heaving by now, I shouldn't wonder, with folk arriving for the ceremony and the Parliament that's been called. There won't be a decent bed to be had for love nor money. My advice is, if you're thinking of going there, wait until after the crowning and thing's have settled down a bit.'

'Oh, I'm not thinking of returning to London,' I said forcefully. 'That's the last thing on my mind. It's my intention not to stir much beyond the Bristol pale for the next few months.'

Jack was shaken with silent laughter. 'I've heard you say stuff like that before, Roger, my lad, and it never works out that way. You tempt providence, you do! I reckon you'll be back in London inside a month. What'll you wager me?'

'Nothing,' I said angrily. 'Stop talking nonsense! I've told you! Adela and the children need me. I'm staying near home for the rest of the summer.'

He grinned. 'Oh, ah! And I might find a pot o' gold at the end of the rainbow.' He got up. 'I must be off. You coming?'

I shook my head. 'I'll stay a bit longer.'

'Please yourself. Josh?'

'Ay' The other man rose ponderously to his feet and they went out together.

'Don't get drunk,' was Jack's parting shot. 'I reckon you've had enough.'

I stuck two fingers in the air, but the gesture was wasted. He was already out of the door. As it happened, I had no intention of spending my money on more ale: I simply wanted to be alone, to think.

I could have sworn, when I left London three weeks earlier, that trouble was brewing. The general mood of the city was edgy and had been, or so I guessed, ever since the heralds had cried the news of King Edward IV's death on April the ninth. Certainly, by the time I rode in through the Lud Gate on St George's Day, there was a febrile atmosphere that was hard to explain. Even the arrival of the Duke of Gloucester with the young king three days after May Day had done nothing to dispel the general sense of uneasiness. Duke Richard's perhaps over-excessive gratitude to his cousin, Henry of Buckingham, for riding to warn him of the Northampton plot, had put many noses out of joint; and, as I said before, I knew for a fact that Lord Chamberlain Hastings had begun plotting almost at once with his old enemies, the Woodvilles, and some of their adherents to overthrow the Protector.

Nothing, however seemed to have come of it. If Joshua Bullman were telling the truth – and there was no reason whatsoever why he should not be – all was quiet in the capital and plans going ahead for the young king's coronation and the calling of his first parliament. And yet . . . I repeat that no one knew better than I that Duke Richard strongly suspected, even if he were not entirely convinced, that the late king had been his mother's bastard by an archer, named Blaybourne. Had he not sent me to Paris the previous year in an attempt to discover the truth of the matter? Unfortunately, the evidence I had uncovered had been sufficient merely to bolster the duke's suspicions without amounting to proof. And as long as the Dowager Duchess of York refused to confirm or deny the allegation she had once made, on the occasion of the late king's marriage to Dame Elizabeth Woodville, then my lord of Gloucester had no alternative but to accept his elder nephew as his rightful sovereign.

I swallowed the dregs of my ale and rose to my feet. But even as I did so, a memory obtruded itself; a memory of the night I had spent at Reading Abbey on my recent journey to London and the sudden flurried arrival, which I had accidentally witnessed, of Robert Stillington, Bishop of Bath and Wells. My lord had appeared unnecessarily agitated, as he had also done when I saw him just over a week later on his way to the service of thanksgiving, for the king's safe entry into his capital, at St Paul's. A third sighting of him leaving Crosby's Place in Bishop's Gate Street, where the Duke of Gloucester had been temporarily lodging, convinced me that my lord bishop had something on his mind. And this, in turn, had provoked the recollection that Robert Stillington had not only been a close friend of George of Clarence, but had briefly been imprisoned around the time of the duke's execution.

I sat down again, much to the annoyance of a man who had been waiting to take my seat, and stared sightlessly ahead of me, twisting my empty beaker between my hands. Here was certainly food for thought. But then, suddenly, resolutely, I once more stood up and made my way outside, breathing in the balmy evening air. What concern was any of this of mine? I asked myself. The capital and its affairs, its intrigues and secrets, were none of my business. Wild horses wouldn't drag me back there. I was home and that was where I was going to stay.

I had been hawking my wares around the manor of Clifton with some success – enough, at any rate, to make me feel at peace with myself and life in general – and was seated on the edge of the gorge, eating the dinner of bread and cheese with which Adela had provided me. Far below me it was low tide, and the sluggish Avon was a narrow thread between its glistening banks of mud, while on the opposite side of the river, as on my own, the towering cliffs were cloaked in the green of trees and shrubs that clung perilously to the rock face. As I watched, a faint breeze tossed the sun-bronzed leaves into patterns of silver and jade and slate-blue, and the distant hills were awash with light, waves of beaten copper rolling towards some celestial shore. The June day was playing at being high summer to make up for the previous evening's wind and rain.

I thought once more of the giants, Vincent and Goram, whom legend credited with cutting the gorge using only one axe between them. The latter, the lazy, gluttonous brother, had suggested that they raise great mounds of rocks mingled with bones of the huge creatures which stalked the earth at that time. Vincent could supply the rocks, he the bones, and incidentally provide meat for their table. The axe, which Goram also used for hunting, would be tossed from one to the other as needed, preceded by a shout of warning, a system that worked well enough until one day the inevitable happened.

Goram, asleep in his chair, failed to hear his brother, who was digging three miles off, call out. The axe split his skull in two and he died instantly, leaving Vincent, grief-stricken with self-blame, to devote the rest of his life to good works, amongst which were the building of the Giant's Causeway in Ireland, the raising of the ancient stone circle at Stanton Drew and even the single-handed building of the Giant's Dance on Salisbury Plain.

Hercules, my dog, who had accompanied me on my excursion, as he so often did, nudged me with his cold, wet nose, indicating his willingness to finish my bread and cheese for me if I really didn't want it. As he had already demolished a large chunk of meat which Adela had thoughtfully packed for him, I ignored the suggestion and, instead, got to my feet preparatory to starting on the homeward journey.

'You're quite right,' I said, addressing him. 'All this brooding on old legends and fairy stories is doing no good whatsoever. I don't know what's got into me lately.'

Hercules wagged his tail in a disappointed sort of way as I crammed the last of the bread into my mouth, but was soon happy again now that we were on the move, snuffling for rabbits among the long grass. (He had never caught one and never would, but he lived in hope.) I strode out across the downs, that high plateau of grassland that shelters Bristol from the northerly winds, keeping it snug in its marshy bed from the worst of the winter weather. In the past ten years, however, since I had been a resident, the city had begun to spread its tentacles ever further beyond the walls, spawning dozens of little communities on the slopes rising towards Clifton and Westbury, so that it was no longer remarkable to encounter children escaping from harassed mothers or to meet with washing drying on wayside bushes, or even blowing about one's ankles on windy days.

As we descended the first of the three main slopes leading homeward, a young lad, some ten or eleven years old, toppled out of the lower branches of a birch tree, landing almost at my feet with a painful thud. Luckily, his fall was broken by a pile of small, leafy branches which he had hacked off previously and which provided a sort of mattress at the base of the trunk.

He picked himself up, cursing, but before I could commiserate with him, a voice from overhead enquired, 'Are you all right, Harry?'

'Of course I'm all right,' Harry said irritably. 'Don' ask stupid questions.'

Another boy of roughly the same age as the first, swung from a lower bough and dropped to the grass. Together, the pair began to gather up the birch branches which I now noticed were far too young and green to serve as firewood.

'They won't burn,' I remarked. 'Your mothers won't be pleased.'

The second lad regarded me scornfully. 'They bain't fer burning, master.' His tone was derisive.

'Naa,' added the boy called Harry. 'They'm fer makin' midsummer crowns. We'm goin' t' sell 'em in Bristol market.'

Of course! I had forgotten the old pagan custom of making wreaths of tender young birch twigs and crowning some local child king or queen of Midsummer Eve. It was a country practice and not much adhered to in cities and towns where the watchful eye of the Church was constantly upon one.

'Better not let too many people catch you at it, then,' I advised. 'You know how many churches and parish priests there are in Bristol.'

'We'm not fools, you know,' the second boy snorted, his contempt for me increasing. He waved a branch in my face. 'Pretty leaves t' decorate your home, sir? Take some home t' your goody. Look lovely in a pot, they will.'

I laughed. 'The priests aren't fools, either,' I warned, 'so be careful. You don't want to find yourselves in the stocks.'

'My da's a carrier,' Harry said, 'and he says in Lunnon they don't care. The priests turn a blind eye. Do you want a sprig? It don't have t' be a crown.'

I thanked him but refused. Hercules was growing restless, anxious now to be home, an anxiety that communicated itself to me. I said goodbye to the two lads, striding out and soon leaving them trailing in our wake until, glancing over my shoulder, I could see them no longer.

Half an hour later, I was at the Frome Gate and, having exchanged a few words with the gatekeeper, was about to pass under the arch when I saw Elizabeth waiting for me, on the opposite side. My heart lurched. Something was wrong.

'What is it?' I asked, gripping her shoulder and hushing the dog who was barking ecstatically in welcome.

Elizabeth lifted her face to mine.

'That man's here again,' she announced accusingly.

THREE

My heart gave a great lurch and sank into my boots. I had no need to ask whom she meant by 'that man', but nevertheless I stalled for time, staving off the actual moment of acknowledgement.

'What man?'

My daughter made no answer, simply staring at me with the large blue eyes that were so like my own. Indeed, she bore such a strong resemblance to me, fair-haired and big-boned with the promise of height to come, that I could see nothing in her of her small, dark Celtic-looking mother. I had often noticed my former mother-in-law, Margaret Walker, searching for some likeness of feature between Elizabeth and Lillis but failing to find one; and I often reflected that it must be a source of great disappointment to her that her one true grandchild had not a single feature to remind her of her long-dead daughter.

We were joined by my stepson, Nicholas, who arrived from the direction of Small Street closely shadowed by his little half-brother, Adela's and my son, Adam. The latter would be five years old at the end of the month and was now of an age to want his siblings' company, a fact which they resented. From the moment Adela and I had married, six years previously, Elizabeth and Nick had been inseparable and had needed no other companions than each other. Now, a persistent little serpent was invading their Eden.

'That man's here,' Nicholas said, unconsciously echoing his stepsister.

'Man,' Adam repeated, his expression hostile. He added, 'You going 'way again, isn't you?'

'No,' I told him firmly. I turned back to Elizabeth. 'I suppose you mean Master Plummer?'

She nodded, her lips set in a thin, inimical line.

'He says you must go back to London with him,' Nicholas said. 'I heard him telling Mother.'

'Well, this time I'm not going.' I took a deep breath and braced my shoulders for the coming tussle of wills. 'I promise you.'

My daughter looked sceptical. 'You always say that, but you always do. Go, I mean.'

'You shouldn't make promises you can't keep,' my stepson reproved me. He had known me long enough, and had so little recollection of his real father, to accept me as his true parent and to treat me with the easy, affectionate lack of respect that my own children showed towards me. It was my fault, of course, being a sad disciplinarian and leaving correction and punishment to Adela. It was inevitable, I suppose, as half the time I wasn't at home, sometimes for months at a time. The only advantage was that when, on occasions, I did lose my temper, I frightened them all to death.

'Where is Master Plummer?' I asked grimly, and was informed in chorus that he was at Small Street, lounging at ease in our parlour. 'I'll soon put a stop to that,' I announced through gritted teeth.

We proceeded in procession to the house left to me five years previously by Cicely Ford, and the cause of a great deal of resentment and envy on the part of some of my former friends who considered me undeserving of such good fortune. The disapproval of the neighbours was of a different sort as they found it demeaning to have a common pedlar and his family living amongst them. We didn't let it worry us, although at times it could prove uncomfortable.

Adela was in the kitchen, sleeves rolled up, making dumplings to add to the pot of sweet-smelling rabbit stew that was bubbling away over the fire. Without looking up, she began, 'He's—'

'In the parlour,' I finished for her. 'Yes, I know. The children told me.'

She did glance up then, recognizing my tone of voice, and gave a rueful smile. 'You can protest all you like, but he isn't going to take "no" for an answer, Roger,' she warned me. 'I've already pleaded your cause and told him you've promised to stay at home for a while.'

'And what did he say?'

She began transferring the dumplings to the stewpot. 'Nothing. He didn't bother arguing. He just produced a warrant signed by the lord Protector and waved it under my nose.'

'Signed by who?' I was so angry, my wits had gone wool-gathering.

'The Protector.' Then, as I still gaped at her, she added impatiently, 'My lord of Gloucester.'

I dumped my nearly empty pack on the kitchen floor and up-ended the plentiful contents of my purse on to the table. 'I'll go and have a word with Timothy,' I said darkly.

'It won't do any good.' My wife came across and gave me a floury kiss on one cheek. Her tone was resigned. 'I know the signs only too well. You won't prevail. Besides,' she added with a laugh, 'half of you doesn't want to.'

'Nonsense!' I declared stoutly.

She laughed again, but said nothing more.

The children, who had crowded after me into the kitchen, now preceded me into the parlour and faced Timothy Plummer before I had time to prevent them.

'He's not coming with you!' Elizabeth exclaimed shrilly.

'No, he's not,' Nicholas corroborated.

'So go away!' roared Adam. Even as a baby he had possessed a fearsome pair of lungs, and although he had grown quieter with age, he still liked to exercise them on occasions.

The Spymaster General looked dazed, which was un-surprising. In the world which he inhabited, children were respectful and deferential to their elders, answering only when spoken to. He was unprepared for this unprovoked, verbal assault.

I shooed the three of them out of the parlour and closed the door firmly in their wake. A voice from the other side shouted, 'You promised!'

I drew up a stool and sat down opposite Timothy, noting resentfully that he had appropriated my own chair, the one with the carved, acanthus-leaf arms. I held up a hand.

'Before you utter a word, my friend, I want to impress upon you that the children were speaking the truth. I am not returning to London with you, so there is nothing more to be said.'

The spymaster cleared his throat. 'I'm afraid there is, Roger. It's not as simple as that.'

I leant forward, stabbing the air with a finger in order to emphasize my point. 'It's just as simple as that. I repeat, I am not going back to London. There isn't any point. For the saints' sweet sake, man, I told you all I know in that letter I wrote to you, and which I presume you've received. You wouldn't be here, else. I swear to you I have no later information.'

Timothy waved a dismissive hand. 'Oh, it's not about Hastings and his treacherous little band of plotters. We know all about them. We're just giving 'em enough rope to hang themselves before we strike. We have our own spy amongst 'em.'

I was interested in spite of myself. 'The lawyer, Catesby, I presume.'

My companion eyed me sharply. 'What makes you say that?'

I shrugged. 'It was obvious when I overheard Hastings and Catesby talking that the lawyer resented the Lord Chamberlain's treatment of him.'

'And how was that?'

'Like an unpaid servant. So, am I correct? Is Catesby your spy?'

Timothy frowned. 'Seeing you know so much, I suppose I might as well admit it. But not a whisper to anyone, Roger! At least, not yet. Once we arrest the ringleaders it won't matter.'

'Who am I likely to tell? I've already said, I'm not going to London with you.'

Timothy heaved a sigh, the long-suffering one he kept specially for when he considered that I was behaving like a recalcitrant child. He reached into the pouch at his belt and produced an official-looking document which he proceeded, slowly and solemnly to unfold. The parchment crackled. He held it up so that I could see the royal seal at the bottom.

'The lord Protector's signature,' he said, tapping with one fingernail the scrawled 'R. Gloucester' alongside it. 'I was instructed to use this only as a last resort; to persuade you if I could, to appeal to your loyalty, to remind you of the

place you hold in the duke's affections and of his continuing friendship. But I can see that you're in one of your
pig-headed moods, in one of your hard-done-by sulks, so
I'm not going to waste my time and breath on persuasion.
It's no use arguing, Roger. We leave for London tomorrow
morning, on horseback of course, and should reach the
capital by Friday.'

I did some rapid calculations in my head. 'That'll be the
thirteenth,' I said. 'June the thirteenth. Friday the thirteenth.
Oh no! With an augury like that, I'm certainly not going.'

'Well, if you prefer being clapped in chains in Bristol
Castle dungeons, that's up to you,' was the sharp response.

'An empty threat,' I argued uncertainly. 'You wouldn't
do it.'

'I won't have any choice,' Timothy retorted. 'Those are
my orders.'

I hesitated. I knew from past experience that my lord of
Gloucester, kind and loyal friend though he could be, had a
ruthless streak in him when it came to getting his own way.
In this, I supposed, he was no different from any other of
our lords and masters. There was no room for weakness and
sentimentality in a position of command, and even less so
when one was governing a country.

For a second or two, I regarded Timothy with a fulmi-
nating eye, my mind scrambling around like a squirrel in a
cage, trying to find some means of escape. But there was
none. Finally, I shrugged and asked resignedly, 'What's this
all about, then? If it's nothing to do with Hastings and his
conspiracy, why do you want me back in London?'

Timothy relaxed and returned the parchment with its royal
seal to his pouch. 'That's better,' he approved. 'Now you're
talking like a sensible man.'

'Just get on and tell me,' I snapped. 'I don't want any pats
on the head.'

At that moment, there was an interruption as Adela knocked
on the door. 'Supper's ready,' she called.

It was a quiet meal. The children, adept at reading my face,
knew at once from my hangdog expression that if I had not
already reneged on my promise, I was about to do so. They

pointedly ignored me and treated all the visitor's attempts to engage them in conversation with scorn, addressing such remarks as they did make either to one another or to Adela. Adela herself was meticulously polite to her guest, but her tone of voice was frosty. Eventually Timothy felt himself bound to reassure her.

'His Grace will, as always, make sure that neither you nor the children are in want during Roger's absence.' He once again rummaged in his pouch, this time producing a couple of gold coins which he placed on the table before her.

My wife eyed them dispassionately. 'I'd rather have my husband's company,' she said at last, 'as probably the duke well knows.'

'Quite possibly,' Timothy conceded gracefully. 'Unfortunately, my lord has need of Roger's extraordinary talent for unraveling mysteries.'

'Not again!' I groaned. 'Doesn't the duke know someone other than myself who's able to use his brains to good effect in these matters? It's not so difficult. Just follow William of Occam's rule – his Razor as it's known – that the obvious answer is generally the correct one.'

'But not always,' Timothy countered swiftly. 'You're too modest, Roger. No one knows as well as you do that Occam's Razor does not invariably apply. And on those occasions we have need of your especial gift.'

Amusement lit Adela's eyes. 'You're a shrewder man than you look, Master Plummer.' The spymaster looked unsure whether to take this as an insult or a compliment and smiled uncertainly. My wife added sweetly, 'You understand that your fellow men are rarely proof against flattery.'

He made no comment, merely passing his bowl for a second helping of rabbit stew while I recharged his beaker with Adela's home-brewed ale. There was, I reflected, nothing to be gained by being unpleasant to Timothy: he was merely the messenger. Besides, if the truth be told, my ready curiosity had been aroused at the mention of a mystery, and I found myself more than a little eager to hear what he had to say.

As soon as we had finished eating, therefore, he and I retired once more to the parlour, leaving Adela to clear the table and wash the dirty dishes, while the children huddled

together deciding which of their many games to play before
being forced up to bed.

'Well?' I asked once we were again settled, the difference
being that this time I was sitting in my own chair and my
companion in the window embrasure, a little less comfortable than he had been before supper. 'What's happened?
What sort of occurrence that the duke thinks it necessary to
send you all the way to Bristol in order to drag me back to
London against my will?'

'Murder and abduction,' was the succinct answer. Timothy
scrutinized me closely as he waited for my reaction.

'Shit!' I said loudly, which was perhaps not the one he
had been expecting.

'It's serious,' he said. 'The boy who's been taken is a ward
of Francis Lovell. You know who he is, I suppose?'

'Of course I know who he is, you fool. Quite apart from
the fact that he's one of the duke's – the Protector's I suppose
I should say – best friends, and has been ever since they
were boys together in the Earl of Warwick's household, I
was with the army in Scotland last year, in case you've
forgotten. And not as one of the poor bloody foot soldiers,
either. As a member of Albany's entourage – and that was
another perfectly safe and simple little job that nearly cost
me my life, I might remind you – I was within daily sight
and sound of most of the leaders of that expedition, including
Francis Lovell.'

'All right, all right,' Timothy grunted. 'There's no need to
get in your high ropes about it. I'm just telling you it's his
ward who's been snatched, so you can see how serious the
matter is.'

'You call him a boy. How old is he?'

'Thirteen. The same age as the king.'

'Is that significant?'

'In a way, but we'll come to that in a minute. The murdered
man is Gregory Machin, tutor to young Gideon Fitzalan.'

'The boy who has been abducted?'

'Yes. At least, the presumption is that he's been abducted.
He's most certainly disappeared.'

'So—' I was beginning, but Timothy interrupted.

'No, wait! The point about Gregory Machin's murder is

that, although he was stabbed, his body was found in a locked room.'

'Suicide, then?' I asked, startled, but Timothy shook his head.

'No. Whoever killed him was standing behind him. The entrance to the wound was at the back. A quick, sharp jab up under the rib cage into the heart with a narrow, stiletto-type weapon. There was very little blood.'

'And the room was locked? You're certain?'

'Of course I'm fucking certain! Do you think I'm a clod-poll? Or that all the other people who've examined the room are clodpolls, as well? The door had to be broken down. It was bolted on the inside.'

'Where and when did this happen?'

'Baynard's Castle, last Friday.' Timothy eased his lean buttocks against the hard stone of the window seat and eyed my chair longingly before continuing, 'The day previously, the Duchess of Gloucester finally arrived from the north – she's staying at Crosby's Place, by the way, where the duke intends to join her eventually – and as far as I can gather, she brought young Gideon Fitzalan with her at the duke's request. Or at Francis Lovell's request, acting on Prince Richard's orders, whichever you please. The following day, the lad was brought to Baynard's Castle with his tutor and nurse to meet his uncle, Godfrey Fitzalan, who's just arrived in London to attend the coronation, and for the present is a part of the Lovell household.'

'Wait a moment,' I said. 'You're telling me that this boy has a nurse?'

'They all have nurses,' Timothy answered with a shrug. 'We're talking about young noblemen, not the street urchins you know. They're not nursery-maids if that's what you're thinking. I suppose you could call them surrogate mothers, making sure my young gentleman is warmly wrapped up if it's cold, that he takes his medicine – if he has any to take, that is – that he has regular bowel movements and physics him if he hasn't; that, in short, he's healthy and happy. Well, maybe not necessarily happy, but you get the general idea. Although I don't imagine Dame Copley will retain her post for very much longer. You're right in thinking that at thirteen

Master Fitzalan is on the brink of manhood. Indeed, many lads of that age already regard themselves as men. But I gather that young Gideon, the Benjamin of a large family of brothers and of a delicate constitution, has been somewhat mollycoddled from infancy onwards. Certainly, Dame Copley is devoted to him, and the way she's carrying on – the tears, the hysterics – you could be forgiven for thinking the boy is her own son.'

I nodded, staring thoughtfully at the empty hearth and wishing, irrelevantly, for the glow of a good fire. Although only two weeks from Midsummer Eve and Day, the evenings still had a tendency to turn chilly, sunlight rarely penetrating the streets and houses in this overcrowded quarter of Bristol.

Finally, I spoke. 'You hinted just now at some particular reason why this Gideon Fitzalan has been brought to London. At the instigation of my lord Gloucester was what you said. Why?'

It might have been my imagination, but I fancied Timothy suddenly looked slightly uncomfortable. The expression was so fleeting that, afterwards, I wasn't really sure I had seen it.

'He and one or two other boys of the same age are to be the king's companions and attend him at his coronation.'

I raised my eyebrows. 'I should have thought His Highness would have his own retinue, his own companions. He can't have lived all those years at Ludlow without contemporaries to share his lessons and leisure time. He can't have been permanently surrounded by his elders.'

'No, of course not.' There was the slightest of hesitations before Timothy proceeded smoothly, 'But they were the children of Woodville adherents, picked by the Queen Dowager and Lord Rivers.'

'So?'

'They have been dismissed. My lord Gloucester wishes the king to be attended by people he can trust.'

I frowned, suddenly uneasy. 'You mean that poor child has not only had his uncle and half-brother forcibly removed and clapped up in prison, but now his attendants, people he's been familiar with all his life – his playmates, his fellow scholars – are also being replaced?'

Whatever his own feelings in the matter, Timothy would never allow even implied criticism of his beloved master. He brought a hand down hard on the stone of the window seat, then winced with pain. 'You don't understand, Roger! Or, worse still, you're not making the effort to understand. That situation at Northampton posed real danger to the duke's life. Oh, I'm not a fool. I have spies everywhere. I know there are rumours among some sections of the populace that the whole story was a fabrication on my lord Gloucester's part; a lie in order to provide grounds for arresting Rivers and Vaughan and Grey. But take my word for it, that wasn't so. The duke knew that he might be in some danger from the Woodvilles, and of course it's true that he doesn't like them; that he has always held them responsible for Clarence's death. But he was still hoping to work with them for a peaceful accession. I can vouch for it that he wasn't truly suspicious even when we reached the rendezvous at Northampton and discovered that the royal party had moved on to Stony Stratford. I don't believe it occurred to him that Stony Stratford was only a short distance from the Woodville's family home at Grafton Regis. When Earl Rivers rode back with an explanation of why the king had ridden ahead by fourteen miles – and a pretty feeble explanation it was, too – my lord was willing to accept it and invited him to supper. If it hadn't been for Lord Buckingham's arrival to warn him of the truth, our duke could well be dead by now. So he dare not trust Woodville sympathizers of what-ever age around the king.'

I said nothing for a moment or two. It was a story I had heard before, and from Timothy, and had no doubt that it was true. But somehow I doubted that the queen's family would have risked killing so popular a figure as the Duke of Gloucester. They could have incarcerated him at Grafton until such time as the king had been crowned and the Woodvilles had assumed positions of power. But even then, there would almost certainly have been trouble on the duke's release.

I sighed. No; taking everything into consideration, I felt bound to admit that my lord Gloucester's reaction, his instinct for self-preservation, had probably been the right

one. As was his present determination to rid the king of all
those of his attendants appointed by, and therefore loyal to,
the Queen Dowager's family.

'So tell me about this murder and the boy's disappearance,' I said.

'I've told you.'

'Only the barest outline,' I protested indignantly. 'Give me
the details. This Gideon what's-his-name . . .?'

'Fitzalan! Try to pay attention.'

I ignored the rider and proceeded, 'This Gideon Fitzalan,
then, arrives in London in the company of the Duchess of
Gloucester, accompanied by his tutor . . .?'

'Gregory Machin.'

'And his nurse . . .?'

'Rosina Copley.'

'And is taken to Crosby's Place for the night. So I assume
that the Fitzalans are a family loyal to the duke?'

Timothy nodded. 'Completely. Their home, Fitzalan Hall,
is in Yorkshire, near Sheriff Hutton. As I told you, young
Gideon is the youngest of a large family of brothers, and
two years ago, Francis Lovell was granted his wardship,
since when the boy has been living at Minster Lovell, in
Oxfordshire, training for knighthood. The duchess stopped
there on her way south from Middleham to collect him.'

'Also his tutor and nurse.'

'Yes. As I mentioned, the lad is of a delicate constitution.'

'And the following day, he is taken not to the royal apartments in the Tower, but to Baynard's Castle. Why?'

'I wish to God you'd pay attention!' Timothy exclaimed
violently. 'I told you just now that one of his uncles, Godfrey
Fitzalan, is in London to attend the young king's coronation
and is temporarily a member of Francis Lovell's household.'

'Francis Lovell is also at Baynard's Castle?'

'He's there to support the duke. My lord is very sensibly
gathering his closest friends around him.'

'Sweet Virgin!' I said. 'That place must be crammed to
the doors. Has Duchess Cicely arrived yet?'

'Yes. That's why my lord went to stay there. He's a devoted
son, as you know. But now that Duchess Anne is settled at
Crosby's Place, he'll naturally join her.'

'Very well, so tell me some more about this murder in a locked room. Locked from the inside, you say?'

'Bolted,' Timothy amended. 'The top bolt only. There was one lower down but that was still open.'

'You must realize,' I pointed out, 'that murder in a locked room is impossible. You are quite sure about this, aren't you?'

The spymaster took a deep breath, his chest swelled and his eyes threatened to pop out of his head, like a frog's. 'I told you, they had to break the fucking door down to get in there!' he shouted, once again doing damage to his knuckles by pounding the window seat. This time I winced for him, but, for the moment, he seemed oblivious to the pain. That, I reflected with inward satisfaction, would come later.

'You're certain the door wasn't just stuck?' He made a gobbling sound as if he were about to choke and I began to be seriously concerned for his sanity, 'All right! All right!' I murmured soothingly. 'I'll accept your word for it that the door was bolted. At least,' I couldn't resist adding, 'that was how it seemed.' I settled more comfortably in my chair. 'So tell me everything you know,' I invited.

FOUR

This time, I thought he might have a seizure.

'What do you mean?' he demanded furiously. 'I've told you! Young Fitzalan has disappeared – vanished into thin air – and Gregory Machin's been found dead – stabbed – in a locked room. What more do you need to know?'

It was my turn to sigh and look superior. 'I need to know when both were last seen and by whom. Were they sighted together or separately? How long was it before either of them was missed? Had the tutor made any enemies among the other members of Francis Lovell's household? Had he any enemies at Baynard's Castle?'

Timothy jerked forward on the window seat. 'Look!' he exclaimed angrily. 'My brief is to take you back safely to London, not try to reply to a lot of foolish questions to which I've not been told the answers. You can make all these enquiries when you reach the castle. And good luck to you! The place is fairly seething with people, as you surmised, what with Duchess Cicely in residence with all her retinue, my lord of Gloucester with his – until he joins the duchess – and the Lovell entourage, as well. Because, of course, none of the latter can move on until this business is resolved. Moreover,' he added gloomily, 'the city itself is bursting at the seams what with the coronation nearly upon us and a session of Parliament in the offing. And don't say you know, because things have got very much worse in the past four weeks since you so cravenly crept away.'

'I did not creep away,' I retorted, nettled. 'I told you in my letter all that I knew. If we'd met face to face, I couldn't have added anything to it. Besides,' I continued in a burst of honesty, 'I had no desire to get mixed up yet again in the duke's affairs. I'd a bellyful of that last year. I've a life and family of my own, in case His Grace doesn't realize it.'

'Oh, he realizes it, all right. For one thing, you're always moaning on about it.' Timothy grinned nastily. 'It's just that you've made yourself so indispensable to him, that he doesn't trust anyone else to deal with these sort of delicate situations.'

'Crap!' I snorted, but I was flattered all the same, as my companion had known I would be.

'I suppose I can answer one of your questions,' he admitted after a moment's charged silence. 'Did this Gregory Machin have any enemies in Baynard's Castle? The simple reply is, he couldn't possibly have done so. He wasn't there long enough. He and young Gideon and Mistress Copley were only in residence one night before the tragedy happened.'

'Which was when?'

'Sometime late Friday night or Saturday morning as far as I know. As soon as the duke was apprised of it, and as soon as he learned from me that you were no longer in London, I was sent pelting off to this godforsaken city to bring you back again. I rode all the rest of Saturday, all day yesterday and most of today practically without stopping, except to change horses and snatch a few hours' slumber.' His tone was aggrieved. 'I'm exhausted, I can tell you. I'm looking forward to a good night's rest.'

He smiled ingratiatingly, but I hardened my heart. I wasn't prepared to have Elizabeth sleep with Adela and me tonight – if, that was, Adela was in a forgiving mood – so that Timothy could have her bed.

'And I'm sure you won't be disappointed,' I said. 'Bristol has many excellent inns and alehouses.' His face fell, but I went inexorably on: 'However, don't lie on too long in the morning. We must leave by first light if, as I want to do, we ride first to Minster Lovell.'

'M-Minster Lovell?' spluttered Timothy. 'Why in the Virgin's name do you want to ride to Minster Lovell? It's fifty miles or so north-east of here, well out of our way. It will add miles to our journey, and the duke has stipulated that we're in London by Friday at the latest. He wants this business cleared up before the coronation.'

'All the more reason for us to start as early as possible tomorrow,' I pointed out smugly.

'But why do you need to go there at all?'

'You said Gideon Fitzalan had been living in the Lovell household until the Duchess of Gloucester fetched him away to London last . . . Wednesday, was it?'

'Yes. They spent a night on the road, arriving in London on Thursday. But you still haven't said why you want to go there. Nothing happened at Minster Lovell.'

'We don't know that,' I argued. 'Something could have occurred there that might prove to be a useful clue.'

I was unable satisfactorily to explain this very strong urge, even to myself. It had come upon me without prior warning, and I suspected that it could have burgeoned partly from a desire to irritate Timothy and to make things as difficult and complicated for him as possible.

He continued to stare at me for a few seconds longer, his lower lip protruding belligerently, and I thought he was going to refuse. But he finally shrugged and gave way. 'Oh, very well.' Then he added, 'If you think you can stand the extra journey! You know you aren't a good horseman. In fact, if you're honest, you'll admit that you're no more at ease on horseback than if you were astride a cow. So don't start whining and wanting frequent rests. I've told you. We have to be in London by Friday, and today's Monday, so we have some hard riding ahead of us.' He rose reluctantly to his feet. 'I suppose now I'd better go and find lodgings at one of your excellent inns –' he managed to make it sound like a sneer – 'and leave you to your fond farewells. I'll see you at sun-up, then, at the livery stables in Bell Lane. Don't be late.'

I lay beside Adela, listening to her gentle breathing and looking up at the moon-splashed ceiling. We had made love and now she was curled into my side, one arm thrown across my chest, one of my arms holding her close. I loved her very much and wished to take a vow never to deceive her again. But, by this time, I knew myself too well and refused to make God a promise that I was aware I might be unable to keep.

And the thought of God reawakened the uneasiness I had been feeling all evening, ever since I had known the over-riding urge to visit Minster Lovell.

'I know it's You, Lord,' I told Him severely. 'Don't think

You're deceiving me for a single moment. You're interfering in my life again, snatching me away from home and family because there's some villain – or perhaps in this case more than one villain – that You want brought to book. I'm not a fool. I recognize the signs by now.'

There was no response. There never was, but sometimes I could swear that I could hear God laughing; a faint, far off chuckling like the gentle tapping of rain against the windows on a summer's night. I sighed and turned to face Adela, resting my chin on top of her head. I could smell the faint scent of the rose petals she had added to the water when she washed her hair. I wasn't looking forward to going back to London, quite apart from this mystery that had been tossed into my lap. There had been something in the general atmosphere of the city during the recent weeks that I had spent there, but what exactly that something was would be difficult to say. Grief, of course, for the death of a king whom the Londoners had particularly loved; a free and easy, open-hearted, generous ruler; a man who loved life and all its pleasures just as they did; someone who ate, drank and made merry just as they did; who lusted after women just as they did; a monarch of flesh and blood (especially flesh). Now, there was uncertainty, as there always must be with a minor on the throne, a young boy totally unknown to them, who had lived since childhood at Ludlow, on the distant Welsh marches. And who would he favour? His father's one remaining brother, the Duke of Gloucester, who was equally a stranger to the capital and the south of England generally, preferring to live secluded on his northern estates? Or his mother's kinfolk, renowned for their grasping ways and insatiable greed for self-advancement? If I had been forced to wager money on it, I would have backed the Woodvilles without a second's hesitation.

And there were so many stories to the Queen Dowager's discredit and to that of her family. I had probably heard more of these rumours and tales than my fellow commoners because of the strange circumstances which had drawn me, mostly against my will, into the inner circle of the royal family and nobility. I was prepared to accept that some of the indictments might be untrue or exaggerated, but there were a couple of highly disgraceful episodes which were given universal credence.

Shortly after the late king's marriage, Thomas FitzGerald, Earl of Desmond, by all accounts a handsome, brave, cultivated and convivial man, had come from Ireland for the new queen's coronation. Immensely popular at the English court, he had struck up a lasting friendship with the young Duke of Gloucester, but he had proved to be a man too honest for his own good. When, during a hunting trip, King Edward had asked his opinion of the new queen, Desmond had replied that while he admired Elizabeth's beauty and virtue, he considered the king would have done better to make a foreign alliance. Edward accepted the answer in the spirit in which it was made, but the queen and her family were not so easily satisfied. Two years later, when the hated John Tiptoft, Earl of Worcester, (nicknamed the Butcher of England) was appointed Deputy Lieutenant of Ireland, he helped the Woodvilles to their revenge. Not only was Desmond beheaded on a trumped-up charge of treason, but two of his small sons were also cruelly murdered.

The second episode had been the arrest of Sir Thomas Cook, also on a charge of treason, because the Woodville matriarch, Jacquetta of Luxembourg, widow of Henry V's brother, John, Duke of Bedford, had coveted Sir Thomas's tapestries depicting the Siege of Jerusalem. The knight had been thrown into prison and his London house ransacked. When he had been brought before Chief Justice Markham, a man famed for his honesty, the jury had been directed to bring in a verdict of misprision of treason only. The queen's late father, the first Earl Rivers, had succeeded in having Markham driven from office and thrown Cook into the King's Bench prison where he had exacted the enormous fine of eight thousand pounds. Not content with this, his daughter had resurrected from the statute books the archaic and lapsed right of 'queen's gold', by which she had been able to claim one hundred marks for every thousand pounds of the fine. Sir Thomas was ruined.

I had heard these two stories more than once and from more than one person, and four times out of five their truth had been attested to from the personal knowledge of the speaker. Moreover, they had chimed with what I, myself, had seen and heard of the Woodvilles, and I had never felt the least inclination to disbelieve them. They had simply strengthened my loyalty to the Duke of Gloucester. But during the past few weeks, I had been uneasily conscious of a growing fear that Prince Richard's desire for revenge – for Desmond, for Sir Thomas Cook and others like him, above all for Clarence – might be escalating out of proportion, especially when it was coupled with the secret belief that his mother's long-ago admission of Edward's bastardy was really true.

The future seemed suddenly insecure, like looking through a glass darkly. I found myself praying that my lord would do nothing rash or foolish, but without any real conviction that my prayer would be answered. I continued to stare at the ceiling, at the shifting patterns made by the moonlight, until, without my knowing it, I fell deeply and dreamlessly asleep.

My first sight of Minster Lovell was about midday, two days later.

Timothy had not exaggerated the speed of our journey, nor its hardships, with changes of horses that left time for nothing more than a stoup of ale drunk standing up, meals of little more than bread and cheese bolted down at wayside hostelries and, on the Tuesday night, a few hours' sleep snatched at an inn whose only lasting impression on me was the countless number of fleabites which reddened my skin and made me itch for long hours afterwards.

The house lies in a hollow, standing on the banks of the River Windrush, the high ground to the north rising towards Wychwood Forest and to the south towards the main Gloucester to Oxford track. It is built – family and servants' quarters and domestic buildings – four-square around an inner courtyard, and, when I first saw it, was only some thirty-five years old. Consequently, it is a house whose function is simply for living in and makes no pretence at defensibility except for some ornamental machicolations on the south-west tower.

We approached it from the east late on Wednesday, across

a small stone bridge spanning the river, and looked down on walls glowing saffron and honey in the afternoon light, scythed through with long amethyst shadows that inched slowly forward across the courtyard. The indignant yelping of dogs greeted us as we rode under the gateway arch, nodded through by a porter who immediately recognized Timothy's blue and murrey livery and the White Boar crest as belonging to the mighty Duke of Gloucester. He even gave me a curt nod as I was looking more respectable than usual, Timothy having insisted that I wore one of the two decent outfits loaned to me for my journey to Paris the preceding year and, to the spymaster's eternal disgust, subsequently presented to me by the duke as a reward for my services. As a result, I was, much against my will, decked out in brown hose and yellow tunic, a velvet hat sporting a fake jewel on its upturned brim, and with a good camlet cloak strapped to my saddlebag.

'I'm not jaunting about the countryside with you looking like a scarecrow,' Timothy had informed me on Monday night. 'So put on one of those expensive tunics my lord's exchequer could ill-afford to give you, a decent shirt and your best boots and, for once, try to look like a gentleman.'

'Expensive my arse!' had been my ungentlemanly response, but I had complied, nevertheless. I could see no point in making the journey even more uncomfortable than it already promised to be by quarrelling with my companion.

Dogs, three or four greyhounds and a couple of mastiffs, were by now circling us, their barking and growling causing the horses to sidle and shift uneasily, but whereas Timothy was well in command of his mount, I was unsure of my ability to control mine. Fortunately, before this was put to the test, a man strolled out of a nearby doorway and called them to heel.

'They won't hurt you, master,' he said grinning up at me and plainly sensing my fear. 'Gentle as milk, they are.' He had all the countryman's contempt for the townsman, particularly for the popinjay that I appeared to be. Then his eyes swiveled to Timothy and took in the Gloucester livery. At once, his manner changed. He tugged his greying forelock. 'William Blancheflower, sir, kennel man to Sir Francis. What's your pleasure?'

'Where's the steward?' Timothy demanded, dismounting. 'You've heard the news from London, I suppose?'

The man's face was suddenly haggard. 'About poor Tutor Machin and the young master? Yes, sir, we heard yesterday. Young Piers Daubenay was sent by Dame Copley with the dreadful tidings. You don't know if Master Gideon's been found yet, do you, sir?'

Before Timothy could reply, I eased myself stiffly from the saddle and asked. 'Who's Piers Daubenay?'

'I am, sir,' announced a voice behind me, and I swung round to see a smooth-skinned youth of, I reckoned, some sixteen or seventeen summers standing at my elbow. Bright blue eyes and a mop of reddish-brown curls were the most outstanding features of an otherwise unexceptional, but very pleasant face. Normally, I imagined, it was the mirror of a happy and sunny disposition, but at present its owner appeared careworn and a little frightened.

'You're a friend of Master Fitzalan?'

'Not a friend exactly, sir, but I'm of his household. I'm a sort of valet, sir. I look after his clothes and help him dress and cut his hair and file his nails. But he was – I mean is –' the voice trembled slightly – 'a friendly young gentleman, sir, and . . . and we got – get – on together, sir.'

This was suddenly too much for Timothy, who snapped irritably, 'For God's sake, lad, stop calling him "sir"! This is Master Chapman and he's no more up in the world than you are.'

But if this was meant to put me in my place, it had exactly the opposite effect. Young Master Daubenay's eyes grew round as saucers.

'You're not the famous chapman, are you? The one who solves mysteries?' He took my answer for granted and clasped my hand. 'Oh, sir! Someone said my lord of Gloucester had sent for you. Oh, you will find him, sir, won't you? Master Gideon, I mean.'

I dared not glance at Timothy. I could see that even William Blancheflower had shifted his respectful gaze from my companion to myself.

'I'll do my best,' I assured Piers Daubenay and returned the pressure of his hand before gently freeing myself. It was a soft hand which had probably never known hard, manual labour. I added, 'I'd like to talk to you as soon as I can. I need to know everything you're able to tell me about the happenings at Baynard's Castle last Saturday.'

At that moment, much, I think, to Timothy's relief, the steward came hurrying towards us, his wand of office tapping the ground as he approached. Again, one glance at the White Boar emblem was sufficient to secure us his immediate and obsequious attention as he ushered us into the house and handed us over to an equally deferential housekeeper.

'Mistress Blancheflower, these gentlemen are in need of supper and beds for the night. I shall leave them in your capable hands. Masters!' He gave us a little bow. 'I shall look forward to your company at the high table in the servants' hall in an hour's time.' He left us, and I almost expected him to shuffle out backwards as if we were royalty.

Timothy, his self-importance restored, smiled pleasantly at the housekeeper and said, 'Blancheflower? Are you related to Sir Francis's kennel man?'

She chuckled. 'Oh, you've met William, have you, sir? Yes, as you've quite likely guessed, he's my husband, We've been married these dozen years or more. And now, if you'll follow me, I'll show you and the other gentleman to your rooms.'

She bustled ahead of us, a slender, upright woman of about her husband's age, which I judged to be somewhere around forty. In contrast to her body, which tended to be angular, her face was softly rounded, its best feature a pair of large brown eyes fringed with sandy lashes beneath delicately arched eyebrows of roughly similar colour. Normally, I suspected she was a jolly soul, but the news brought from London by young Daubenay had cast a gloom over the entire household. She made no further attempt to engage us in conversation until she had seen us safely installed in two adjacent guest-rooms on the ground floor and assured herself that all was in order. Only then did she allow herself the luxury of an anxious question.

'I suppose you've heard no more about poor young Master Gideon, sirs?'

Timothy shook his head. 'Master Chapman and I are on our way to London now and hope to reach there sometime

Friday morning. We must spend another night on the road after leaving here tomorrow, but it may be that there will be some good news by the time we get there.' He was plainly loath to draw attention to me, but, seeing no help for it, went on: 'Master Chapman has been called in by my lord Protector to try to find the boy and throw some light on the mysterious circumstances of Tutor Machin's death. The reason we're here is because Master Chapman feels it necessary to discover something about his and young Master Fitzalan's life in the days before they left for the capital last week, in company with the Duchess of Gloucester.'

The housekeeper turned to me, looking bewildered. 'There's nothing to tell, sir. There were no unusual happenings, nothing out of the ordinary until the sudden summons for Master Gideon to go to London to wait upon the new young king. That was a surprise, I admit. None of us had foreseen such a request, as indeed why should we? If we'd thought about it at all, we'd assumed that His Highness would have his own attendants, brought with him from Ludlow; boys who'd grown up with him and been his playmates and fellow scholars for most of his life.'

I glanced at Timothy and raised my eyebrows, but he at once gave a discreet shake of his head. There was no need, his look implied, to say more than necessity demanded.

Mistress Blancheflower meantime rattled on, 'He didn't want to go at first. Master Gideon, I mean. And Gregory – Tutor Machin – was even more put out than he was. Carried on something dreadful about the lad falling behind with his lessons and growing up a dunderhead with his noddle stuffed full of nothing but pleasure and fine food and new clothes. That was when I saw the boy's attitude begin to change. He suddenly decided that going to London might not be such a bad thing after all as long as Mother Copley and Piers were allowed to accompany him to attend to his well-being. He wasn't best pleased, though, when he discovered that Gregory was also going with him.'

'And Dame Copley?' I enquired. 'How did she feel about London?'

The housekeeper cocked her head on one side, absent-mindedly jingling the keys at her belt.

'To my surprise, she quite liked the idea. I'd expected her
to complain that Gideon was too delicate – she was always
dosing him with some concoction or another, poor child –
and shouldn't be exposed to the foul London air. But she
didn't. In the end, she was as eager to be off as he was.
Although, she wouldn't have been, of course, if she could
have foreseen what was going to happen almost as soon as
he got there.'

Neither Timothy nor I volunteering any opinion on the
matter, she finally took herself off with a parting instruction
to present ourselves in the servants' hall for supper in about
an hour.

'Anyone will tell you where it is. Meantime, I'll send one
of the girls with hot water for you. You'll no doubt be in
need of a wash after your journey.'

She was as good as her word, a young kitchen-maid
arriving shortly afterwards, staggering under the weight of
a heavy pail full of gently steaming water. A little later,
having washed and changed my yellow tunic for the green
one with silver-gilt buttons, I knocked on Timothy's door
and suggested that we spend the intervening time until supper
by a turn in the fresh air.

'I need to stretch my legs. They feel cramped from all
that riding.'

Minster Lovell proved to be even bigger than I had at first
imagined.. While the bakery, buttery, laundry, pantry and
kitchens were all housed in the east wing, the stables, kennels
and a handsome pigeon loft were located outside the main
gateway. And it was while Timothy and I were idly watching
the birds fly in and out of the loft, happy for five minutes
or so to let our overcharged minds go blank, that young Piers
Daubenay found us.

'I saw you go out of the gate,' he said, 'and I knew you
wanted to speak to me, Master Chapman.'

I bowed to the inevitable. 'Let's sit over here,' I suggested,
moving towards a stone bench set against a wall of the outer
compound. And once we were settled, I commanded, 'Now,
tell me everything you know.'

Piers grimaced. 'It's not very much,' he admitted and then
fell silent.

'You spent one night at Crosby's Place,' I encouraged him, 'before visiting Baynard's Castle?'

'Yes. Master Gideon, Tutor Machin, Dame Copley and myself joined Her Grace of Gloucester's entourage earlier in the week, when she stopped here on her journey south, and we reached London and Crosby's Place late last Thursday. But the day was too advanced for us to do more than tumble into bed wherever we could find one.'

'You didn't share Master Fitzalan's?'

'No. Mind you, he offered. He's a kindly lad. But I don't like sharing beds with people.' Piers gave a mischievous grin. 'They either snore or their feet smell.'

Timothy snorted. 'A bit particular, aren't you, my lad? There aren't many who'd pass up the chance of sleeping in a soft bed instead of making shift in some corner or other.'

The boy grimaced. 'Perhaps not. But I prefer my own company whatever the discomfort. I've told you. I'm like that.'

I broke in impatiently on this exchange.

'So next day, you and the tutor and nurse accompanied your young master to Baynard's Castle so that the boy could meet his uncle – er . . .'

'Godfrey,' Timothy supplied.

Piers nodded agreement. 'And also two of his brothers, Blaise and Bevis, who are in attendance on their uncle.'

'There seem to be a lot of these Fitzalans,' I commented drily.

'Oh, there are. A lot of them,' my younger companion commented happily.

'And did Master Gideon meet his kinsmen?'

'I think so. I wasn't present, of course. Well, he wouldn't need me to say hello to his uncle and brothers, now would he?'

'And then what happened?'

'Sir Francis informed Gideon that he was to join the king in the royal apartments in the Tower the following day, but that we would be spending that night, Friday night, at the castle. But –' he shrugged – 'we never did get to the Tower. The next morning, Tutor Machin was found dead in his room

– his locked room – and Master Gideon had disappeared.'
He was silent for a moment, biting a thumbnail, then added,
'It must be magic. I reckon it was Mother Copley. I've always
said she was a witch.'

FIVE

Timothy glanced up sharply.

'You shouldn't say things like that,' I reprimanded Piers, 'not even in jest. Particularly not in jest. You know very well that witchcraft is a hanging offence. Burning at the stake for a woman.'

The boy looked frightened. 'I – I didn't mean it,' he stammered. In – in Yorkshire, where I come from, "witch" can be a term applied to any old woman.'

I didn't believe him. Neither did Timothy.

'You also mentioned the word "magic",' he pointed out sternly.

'It was a joke,' was the desperate reply.

I turned the conversation. 'Dame Copley is an old woman, then?' Piers hesitated. I surmised that the nurse was most probably somewhere in her late forties or perhaps early fifties. Such an age, though old, would doubtless seem ancient to a lad in the first flush of youth. 'Older than Mistress Blancheflower?' I suggested.

'Maybe, a little,' he admitted, adding defensively, 'Well, *she's* old.'

'Not when you're my age or Master Plummer's.' I saw the spymaster shoot me a look and grinned to myself. I was never quite sure how old Timothy really was. Older than he was prepared to acknowledge was my guess. I went on: 'You say you spent Friday night at Baynard's Castle. Where did you all sleep?'

Piers scratched his curly head. 'I know Tutor Machin had a room of his own. If,' he added derisively, 'you can call it that. Have you ever slept in the castle, masters?'

'I have,' I said feelingly, before Timothy had a chance to explain to this ignoramus that he knew the place like the back of his hand. 'Some of those so-called rooms are smaller than a monk's cell. And, believe me, I know what I'm talking about. I was once a novice at Glastonbury Abbey.' Piers's face lit with interest at this piece of information, so before he could start asking irrelevant questions, I hurried on: 'You're certain, are you, that the tutor had a separate room?'

The boy gave me a withering stare. 'Naturally I'm fucking sure,' he answered, using the swear word coldly and deliberately as though to impress me with his manhood. 'That was where his body was found, Saturday morning – stabbed through the heart and the door bolted on the inside.'

Of course! I could have kicked myself for forgetting such an important fact. I must be more fatigued than I had realized. The long, hard ride yesterday and most of today, with very little sleep in between, had taken its toll,

'Right!' I said briskly, trying to sound like a man in full command of his wits. 'Where did young Fitzalan sleep? With Dame Copley?'

'When we were at home in Yorkshire, he did. But since we came here, to Minster Lovell, he had a chamber of his own. Sir Francis's instructions. He said if Master Gideon was in training for knighthood, he couldn't still be sharing a room with his nurse. Lord! What a squawk she set up! Said Master Gideon wasn't strong, that she'd been entrusted with his welfare by Lady Fitzalan, that if anything happened to him she'd hold Sir Francis personally responsible. In the end, she wore the poor man down until he let her have the adjoining room. But at Baynard's Castle, I don't know where he slept, sir. Not with her, that's for certain, because it was she raised the alarm the following morning when she discovered he was missing.'

'Does anyone know where he spent the night? Or where he had intended to spend the night?'

Piers shook his head. 'I don't know. No one said anything to me. And after Tutor Machin's body was found, the door of his room being locked and all, everything was confusion.' He nodded at Timothy. 'I expect Master Plummer can confirm that, sir, if he was there. Everyone was running about like chickens about to get the chop. Even my lord Gloucester put in an appearance, and someone told me they heard him telling Sir Francis it was a matter of the first urgency that the affair be cleared up, and swiftly. Then, the next day, I was sent down here to inform Sir Francis's people what had happened.

I suppose someone else must have been despatched to Yorkshire to give Sir Pomfret and his lady the terrible news.'

'And I,' Timothy cut in bitterly, 'was sent to Bristol to fetch you. But the lad's right. There was so much panic, so much . . . as he says, so much confusion that I don't think any of us had time to glean any details. I certainly didn't. I left the castle on the Saturday afternoon, by which time, practically nothing was known except that Gregory Machin was dead and the boy missing, unable to be found.'

I turned back to young Master Daubenay. 'And where did you sleep on Friday night? In the common dormitory with the other male servants?'

'No, I did not!' He was indignant. 'Not with that stinking lot! I've explained to you, I don't like sharing a bed with other people. I'd rather put up with a bit of discomfort and find a quiet corner out of other folk's way. There's always somewhere, either in the kitchens or the stables where you can find a little privacy.'

'So you were on your own,' I murmured thoughtfully.

He eyed me uneasily, as though trying to interpret my words. 'I was in the stable loft, if you must know. There were a couple of stable boys up there with me. Does it matter?'

'It might do. Or it might not.' I shrugged. 'I can't say at this stage what is important and what isn't. Anyway –' I got to my feet – 'we'd better be getting into supper.'

Timothy rose with alacrity, but Piers hesitated a moment longer. 'I must return to London,' he said, 'so will you and Master Plummer take me with you tomorrow?'

'We'll have to spend tomorrow night on the road, you know.' I laughed. 'But we won't force you to share a bed with either of us.'

'We'll most likely be forced to share a bed with one another,' Timothy grunted, obviously none too pleased at the prospect. 'People are crowding into London from all quarters of the country at present. We'll be lucky if we're not sleeping under a hedgerow or in a barn somewhere.'

'Oh, not with you in the Protector's livery, surely!' I mocked him. 'Someone will be kicked out to make room for us.'

What he might have said as a rejoinder, I don't know.

What he did say, barely moving his lips, was: 'Stand perfectly still, Chapman.' He himself, I noted, had gone rigid as had Piers, still seated on the bench.

For a fleeting moment I wondered if they were trying to make a fool of me. But then I heard it: a vicious, blood-curdling growl just behind me.

'It's Beelzebub,' the lad whispered, his face chalk-white. 'And he isn't wearing a muzzle.'

I felt the hairs rise on the nape of my neck as an enormous mastiff, a veritable brute of a dog, circled into my line of vision, positioning itself halfway between Timothy and me, its evil, yellow gaze flicking from one to the other of us, saliva dripping from the corners of its mouth. I could smell its breath, stinking of raw meat, from where I was standing. The situation had a strangely familiar feel to it, as though I had experienced something similar, and that very recently – something 'already seen' as the French would say – but I was too paralysed with fear to remember where and when. Timothy stood like a statue.

There was another growl, followed by a snarl and the sudden snapping of jaws. I saw the spymaster close his eyes, evidently anticipating the worst. Piers gave a choking sob. I sent up an incoherent prayer . . .

'Here, Beelzebub, here!' yelled a voice, and the animal turned, fangs bared, ready to deal with this latest enemy. While his attention was thus distracted, I allowed myself to swivel slightly to my right to see who was foolhardy enough to risk the creature's anger. William Blancheflower was a few yards away, holding out an enormous hambone which he waved enticingly from side to side, retreating slowly step by step as he engaged the dog's interest. Then, as Beelzebub sprang forward, he dropped the bone and, as it was seized and savagely shaken, moved swiftly behind the animal, jerked its head back with his left hand and clapped on a muzzle with his right. One of the three kennel-boys, trembling with fright, fastened the straps, jumping quickly out of the way as William grappled with the by now enraged beast and forced it back inside its kennel, slamming and bolting the door after it. He then vented his wrath on his trio of subordinates.

'Which of you cross-eyed little numbskulls left that fucking kennel door open?' he screamed. He strode towards them and knocked their heads together with a ferocity that made me wince. 'You know how dangerous that bastard is! Now, which one was it, eh?'

Of course, they vociferously denied responsibility, each one blaming the other two, with a wide-eyed innocence that made it impossible to tell who was lying and who was not. In the end, the kennel master gave it up, but threatened them all with instant dismissal if such a thing ever happened again.

'My abject apologies, masters,' he said, turning to Timothy, Piers and myself, the three of us fast regaining our courage now that the danger was past.

'Think nothing of it,' Timothy assured him grandly. 'I daresay the dog would have done us no harm.'

'If you believe that, you're a fool,' was the curt reply. 'Forgive me, sir, for speaking so bluntly, but that animal is one of the most dangerous creatures it has ever been my lot to encounter. By rights he should be put down before he does someone a serious mischief, but Sir Francis won't hear of it. Says the place is completely safe from marauders as long as Beelzebub is allowed to roam free at nights.' He laughed at what must have been the look of consternation on our faces. 'Oh, don't worry, masters. He's only allowed to roam around the outer walls. The courtyard gate is shut and locked at sundown. The dog can't get inside. And I'm out to muzzle and return him to his kennel at daybreak. You can sleep sound.'

'Nevertheless, I'm bolting my chamber door tonight,' I remarked quietly to Timothy as we returned to the inner courtyard and so into the house for supper.

He nodded in agreement, but Piers Daubenay, who had the excellent hearing of the young, assured us blithely, 'You've no need to be afraid, you know. Kennel master Blancheflower is quite right when he says Beelzebub can't get in. The gate between the inner courtyard and the outer compound is always securely locked at sunset every night. And there's a small side door, also bolted from within, which William can slip through each morning without any danger that the dog can push past him and come inside.'

'And in the evening?' I was still worried.

'In the evening?' Piers frowned, then smiled. 'Oh, I see what you mean. William gives Beelzebub his meal last thing, and, while the dog's sniffing at his food, he removes his muzzle, then quickly enters by the side door and bolts it top and bottom. You'll be perfectly safe, you know.'

'I never thought otherwise,' Timothy replied with a nonchalance that did him credit. But I guessed that he intended to lock his chamber door just the same.

Supper in the airy servants' hall had been a pleasant meal. The spymaster and I had been given seats of honour, one on either side of the steward, and the food had been worth waiting for: an oyster soup followed by roast mutton in onion sauce, with beef patties and mustard curd as a remove, the whole being rounded off with a pear syllabub garnished with crystallized rose petals. Both ale and wine had been served, and I had partaken liberally of both. I remember wondering at the time if I had been wise to do so.

The conversation, on the high table at least, had been subdued, all of us thinking of the missing Gideon Fitzalan, wondering if he had yet been found and, if not, what could possibly have become of him. This latter consideration had troubled me, perhaps, more than the others, the discovery of his whereabouts having been laid squarely on my reluctant shoulders. I had listened enviously to the careless hum of talk and the occasional shout of laughter from the lower tables and resentfully wondered, not for the first time in the past couple of days, how it was that I found myself mixed up in the Duke of Gloucester's affairs yet again.

Now, lying naked on top of my mattress – for the little guest chamber, though comfortable, was hot and airless and I had pushed the coverings on to the floor – I felt that resentment forming itself into a great knot inside my belly, churning away as though it were a live thing. After a while, however, I realized that it wasn't rancour that was causing my discomfort, but something far more physical. The wine and ale were at war with one another, and a third helping of syllabub was also putting up a fight of its own. As always where food and drink were concerned, my eyes had proved to be too big for my innards. I could feel the sweat pouring off me and knew that I was about to throw up. I slid off the bed, wrapping the discarded sheet around me as I did so, unbolted my door and stepped out into the passageway. Timothy's drunken snores sounded clearly from the room next to mine.

I recalled that the door at that end of the corridor gave on to the courtyard, and was relieved to see that, although locked, the key hung on a nail beside it A second or two later, I was breathing in the cool midsummer night air, and the threat of immediate sickness had receded. Everything was silent except for the hoot of an owl somewhere amongst the trees bordering the estate, their heads nodding above the roofs of the various outbuildings. A three-quarter moon was riding high in the heavens, bringing the shadows moving stealthily out of their corners to creep across the courtyard floor and give everything a somewhat sinister aspect.

Suddenly, out of the corner of one eye, I thought I saw a movement in the blackness near the gateway arch. I turned my head sharply, straining to see more clearly, but all appeared still. And yet so strong had been the impression that I forced myself to walk across the moonlit space of the enclosure, feeling very vulnerable and exposed, until I reached the wedge of all-concealing shadow by the gates themselves. These, I was pleased to note, were firmly closed, the massive crossbar in place and the great top and bottom bolts securely rammed into their sockets.

I turned to the door at the side of the gateway that Piers had mentioned, peering through the gloom to make certain that it, too, was fastened. I was startled to see that it was not: neither bolt had been shot. Not, of course, that there was any real need for anxiety I told myself. It was firmly closed and even Beelzebub's brute strength would be unable to batter down the solid oak of which it was made. All the same, I decided, it would be wise to make sure, and the sooner the better. I had suddenly recollected that I was wearing nothing but a sheet and, even though the night was warm, I was beginning to shiver. In spite of this, I hesitated a moment or two longer, peering around me for some sign of life, but there was none that I could see. All the doors to the outbuildings were firmly shut; not even the baker or his assistant as yet

out of bed to light the ovens for the new day's batch of bread.
The movement I fancied I had seen had been nothing more
than a trick of the light, a flicker of shadow in the gateway's
arched depth. All the same, I decided that someone had been
lax in doing his duty; probably William Blancheflower when
he had returned the previous evening from taking Beelzebub
his supper. So I first reached up and then stooped to fasten
the side-door's bolts, both top and bottom.

Satisfied, I wrapped the sheet more firmly about me and
went back to bed, the rough stones of the courtyard chafing
my bare feet. This time, thoroughly chilled, I picked up the
coverings from the floor and spread them over me. Ten minutes
later, I was sound asleep and remained so until morning.

I was awakened not by the cock crowing nor by the careless clatter of servants as they went about their morning's
work, but by the sound of raised voices just outside my
chamber door.

'Well, where in God's name is she?' the steward – I could
easily recognize his edgy tones – was demanding angrily.
'The kitchen's a shambles with Mistress Cook waiting for
the pantry and buttery to be unlocked, not to mention the
linen press and still room being inaccessible! For heaven's
sake, man! You ought to know where your wife is, surely!'

'I haven't set eyes on her since I got up,' came William
Blancheflower's voice in answer. 'Nell's always up before
me – up with the dawn, as you're well aware, Master Steward
– so I assume she's around somewhere doing her duty.'

'But that's just what she's not doing,' came the impatient
reply. 'I keep telling you! None of the internal doors have
been opened and no one can get on with their work. I suppose
I'll have to fetch the spare set of keys myself, but it's
extremely annoying! When you find her, man, tell her I am
excessively put out.'

'You can tell her so yourself,' was the truculent rejoinder.
'I've the dogs to see to, their feed to make up and Beelzebub
to muzzle and get back in his kennel. Nell must be about
somewhere or other. Though I admit it's not her way to
neglect her duties like this. If I come across her, I'll give her
a flea in her ear.'

The voices subsided and I started to dress. A maid arrived a few minutes later with hot shaving water for both Timothy and myself (I heard her knock at his door and the scrape of his bolts in response) so things in the kitchen were obviously straightening themselves out. By the time I was ready for breakfast – blue hose, clean shirt, yellow tunic – Timothy was waiting for me outside my door, ready to make his way to the servants' hall, where the smell of hot oatcakes suggested that Master Steward had found his spare keys and unlocked all necessary cupboards. But still there seemed to be no sign of the housekeeper.

Piers Daubenay, looking very smart in what I took to be the Fitzalan livery of green and orange, joined us as we were sitting down on one of the benches at the upper table. (The lower trestles were empty, the lesser servants presumably being already about their business.) While we ate, the daylight, seeping in through the unshuttered windows strengthening from purple to opalescent blue, I told my two companions about the apparent disappearance of the housekeeper.

'Keeping a love tryst somewhere,' Timothy sniggered, 'and forgotten the time.'

But young Daubenay was much more disturbed. 'You say it's Mistress Blancheflower who's missing?' he asked, frowning. 'You heard Master Steward and William talking? You're sure about that?'

'As sure as I can be without having looked out of my door,' I answered positively. 'I'm certain I recognized the steward's voice and almost as certain that it was the kennel man with him. Why do you doubt me?'

'No . . . No reason,' Piers stammered. 'It's just so unlike Nell Blancheflower to fail in her duty, that's all.'

I was just trying to work out if this was an answer to my question or not, when I heard – when, indeed, we all heard – someone shouting at the top of his voice and someone else, a young lad by the sound of it, screaming. The noise was coming from the courtyard and Timothy, Piers and I rose as one man, crowding out into the passageway and clustering around the main door where we were immediately joined by Master Steward, the cook, still with a spatula in her hand, and three kitchen maids, all looking suitably alarmed.

William Blancheflower was running towards us, his face a
mask of horror and his jerkin streaked with blood. There was
blood on his hands, as well. Behind him, one of the kennel
lads had stopped to throw up on the cobbles. The steward
started forward to meet them.

'William, what in God's name has happened?'

'Nell!' the kennel man gasped, and leant against the wall
of the house, fighting for breath.

I could see now that he was grasping a hunting knife in
his right hand and that this, too, was covered in blood. For
one awful moment, it flickered through my mind that William
had murdered his wife, but I instantly dismissed it as he
turned his ravaged face towards us.

'What about Mistress Eleanor?' the cook demanded, her
voice trembling and her eyes beginning to reflect the horror
in his.

'Dead!' William croaked. 'Her throat torn out by that
savage dog,' He held up the dripping knife. 'Well, he won't
kill anyone else. I've done what should've been done years
ago, only Master wouldn't hear of it. I've cut his throat an'
all.' He collapsed on to his knees, wracked by noisy sobs.

'But . . . But I don't understand,' the steward protested.
'Whatever would take Mistress Blancheflower outside the
walls during the hours of darkness? Like the rest of us, she
knew how dangerous Beelzebub was.'

At this point, my attention was distracted by a noise behind
me, and I turned just in time to see Timothy catch the slender
form of Piers Daubenay in his arms as the boy crumpled in
a faint. With an exclamation of impatience, the spymaster
pushed his burden at me, saying, 'Here, you hold him, Roger,
while I go and investigate. Master Steward, follow me!'

It was just as well that he didn't require my company. I
was standing as though rooted to the spot, my mind in a
turmoil. I had no doubt at all that I was the unwitting cause
of the housekeeper's death. My eyes had not deceived me
last night. For reasons of her own, Eleanor Blancheflower
had been up and about during the small hours, but when she
had seen me crossing the courtyard to investigate, and being
trapped in the gateway with no place to hide, she had unbolted
and slipped through the side-door, intending to come in again

as soon as the coast was clear. Unfortunately for her, I, in my usual busybody fashion, had repaired what I believed to be a serious omission and thus locked her out – with fatal consequences. Did I own up? Or did I lie low and say nothing? I must speak to Timothy as soon as possible.

Luckily, Piers recovered consciousness in a very short space of time, but his looks were so ghastly that I was reluctant to leave him. The cook had her hands full with two of the kitchen maids in hysterics and the kennel boy clinging to her skirts and shaking from head to foot. Fortunately, he had, for the moment at least, stopped vomiting.

Piers freed himself from my clasp with more speed than gratitude and gave me a push. 'For heaven's sake go and find out what's happening, Master Chapman. See if there's anything to be done. Perhaps things aren't as bad as William thinks.'

There was a desperation in his voice. He knew perfectly well that his hopes could have no foundation. As indeed proved to be the case. One glance at the housekeeper's ravaged throat was enough to tell me that there was no chance of her being alive: the dead mastiff had done his evil work all too thoroughly. I wasn't surprised that the bereaved husband had hacked him to death so savagely.

Timothy was looking green as he watched while two stable-hands loaded the corpse on to a hurriedly improvised litter – a large piece of sacking knotted at each corner – and then, with two others, bore their gruesome burden back to the house.

I gripped Timothy's elbow. 'I must talk to you,' I whispered.

'Not now,' he answered testily. 'Are you and that boy packed and ready to go? It's no good looking at me like that. I'm on the Protector's business and I can't let an unfortunate accident like this delay me. There's no question of foul play that I can see. Although what the woman was doing up and about and outside in the compound before the main gate was unlocked is another matter. However, that's not our business, praise be! Get hold of young Master Daubenay, if he still wants to accompany us, and tell him we're off.'

Fast recovering the tone of his mind, Timothy strode through the gateway and across the courtyard with me following at his heels, wondering what to do for the best. It struck me that William Blancheflower had not as yet mentioned the fact that the side-door had been bolted from within, and guessed that in all the ensuing horror and confusion, he had most probably forgotten the fact. He might remember it later, or he might think himself mistaken, depending on how much grief warped his memory and clouded his judgement. Taking everything into consideration, most notably Timothy's urgent desire to get away, I decided, not for the first time in recent weeks, to say nothing; although it disturbed me a little that I was growing so practised in the art of deception.

I thought at first that Piers Daubenay was going to refuse to go with us, his grief at the housekeeper's death seeming so extreme. But in the end, realizing that there was nothing he could do if he stayed, he decided to accompany us. Besides which, he was anxious to discover if Gideon Fitzalan had been found.

For my own part, I could not help wondering at the intensity of his mourning for Eleanor Blancheflower's death. True, it had been unusually gruesome, but I could not rid myself of the suspicion that there was more to it than that. Had they, at some time, been lovers? She, I judged, was somewhere nearer forty than thirty, while he was a mere stripling. But that meant nothing. I had known many a lad attracted by older women, and many a woman, especially if she were married to an older man, excited by youth and fresh looks. And maybe his earlier remarks about her age had been an attempt to mislead us concerning his true feelings for her. Well, I didn't suppose he would tell me if I asked him. And it was not my place to intrude.

We spent Thursday night at a small hostelry bordering the London road, Piers, true to his boast, refusing to share a bed with Timothy and me, preferring a stable loft where he could cry himself to sleep in private. His eyes were still swollen with weeping when we set off the following morning at cockcrow. Timothy reminded us both that it was Friday the thirteenth and begged us, although not himself superstitious, to be extra careful.

We reached London without mishap, riding through a busy

and overcrowded Westminster and along an even busier Strand, entering by the Lud Gate a little before noon, not having stopped, to my great annoyance, for dinner. I was still sulking about this as we came within sight of St Paul's. But suddenly all other considerations were put to flight. People were running through the streets waving their arms and shouting, 'Treason! Treason at the Tower! High treason!'

SIX

Timothy, Piers and I reined in our horses and pulled them into the side of the road. I looked questioningly at the spymaster.

He shook his head, indicating that he was as much at a loss as I was. Then he leant from the saddle and grabbed a blue-capped apprentice who was shouting as loudly as anyone, 'Treason! High treason!'

'What's happening?' he demanded. 'What treason?'

The lad regarded him vacantly for a moment or two before shrugging his narrow shoulders.

'Lord, I don't know, master. But everyone's saying it. I just joined in.'

Timothy pushed him away with a snort of disgust and raised himself in his stirrups, peering over the heads of the people around us, obviously hoping for the sight of someone he knew. The little crowd had greatly increased even in the short time that we had been there, shop-owners and house-holders pouring out of doors, attracted by the rumpus and anxious to discover what was going on. Everyone milled around aimlessly, begging enlightenment of his neighbours, but getting no satisfaction and growing more frustrated and alarmed by the second.

Suddenly, Timothy's gaze sharpened and homed in on a small, sandy-haired man struggling through the crowd from the direction of Cheapside. He was wearing the Duke of Gloucester's livery.

'Simon! Simon Finglass!' Timothy bellowed in a stentorian voice which I hardly recognized as his; indeed, until that moment, I would have thought him incapable of making so much noise.

In spite of the hubbub, it was loud enough to attract the other man's attention. He lifted his head and stood on tiptoe, trying to locate the source of the summons. After a while he spotted Timothy's frantically waving arm and fought his way through the mob to our side. A little breathlessly he gripped the horse's reins to steady himself and looked up enquiringly into Timothy's face.

'What's happening?' the spymaster reiterated. 'Treason at the Tower? What are these fools talking about?'

'You're back, are you?' The sandy head nodded approval. 'Good thing. If half what's being rumoured is true, I guess you'll be needed at the Tower. Where've you been?'

'On the duke's business,' Timothy snapped, 'and none of yours! Just answer my question, will you? What is this all about?'

Simon Finglass shrugged. 'Don't know for certain,' he admitted. 'Only know what they're saying.'

He paused, sucking his teeth. Timothy turned purple in the face and, to save him an apoplexy, I leant forward, gently stroking my restless mount between the ears, and asked, 'What is it "they" are saying?'

The cacophony around us was now deafening and, once again, as just a few weeks previously, I sensed the near-hysteria of the crowd, a product of that febrile atmosphere which had lain like a pall over the city ever since King Edward died. I dismounted, indicating that Timothy and Piers should do the same, and led the way into the comparative peace and quiet of St Paul's churchyard. Here, at least, we could hear ourselves speak.

Timothy addressed himself to his acquaintance. 'Simon, what is going on? Tell us, man, for God's sake!'

The man screwed up his small russet apple of a face in an apologetic grin. 'I don't know for certain. I was at Baynard's Castle collecting some of the duke's gear he'd left behind when he moved to Crosby's Place. I knew there was an important meeting at the Tower this morning – the duke, the Lord Chamberlain, the Archbishop of York and some others – but what it was about I knew no more than the next poor sod who ain't privy to the councils of the high and mighty.'

'For Christ's sweet sake, get on with it!' Timothy groaned.

Master Finglass looked hurt. 'I am! I am! Well, I'm minding my own business down in the main courtyard, packing the duke's stuff into a couple of saddlebags, when two of our fellows come bursting in from the Thames Street gate, looking like they've seen a bloody ghost. The Archbishop, the Bishop of Ely, and some lord or other have all been arrested on a charge of high treason. And also . . .' He paused momentarily for dramatic effect before continuing, 'And also arrested is the Lord Chamberlain. Same charge! Treason!'

'Ah! At last!' Timothy let out a grunt of satisfaction and nodded at me. 'We've seen that coming.'

Simon Finglass gripped the spymaster's wrist. 'Wait! That's not all they're saying. They're saying that Lord Hastings is dead. That he was rushed to Tower Green and beheaded there and then by one of the executioners who'd been brought to the Tower, special-like, for that purpose. That the chamberlain was barely given time to be shrived and that they didn't even use the proper block. They used a piece of timber that was lying around after some recent building repairs.'

There was dreadful silence. Timothy, Piers and I stood as though struck dumb. I was conscious of the drumming of my heart, of a deep sense of foreboding and of the high, shrill singing of a bird in a tree behind me. Finally, after what seemed an age, Timothy cleared his throat and at the second attempt said, 'His Grace of Gloucester wouldn't do that. He wouldn't condemn a man to death without trial. It's illegal. It's against the laws of Magna Carta. Even the king himself couldn't do it, and my lord is only Protector.' He suddenly gained in confidence and his voice became stronger. 'There must be some mistake. You must have misheard, Simon.'

The other shook his head. 'I didn't mishear nothing. Nor did anybody else. 'Cause we were all saying the same as you. As how it was against the law. As how the duke, who's a stickler for doing things right, wouldn't go against his conscience by executing a man without trial.'

Timothy chewed his lower lip. 'What do you think, Roger?'

It demonstrated the extent of his perturbation that he should ask for my opinion. In normal circumstances, his own was all that counted with him.

I hesitated before answering. The truth was that I didn't really know what to think. On one hand, the man whose birthday I shared, whom I had known and deeply admired for the past twelve years, who was renowned everywhere for his sense of fair play, would surely never have permitted, let alone ordered, such a travesty of justice; but on the other hand, ever since the previous year's expedition to Scotland, I had been conscious of a growing ruthlessness beneath the cultured and civilized front which the duke presented to the world.

He had cause, heaven knew, for being embittered. Richard of Gloucester had a strong, puritanical streak in his nature and he had been forced to stand by and watch his adored elder brother, the magnificent, golden warrior of his youth, transformed into a man devoted to hedonism, his health slowly but surely destroyed by the pleasures of the flesh. The chief companions of the king's overeating, drinking and whoring had been his best friend, William Hastings, and his two stepsons and their uncles, members of the queen's hated Woodville family, all of whom the duke held responsible for the death of his other brother, George of Clarence. Yet even so . . .

'There must be some mistake,' I replied at last. 'A rumour that's been taken as fact.'

Timothy grunted, presumably in agreement, but said nothing, an omission that made me uneasy. I was about to press him for his own thoughts on the matter when there was a sudden shifting of the crowd as people began invading the churchyard, stampeding towards St Paul's Cross in the north-east corner.

'There's a herald coming,' Simon Finglass announced, and made off after the rest.

Timothy, Piers and I remounted, giving us a distinct advantage over our fellows, and simply turned our horses to face the right direction. Sure enough, a herald in the royal livery appeared, preceded by a trumpeter whose piercing blasts on his instrument commanded not just silence from the crowd, but threatened to waken the dead all around us and raise them from their graves. But they had the necessary effect. The people fell silent.

'Oyez! Oyez! Oyez!' The herald eyed us all severely to make certain that he had our attention before proceeding to unscroll and read from the parchment in his hand. It seemed that during a meeting of the Privy Council that morning, the Duke of Gloucester had suddenly turned on Lord Hastings, Lord Stanley – Henry Tudor's stepfather – the Archbishop of York and the Bishop of Ely and accused them of plotting his own and the Duke of Buckingham's deaths with the intention of then taking control of the king. The plot also involved the queen dowager, at present in sanctuary, with Mistress Shore, the late king's mistress, acting as go-between. All the accused – Queen Elizabeth, of course, excepted – were now in custody. There was no need for alarm. Everything was under control. People were to return to work and proceed with their daily tasks.

And that was all. The herald and trumpeter departed. Timothy heaved a sigh of relief and turned to me.

'No mention of any out-of-hand executions,' he said. 'There will be some, no doubt of that. But all legal and above board.'

I nodded, feeling as though a great weight had been lifted from my mind. If Hastings and the other conspirators got what was coming to them that was only a fitting punishment for their crime. But it would be by due process of law and that was what mattered.

'What do we do now?' I asked as the crowds, somewhat disappointed at this tame ending to all the excitement, began to disperse.

'I must get to the Tower as fast as possible. I may be needed.' Timothy's little air of self-importance made me struggle to suppress a grin. 'In any case,' he went on, 'I must report your safe arrival to the duke. You and Piers had better go straight to Baynard's Castle and see if there's any news concerning Master Fitzalan. If not, Roger, you'd best begin your enquiries right away.'

I said nothing. He could take my silence for acquiescence if he liked. But I intended to procure myself some refreshment first. Like the rest of my countrymen, I believed in a sufficient amount of rest and recreation.

The main courtyard of the castle was thronged with guests and servants alike, all avidly discussing the reports from the Tower. I guessed that Gideon Fitzalan's disappearance and the murder of Gregory Machin had been superseded as the general topic of concern and conversation.

'Follow me,' Piers said briskly as he dismounted, at the same time signalling to one of the grooms to come and take our horses. 'I'll take you to Dame Copley. She's bound to be in her room. Or – wait a minute! I can see Godfrey Fitzalan over there. You know, Gideon's uncle.'

I shot out a hand to detain him, my mind still running on food, but I was a second too late. Piers was already plunging through the knots of people towards a tall man with a shock of curly brown hair and a pair of very light bluish-grey eyes that contrasted oddly with his very dark, almost black eyebrows.

'Master Fitzalan,' he cried, grabbing the man by his sleeve. 'It's me. Piers Daubenay, Master Gideon's servant. You know! I was sent to Minster Lovell to apprise them of the news—'

The man held up an imperious hand, checking Piers in full flow. 'Young man, you have made a mistake. Excusable, I'll allow. You probably think I'm Godfrey. Well, I'm not. I'm his twin, Lewis. I've ridden post-haste from Yorkshire at my brother Pomfret's request, to find out what's going on. Pom's having to travel more slowly to accommodate my sister-in-law, who's been suffering from fits of hysterics ever since she heard the news of her precious son's disappearance. Poor soul,' he added perfunctorily, leaving me with the distinct impression that there was little love lost between him and Gideon's mother. He added vaguely, 'If you want Godfrey, he's probably indoors somewhere or other. Maybe with Sir Francis.' And he turned back to continue his conversation with another man.

'How many of these damned Fitzalans are there?' I demanded peevishly and not for the first time, as we fought our way to the main door, where two of Duchess Cicely's guards, wearing the badge of York, challenged our right of entrance. But this was because they were bored and wanted something to do. A second glance at Piers's green and orange Fitzalan livery and they let us through.

'I told you,' Piers flung over his shoulder, 'there are a lot of them. I'd forgotten that Master Godfrey has a twin brother.'

'Stop!' I ordered, leaning against the wall of the passage we were traversing and refusing point-blank to go any further. Piers paused, staring at me in surprise. 'I'm hungry and tired,' I explained. 'Before we go looking for anyone else, I intend visiting the kitchen to see what I can scrounge in the way of food. Then I'm going in search of the steward to find out where I'm to be housed.'

'But we need to know if Gideon is still missing,' my companion protested indignantly.

'No, we don't,' I sighed. 'Use your head, boy. If he had been found, his uncle would have told us so, don't you think?'

'I suppose so,' was the reluctant agreement. 'Do you know where the kitchens are?'

'I do,' I answered simply, and led the way to the vast servants' hall which adjoined the furnace-like hell, where most of the cooks worked stark naked because of the heat. 'I knew this place when it was presided over by one of the biggest men you've ever seen. His nickname was Goliath. He's dead now'

If Piers was impressed by my knowledge, he hid it admirably, lounging at one of the tables, a petulant expression on his handsome face, while I ventured into the kitchen in the hope of encountering a friendly face. I was fortunate and, ten minutes later, Piers and I were each tucking into a plate of broken meats left over from the sausages and pies that had been served at dinner. I was pleasantly surprised at their quality, the dowager Duchess of York being a notoriously parsimonious hostess. Even my companion, impatient as he was to get on and find Dame Copley or Godfrey Fitzalan, permitted himself to relax and enjoy his meal.

'I was hungrier than I thought,' he acknowledged.

'Tell me,' I said, emptying my mouth of a wedge of beef pie and taking a draught of ale, 'is Gideon's father, Sir Pomfret, the eldest of these Fitzalan brothers?'

Piers shook his head. 'I think he's the youngest.'

'So he's been knighted?'

'Yes. After Tewkesbury, along with Sir Walter Tyrell and some others.'

I knew Sir Walter, as I did so many more, from the Scottish campaign of the previous year; a big, blond, self-confident man, son of a Suffolk gentleman and one of Duke Richard's most loyal and devoted servants, the holder of various important offices within the duke's gift. But Sir Pomfret Fitzalan held no place in my memory so I guessed he had taken no part in the brief war which had seen Berwick recaptured from the Scots to become an English town once again.

'So he fought at Tewkesbury, did he? Obviously on the winning side.'

My feeble little joke fell flat, Piers firing up in instant defence of the family he served.

'You don't suppose any Fitzalan would fight for the Lancastrians, do you? Why, man, Henry of Lancaster was a usurper, for all he and his son and grandson called themselves kings. The true heirs of Richard II were the House of York . . .'

'All right, lad! All right! I was being funny. I hold no brief for old Gaunt's descendants any more than you do. Look, finish your ale and we'll go to find this Rosina Copley, and anyone else who can give us information about the tutor's murder and young Gideon's disappearance. Drink up! Come to think of it, we'd better discover Sir Francis's whereabouts, too, and let him know about the happenings at Minster Lovell. I'm talking about Eleanor Blancheflower's death. And Beelzebub's.'

And having a somewhat jaundiced view of how a nobleman's mind works on these occasions, I was willing to wager Sir Francis would be more upset about the dog.

Ten minutes or so later, having negotiated some of the warren of narrow corridors and twisting staircases that comprised the better part of Baynard's Castle, I found myself yet again on the ground floor. (One was forever going upstairs only to descend once more.) Piers and I were standing outside a room at the end of a short passage whose open door gave on to the castle's water-stairs and landing-stage. The noise of the river traffic and the shouts of the boatmen, as they plied for trade, came clearly to our ears.

Piers rapped on the door and, after a few seconds, a doleful voice bade him come in. He gave me a quick, almost furtive glance, which I was at a loss to interpret, before entering the room and announcing loudly, 'Dame Copley, I've brought someone to see you.' He stood aside and waved me in.

'Who's this?'

I found myself face to face with a tall, very upright woman of perhaps some forty to fifty summers, her most notable feature being a pair of fierce blue eyes which blazed on either side of a sharp, pointed nose, quivering now with suspicion and, I felt, dislike. Although how that could be when she knew nothing about me, I was uncertain. But the feeling was strong. And the thin, lined cheeks, skeletal in their lack of flesh, were rigid with tension, the narrow lips almost invisible.

'Who's this?' she demanded for a second time.

Piers laid a gentle hand on the woman's arm. 'This is Roger Chapman, mistress. He's been sent for by the Duke of Gloucester to look into the young master's disappearance and the murder of Tutor Machin. He arrived at Minster Lovell while I was still there and I travelled back to London with him and Master Plummer.'

'Master Plummer?' The hostile scrutiny continued.

'His Grace's spymaster general,' I said, giving back look for look.

In spite of all that I had been told of Dame Copley's grief for her missing charge, of her bouts of hysteria, she seemed to me to be fully in control of her emotions. I could see no trace of redness around her eyes, no swollen eyelids, no tear-streaked cheeks. And as though suddenly conscious of this fact, the nurse turned away abruptly, pressing a handkerchief to her face. (I was impressed. Even though King Richard had introduced this article to England well over ninety or more years ago, it was still something of a rarity. Most people like me continued to use their fingers or their sleeves.)

The room was typical of the castle's servant quarters, more like a monk's or a nun's cell than anything else. There was just space enough for a narrow bed and a clothes chest that also doubled as a bedside table, its curved lid entailing a careful balancing act when used for this purpose. (What, after all, did our masters and betters know of such inconveniences?) A shelf supported tinderbox and candle, and I could see what appeared to be a half-full chamber-pot pushed nearly, but not quite, out of sight beneath the bed.

Dame Copley sank down upon the chest, her eyes covered and her body shaking, while Piers crouched beside her, awkwardly patting her free hand.

'Master Chapman will find Gideon somehow,' he assured her. 'That's what he's here for.'

I wished I could share his optimism, but there was nothing to be gained by voicing my doubts on the matter. I, too, crouched down, and although balking at actually touching the dame – there was something I found slightly repellent about her – I nevertheless said in the sort of gentle, encouraging tone I normally used for children, 'Tell me what you know. Who was the last person to see Gideon before he disappeared?'

Dame Copley gave a sniff and ostentatiously wiped her nose (although I noted that she was still dry-eyed). 'It was that girl, Amphillis Hill.' She gave a significant nod in Piers's direction, as much as to say he would know who was meant. For my benefit, she added, 'Amphillis Hill is one of the castle seamstresses. A pretty young thing. Or, at least, she thinks she is.'

Piers gave a chuckle. 'Now, be fair, Rosina, you know very well she is.' He grinned at me and made curves in the air with his hands. 'She has a shape like that as well as the most beautiful blue eyes and dimples. You'll love her, Roger. All the men do.'

I ignored this and pressed Dame Copley for further information. 'Where and when did this Mistress Hill see Gideon?'

'On the Friday evening after supper, in company with Gregory Machin. It was in the corridor outside, at the other end where there's a flight of steps that lead to a landing and a number of rooms similar to this one. Tutor Machin had been allotted one of them for the night.'

'Had the boy been to see you?' I asked.

She nodded miserably. 'He came to say goodnight.'

'Did he sleep with Tutor Machin?'

Dame Copley shook her head vigorously. 'Oh, no! Gideon was sharing a chamber with his uncle, Godfrey. And the following day, he was going to the Tower to become part of King Edward's household.'

I nodded. 'So I've been given to understand. So Tutor Machin was taking him to find his uncle, was he?'

'Not immediately. Although I suppose he would have done,
eventually. Gregory was fussing unnecessarily, as usual. He
said that in all this upheaval, Gideon was missing too many
lessons; that his mathematics and philosophy were falling
behind and that his reading ability was abysmal. And if he
was going to serve the king, who is noted for his learning,
he must not appear an ignoramus.' The nurse tossed her head.
'Of course, Gregory was really only concerned with his own
reputation.'

'And Master Machin was intent on giving the lad some
extra tuition, was that the idea?'

'Oh dear me, yes! I told him to let the child run out of
doors before he went to sleep. It would do him far more
good than poring over musty old school books. Besides,
Gideon was overtired, I could see that. He's always been
delicate, a fact no one has ever seemed to understand,
except his mother and myself. All this excitement, all this
junketing about, has been bad for him. He needs a quiet
life.'

'Now, Rosina, admit you mollycoddle him,' said Piers with
a smile, and for the second time I felt a slight sense of
surprise that the lad should use Dame Copley's Christian
name so freely. I would have expected the nurse to be shown
some deference from an obvious inferior in the domestic
hierarchy. But as the dame herself took no offence, who was
I to cavil? Some households are laxer than others.

I returned, as the French say, to our sheep. 'So Master
Gideon, after bidding you goodnight, left this room in
company with Tutor Machin. Did you watch them to the end
of the passageway?'

Dame Copley shook her head. 'No. I was tired and wanted
to doze. Gideon promised to come to see me again in the
morning before he left for the Tower, and I told Gregory to
shut the door behind him. And that –' she pressed the handkerchief to her lips with shaking fingers – 'was the last time
I saw my precious boy. And the last time I saw Gregory
Machin alive.'

Piers rose from his knees and, seating himself on the bed,
leant over and put an arm around the nurse's shoulders.

'Don't worry, my dear. I've told you, Master Chapman is

here to find him. Master Gideon, I mean. There's nothing he can do for Tutor Machin.'

'Except find his killer,' Dame Copley pointed out.

There was a short and somewhat pregnant pause while I contemplated the task ahead of me. Then I took a deep breath and gathered my forces together.

'You say that this Amphillis Hill, this seamstress, saw both Gideon and his tutor at the far end of the passageway outside. Do you know how she came to see them? What she was doing there? Why she was there?'

It was Piers who answered. 'I believe she'd been out, across the river, and had just landed back at the water stairs. She entered the castle by the door you must have noted as we came in.' He paused, shrugging. 'I may be wrong. I had precious little time to gather much information in all the panic and flurry after the discovery of poor Master Machin's body.'

'No, you're quite right,' Dame Copley confirmed. 'It seems Amphillis saw them from the door as they were mounting the stairs at the other end. They disappeared round the bend, going up to Tutor Machin's room, but by the time the girl herself reached the top of the stairs, there was no sign of them. Not surprising, of course, as Gregory's chamber – if,' she snorted, 'one can dignify it with that name – was only the second one along. Not that the girl knew that, or cared. They were nothing to her. She didn't even know their names – at least not then – or what they were doing in Baynard's Castle. She just happened to be the last person to see them both.' Once again, the handkerchief came into play.

I got thankfully to my feet and stretched my legs. 'The best thing I can do is to see this Amphillis Hill for myself,' I said. I looked at Piers. 'Do you know where I can find her?'

SEVEN

Dame Copley sniffed loudly.

'If she's at her work, where she ought to be,' she said waspishly, 'and not gadding around the castle or taking trips across the river, as these young girls seem prone to do, she'll be with the other seamstresses in the sewing room. Piers knows where that is. He'll take you.'

Piers rose from his seat on the bed.

I shook my head. 'Don't bother, lad. I can find it. I've a tongue in my head. You'd be better employed seeking out Sir Francis and informing him of Mistress Blancheflower's death. And that of his dog.'

At my words, the nurse gave a piercing scream and staggered to her feet. 'What do you mean? What's he talking about, Perry?' She laid a trembling hand on Piers's arm. 'Nell? Dead? There-there must be some mistake. Tell me! Tell me!'

Piers threw me a reproachful glance. 'She doesn't know yet. I was going to break it to her gently, later. Dame Copley and Mistress Blancheflower were particular friends, you see. They took to each other straight away after we arrived at Minster Lovell from up north.'

'It can't be Nell!' Rosina Copley had seized the young man by the shoulders and was shaking him violently. 'You mean it was William.' She drew a ragged, gasping breath and then seemed to take herself in hand. 'What did Master Chapman mean about the dog? Is he talking about that brute, Beelzebub? But Nell had nothing to do with the dogs.'

'It-it was an accident,' Piers said, obviously upset by the nurse's distress. 'She . . . Well, no one knows quite how it happened. Mistress Blancheflower went out of the main courtyard the night before last or sometime during the early hours of yesterday morning. The dog savaged her. T-tore her throat out.'

I stepped forward quickly, afraid that Dame Copley was about to faint. But she was made of sterner stuff than that, and although she was ashen-white, her lips bloodless, she managed a faint, rueful smile at her own weakness.

'Tell me all about it,' she whispered to Piers, who nodded and sat down on the bed again, inviting her to sit alongside him.

'I'll go and seek out this Amphillis Hill,' I said, not merely because I wished to avoid a painful scene, but also because my own secret guilt was making me deeply uncomfortable. Piers volunteered no answer, being busy consoling Dame Copley like the good and caring lad he seemed to be, so I slipped out thankfully into the passage, closing the door quietly behind me.

I leant against the wall for a moment or two, convincing myself that there was nothing to be gained by confessing my unfortunate part in Eleanor Blancheflower's death to Piers and the nurse – or indeed to anyone. It would only complicate an already fraught situation. Silence, I decided for the second time, was my best, really my only, option. I had other things to occupy my attention.

I felt better for this decision and walked forward to stand in the open doorway at the end of the passage, staring out at the familiar landing-stage and water-stairs of Baynard's Castle. It took me back a year to the events following my return from Scotland, and for a minute or two I was lost in memories of a pair of large, violet-blue eyes, fair, wavy hair and a seductive, willowy form that invited embrace. Eloise Gray. I found myself wondering where she was now and what she was doing . . .

I shook my head angrily, freeing my mind from memories I had no business to be harbouring, and turned round to face the opposite direction. Ahead of me stretched the passage, empty now of all but shadows cast by the afternoon sunlight, and, at the far end, the first few treads of a flight of stairs that twisted up and out of view. That was where Amphillis Hill had seen young Gideon Fitzalan in company with his tutor, Gregory Machin, as they disappeared out of sight around the bend. By the time she herself reached the landing at the top, they had vanished, one to be found murdered in a locked room, the other . . . The other seemingly dissolved into thin air.

*   *   *

The sewing room of Baynard's Castle, which, after a number of enquiries and conflicting directions, I discovered on the third floor of one of the towers overlooking the river, was a bright, sun-filled room full of chattering girls seated around several long trestle tables littered with skeins of cotton, embroidery silks, pieces of material, parchment patterns, pin boxes, needle boxes, scissors and all the rest of the paraphernalia necessary for making and mending in a household as large as the Dowager Duchess of York's.

The pleasant-faced, elderly woman who was in charge readily acceded to my request to speak to Amphillis Hill without evincing any interest in who I was or what was my authority. Here was no strict taskmistress, and it was small wonder that the girls all seemed happy and relaxed. But whether as much work got done in any one day as the duchess had a right to expect, was debatable. I decided that the answer was probably not.

Amphillis Hill was very much as Piers had described her, if not prettier. She certainly had a buxom figure, although in my opinion just a little too buxom for her height. Another inch or two would have made her perfect. As it was, the first word that came to my mind was 'squat'. But I soon realized that this was an over-exaggeration and that most people would find nothing to criticize. Perhaps it was my recent memory of Eloise Gray that was making me too particular. As for Mistress Hill's face, with its rosy, rounded cheeks, wide blue eyes, long, fair lashes and delicate, overarching, equally fair eyebrows, only your true misanthrope could have found fault with that.

I beckoned her away from the table where, with tiny, almost invisible stitches, she was mending a rent in a black velvet skirt, and drew her to one of the windows, thrown open on this warm June day to let in both sunshine and the stench of the river. I explained as briefly as I could who I was and what was my mission at Baynard's Castle, expecting her to be puzzled and question my identity, or at least to ask a few pertinent questions. But she just laughed.

'Oh, I've heard of you,' she said. 'In fact a lot of people have heard of you. You're the man Duke Richard always sends for when he has a problem to be solved. You went to

Scotland with him last year in the company of his cousin, the Duke of Albany. You're the notorious Roger Chapman.'

I was taken aback. It had never occurred to me that my association with the duke had been so noticed and commented upon; but when I gave the idea my serious consideration, I could see that it was probably well-nigh inevitable after so many years. I wasn't sure I cared for her choice of the word 'notorious' though.

Amphillis went on, 'I suppose you want to ask me about that poor man who's been murdered? And the boy, the one who's disappeared?' I nodded and she shrugged. 'I'm afraid I can't tell you any more than I've already told the duke, Sir Francis, the lad's uncle, his two brothers and the Virgin alone knows how many other people who've interrogated me on the subject.'

I smiled down at her, my special, winning smile that I persuaded myself could always melt the heart of a pretty young girl. (Oh, the conceit and folly of youth!)

'Could you bear to tell me again, for one last time?'

She sighed with exaggerated weariness, but a dimple peeped. 'I suppose so.'

'You were coming in from the landing-stage,' I prompted. 'You'd been out, I understand, across the river.'

'Yes. I'd been on an errand for Dame Claypole there.' She indicated the head seamstress. 'There's a shop in Southwark that sells extra fine linen, which we needed to repair one of Her Grace's nightgowns.' She added irritably, 'Duchess Cicely really ought to have new ones made, but she won't. They say that when she was younger, she was terribly extravagant. If that's so, she's certainly atoned for it since.'

'So what did you see when you came in through the landing-stage door?' I asked, putting an abrupt end to this digression.

'What? Oh! Yes. I saw a man and a young boy mounting the stairs at the other end of the passageway.'

'Did you know who they were?'

'No. There are so many people in this place, you can't possibly know everyone. And anyway, it turned out that those two had only arrived late the day before. If I'd recognized them, it would have been a miracle.'

'You hadn't noticed them previously? I mean they hadn't been ahead of you as you crossed the landing-stage?' I wanted to test Dame Copley's story.

Amphillis shook her pretty head. 'I was the only person in the boat that brought me back from Southwark and when I got out, the landing-stage was deserted. There was only one place they could have come from, and that was one of the rooms opening on to that corridor.' She glanced at me sharply. 'I've been told since that the lad's nurse – although he looked too big to me to have a nurse – has been given a chamber there. And if that's so, he and that tutor of his must have been visiting her. It was some time after supper, so perhaps they'd been to wish her goodnight.'

I didn't confirm this, saying merely, 'And when you your-self mounted the stairs, both man and boy had disappeared?'

'Yes. But that wasn't surprising. There are rooms there, also used by visitors. I just presumed they were in one of them.'

'You didn't see anything out of the ordinary?'

'No. But then,' she added astutely, 'that doesn't neces-sarily mean there was nothing to see. I wasn't looking for anything, was I?'

'No,' I agreed, 'I suppose you weren't. Thinking back now, is it possible that there might have been something?'

She puckered her pretty brow in concentration, but this was almost impossible amidst the chaff and general banter coming from the girls on the tables behind us. Intrigued by my presence and the low-voiced conversation with Amphillis, they were agog to know what it was all about.

'Don't keep him all to yourself, my dear. A good-looking fellow like that should be shared around,' a snub-nosed girl with bright brown eyes called out, occasioning a gust of laughter.

'There's enough of him in all conscience,' another girl cried, this time provoking an absolute gale of merriment.

'More than enough,' someone else sniggered.

I realized it was time to be going. Experience had taught me that women in a crowd could be far cruder than men, however sweet and modest they might be singly. Before I could take my leave of Amphillis, however, the snub-nosed

girl had left her table and come across to us, throwing one
arm around her friend's shoulders and raking me from head
to foot with those bright brown eyes.

'Well, well!' she said. 'We don't often see your like at
Baynard's Castle. And never at Berkhamsted.' This, I knew,
was the dowager duchess's other castle, where she lived in
semi-reclusive, semi-religious retirement, only coming to
London for important occasions. The forward young minx
continued, 'You need speaking for, and I don't see why little
Philly here should have you all to herself. So, I shall give
you my favour as if I were a grand lady and you my knight.'
And giggling and blushing in equal measure, she unpinned
a sprig of leaves from the bodice of her gown and fixed it
to my jerkin. Then with eyebrows coquettishly raised, she
waited for my reaction.

I'm afraid I disappointed her. I was more interested in
what she had given me than I was in her.

'Birch leaves,' I said, squinting down at them. 'Of course!
It can't be long now until Midsummer Eve.'

'Just over a week,' Amphillis cut in, frowning furiously
at her friend.

'This coming Monday sennight,' brown-eyes confirmed.
She gave a delicious shiver. 'They say that if you walk seven
times clockwise round a church at midnight, sowing
hempseed as you go, and then look over your left shoulder,
you'll see the person you're going to marry.' She cocked her
head to one side and laid a hand on my arm. 'Is it possible,
sir, that you might be somewhere near a church on
Midsummer Eve?'

'He's married,' Amphillis said tartly, before I had time to
answer. 'And if you're going to ask me how I know, Maria
Johnson, I have a nose for these things. Master Chapman
looks married. You can always tell. Men who are leg-shackled
don't behave in just the same way as men who aren't.'

The other girl's face fell ludicrously. 'Are you?' she asked,
addressing me. And when I nodded, snatched back the birch
leaves and pin. 'No use giving you my favour then,' she
snapped, and returned to her table amid the jeers and laughter
of the other girls.

The head seamstress, suddenly aware of behaviour getting

out of hand, came hurrying across, her pleasant face creased with concern. 'Amphillis—' she began anxiously, but I forestalled her.

'I'm leaving now, mistress,' I said. And, with a smile and a quick general word of farewell, departed.

My immediate intention was to go in search of Piers until I realized that I had no idea where to find him. So, instead, I went to look for the steward to find out where I was housed. To my astonishment, I discovered it was the same costive little chamber that I had occupied the previous year before I was despatched to France: damp, chilly, high up, with the same narrow window overlooking the water-stairs. Someone had fetched my saddlebags and dumped them on the bed, and the young lad who had been deputed by the steward to be my guide, informed me that supper would be served in the servants' hall in half an hour.

'Never mind that,' I said, rather to my own surprise as well as the boy's (food being of paramount importance in any underling's day). 'Do you know where the murder took place last week?' He nodded mutely, his eyes suddenly wide with alarm. 'Good. Can you take me there?'

'N-now?' he gulped.

'Yes. Now.'

He was reluctant to do so, but gave in to my bullying, and I eventually found myself back at the top of the stairs which led down to the passage where Rosina Copley had her room.

'That one,' the lad said, pointing to the second door along. 'That's where he was murdered, except . . .'

'Except?'

The boy shuddered. 'Except it couldn't have been by no mortal hand, could it? Stabbed in the back, he was. But the door was bolted on the inside.' He pointed with a grubby, trembling forefinger. 'Well, you c'n see for yourself, master. They had t'break it down.'

And suddenly I saw what I should have perceived at once had the gloom of the landing not made observation difficult. The entrance to the second room from the stairhead was nothing but an empty space, although quite a number of large splinters and shards of wood still lay around. The hinges hung jaggedly from their sockets, bearing silent witness to the force which had been necessary to get inside. The lad edged up behind me, peering over my shoulder and staring with morbid fascination.

'They say he were lying right across the door, stiff as a poker,' he whispered. ''Course, I don't know that for certain. I didn't see him. But it's what they're saying, those that did.'

'Who found the body?' I asked, but he didn't know.

'Them that broke down the door, I suppose,' was his somewhat fatuous reply. And yet it had logic to it.

I stepped inside and glanced around, but there was nothing to see. All the tutor's personal belongings seemed to have been removed, and what remained was simply the sparse furnishings of the cell-like chamber. There were no stains on the flagstones and the scattering of straw was none other than those which might have been expected from the trampling of many feet. Gregory Machin obviously hadn't bled much, a fact consonant with what I had been told of a quick stiletto thrust through the back into the heart. But who could have done it? Who could have managed to enter and vacate the room, bolting the door behind him?

I glanced up. The bolt was still slammed home in its wards; a good, solid iron bolt which had evidently resisted being shaken loose when, as must certainly have happened, someone first tried to rouse the tutor by banging and shouting in order to awaken him. I walked over to the window where I opened the shutters and leant out. I was only one storey above the ground, but I could see no foothold, no projecting stones that would have made for easy climbing. Moreover, the window – even had the shutters been open, which was possible on a warm June evening – was far too narrow to permit of easy access. Tutor Machin must have been alerted to anyone trying to gain entrance by that method, and a single push would have sent the intruder sprawling on the landing-stage below.

'Them shutters were closed,' said the lad's voice behind me. He had ventured in, his courage fortified by my presence, and was staring warily about him. 'So they say,' he added, careful to deny any personal involvement in the matter.

'And who are "they"?' I asked.

He shrugged. 'No one in partic'lar. It's just what everyone's saying.'

I could see that I was unlikely to get any information worth the having, so I encouraged him to return to his duties, whatever they were, and leave me in peace.

'Master Steward's probably looking for you. With all these visitors thronging the castle, there must be quite a few errands to run.' He agreed and was moving reluctantly towards the door, when I remembered Piers and stopped him. 'Do you know where young Master Daubenay's lodging?'

When he had finally identified Piers, the boy gave a disparaging sniff. 'Oh, him! Should by rights be dossing down in the male dormitory, but I ain't seen him there, leastways not yet, and he's been here more'n a week now. Don't know where he goes. Law unto himself, that one.'

That tallied with what I already knew of Piers, so I nodded dismissal and gave my full attention to the room. A second inspection, however, yielded no more clues than the first, nor any further inspiration as to how a man could be stabbed in the back in a chamber shuttered and bolted from the inside. I again looked closely at the window, but even had it been wide open at the time – although 'they', it seemed, said definitely not – I still deemed it impossible for the murderer to have entered that way.

Witches? Demons? The Black Arts? I shivered. It was possible, I supposed. We all knew that these things existed, and yet, somehow or other, I could never bring myself to a wholehearted belief in any of them. I thought of the demons who had once, according to legend, inhabited this island, but found I could give them little credence, either. Nor the giants. Nor the thirty-three Daughters of Albion. And yet, was I right? If one believed in God, should one not believe in Satan also? There was undoubtedly good and evil everywhere one looked in the world. But there again, was my definition of evil the same as the next man's . . .?

I took a great gulp of river-scented air – enough to sober any man – and gave myself a mental shake. What in God's name did I think I was doing, standing here philosophizing, when there was work to be done and a murderer to be caught and an abducted child, whose life was most probably in danger, to be found? I gave one final searching glance around the room, grudgingly admitted that there really was nothing to be gained by prolonging my stay, stepped across the shattered splinters of wood that had once been a door and emerged into the passageway.

As I did so, a trumpet sounded in the distance summoning the castle's underlings to supper. It occurred to me that I was bound to be reunited with Piers in the servants' hall and turned towards the stairs with a certain amount of relief. As I did so, a young girl appeared from the opposite direction, sweeping the passage clean of what looked like several days' dust and litter. But as soon as she heard the trumpet, she propped her besom against the wall and slipped past me with a sweet, half-guilty smile, running fleet-footed down the steps, knowing from long experience that she who came first was most likely to be first served. I was about to follow her example when something among the pile of rubbish beside her broom caught my eye. Stooping, I carefully picked it up.

It was a little twig of birch leaves such as the seamstress, Maria Johnson, had been wearing – and someone else, although I couldn't, for the moment, think who – a token of that night of magic and mystery, Midsummer Eve, which was now only ten days away. It must, I reckoned, have been dropped quite close at hand, having been one of the last things, if not the last, to be swept up by the young girl's broom before she abandoned it to go to supper.

I stared at the twig thoughtfully where it lay in the palm of my hand, wondering what significance its discovery had so near to the room where the murder had been committed. In the end, I was forced to the conclusion that it probably had none. Nevertheless, I put it into the pouch at my belt, then made my way to the servants' hall for supper.

The first person I saw on entering was Piers who was on his feet, keeping a look out for me. With a sweeping wave of one arm, he indicated that I should join him at a table halfway down the hall where he had evidently saved me a place.

'Where in God's name have you been?' he demanded as I eased myself on to the bench alongside him.

'I was just about to ask you the same question,' I retorted, helping myself from the big basin of pottage which the servers had placed in the centre of the table. Having sampled it, I grimaced. 'The food doesn't improve. It's still the same, tasteless mush that was being served up last year.'

A young woman sitting opposite to me said bitterly, 'It never changes. Just be thankful you don't live here.'

I realized it was the girl who had been sweeping the passageway, and that in spite of her complaint, she was just about to help herself to a second bowlful of stew. But then, however bad the food, one had to eat.

'I saw you just now,' I said. 'You were sweeping the corridor outside the room where Master Machin died. How often do you clean it?'

She grimaced and stuffed another spoonful of pottage in her mouth as though afraid that someone might deny her right to it. When, however, she was able to speak, she deigned to reply. 'Not often,' she admitted, raising her voice slightly in order to make herself heard above the general din of conversation, adding defensively, 'There's miles o' passageways in this here place. A girl can't be expected to be everywhere at once.'

'Of course not,' I agreed sympathetically. 'And surely no one of any sense would expect it of you.' She looked mollified and I continued, 'Would you say that today was the first time you've swept it since the murder? Since last Friday, that is?'

'There ain't been no point in sweeping it before,' she answered indignantly. 'What with the door of that room being broken down and everything, I just been waiting for the dust to settle.'

'Very sensible, too.' I smiled, and bent my head to get on with my own rapidly cooling supper.

The girl stared at me for a moment or two, obviously waiting for me to explain the reason for my questioning, but when I didn't, she soon lost interest and began speaking to the man sitting beside her.

'What was that about?' Piers hissed in my ear, but I waved him to silence.

'I'll tell you later. Did you find Sir Francis and inform him of events at Minster Lovell?'

'I did.'

'And?'

'He wasn't best pleased about any of it, especially William Blancheflower's decision to kill Beelzebub.'

'What did I tell you?'

Piers shook his head. 'Oh, he was upset about Nell's death just as much. Coming on top of all the rest, he so far forgot himself as to say straight out in front of me that he wished he'd never set eyes on any of the Fitzalans and that he rued the day young Gideon crossed his threshold. Of course, he quickly recollected himself and put me on my honour not to repeat what he'd said to Godfrey or Gideon's brothers. He looked harassed, poor man, and muttered something about "this business at the Tower", and something else about having been summoned by the Lord Protector.'

I picked the meat from between my teeth and wondered if I was hungry enough to risk a second bowl of pottage, and decided that I wasn't.

'Let's get out of here,' I said to Piers, as the sound of several hundred people all talking at once threatened to deafen me.

He agreed, but as we turned to swing our legs over the bench, I became aware that someone was standing directly behind me.

'I thought I should find you stuffing your guts as usual,' Timothy Plummer remarked crudely. But without giving me time to reply in kind, he went on, 'You're wanted at Crosby's Place. Now. The Protector wants to see you.'

EIGHT

M y first thought was that he had aged, suddenly.
I had encountered Duke Richard briefly only a
few weeks previously, and even then he had seemed
careworn; hardly surprising considering all that had happened
in such a short space of time. The death of his adored elder
brother and the Woodville conspiracy against himself had
been shocks from which it would take any man a while to
recover. That was only to be expected. But now, standing
before him in the superb hall of Crosby's Place, the evening
light filtering in through the great oriel window, the magnificent red and gold ceiling arching above us, the splendour
of marble flooring beneath our feet, his face, always thin,
looked even more drawn with anxiety. And there was something feverish about him; his dark eyes glittered and he played
even more constantly with the rings on his fingers.

During our ride through the London streets from Baynard's
Castle to Crosby's Place, I had taken the opportunity to quiz
Timothy on what had happened at the Tower that morning.
Was it, after all, true that Lord Hastings had been summarily
executed?

'No, of course not,' the spymaster had snapped, adding
bitterly, 'although it won't stop the rumour spreading and
being repeated as fact over and over and over again until
some people are convinced of its truth.'

'So what did happen?' I wanted to know.

Timothy grunted. 'There was a conspiracy, of course. We
knew that – well, you knew that – with Mistress Shore trot-
ting to and from Westminster Sanctuary to keep the queen
dowager apprised of events. For the moment, all the conspirators are in custody in the Tower. What will become of most
of them, I can't say. But I'm sure that Hastings will be tried
and executed.'

'How do you know he'll be executed?' I had queried
uneasily. 'How can you possibly anticipate the verdict?'

'Oh, don't pretend to be naïve, Roger,' he retorted angrily, as we had turned from Thames Street to ride up Old Fish Street Hill. 'The man's guilty. You alone could testify to that. Jealousy of Buckingham is what's at the bottom of it. Hastings has always been at daggers drawn with the Woodvilles, and until a week or so ago he was my lord Gloucester's closest ally. Until, that is, he discovered that the place he had assumed was lawfully his, as the Protector's right-hand man, had gone to my lord Buckingham, along with God only knows how many perquisites and concessions that Hastings had counted on as his by right. So he threw in his lot with the queen dowager and her adherents in another attempt to get rid of my lord. And if there's one thing more than any other that Duke Richard can't pardon it's betrayal of trust. "Loyaute me lie" is his motto, and he expects the same of others. He won't let the Lord Chamberlain – ex-Lord Chamberlain – escape to plot again. Hastings will die, but at least he'll have been given the dignity of a trial.' I saw Timothy glance sideways at me. 'Now what's the matter?'

I had shaken my head; I couldn't explain without incurring his further anger. Indeed, I had felt angry with myself for quibbling because I could clearly understand the necessity for Hastings's removal. (One of the things I had noticed since my arrival in the capital that morning was how many of the Lord Chamberlain's retainers were thronging the London streets. They constituted a small army and could undoubtedly, if called upon, pose a serious threat to civic stability.) All the same, there seemed little difference to me between condemning a man to the block out of hand and letting him stand trial when the verdict had been prearranged.

'Roger!' I realized with a start that the duke had extended his hand and I dropped to one knee to kiss it. It was icy cold in spite of the warmth of the evening. He laughed. 'You were miles away, my friend.'

I glanced up guiltily and wondered how many other princes of the blood royal would dismiss such negligence with a smile. But his always unexpected sense of humour shone through to lighten what, for me, could have been a very nasty moment.

'Your Highness, forgive me,' I said, rising to my feet. 'You must blame my rudeness on lack of sleep. I only arrived in London this morning after a night spent in a very indifferent wayside inn.'

He nodded. 'I hear from Timothy that you insisted on going to Minster Lovell before coming here. Did your visit offer up any resolution to this mystery?'

'Not that I'm aware of at the moment, my lord.' I saw him arch his eyebrows and added, 'I can never tell what might prove to be useful in time.'

'No, I suppose not.' He waved me towards a cushioned stool with armrests and resumed his own seat in a carved armchair. 'I can only ask you to do your best and to do it quickly. However, that's not the reason I summoned you here.'

At this point, he turned his head and glanced at someone whose presence I had so far failed to notice, and I was somewhat disconcerted to find that the duchess was also in the room.

I had not seen the Her Grace of Gloucester for some time, and then only at a distance when the duke's sister, Margaret of Burgundy, had visited London two years previously. Like her older sister, Isabel, the long-dead Duchess of Clarence, she was a delicate, almost childlike woman, and I reflected yet again how strange it was that the line of that mighty, vigorous man, Richard Neville, Earl of Warwick, had run to seed in these two fragile daughters. I had once, more than a decade ago, done the Lady Anne, as she then was, a service, and she smiled at me now in instant recognition.

'I'm happy to see you again, Master Chapman.'

'And I you, Your Grace.' I got clumsily to my feet and made my obeisance.

'Oh, sit down, man. Sit down.' Her husband waved an airy hand. 'We're not standing on ceremony this evening. This is a meeting strictly off the record. It's never taken place. You hear me, Roger?'

'I do, Your Highness,' I said, wondering what on earth was coming.

There was a protracted pause; so protracted that although it was not my place to do so, I felt obliged to fill it.

'I trust Prince Edward is well, Your Grace,' I said to the duchess.

A shadow crossed her face. 'We think him a little better now that the warmer weather is here, I thank you, Master Chapman. He has had a nasty cough this past winter, as indeed have I, but we look to the pure air of the Yorkshire moors to cure it. He will stay at home for the present.'

'Sweetheart, the boy's strong enough if he isn't coddled into ill health by you and that nurse of his.' The duke spoke with all the irritation of someone who knows full well that what he is saying is what he wishes to believe and not what he knows to be the truth. He turned towards me and cleared his throat. 'Roger, when you went to France for me last year, on that . . . that mission. When you spoke to . . . oh, I forget her name. The Frenchwoman married to the English soldier . . .'

'Mistress Gaunt. Yes, Your Grace?'

The duke was twisting the ruby ring on his right-hand little finger even more rapidly than before, but quite unaware that he was doing so. He went on, 'She told you the story of my two eldest brothers' christenings. What . . . what did you make of it?'

'What did I make of it, Your Highness?'

'Yes, man, make of it?' Agitation and impatience were blended in equal measure.

'In what particular, my lord?' I was confused, groping my way down an as yet blind alley. What was it he wanted me to say? In my experience, the duke rarely showed exasperation with underlings, but I sensed that at this moment he was close to losing his temper.

The duchess took pity on me, leaning forward in her chair. 'Master Chapman,' she said in her low, sweet voice, 'do you believe that the story of those two Rouen christenings – that of the younger child being so much grander and better attended than that of the elder – is proof of my mother-in-law's ancient claim that the late king was her bastard child by the archer Blaybourne?'

I drew a deep breath. I was on quicksand here and had to tread carefully. I addressed the duke. 'My lord . . .' I hesitated, then plunged. 'Yes, I believe that the story does in some measure support the Duchess of York's claim. But it is not even proof, let alone proof positive. There could be other valid reasons why the lord Edmund's christening was made so much more of than the lord Edward's.'

'Such as?'

I thought quickly. 'The duchess may have been unwell after the late king's birth and not in the mood for a great celebration.'

The duke looked sceptical. 'My mother was never unwell after giving birth to any of us. But let's presume your theory's true. Why would she and my father not wait until she was in better health to hold the christening? Edward was the much longed-for son; a healthy boy following the early death of an older brother at Hatfield before my parents left for Normandy. And why was my father always so much fonder of Edmund than of Edward? They went everywhere together – until they died together, at the battle outside Wakefield.'

I grimaced. 'When Your Grace puts it like that . . .' I glanced imploringly at the duchess.

She did not fail me. 'I think, sweetheart, that what Master Chapman is saying is that while the story is a very strong indication that you are the rightful king, and have been ever since George was executed, it isn't sufficient proof in itself. And didn't you tell me that this woman, this Mistress Gaunt, is dead?'

The duke nodded, his naturally thin lips compressed to an almost invisible thread. 'She was murdered by a Woodville spy. Isn't that so, Roger?'

'Unfortunately yes, my lord.'

'Further proof, wouldn't you agree, of the story's significance?'

For answer, I asked him again, as I had asked him on various occasions the previous year, 'Is there no possibility of persuading the dowager duchess either to confirm or deny what she said at the time of the late king's marriage?'

The duke sighed. 'As I've told you before, my mother refuses to discuss the subject. One can see why, of course. For a start, she is a very different woman to the one she was nineteen years ago. She has embraced the religious life and would no longer find it acceptable to be seen as a woman who once cuckolded her husband. And then again, young Edward is her grandson, even though he is half Woodville.'

Duchess Anne said bitterly, 'My mother-in-law is a very obstinate and difficult woman, Master Chapman.' She coloured and gave a little gasp, realizing the magnitude of her indiscretion.

The duke laughed. 'Just be thankful, my love,' he admonished her, 'that your very unwary opinions were expressed to someone as trustworthy as Roger. But it wouldn't do to make them generally known.' He looked across at me. 'And now, my friend, I am going to be equally indiscreet because I know you can keep your mouth shut. I must tell you that in spite of her steadfast refusal to repeat her words concerning my brother Edward's bastardy, my mother does consider that . . . that I should lay claim to the throne.'

'My-my lord?' I felt as if someone had punched me in the guts.

'Particularly,' the duke continued as if I hadn't spoken, 'in view of Bishop Stillington's testimony.'

Robert Stillington, Bishop of Bath and Wells! How that man kept cropping up in the family history of the House of York. His friendship with the late Duke of Clarence had been marked, and his imprisonment in the Tower at the time of Clarence's downfall and execution – a downfall undoubtedly brought about by the Woodvilles – had suggested some kind of collusion between the two. And a few weeks earlier, during my first journey to London in pursuit of Adela, the bishop had arrived at Reading Abbey, late one night while Jack Nym and I were lodging there, in a flurry of agitation and self-importance. He and his retinue had also been highly visible, riding around the streets of the capital during the days that followed. And now it seemed he possessed knowledge which could bolster my lord Gloucester's entitlement to the throne. If so, it must be secret knowledge that he had shared with the Duke of Clarence in the past; knowledge that had led to that rash young man's undoing.

Yet again I hesitated, unsure of what I was supposed to say. But the duke's expectant look encouraged me to ask the necessary question.

'What – er – testimony is that, my lord, if I'm not being too presumptuous?'

The duke smiled. 'It will be common knowledge in a day or two, in any case, but until then, Roger, I trust you to keep silent, at least, to outsiders. My own people know what's in the wind.' He glanced at his wife, who nodded her approval, and then went on, 'Bishop Stillington informs me that the late king's marriage to the Widow Grey wasn't legal. Edward had already secretly plighted his troth to, and solemnly promised to marry, the Lady Eleanor Butler, daughter of the Earl of Shrewsbury. No one knew of this except my brother, the lady herself and Bishop Stillington who conducted the ceremony of betrothal.'

'And as you must be aware, Master Chapman,' the duchess put in, 'a betrothal, in the eyes of the Church is as binding as are the vows of marriage. The children of my late brother-in-law's so-called marriage are therefore illegitimate, and as my nephew Warwick is barred from the throne by his father's attainder, my husband is undoubtedly king. I tell him that he must immediately claim what is rightfully his.'

I was more than a little surprised at how forcefully the duchess spoke. She had always struck me as so self-effacing a person as to be almost a cipher, as having no existence beyond her husband's shadow. I suppose I had failed to realize that under her gentle exterior she was her father's daughter. During his final years, Warwick had fought and died so that one of his girls might be consort to England's king, and she could see the present opportunity only as the vindication of all his hopes. And her son – Warwick's grandson – would one day wear the crown.

I was startled by the duke's voice cutting across my tumultuous thoughts.

'Well, Roger, has the cat got your tongue?'

'Your Grace, I . . . I . . .'

'Don't know what to say, is that it?' He looked disappointed. 'I had hoped that your reaction would give me some indication of how the world in general would regard my assumption of the crown.'

'The country will be safer –' again it was the duchess who spoke – 'with a strong man to rule it than with a young king who will be at the mercy of his squabbling relatives, all vying for power.'

'I-I suppose so,' I answered feebly, my head reeling from the impact of the news.

I thought of that angelic-looking, fair-haired, blue-eyed child riding to St Paul's and also of the way the women in the crowd had drooled over him, their maternal instincts at fever pitch. I wondered how they would accept his being put aside, his being proclaimed a bastard, in favour of a man of whom the Londoners knew so little. And what would happen to him and his brother and numerous sisters once their uncle had usurped the throne? Some detached part of my mind noted with interest my choice of phrase. Did it mean that I didn't believe Bishop Stillington's story? That I thought it a fairy tale concocted between him and Duke Richard?

And yet the story had logic to it. Had not King Edward's marriage to Lady Elizabeth Grey been a secret known only to themselves and the Woodville family for many months? The king's closest advisers, his own mother, brothers and sisters had been kept in the dark until his betrothal to Bona of Savoy had been arranged and he could no longer conceal the fact. So was it not possible that Edward had gone through an earlier equally secret ceremony with another woman? Except, on that occasion, he had persuaded her into bed without actually having to marry her. But if he had promised marriage, it was true that the Church would regard it in a serious light.

But serious enough to depose a king by declaring him and all his siblings bastards? I wasn't at all sure about that.

'Your Highness could refer your argument to an episcopal court,' I suggested. 'To Rome, if necessary.'

The duke shook his head. 'There isn't time, Roger. This dilemma needs resolving as soon as possible.' There was a moment's silence before he added, 'I must admit your attitude saddens me. I had hoped, knowing what you do, that you would be glad that I can rightfully claim what you surely must feel is really mine.'

'Your-your Highness,' I stammered, 'I'm sorry. It-it's just that I wasn't prepared . . . It's been a shock . . .'

He got up and I rose with him. He put a hand on my shoulder. 'No, don't apologize, my friend. For I count you as my friend, you must know that. We share more than just

the same birthday: we share trust, you and I. I shouldn't have
used you like this, as a sounding board, when I haven't even
come to a final decision, myself. Now, sit down again and
tell me how your enquiries are progressing. This unfortunate
affair must be resolved before . . . Well, let's say as soon as
possible. It's not the sort of cloud I want hanging over me
at present. I refer, of course, to the disappearance of Master
Fitzalan and the murder of his tutor.'

I resumed my seat. 'Your Grace, I only arrived in London
this morning. I've hardly had time—'

'No, no!' he interrupted sympathetically. 'I appreciate that.
But the locked room, do you consider that an insurmount-
able obstacle?'

With a great effort of will, I forced myself to concentrate
on the matter now under discussion, attempting desperately
to control my whirling thoughts which were everywhere at
once, still trying to assimilate the implications and possible
consequences of what I had just been told.

'My lord, unless you believe in the agency of supernatural beings, there has to be a rational explanation. But exactly
what that is, I must confess, for the moment eludes me.' His
smile and nod of encouragement began to settle my mind.
This was the master and friend I had known for so many
years; a man of understanding, intelligence and courtesy. I
went on, 'Sir, do you know the ancient custom of the crown
and the bough?'

'I do,' said the duchess, as her husband hesitated, frowning.
'It is, as you say, Master Chapman, a very old custom indeed,
probably dating from Saxon or pagan times.' (Which, I
guessed, to someone of her exalted Norman lineage, would
probably amount to much the same thing.) 'It has to do with
Midsummer Eve,' she explained to the duke, 'when people
wear garlands of leaves or a spray pinned over their hearts.
Someone is crowned Midsummer king or queen, just as, at
the beginning of spring, a girl is selected as Queen of the
May.'

'And you think, Roger, that this custom has some bearing
on the case?' As he spoke, Duke Richard's eyes met those
of his wife and they both broke into spontaneous laughter.
It was the intimate merriment of a couple who had known

each other a very long time, the roots of whose friendship went back deep into their childhood; a couple who could read each other's thoughts as easily as if they were their own.

'An omen,' said the duchess delightedly, and the duke nodded.

I said hastily, 'My lord, I have no reason – no positive reason – to believe that this custom has any bearing on either the murder of Gregory Machin or on Master Fitzalan's disappearance.'

'I understand.' Smiling, Duke Richard again rose to his feet and, for the second time, I jumped up with him. 'You like to keep your own counsel until you suddenly astound us all with the answer. Save your protestations, my friend. You've never failed me yet and you won't now.' I groaned silently under the weight of his confidence. He continued, 'And concerning that other matter, I know I can trust you to say nothing until it becomes public knowledge.'

'Not even to Master Plummer?' I couldn't help asking.

'Oh, Timothy!' The duke gave a sudden mischievous grin. 'He knows everything. Or thinks he does.'

A beringed hand was extended for me to kiss. This time it really was the end of my audience. I was being dismissed. I knelt once more and pressed his fingers to my lips. The duchess, too, proffered her hand and as I bowed over it, I was rewarded with a glowing smile.

'I am so happy to have renewed our acquaintance, Roger,' she said, using my Christian name for the first time.

'And I, Your Grace.'

Timothy was waiting for me in the courtyard with the horses, now rested and fed. He was plainly agog with curiosity.

'You were gone long enough,' he accused me. And when I didn't answer immediately, he added, 'You must have spun a good tale, for by my reckoning you can have found out very little as yet.'

I gave him a sharp look as I mounted my brown cob, wondering if he were being disingenuous.

'The duke realizes that,' I said. 'It wasn't why he asked to see me.'

The spymaster raised his eyebrows. 'No?'

'No. He wanted to know if the information I'd gleaned in France last year had convinced me of his right and title to the crown.'

Timothy sucked in his breath. 'And you answered . . .?'

'That whatever I thought didn't matter because it wasn't proof. But now . . .' I paused significantly. 'But now, it seems it isn't important. Bishop Stillington has convinced the duke – and the duchess – that the marriage of the late king and the queen dowager was invalid anyway, and that all the children are therefore bastards.'

Timothy gasped. 'He told you that?'

'Under a promise of secrecy, of course. Although it seems it won't remain a secret for very long. If I understood the duke aright, he intends to lay claim to the throne and depose his nephew any day now.'

We clattered down Bishops Gate Street Within, crossed the Poultry and entered Grasschurch Street almost directly opposite. The June evening was edging toward dusk, the sun trailing long fingers of coral and orange and pearl as it sank towards the western horizon. Many of the night-soil workers, who preferred to get their unpalatable task over early, were in and out of the houses, clearing privies and cesspits, loading the unsavoury contents into tarred barrels which were then carted outside the city before the curfew bell shut the gates, ready for disposal the following day. The taverns and alehouses were full and, judging by the noise emanating from every one we passed, doing their usual roaring trade. There would be a good few thick heads come the morning.

Timothy remained silent, wrapped in his own thoughts, until we had crossed Eastcheap and were nearly at the turning into Thames Street. Then he said slowly, 'He trusts you, Roger.' But then he could not help adding, 'What made him tell you, I wonder?'

'Well, my guess would be that he wanted to test my reaction. Duke Richard regards me in the light of his Everyman. What I feel today the world will feel tomorrow.' Even to my own ears, my tone sounded bitter.

Timothy turned his head to consider my profile. 'And what will the world feel tomorrow?' he asked eventually. 'Nothing to rejoice my lord's heart if the grim look on your face is anything to go by. Kings have been deposed before – the second Edward, the second Richard, the late King Henry – so why the expression of disapproval?'

I hesitated while I marshalled my turbulent thoughts. 'They were all grown men,' I said at last. 'Men who had reigned long enough to prove themselves inept and unfit to rule. Many people were tired of them. They weren't angelic-faced young boys who had antagonized no one. I tell you, Timothy, however much I'm convinced in my own mind that Duke Richard truly is the rightful king – if, that is, you discount Clarence's son because of his father's attainder: an attainder that could be reversed, by the way – I still believe he's making a terrible mistake. And another thing,' I added as he opened his mouth to speak, 'all three kings you mentioned died in mysterious circumstances. Probably murdered.'

'You're not suggesting . . .' my companion began hotly.

'I'm not suggesting anything,' I snapped back. 'I'm just stating a fact.'

'I hope you didn't say all this to the duke's face!' The spymaster's anger was palpable.

'Do you think I'm that sort of a bloody fool?' The bile was rising in my own throat. 'But maybe I should have done. At least it would have been more honest. And if, as I think was the case, he really did summon me to Crosby's Place to test my opinion as that of the common man, then I've probably left him with a false impression.'

'You don't understand, Roger,' Timothy said in a low voice, trembling with passion. 'You just don't comprehend the danger Duke Richard is in, and has been in, ever since his brother died. The Woodville faction will do anything – anything, I tell you! – to get the king in their power. And that means nothing less than my lord's death, and quite probably that of the duchess and their son, also.'

'Then he should appeal to the people,' I answered, equally low, equally passionately. 'They don't like the Woodvilles. They never have. But deposing his own nephew and usurping the crown? No! The populace at large won't like it.'

'Bishop Stillington can prove—'

'They're not familiar with Stillington! He could be in collusion with the duke for all they know!'

We were both shouting by now and passers-by were turning their heads to stare. I took a deep breath. We were almost at our destination. The towers of Baynard's Castle were visible ahead of us, and it was time to call a truce. Timothy felt so, too, and held out his hand, which I grasped.

But we parted in silence as he turned his horse about to ride back to Bishop's Gate Street.

NINE

The next two days yielded nothing of any worth. By the end of the second, when I retired to my cell-like chamber for such sleep as the long, light evenings, my frustration and the hardness of the mattress would allow, I was almost ready to declare the mystery unsolvable.

On Saturday morning, half my mind still taken up with the duke's revelation of the day before and its possible consequences, I had again closely examined the room where Gregory Machin was killed, but the most minute inspection had failed to reveal anything new. There seemed to be no way the murderer could have entered from either within or without the castle if the chamber door had been bolted; and everyone concerned, plus the evidence of the smashed door, testified to the fact that it had been. I again looked closely at the bolt and its socket, two fine examples of the iron worker's art, which even the shattering of the wood with an axe had not budged; while no wishful thinking or silent prayers could make the window any wider or any easier of access than it had been the previous afternoon. It was impossible that the murderer could have lain in wait inside the chamber and then, having done the deed, escaped by that route. Besides which, the lad who had accompanied me on Friday had sworn that the shutters had been closed. Even a second reconnoitre of the window from the landing-stage offered no sudden enlightenment. No footholds had miraculously appeared on the outside wall during the night. The mystery remained as baffling and bewildering as ever.

Yet, I told myself, there had to be an answer apart from that of some supernatural power at work. And I refused, in this case at least, to believe in demons and ghosts. The reason for this certainty was hard to explain other than my conviction that God's hand was in this, as it usually was in everything I did, and that He would not pit me against unseen forces. This was a human crime and I was here to solve it.

'All right, Lord,' I said, strolling back indoors, 'then give me a little help.'

Why had the tutor been murdered? A few moments' reflection suggested that the most probable solution was to enable the boy to be snatched and abducted without interference from the man. But that meant Gideon Fitzalan must also have been inside the room. Had he, too, been killed? But why, therefore, had he been taken away? And why had he not made an outcry? Could it mean that he had gone willingly? Had he been a party to the plot, whatever it was?

By this time, my head was reeling, and I had decided to abandon this aspect of the mystery, going, instead, in search of the uncle, Godfrey Fitzalan, whom I managed at last to run to earth in the tilting-yard, where he was putting in a little practice with the quintain.

'Stand clear!' he yelled as he galloped up on a showy grey and hit the sand-filled bag an almighty clout with his lance. He then turned on me. 'Don't you know better than to get too close, you fool?'

'I was nowhere near the thing,' I retorted angrily, and was about to trade insult for insult when I recollected that I needed the cooperation of this man and that putting up his back was not the most sensible way to go about it. 'A beautiful hit, sir,' I toadied, despising myself as I did so.

He nodded, accepting such praise as his due, couched his weapon and dismounted, eyeing me up and down.

'Were you looking for me?'

'Yes, sir. I'm enquiring into the disappearance of your nephew for the Protector.'

He grunted. 'Oh, you're this chapman fellow, are you, that I've been hearing about? Quite one of my lord Gloucester's favourites, by all accounts. Sir Francis tells me the duke sets a lot of store by your ability to solve these sorts of mysteries, so what do you want to know? And poor old Gregory Machin dead! A bad business! A bad business!'

He was very like his twin whom I had met the preceding day, with the same shock of curly brown hair and light blue eyes beneath surprisingly dark, almost black, brows. But he was not quite so tall and somewhat broader than his brother.

What did I want to know? 'Anything you can tell me, sir,'

I said after a second's hesitation. 'Anything you think might have a bearing on Master Gideon's disappearance.'

'Why in God's name should I have any information?' he demanded irascibly. 'You'd do better to ask his brothers, young Bevis and Blaise.' He waved an airy hand. 'They're around somewhere. Half the damn family seems to be here for one reason or another. And Bevis and Blaise are the two boys nearest to Gideon in age. He's the baby of Pomfret's family. You'd never have guessed that that whey-faced creature Pom married would have bred so prolifically. Seven of 'em she's produced as easily as falling off a log.' Godfrey looked glum. 'And there's my old mare can't get one. Not for lack of trying, mind you,' he added with a lascivious wink.

I ignored this. 'And you can't think of any reason, sir, why someone might want to abduct your youngest nephew?'

'Gideon ain't my youngest nephew,' he replied almost gloomily. 'He was, mind you, until a short time ago. But last month my brother Henry's new wife presented him with a bouncing boy. And Hal's the eldest of all of us, sixty-one if he's a day, and she's a third of his age, if that. My old mare says it's disgusting –' he shrugged – 'but I don't know! If a man's up to it, well, why not? If he's able to bed a young filly, good luck to him, is my motto. But another boy! Our family runs to boys. Can't seem to get a single girl between us. Shouldn't complain, I suppose. There's many a king and nobleman who'd envy our family, I daresay.'

'So you can't help me, sir?'

He shook his head. 'Though I feel sure Pomfret will manage to blame me or Lewis for the boy's disappearance when he finally arrives. Still on his way down from Yorkshire, you know.' I nodded. 'You'd better find my nephew, Blaise – or the other one, Bevis. Like I said, they're about somewhere.' He added vaguely, 'They're in attendance on Sir Francis.'

But when I at last managed to track down these two young gentlemen, I found them kicking their heels in the servants' hall, playing a desultory game of three men's morris. It appeared that Sir Francis Lovell had been urgently summoned to Crosby's Place to wait upon my lord of Gloucester – and, well, I could guess what for! The duke would gradually be testing the opinions of his friends, gaining their support for what I feared was no longer just an idea at the back of his mind, but a definite and fully-fledged plan.

I tried not to think about it – after all, there was nothing I could do – and seated myself beside one of the boys, both of whom bore a strong family resemblance to their twin uncles. Briefly, I explained what I wanted to know.

Neither was purposely unhelpful. It was just that they had no idea what could have happened to their youngest brother or why.

'Did Tutor Machin have any particular enemies?' I asked in desperation when they showed signs of tiring of the subject and returning to their game.

They shook their curly heads in unison.

'Nobody liked him enough to dislike him,' the elder, Bevis, said, adding, 'if you know what I mean.'

'He was a dry old stick, but a good teacher.' This was Blaise's contribution. 'But harmless enough. He never quarrelled with anyone to my knowledge.'

'Except Mother Copley,' his brother added with a grin.

I seized on this. 'He and Dame Copley didn't get on?'

Bevis hunched his shoulders. He was a handsome lad of, I judged, about nineteen or twenty summers.

'They fought over Gideon. He's always been the old girl's favourite, just as he's our mother's. He's a sickly little beast, although not near as sickly as he likes to make out. At least, that's my opinion.'

'It's everyone's opinion,' Blaise concurred heartily. 'Gid's a bit of a weasel. Likes to be coddled and made a fuss of. God's toenails! Wasn't there an almighty row when Mother insisted that Dame Copley accompany him to Minster Lovell?' He chuckled reminiscently. 'I thought Father was going to die of an apoplexy. Never seen anyone so mad in all my life.'

'But the women carried the day,' his brother pointed out. 'In the end, Father was no match for them, with their wailing and sulking and wringing of hands. And of course, Tutor Machin didn't like it much, either. In fact, to say truth, he was furious. He'd hoped to get Gideon to himself, toughen him up a bit. And get some book learning into his silly little noddle.'

'What about young Piers Daubenay?' I asked.

But it seemed that there had been no objection to Piers.

'He's Gid's servant,' the older boy replied with a shrug. 'Gid has to have a servant. We all do. Nothing wrong with Piers. Bit vain, mind you. Prinks and preens in front of any mirror he happens to come across. But I think he has Gideon's measure. Or had,' he added, suddenly sober.

It seemed to hit both of them at once that they might never see their youngest brother again. They discarded their mocking tone and Bevis asked seriously, 'Do you think he's dead?'

'I don't know,' I told them truthfully. 'It's possible, but in that case, I can't see any reason why he would have been abducted. If it was necessary to get rid of him because he'd been a witness to murder, then he could have been disposed of on the spot. Why go to the trouble of taking him away?'

'So what do they want with him? Whoever "they" are?'

Regretfully, I shook my head. 'I'm afraid I don't have an answer for you just at present.' Or in the near future at this rate, I added mentally, but was careful not to express my thought aloud.

And that was as far as I got on Saturday, while the Dowager Duchess of York's insistence that everyone under her roof should attend Mass at least twice, if not three, times on Sunday, as well as observing a Sabbath calm throughout the intervening hours, effectively put a stop to my investigation until the following day. I used the respite by trying to assemble my thoughts and impressions in some sort of order, but found that, at the moment, they were too jumbled to form any kind of pattern. The murder of Gregory Machin in his locked room frustrated me at every turn for the simple reason that although it was an impossibility, it was also a fact. But how could one have an impossible fact? It was a paradox, a contradiction that sent my mind reeling. There would appear to be only one answer; that some supernatural agency was involved, but that I refused to allow. Once again, I examined the reason as to why I was so adamantly set against this solution, and again accepted that my instinct told me it wasn't so. And over the years, I had learnt to trust that feeling which seemed to emanate from somewhere deep down in my guts.

I saw very little of Piers during these two days. Once or twice, I recognized him at a distance during meals in the servants' hall, but he made no move to come over to my table; indeed, he returned my salutations with the briefest of nods or waves. He was in company with a group of younger men, all about his own age, and there was a good deal of laughter and joking as well as a certain amount of horseplay when the steward's stern eye was not upon them. It made me uncomfortably aware that in a few months' time, on October the second, I would be thirty-one years old. I was approaching middle-age.

And it was this realization as much as anything that made me so restless that Sunday night, chasing sleep from my pillow and keeping me awake into the small hours of Monday morning. And when I did finally fall asleep, it was to dream of Eloise Grey of all people; a muddled farrago of nonsense in which I was chasing her through the twisting passage-ways of Baynard's Castle, never quite catching up with her, but always a frustrating step or two behind. I woke just before dawn with the changing of the light, then slept again almost immediately to resume the same dream. Although not quite the same. This time it was Piers Daubenay whom I was pursuing – but still with the same lack of success . . .

I awoke with a start to find the morning well advanced if the bustle and clatter and raised voices within the castle were anything to judge by. And when I had eased my aching body from my hard pallet and opened the shutters of my cell-like room, the sun streaming in upon my face, the amount of traffic already on the river and the shouting of the boatmen as they vied with one another for trade convinced me that it was even later than I had thought.

I dressed as quickly as I could in my own comfortable old clothes, leaving the better stuff in my saddlebags, which I stowed away in a dark corner to reduce the possibility of theft. Next, I went down to the kitchen courtyard to stand in line for my turn at the pump, before making my way to one of the sculleries where bowls of hot water had been set out for shaving. By this time the water was tepid and my knife blunt, so I managed to cut myself twice, once on my cheek and once on my chin, and went to breakfast in a foul mood not improved by the usual meal of porridge, dried fish and yesterday's stale oatcakes. Silently, I cursed the dowager duchess and her parsimonious ways.

While I munched laboriously at my final oatcake, swilled down with some exceedingly weak small beer, I decided that I must speak again with Amphillis Hill. Accordingly, when I had finished, I directed my steps towards the sewing room.

'I'm sorry, Master Chapman, but I can't spare any of the girls just now.' The pleasant, elderly supervisor looked genuinely upset at having to deny my request, but her tone was determined. No blandishments or persuasion were going to make her change her mind. She indicated the silent girls, their heads bent diligently over their work, not a word or a giggle to be had from any of them. 'The duchess has ordered extra embroidery on the train of her coronation robe, and we're going to be hard pressed to get it done in time. If you wish to speak to Amphillis, you must do it later. Perhaps this evening.'

I glanced round the room, but there was no telling which girl was which. None of them looked up or gave me greeting. I could have urged it, citing my work for the Duke of Gloucester as my authority, but the dame in charge appeared harassed, overburdened with responsibility, so I gave in with as much grace as I could muster.

Once outside the room, I paused, wondering what to do next. Finally I decided to visit Dame Copley again in the hope that she might, now that she was calmer, remember something of value.

As I approached the twisting stair leading to the nurse's chamber, I heard the soft murmur of women's voices and then the gentle closing of a door. Two swift strides brought me to the head of the steps and I tiptoed down them, steadying myself with a hand against the left-hand wall, just in time to see Amphillis Hill let herself out of the door at the end of the passageway which gave access to the landing-stage. That same Amphillis Hill who, according to the sewing-mistress was busily plying her needle somewhere upstairs with the rest of the seamstresses.

For half a second I toyed with the notion that I must be mistaken, but the evidence of my own eyes assured me I was not. There was something immediately recognizable about the girl. Besides which, the faint echo remaining in my head of the voices I had heard told me that one of them was hers. She must have been visiting Rosina Copley. There was no alternative: the nurse's room seemed to be the only one occupied along this corridor.

Abandoning my original intention of going to see the dame myself, I followed Amphillis out of doors. She was in the act of summoning a passing boat and, keeping to the shadows cast by various small buildings to my left, I was lucky enough to hear her direction to the oarsman.

'Westminster. And hurry!'

I waited until the vessel was in midstream before descending the water-stairs and shouting to another boat. I gave the same direction.

As we pulled away, turning upstream, the oarsman grumbled, 'Westminster! Westminster! No one's going anywhere else today it seems. You're the fifth person I've taken there this morning, and the day's hardly begun. Doing the same run all the time gets monot'nous. I'm the sort what likes variety in me work, I am. Howsoever –' he shrugged resignedly – 'it's only t' be expected, I suppose.'

'Why?' I asked, listening to him with only half an ear while my eyes strained to keep Amphillis's boat in sight.

'D'you mean you don't know?' He sounded incredulous. 'Why you going there, then?'

I ignored this intrusion into my private affairs and asked again, 'What's happening?'

'They're bringing the young Duke o' York out of sanctuary. They say the Duke o' Gloucester – him what calls himself Protector now – has ordered it. Says he wants the lad to be with his brother in the Tower, ready fer the little king's coronation.' He sniffed. 'You really mean you ain't heard?'

I shook my head. 'I've only been in London since Friday.'

'Ho! Friday is it? In that case, you surely must have heard about the 'heading o' the Lord Chamberlain in the Tower.'

'He wasn't beheaded,' I said loudly. 'He's awaiting trial.'

The man gave a sort of snorting hiccough which I took to be a laugh. 'Who told you that fairy story? Them little elves at the bottom o' the garden? You don't want to believe everything you hear, y' know.'

'And neither do you!' I could feel my temper rising. Timothy had been right. Once those sorts of lies were disseminated, they quickly took root. 'You don't like the Protector?' I asked in a quieter tone, noting with relief that Amphillis's boat was still within view. The influx of river traffic was making it difficult to proceed with any speed.

'Don't know much about him down here, do we? Barely set eyes on him these past few years. Caught a glimpse or two of him last year, o' course, when there was all that fuss about him having won back some godforsaken, piddling little town in Scotland. What I say as a good Englishmen is bugger the Scots! Barbarians, all o' them. No good t' man nor beast. Same with northerners,' he added darkly, speaking as a man of the south. 'Weird, they are. Who knows what goes on up there? And he's one o' them. The Duke o' Gloucester, I mean.'

There seemed to be no argument against such entrenched prejudice, so I held my tongue, concentrating instead on keeping the other boat in sight. I became aware, however, that we and all the smaller vessels on the northern side of the river were being forced closer to the bank as a number of great gilded barges rowed past. And I noted that the leading barge flew the Gloucester standard, while others sported those of the Duke of Buckingham and Lord Howard. But the most worrying aspect was the boatloads of armed men following in their wake. It at once suggested to me, as it most certainly must to others, that the queen dowager was not willingly parting with her younger son. My heart sank. If force were to be the order of the day, Prince Richard would forfeit a great deal of goodwill.

My boatman suddenly rested on his oars.

'Might as well let 'em go,' he grunted. 'It'll be easier when that lot have landed.'

'Nonsense!' I said sharply. 'Go on, man! Go on!'

But he was not to be shifted, with the inevitable result that, by the time I did disembark at Westminster stairs,

Amphillis was nowhere to be seen, having vanished into the crowds that were assembled in front of the sanctuary. I stood still perforce, but even though I was a head taller than most of my neighbours, looking for her was as much use as searching for a needle in a bottle of hay.

I could see that the sanctuary was surrounded by my lord of Gloucester's men-at-arms. My lord himself, the Duke of Buckingham, Lord Howard and various other exalted personages, whom I failed to recognize, seemed to be locked in a violent altercation with a member of the queen dowager's household. The lady was obviously proving recalcitrant, refusing to release the little Duke of York without a fight. Indeed, no one could force her to give up the boy without violating the law of sanctuary.

A fat, red-cheeked woman standing next to me yelled out, 'Leave the child alone! He needs to be with his mother! Don't you let him go, my dear!'

There was a murmur of agreement from the crowd and other voices, mainly women's, were raised on Elizabeth's behalf.

'What's he want with the lad, anyway,' someone else, a man this time, grunted. 'Seems suspicious to me.'

'He' I took to be the Duke of Gloucester, and there was a further mutter of assent, now definitely hostile. I could feel the charge of menace in the air, and began to sweat uncomfortably, as if my affection for the duke made me culpable as well.

As well? Did I then believe that my lord was wrong to wish for the brothers to be together on the eve of the elder's coronation? Or, deep down, did I believe that Edward V would never be crowned? Did I secretly fear that there was a more sinister motive in removing little Prince Richard from sanctuary? Hastily I suppressed the idea. I had known Duke Richard for years and recognized him as a man of principle and honour. Whatever he did would never be from any ulterior motive.

Something was happening. My lords Gloucester, Buckingham and other dignitaries now withdrew to the nearby building which housed the Star Chamber, while Lord Howard and an old grey-haired man in episcopal robes – identified by the red-cheeked woman as Thomas Bourchier, Archbishop of Canterbury – disappeared in the direction of the abbot's quarters, presumably to confront the queen dowager herself.

It was at this moment that I spotted Amphillis at the back of the crowd in earnest conversation with another woman whose back was turned towards me. Neither seemed to be interested in the drama unfolding in front of them, nor, I was certain, had Amphillis noticed me. Cautiously, and with bent knees in order to reduce my height, I began to push my way through the crowd. It was a struggle, but I had the advantage of moving in the direction no one else wanted to go, everyone being eager to get nearer the sanctuary rather than further from it. But even so, my passage was necessarily slow, and by the time I found myself close to the door of St Margaret's church, where I had seen the two women, they had vanished.

Hot, frustrated and angry, I propped myself against the wall, stretched my bent and aching knees and once more looked about me. There was a sudden sibilance, a hissing that ran through the crowd like wind through corn, and I could see that the Archbishop had emerged from the sanctuary, the nine-year-old Duke of York clutching his hand; a small, bewildered and plainly – even from where I was standing – frightened child, his fair hair shining in the morning sun and what looked like tears glistening on his cheeks.

I saw my lord Gloucester go forward to greet his nephew, stooping to take the boy's hand in his and obviously trying to reassure him that all was well: he was being taken to be with his brother in the royal apartments in the Tower. I could hardly imagine that either boy was looking forward with any eagerness to the encounter. They didn't know each other. The king had been brought up in his own household in faraway Ludlow, on the Welsh marches, while Prince Richard had lived with his mother and ever increasing brood of sisters, all of whom no doubt had made a great pet of him, as women will.

The royal party moved off to the water-stairs and the waiting barges and the crowd began to disperse. In what seemed like only a few minutes, the space in front of the abbey had cleared, and suddenly there was Amphillis again, walking with her companion towards Westminster Gate. The second woman still had her back to me, but there was something familiar about it. I felt sure I had met her before somewhere, but without seeing her face, I couldn't be certain. Dodging around the street vendors with their trays of hats and spectacles, and keeping a firm grip on the pouch at my waist – Westminster was notorious for the speed and dexterity of its thieves – I tried to catch up with the two women, but they were moving too swiftly. For several moments I lost them as a troop of jugglers and mummers headed into Westminster with a great deal of unnecessary rattling of tambourines and blowing of trumpets in order to announce their arrival. And when I did at last catch sight of Amphillis again, she was alone, munching a pasty at one of the dozens of cook-stalls that proliferate around the gate.

It reminded me that I, too, was hungry, and although it was not yet dinner time, I bought a couple of eel pies which I ate standing up while never taking my eyes from my quarry. At least, that's what I thought, but between one blink and the next it seemed that she had gone, and there was still no sign of the other woman, either. Disgusted with myself, telling myself that I was getting old and slow, I finished and paid for my meal, bought a cup – well, two cups – of ale from a neighbouring stall and decided there was nothing for it but to return to Baynard's Castle and see if any more was to be discovered there.

As I walked back along the Strand towards the city, I wondered why I had been so reluctant to accost Amphillis openly, and came to the conclusion that there had been something furtive in her manner that had aroused my suspicions, although exactly what I was unable to say.

And then I saw her, ahead of me, passing the Chère Reine Cross. Every now and then, she glanced over her shoulder as if to make certain that she wasn't being followed. I was right. She was uneasy.

I dodged into the shadows cast by the overhanging houses and went after her.

TEN

Amphillis entered the city by the Lud Gate and walked up as far as St Paul's, with me still keeping a careful distance of perhaps some ten or fifteen paces behind her.

Once inside the city wall, the crowds thickened and she was forced to slow down, making it easier for me to keep her in view. Moreover, she ceased looking over her shoulder, seeming to gain confidence from the close proximity of other people. Not that I thought her really nervous of being followed: she appeared simply to be taking precautions against . . . Against what? Was it just my imagination that this expedition of hers had some nefarious purpose? Or was she merely playing truant from her duties in the sewing room? And if that were so, did she have the cooperation of the head seamstress, or was her absence being cleverly concealed by her companions?

At the top of Lud Gate Hill, Amphillis turned right down Old Dean's Lane and continued walking, past the house and gardens of the Dominican friary, finally turning left into Thames Street. It seemed that she was returning to Baynard's Castle – its bulk was already looming just ahead of us – and I felt an acute sense of disappointment. It had been nothing but a pleasure jaunt after all then, a cocking of her nose at authority in order to prove, no doubt, that she could do it. I could well imagine that an independent spirit such as hers would derive great pleasure from the notion. She had been to see a friend: that was all there was to it.

I had begun to slacken my pace when, with a sudden quickening of my heartbeat, I realized that Amphillis had passed the castle gate and was proceeding on her way. Indeed, she was almost out of sight. Cursing myself for a dolt, I hurried to regain the ground I had lost, but it wasn't easy. Thames Street is always a nightmare of overcrowding. On one side lie the great wharves and warehouses and on the other the mansions of the wealthy merchants and traders. The middle of the roadway is one long traffic jam of drays and carts and sumpter-horses, the drivers and riders abusing each other in the most colourful of epithets and even willing, on occasions, to dismount and use their fists. And if you are on foot, you are jostled by grinning sailors of every nationality, while your ears are assaulted by a veritable Babel of sound as all the languages of Europe (and beyond) seem to vie for dominance.

I had lost her. At the bottom of Old Fish Street Hill, I paused, sweating, but could no longer see Amphillis anywhere ahead of me. Of course, she was short; she was easily overlooked in a crowd. Then I noticed a water trough at the side of the road and stepped up on its rim. The added height enabled me to see well past the turning to Cordwainer Street, and just as I was bemoaning the fact that I had lost my quarry for good, I saw her a few yards further on, a small, quick-moving figure in a blue gown and white coif, hurrying in the direction of Dowgate Hill.

I caught her up, still being careful to stay a good few paces behind her, as she took the short cut through Elbow Lane. This brought her out perhaps some thirty or forty yards up the hill which she climbed steadily, heading for the junction with Wallbrook. It was not so simple to remain unnoticed here where the crowds were thinner, but not once did Amphillis turn her head or give any further indication that she was afraid of being followed.

Suddenly, without warning, she crossed the road from left to right, incurring, as she did so, the righteous wrath of a drayman descending the hill, and plunged into a side turning where the upper storeys of the houses on either side met almost in the middle, shutting out the daylight. At the entrance to the alleyway, I hesitated. It might be dark, but it was also quiet and offered very little cover. A few people were about, but not enough to conceal my bulky figure, and I wondered what excuse I could offer for my presence if Amphillis finally turned and saw me.

My dithering cost me dear, for when I did make up my mind, I found that I had lost her for a second time. Not caring now whether she spotted me or not, I quickened my stride, but she was nowhere to be seen. I soon discovered that the alley was quite short, bearing to the left and, at the further end, opening into the bustle of Candlewick Street. And now I really did curse my bungling ineptitude, calling myself all the names I could lay my tongue to. Why had it not occurred to me that she had merely taken another short cut, just as she had done through Elbow Lane? Why had I jumped to the unreasonable conclusion that this alleyway was Amphillis's destination? I was getting old and stupid.

At last I decided it was no good standing there. I might as well accept defeat. This time I wasn't going to catch her up again as I had done before. I had no idea which way she had taken, left towards Wallbrook or right in the direction of Eastcheap and any of the half dozen streets that lay between. I might as well return to Baynard's Castle.

I turned back into the alleyway, then, with a sharp intake of breath, stopped, hiding in the shelter of a doorway. Amphillis had suddenly reappeared just ahead of me, as if from nowhere, evidently in a hurry and retracing her steps towards Dowgate Hill.

I waited for her to vanish round the bend in the road, then eased my way forward, eager to discover where she had come from. It surely had to be one of the houses on the left-hand side, for there was no opening between any of them that I could see, but how to identify the particular house seemed almost impossible. I could hardly start knocking on doors enquiring whether anyone within was acquainted with Amphillis Hill.

And then I saw it, the narrow frontage of a tiny church huddled like a frightened spinster between two of the larger houses, its well-worn door of weathered oak very nearly invisible in the shadows. Could this be the answer? Had Amphillis simply come all this way in order to pray to a favourite saint?

I turned the ring-shaped handle, half expecting to find the door locked, but it gave easily and silently under my hand, as if it were kept well oiled, suggesting that the place was frequently used. But when I entered, the musty smell of decay met my nostrils, and I noticed that the dust was thick around the perimeter of the floor, although a pathway of scuffed footprints led as far as the altar and back again.

The altar itself was a plain stone slab adorned with nothing more than a couple of wooden candlesticks, holding two sickly-looking candles, and a poor plaster image of the saint to whom the church was dedicated. In the shaft of daylight from the still open door, I could just make out the name carved into its base.

Saint Etheldreda.

I cudgelled my brains to remember what I knew of her and, thanks to Brother Hilarion's good teaching during my novitiate at Glastonbury, found that I could recall the lady surprisingly well. For those who found Saxon names particularly daunting – which, of course, over the centuries, had included our Norman masters – she was also known as St Audrey. But, being myself of Saxon descent, in spite of the French name my mother had inflicted on me, I preferred to think of her as Etheldreda.

If memory served me aright, she was the daughter of an East Anglian king called Anna, and had been twice married. But marriage was not at all to Etheldreda's taste and she had rebelled against what she saw as the tyranny of the wedded state until released from its bonds by the death of her first husband. Unfortunately for her, she had then been forced into a second marriage, but this time had been able to persuade her new husband that God wished them to live together only as brother and sister, an arrangement that had led him to renounce her at the end of twelve years. (And who could blame him, poor fellow? I wouldn't have tolerated such a situation for as much as twelve months.) This had at last left the saint free to go and live a solitary life on the Isle of Ely, where she founded a monastery and also a nunnery of which she became the first abbess. The Venerable Bede tells us that Etheldreda suffered from a disfiguring neck tumour which she regarded as a punishment for having once worn a valuable necklace for her own self-glorification. But when her body was exhumed, some years after she died of the plague, the tumour had miraculously vanished and her flesh was sweet and wholesome. She was, inevitably I felt, the patron saint of all neck and throat ailments.

Was it possible then that Amphillis suffered from such trouble? Was that why she came here, to pray to the saint for a cure? And yet I found it hard to believe. The little seamstress was surely too full of life to be suffering from any kind of illness. But why else would she come so far? For what purpose?

Perhaps she just favoured the saint. Perhaps Amphillis herself was no friend to matrimony. And if so, was she naturally celibate by nature or did she prefer her own sex? That there are such women – and of course men – we know from the ancient Greeks, although the law and the Church forbid such love on pain of death.

I wandered around the church, scuffing up more dust, turning the matter over in my mind and finally reaching the conclusion that it was not my concern. I felt reasonably certain that it was St Etheldreda's that Amphillis had been visiting, and not one of the neighbouring houses, although why this conviction was so strong I couldn't really say. It was just my instinct guiding me again.

I suspected that my morning had been wasted on a wild goose chase, and that this place, that Amphillis herself, had nothing to do with either the murder of the tutor or the disappearance of young Gideon Fitzalan. I cursed silently before recollecting that I was in God's house and, with a sigh, turned back for one last look at the altar.

It was then I noticed for the first time that someone had put a garland of meadow flowers around the statue's neck, and remembered suddenly that her feast day was June the twenty-third, Midsummer Eve. And Midsummer Eve was fast approaching. It was exactly a week away. Someone had thought it worthwhile to deck the saint for her coming festival.

Amphillis? But the flowers looked too faded to have been placed there this morning. Judging by appearances, they had been there several days, but I stepped closer to make certain.

'What you doing here then, my young master?' queried a voice behind me.

I whirled about to find myself confronting an old woman in a rusty black gown and none too clean apron and coif, with a few wisps of grey hair escaping from beneath the latter. Several of her front teeth were missing, so that when she spoke, she made a kind of whistling sound, but her blue eyes were still as bright and sharp as a young girl's. She was carrying a garland of wild flowers, similar to the one already gracing the saint's slender neck

'I . . . er . . . I was paying my respects to the saint,' I answered, feeling like a schoolboy who had been caught in some suspicious act.

'Know who she is, do you?'

'Yes. Saint Etheldreda.'

The woman gave a cackle of laughter that turned into a whistle as it died away. 'Any fool could tell that. It says so underneath.'

'Also known as Saint Audrey,' I retorted, and went on to give the saint's history.

My interlocutor looked impressed. 'You don't look like an educated man. Not in them clothes,' she added frankly.

'I was once a novice at Glastonbury Abbey.' I bowed. 'May I have the honour of knowing to whom I'm speaking?'

That made her cackle even louder. 'My, my! Quite the gen'leman. My name's Etheldreda, too. Etheldreda Simpkins. She's my name saint.' The woman nodded towards the altar. 'That's why I keeps her decked with flowers. "Ethel" means "good" in the old language, you know. And what are you called, my fine young cockalorum?'

'Roger.'

My new acquaintance eyed me up and down. 'That's a Norman name for a Saxon boy like you.'

I laughed. 'Surely after four hundred years we're pretty much one and the same.'

My companion snorted contemptuously and whistled even louder. 'If you believe that, young man, you're a bigger fool than you look. How many of our lords and masters do you know called Smith or Wright or Carter?' She answered her own question. 'None, I'll be bound. They all have danged Frenchified names – Neville or Beauchamp or de Vere.' She spat the words out like a mouthful of cherry stones.

'Very true,' I answered with a grin. 'You're an astute woman, Goody Simpkins.'

'Dunno about that.' She regarded me cautiously. 'But I know what I know,' she added fiercely.

'This church doesn't look as if it's much used,' I said, indicating the dust. 'But I don't suppose many people outside this alley know that it's here. I nearly missed it myself, it's so narrow and so hemmed in by the houses on either side. Does it have many worshippers?'

'More'n you'd think. But mostly women, those that aren't happy with their menfolk or their marriages, I reck'n. There've been a few strangers around here lately.'

'There was a young girl in here awhile ago,' I said. 'Short, plump.' Although as a description it didn't really do Amphillis Hill justice. 'It was because she came out of the church that I noticed it, and came inside myself to have a look around. And offer up a prayer, of course,' I added hastily.

I received a deservedly sceptical look, but the old dame made no comment. 'I don't recall seeing her today,' she said. 'But I know who you'm talking about. I've seed her once or twice lately. Don't know who she is, mind. Ain't from this part o' the city. I was born here and I knows most folk from Candlewick Street and the hill. Dowgate, that is.'

I nodded, but absently. I had been vaguely aware for some minutes of a sound, faint and far off, that I couldn't quite identify. Finally, as Goody Simpkins was speaking, I recognized what it was.

'I can hear running water somewhere,' I said. 'At least, I think that's what it is. It's hard to tell.'

My companion once again gave her ear-splitting cackle. Her paroxysms of mirth were doing serious damage to my ears.

'You got sharp hearing, young master. I can't make it out nowadays, although I could once, plain as plain. But now I'm nigh on sixty. My time'll soon be up and my ears ain't what they used t' be. It's only natural. What you c'n hear is the Wallbrook gurgling away deep underground. Centuries ago it were built over. They do say as it flows out of a pipe somewhere along the banks o' the Thames.' She reverted to our previous topic of conversation. 'Mind you, I did glance in here earlier this morning, and there weren't nobody here then. O' course, it don't mean that girl weren't here. She could've been down in the crypt.'

'The crypt?' I questioned sharply, staring around. 'I don't see any entrance to a crypt.'

'Not from where you're standing, you wouldn't.' The old

woman advanced and, reaching up, removed the garland of dead flowers from about the saint's neck, replacing it with the fresh one. 'It's behind the altar. Here, I'll show you.'

Between the back of the altar and the inner wall of the apse was a narrow space just wide enough to allow one person at a time to squeeze into the gap, and set in the floor was a heavy slab of stone which plainly could be lifted by a length of rope tied at one end to an iron ring.

'Pull it up, then,' said the crone over my shoulder.

I stooped and heaved on the rope with a force that sent me staggering back, so that both Etheldreda Simpkins and myself ended up in a tangled heap on the dusty floor. Etheldreda swore with a fluency that commanded my admiration. I knew few men, including myself, who could have equalled her vocabulary.

'You didn't have t' pull on it like that,' she reprimanded me when once she had caught her breath. 'It do come up easy.'

'I realize that now,' I snapped. 'I didn't expect it to. I thought it would be difficult to move.'

I picked myself up and helped my companion to her feet. Cautiously she felt herself all over to ensure that nothing was damaged.

'You can't be thrown around like that at my age, young master,' she complained, whistling louder than ever. 'It ain't right nor seemly.'

I apologized before again turning my attention to the trap-door. This now lay inner side up, flat on the floor. I crouched down and examined the enormous iron hinges. They gleamed with oil fairly recently applied and I glanced up at the old woman.

'The crypt must be in fairly frequent use,' I said. 'So what's it used for?'

She shrugged her thin shoulders. 'I think the priest do let people store their rubbish down there.'

I nodded. There was a church, St Giles, not far from where I lived in Bristol, where the crypt was similarly rented out by the local incumbent to supplement his starvation wages.

'If you want t' ask him,' Etheldreda went on, 'he'm about somewhere. We do share him with St Mary Bothaw, St Swithin and St John Wallbrook.'

'That won't be necessary.' I could see a flight of steps descending into the darkness. 'Where are the candles and tinderbox kept?'

'You going down, then?' When I nodded in affirmation, she sniffed. 'What you do need's a lantern. It be draughty down there. A candle'll blow out easy. Stay here. I'll go and fetch one. My house is just across the street. I won't be two shakes o' a lamb's tail.'

She was as good as her word, moving with a celerity that belied her years. And if she took a little longer than the promised 'two shakes' I barely noticed it as I crouched on my haunches staring into the chasm below me, trying to identify the smell which rose from its depths. Must and decay and damp made up the greater part of it, but there was something else; something I could not place and yet was oddly familiar; something that made me strangely uneasy.

I was still puzzling over it, but still without an answer, when Etheldreda returned carrying a lighted lantern which she handed to me.

'You go first,' she said.

I was taken aback. 'You're coming down with me?'

'Why not?' She cackled again, this time full in my left ear, making it sing. 'Never been down there, so here's my chance. And with a handsome young fellow like you, as well! Mus' be my lucky day!'

'Mind you don't slip,' I warned her, holding the lantern higher.

To my surprise, there were at least a dozen steps: the chamber was deep underground. And the old woman was right. It was devoid of any tomb, so the priest allowed his parishioners to use it as a repository for unwanted odds and ends. The feeble rays of my raised lantern showed the same jumble of broken furniture as could be found in St Giles's crypt. Here and there were more useful items, such as a pile of wooden planks and a stack of undamaged tiles, but in general there was little of value and certainly nothing worth stealing. No thief would find it worth his while to risk the steep descent for such rubbish. And the church itself offered nothing to tempt the light-fingered. The door could be left unlocked with perfect safety.

The noise of running water was louder down here. I noticed that the walls glistened with damp and were patched with mould. The Wallbrook must be very close. The smell, too, was slightly more pungent, but my nose was growing used to it, and after a very few minutes failed to be irritated by it any longer.

'They do say,' Etheldreda volunteered, peering about her, 'that there did used t' be a Roman what-d'you-call-it here-abouts. Wouldn't be a church, now would it? Not with them worshipping all them heathen gods.'

'Temple?' I suggested

'That'd be it.' She whistled again through the gap in her front teeth. 'Old John Marchant, him what lives in one o' the end houses, reck'ns it had summat to do with a bull. Sounds a rum do t' me, but you c'n never tell with them folks from ancient times.'

'Mithras,' I said. 'Your friend reckons that this – or near here – was the site of the Temple of Mithras?'

I knew all about Mithras, the soldier's god; the god of the Roman legions. His story had been told in one of the forbidden books in the Glastonbury library whose locked clasps had been picked by my fellow novice, Nicholas Fletcher. And having read it, I could see why, in many ways, it was far more disturbing than the lascivious tales of the daughters of Albion and their ilk, and why Brother Hilarion had been far more upset by our reading it than all the rest put together.

A thousand years ago, Mithras had been born in a cave in Persia in midwinter, while shepherds watched nearby and a star shone in the heavens. He was represented with a torch in one hand and a knife in the other, and with the knife he had single-handedly killed a great white bull, cutting its throat so that its shed blood should bring fertility to the earth. And then, after a last meal of bread and wine, he had been taken up to heaven. His name meant 'friend' because he was the protector of mankind in this life and guarded him from evil spirits after death.

'What d'you say he was called?' Etheldreda's voice cut into my thoughts and made me jump.

'Mithras,' I said, and told her the legend.

She frowned, sucking her bottom lip. 'Sounds blaspheemious

t' me,' she opined at length as she puzzled over the familiar
elements of the story. 'Didn't ought to be taught to young
folk like you.'

'It wasn't.' And I regaled her with the circumstances which
had attended my first reading of the tale. This amused her
greatly and diverted her attention, as I had hoped it would.
She was too old to be bothering her head over questions of
religious belief. And anyway, such questions were dangerous.

'There don't seem t' be much down here worth looking
at,' she finally remarked. 'And I'm getting cold. 'T ain't good
for we old 'uns t' get shivery. I'm going now. You c'n poke
about a bit more if you want. You c'n return the lantern when
you'm finished. It's the house opposite the church door.'

I thanked her and lighted her progress up the steps until
she disappeared through the trapdoor at the top before
returning to my survey of the crypt. At first glance – or, in
this case, at a second and third glance – it seemed as though
Goody Simpkins was correct; there was nothing more to see
than we had already discovered. But my natural stubborn-
ness made me prowl around yet again, the lantern's pale rays
fitfully illuminating the broken or unloved bits of old furniture that had been stored down there: a three-legged stool,
a chair with an awkward back, a hideous pot which had probably been someone's wedding gift and hated on sight. And
certainly there was nothing to have tempted Amphillis Hill
down there. I decided that the old woman must have peeped
into the church before Amphillis arrived.

I held the lantern higher for one last fleeting glance around,
and was about to make for the steps when there was a scraping
sound followed by the crash of something falling. I swung
to my right, my heart beating furiously, the beam from the
lantern careering madly up and across the walls and finally
coming to rest on a number of wooden planks that had been
propped vertically in one corner. One of them must have
toppled over – maybe I had accidentally brushed against it
– bringing a second one down with it. The noise in that
confined space had been deafening, making me jump and
my heart hammer in my chest.

Disgusted with myself for being so easily frightened, I put
the lantern on the floor and went to lift the fallen planks,

propping them once more against the wall. It was as I was positioning the second of the two that I suddenly noticed what seemed to be a latch and realized that I could be looking at a door. It was partially concealed by the wood which had to be removed by anyone wishing to make use of the entrance. I guessed that whoever had closed the door last had been in something of a hurry and had failed to prop one of the planks upright.

With shaking hands, I began to shift them, half expecting that my eyes were playing me tricks, and that what, in the gloom, appeared to be a latch would prove in reality to be nothing but a shadow. But when the planks had all been moved some foot or two to the left, a thick oaken door, studded with iron nails and opened by a substantial iron latch, stood revealed.

I opened it. The door swung inwards without a sound, suggesting that its hinges had also been carefully oiled. I retrieved the lantern and held it aloft, its beam lighting the walls of a second chamber. This was even further below ground than the crypt and entailed the descent of another half dozen steps before floor level could be reached. The sound of running water was quite loud now, indicating that the Wallbrook was somewhere close at hand. Moreover, the peculiar smell I had noticed was stronger here and made me want to retch.

Someone – I forget who – had once told me that beneath the London streets there still existed a warren of subterranean passages and vaults from the city's ancient past, and here, had I doubted it, lay the proof of those words. Far above me, the hustle and bustle of the everyday world went on, but down in this stinking and fetid darkness I was in another place, another time, another life . . .

With an effort, I pulled myself together and harnessed my wandering thoughts. I lifted the lantern higher and examined my surroundings. The chamber was empty, but in one corner I could see a large, semicircular aperture which, when I crouched beside it, showed itself to be a downward-sloping drain, and the sound of water gushing past was now loud in my ears. It was a channel, quite possibly Roman in origin, connecting this chamber with the stream and serving the

Temple of Mithras which, according to Goody Simpkins's friend, had once stood on or near this site.

I stood up and held the lantern above my head for one last look around, but there was nothing more to be seen. Dark stains mottled the floor, patches of fungus sprouted from the walls and quite suddenly, for no apparent reason, I could feel my flesh begin to creep. I shivered, feeling inexplicably depressed and weary.

I turned and made for the stairs.

ELEVEN

I flung wide the shutters and shouted, 'Well? Can you see any way to get in?'

It was the following morning and I had recruited Piers Daubenay to assist me in a small experiment. I had, without its occupier's knowledge or permission, locked, or rather bolted, myself into the room next door to Tutor Machin's, having previously directed Piers to remain outside on the castle's landing-stage. Now, as I leant out of the open casement, his youthful, smooth-skinned face was upturned to mine, the morning sun catching the red glints in his curly hair and turning it to copper.

'Well?' I demanded again testily. 'Is there any way in which you can climb up the wall to this window?'

He shook his head. 'I can't see one,' he reported cheerfully. 'This stretch of wall is smooth, But you must know that. You must have inspected it already.'

'I just wanted a second opinion, that's all. You would agree with me, then, that no one could have climbed into any of the rooms along this passageway from outside?'

'Impossible,' he confirmed.

'Now come in and see if there is any way – any way at all – that you can get inside this room without me unbolting the door.'

'You know fucking well it can't be done.'

As once before, at Minster Lovell, the swear word jarred, not because I was a prude and didn't use it myself on occasions – quite a few occasions, if I'm honest – but because it seemed deliberately chosen to prove a point. But what point? That the soft-cheeked boy was really a man who could hold his ale and curse along with the next fellow? Probably. He couldn't possibly believe it would shock me.

'Just come in and do as you're told,' I said.

A few minutes later, the latch rattled, then there was a thump as Piers presumably threw his weight against the door.

Nothing happened, of course. The bolt didn't even tremble. Like its counterpart in what had been Gregory Machin's room, it was too stoutly made. I partially loosened it, so that only the tip of the shaft remained in the socket.

'Try again,' I ordered my helper. 'Harder this time.'

Piers obliged, but once more there was no appreciable result. No one could have entered the tutor's room even if the bolt had not been properly rammed home. I sighed and opened the door.

'So what's the answer?' Piers asked as I stepped outside and went to look yet again at the neighbouring chamber.

This had at last been swept clean of the shards of wood from the broken door, although the castle carpenter had not so far had time to make and fit a new one.

'I don't know,' I admitted. 'There doesn't seem to be one.'

Piers crossed himself and made the sign to ward off the evil eye, his jaunty air suddenly deserting him.

'There's only one explanation then, isn't there?' he demanded unhappily. 'This was the Devil's work.'

I didn't reply because there seemed to be no satisfactory alternative solution. And yet I still couldn't bring myself to accept it. I felt strongly that the murder was human handiwork. For one thing, if the Devil, for whatever reason, had wanted to take Gregory Machin's life, he would have had no need to use a dagger. Old Nick would simply have appeared and frightened the poor man to death. Or just ripped his soul from his body. No, no! The more I thought about it, the more I was convinced that there was a rational explanation. But what it was, I had as yet no idea.

An exclamation from Piers made me turn sharply in the hope that he might have discovered something I had overlooked. But he had wandered over to the window and flung wide the shutters to let some air and light into the claustrophobic atmosphere of the room.

'What is it?' I asked.

'Sir Pomfret and Lady Fitzalan have just arrived at the water-stairs with all their baggage. They must have come up river by barge.' He turned, a slight smile on his lips. 'Now there's likely to be some wailing and gnashing of teeth. Poor Sir Francis will be held entirely responsible for Master

Gideon's safety and will feel the full force of her ladyship's tongue.'

A young lad, one of the household pages by the look of him, who had just mounted the stairs from the lower passageway, glanced towards us, obviously having overheard what Piers was saying.

'Not Sir Francis any longer, if you please,' he admonished us. 'Word arrived from Crosby's Place not half an hour ago that my lord's been made a viscount and appointed Lord Chamberlain in Lord Hastings's place.'

Piers gave a long, low whistle, and once again I felt as though someone had punched me in the chest. Things were beginning to move. The duke was taking steps to surround himself with his friends, appointing them to key positions in the government. It surely could not be long now before he took the biggest step of all and laid claim to the crown.

Piers gave an uncertain laugh as he studied my face. 'What's the matter, Master Chapman? You look as though you've lost a shilling and picked up half a groat.'

At his words, the page, who had been about to move on, swung round and examined me carefully from head to foot. 'Are you Roger Chapman?' he asked doubtfully. I inclined my head. 'In that case,' he went on, 'Sir Pomfret and Lady Fitzalan want to speak to you. I've been sent to find you. They're in the great solar. If you'll follow me, I'll show you where it is.'

Piers chuckled unfeelingly. 'Now the fur will fly. You'll be subjected to all her ladyship's hysterics. And neither she nor Sir Pomfret will believe you're the duke's choice to investigate this mystery. Not in those clothes! What a pity you're not wearing one of your gentleman's outfits.'

The page was sympathetic. 'I'll wait,' he offered, 'if you wish to change.' And he leant his shoulders against the passage wall. 'They won't know how long it took me to find you. I certainly didn't expect to run you to earth so soon.'

'My room is several landings up,' I warned him.

He shrugged. 'I'm in no hurry.'

Of course he wasn't. I'd never yet met the domestic servant who was, unless he was threatened with condign punishment for dawdling.

'I'll come with you,' Piers offered. 'I ought to accompany you to the solar anyway. I daresay Sir Pomfret and Lady Fitzalan will want to see me.'

And without waiting for my agreement, he followed me along the passage, up two more flights of cold stone stairs, under an archway and on to a landing which I immediately recognized as the one outside the sewing room. And there, facing me, standing by the door talking to another woman whose back was towards me, was Amphillis. I hadn't seen her since the previous day, nor had I sought her out after my return to Baynard's Castle, but I thought the gaze she turned on me now was both guilty and startled. I was not, however, much concerned with her at that moment. I had realized with something of a shock that her companion was the same woman she had been talking to at Westminster the day before when the little Duke of York had been delivered from sanctuary. And for the second time, I felt that that back was somehow familiar.

'Amphillis!' I said, and was about to start forward when a cry of pain behind me made me turn abruptly to find that Piers had stupidly taken a step backwards and slipped down a couple of stairs. He was propped against the wall, hopping on one leg and cradling his left foot in both hands.

'I've twisted my ankle,' he moaned. 'When you stopped suddenly like that, I wasn't expecting it.' He lowered the afflicted member to the ground and gingerly tested it with his full weight. 'No harm done,' he added with a sigh of relief. 'It will be better in a minute or two.'

I gave an unsympathetic grunt and swung back to speak to Amphillis, but neither she nor the woman with her were anywhere to be seen.

Cursing, I stepped towards the sewing-room door.

'I must speak to Mistress Hill,' I said, but Piers hobbling after me, grasped me by the elbow.

'You can't waste time talking, Roger,' he said urgently. 'You still have to change and Sir Pomfret and Lady Fitzalan won't tolerate being kept waiting much longer. You'll get that young page into trouble. So come on! Let's get up to your room.'

I ignored this.

'Did you see them?' I demanded. 'Amphillis Hill and another woman! Did you see where they went?'

'No, I did not,' Piers answered crossly. 'Thanks to you, I was too busy falling downstairs. But I'm telling you, you haven't time to go looking for anyone now. You can speak to Amphillis later if it's urgent.'

'It's not her, it's the other woman I want. That's the second occasion I've seen her, but unfortunately only her back view each time. All the same, I feel certain that I know her – or at least that I've seen her somewhere before. Let go of me! I'm going into the sewing room to see if they're there.'

But when I glanced around the door, there was no sign of Amphillis or her mysterious friend. Moreover, I got very short shrift from the chief seamstress, who was plainly growing impatient with my frequent and unwelcome appearances in her domain. In reply to my query, she snapped that Amphillis was out on a commission for Her Grace of York and was not expected back for some hours.

When I would have argued the point, Piers hissed in my ear, 'For God's sake, come on! Just remember that poor lad waiting for us downstairs.'

Reluctantly, I tore myself away. As I had at least one more flight of steps to ascend, Piers excused himself from accompanying me on account of his ankle.

'I'll wait here,' he said. 'Don't be long.'

His peremptory tone annoyed me, and once in my narrow cell of a room, I took my time shedding my comfortable attire and donning brown hose and yellow tunic, not forgetting my velvet cap so that I could doff it respectfully in Sir Pomfret's presence. Then I loitered some more, staring out of my window . . .

I caught my breath. Two women were hurrying towards the water-stairs. One was definitely Amphillis and the other almost certainly her mysterious companion. A passing boat having been hailed and rowed to shore, the pair embraced, a little perfunctorily it was true, but with enough affection to warrant a kiss on both cheeks and a quick hug. The second woman was now facing me, but too far away for me to make out her features with any clarity. And yet I was again seized by the conviction that I had seen her somewhere before:

there was something about her build and her stance that teased my memory, but cudgel my brains as I might, I could not place her. Where and when we had met continued to elude me.

The woman turned and went down the steps, the boatman steadying his craft as she stepped into the bows and took her seat. A final wave, and she was being rowed upstream towards Westminster, while Amphillis walked slowly back towards the castle. But before she could reach the landing-stage door, another figure bustled out to meet her.

Dame Copley!

The nurse took Amphillis by one arm and turned back with her towards the building, her head bent to catch what her companion was saying. This seemed to be a great deal, which surprised me. I had not gathered from Dame Copley's previous remarks on the subject that she and Amphillis were anything but nodding acquaintances; certainly not on the friendly terms that now appeared to exist between them. And twice during the short walk, Amphillis paused, gesturing behind her towards the water-stairs and obviously imparting information about the woman who had just left her. I cursed my bad luck that from my eyrie I was unable to hear a single word that was being exchanged. (And I dared not lean out of the window for fear of being seen.)

I returned to the sewing-room landing to find Piers hobbling up and down in frustration. 'What, in the name of all the saints, have you been doing?' he demanded without waiting for me to offer an explanation. 'In spite of the pain I'm in, I was just about to go up to look for you. It hasn't taken you this length of time, surely, just to change your clothes?'

I made no answer to this reprimand, but asked instead, 'How well does Dame Copley know Amphillis Hill?'

Piers blinked a little at this abrupt change of subject and stammered, 'Sh-she knows her. Well, you know that she does. It-it was Rosina who mentioned her to you as being the last person to have seen Tutor Machin alive. You must remember!'

'Of course I remember!' Once more I was startled by Piers's easy use of the nurse's Christian name. 'But I didn't get the impression that they were friends.'

'They're not.'

As we began descending the stairs, I told him what I had just observed, reiterating my conviction that I had met the third woman at some time in the past, but not that I had seen her the previous day. Indeed, I continued to keep the whole of yesterday's adventure a secret. Why, I wasn't sure.

Piers refused to be impressed or see any significance in what I had recently witnessed. 'They were simply having a gossip, that's all. You know how women love to chat.' He waved a dismissive hand. 'And now for heaven's sake hurry up! Sir Pomfret will be having an apoplexy by this time and that poor page will be in trouble.'

Neither prediction came true.

The page, having conducted us to the great solar, had the good sense merely to announce us as quickly as possible before making himself scarce. As for Sir Pomfret, he was plainly too travel-weary, and had his hands too full comforting his wife to be concerned with any tardiness on our part. Besides which, both his brothers, Godfrey and Lewis, and his sons, Bevis and Blaise, were already with him, making the room feel uncomfortably full of people. For several minutes our presence was ignored, while Lady Fitzalan was coaxed into abating her sobs with a platter of doucettes and another goblet of wine. Finally, however, young Bevis, prodded in the back by Piers, condescended to notice us and announced our arrival again to his father. The huddle of anxious relatives drew to one side.

My change of raiment evidently failed to impress Sir Pomfret, because he eyed me up and down with obvious suspicion, and his tone, when he spoke, was decidedly chilly.

'So you're this . . . this . . . this chapman –' the word when he at last produced it was redolent with contempt '– that the Lord Protector has appointed to look into my son's disappearance, are you? Well, I suppose Duke Richard knows his own business best. Although I shouldn't have thought—'

Blaise interrupted him. 'Master Chapman has a great reputation for solving these sort of mysteries, Father. At least,' he added ingenuously, 'so I'm told.'

I saw Piers, standing a little ahead of me, suppress a grin.

Sir Pomfret, having digested this, inevitably posed the question I was dreading. 'So what have you discovered, my man?'

I was saved from immediate reply by the sudden entrance into the solar of Dame Copley, coming to pay her respects and duty to her employers. At the sight of her, Lady Fitzalan gave a little scream – rising to her feet and spilling wine down the front of her gown as she did so – and stumbled towards her.

'Rosina!' she sobbed. 'Where is he? Where's my baby boy?'

Bevis and Blaise exchanged glances, the former making a gagging sound which, mercifully, was heard by neither parent.

The two women clung together, mingling their tears and making sufficient noise to call forth a terse reprimand from Sir Pomfret, demanding quiet. He then, as I had been afraid he would, turned his attention back to me.

'Well, Master Chapman, I'm waiting to know what you've discovered.'

I had, by this time, marshalled my thoughts into some sort of order and was ready with my excuses. 'Sir Pomfret, I regret that I cannot, just at present, reveal any details. Protocol compels me to present my findings first to my lord of Gloucester before telling anyone else. Also secrecy at this point in my investigation is vital.'

Out of the corner of one eye, I saw Piers's head jerk round, his eyebrows raised, but I stared doggedly ahead, refusing to meet his gaze.

'So you have discovered something?' the knight demanded.

I made no direct answer, but smirked knowingly. Sir Pomfret could make what he liked of that.

He was not disposed to make anything of it and barked at me that he supposed, as Gideon's father, he had as much right to be informed of my discoveries as anyone, including the Lord Protector.

There was a general all-round nodding of heads, but once again, I was saved by the opening of the solar door. A diminutive page announced the Dowager Duchess of York and Cicely Neville made her stately, unhurried entrance, leaning on an ebony, silver-handled cane and attended by two of her women.

There was an immediate flurry of bobbing and bowing, in acknowledgement of which she gave an impatient wave of her hand as if bored by such homage; as no doubt she was, I reflected, after a lifetime of adulation. In her youth, she had been known as the Rose of Raby, one of the loveliest women in England; and remnants of that beauty still showed in a face that wore its age with dignity, making no attempt to hide the wrinkles beneath a layer of white lead and paint.

I studied her carefully as she advanced on Sir Pomfret and his lady, holding out a gnarled hand for them to kiss. She was dressed austerely in a black gown and white coif, as nearly akin to a nun's habit as was seemly in a woman still very much of her world, however much she might wish people to think otherwise. I imagined that the shrewd, keen eyes missed very little, and had no doubt whatsoever that she was wholeheartedly behind her remaining son's bid – if that was indeed what it turned out to be – for the crown. She had never made any secret of her dislike of her daughter-in-law, the queen dowager, and her cohorts of Woodville relations, and was outspoken, so rumour had it, in holding them responsible for the execution of the Duke of Clarence. The young king might be her grandson, but he had been raised surrounded – smothered one might almost say – by his mother's kinsmen from early childhood. The poor boy could not help but be more Woodville than Plantagenet.

'Sir Pomfret!' After a brief nod, she ignored Lady Fitzalan. (I fancied she did not care overmuch for her own sex.) 'I cannot express how deeply distressed I am that this terrible murder should have taken place in my house. And the disappearance of your son! I, too, have lost children. I can enter into your feelings.'

This assumption that Gideon must be dead was of no help to his parents, Lady Fitzalan immediately falling into another fit of hysterics, which her agitated husband strove vainly to assuage. In the end, it was a sharp word from the duchess which stemmed the flow of tears.

'Control yourself, madam!' She then bent her disapproving gaze on Bevis and Blaise who were trying to make themselves as inconspicuous as possible. 'Are these your sons?' Sir Pomfret assented. 'Then one of them must take his brother's place. You!' She pointed at Bevis. 'You must present yourself at the royal apartments at the Tower as soon as possible to wait on the k– on my grandson.' I wondered if anyone else apart from myself had noticed her balk at the word 'king', but there was nothing in any face to suggest that someone had. She went on, 'My son wishes Edward to have people he can trust around him.'

Lady Fitzalan stretched out a trembling hand. 'Your Grace, Bevis won't . . . won't disappear, as well, will he?'

The duchess deigned no reply to this, merely snorting impatiently before suddenly swivelling round to confront me.

'Ah, Master Chapman, we meet again. It's been a long time.' She looked me up and down. 'You've put on weight. And smarter, too, I notice.'

To my annoyance, I found myself colouring up under that keen scrutiny. I managed an ingratiating smile.

The duchess continued, 'I understand my son has summoned you to London to unravel this mystery. Have you done so?'

'N-not yet, Your Grace,' I stuttered, feeling like an errant schoolboy. (Or should I say a fat errant schoolboy? Had I put on weight? Probably. I liked my food too much and Adela fed me too well.)

'Do you have any ideas?' the duchess shot at me. 'We need this unfortunate matter cleared up before the coronation.'

She forbore to say whose coronation, and once again I wondered if I was the only one to think the omission significant.

I gave the silent smirk another airing, but it had as little effect upon my interlocutor as it had done on Sir Pomfret.

'Well? Yes or no?'

I lied through my teeth: there was nothing else to do.

'For the moment, my lady, I prefer to remain silent. I need first to speak to my lord the Protector.'

She regarded me thoughtfully for a second or two, pursing her lips, then nodded briefly. 'I understand,' she said. (I prayed to God she didn't.) 'Sir Pomfret, rooms have been prepared for you and your lady. I will send my steward to conduct you to them. Meanwhile this young man –' she once more indicated Bevis – 'can be escorted to the Tower.' She looked

at Blaise. 'And his brother may as well accompany him.'
The duchess seemed to become aware of Godfrey and Lewis
Fitzalan for the first time. 'Ah! The twins! You are in good
health, sirs?' They both acknowledged the question, each
with a deep bow. 'And the rest of the brood? Henry? Warren?
Raisley? George?'

There was a general gasp, and Godfrey said admiringly,
'Your Grace is a marvel to remember all their names.'

The duchess smiled. 'I never forget the names of our loyal
adherents. The House of York has reason to be grateful for
your family's support over the years.' She turned to Sir
Pomfret who had momentarily forgotten his troubles and was
goggling at her with admiration quite as open as his brothers'. 'You, too, I believe, have four other sons besides these
two lads here and . . . and Master Gideon?'

As the last name was uttered, Lady Fitzalan gave a convul-
sive sob, and the duchess, without waiting for a reply, took
her leave on a somewhat hurried note.

'God be with you all,' she said, and swept from the solar
as quickly as her rheumatic limbs would allow.

I decided it was time to beat a hasty retreat of my own
before the bereaved father could question me further. Fortunately, Lady Fitzalan's renewed attack of the vapours gave me
an opportunity to slip away quietly while her husband's attention was otherwise engaged. Piers followed me out.

'A little of that caterwauling goes a long way,' he remarked
callously as he caught up with me and slipped a hand through
my arm. 'Let poor old Sir Pomfret and Mother Copley deal
with my lady.' He looked sideways at me. 'Did you really
mean what you said in there? Have you found out anything?'

I hesitated, tempted to admit the truth, but pride held me
silent. 'Perhaps,' I said.

'You know how the murder was committed? What's
happened to Gideon?'

I disengaged myself. 'You ask too many questions. Listen!
There's the trumpet sounding for dinner. I don't know about
you, but my encounter with Duchess Cicely has left me
extremely hungry.'

'You're always hungry,' Piers laughed. And mimicking the
duchess's voice, added, 'You've put on weight.'

I treated this jibe with the disdain it deserved and quickened my step, leaving him to make his way to the servants' dining hall in his own good time. I heard him laugh as I rounded a corner.

Later that day, in the warmth of the June afternoon and to ward off the somnolence that threatened to overcome me after two large helpings of pottage followed by oatcakes and goat's milk cheese, I left Baynard's Castle and went for a walk through the crowded city, pausing every now and then to watch the erection of stands and decorations for the forthcoming coronation. But nowhere did I see the name Edward or any reference to the young king at all. It was almost as though he had ceased to exist. And what of his mother and sisters? They were all still in sanctuary, and I had heard no rumour that they were about to come out.

I wandered on, lost in thought and taking no real heed of where I was going until I suddenly found myself in Bucklersbury, outside the inn of St Brendan the Voyager. I was standing staring at the painted sign over the door of the saint in his cockleshell boat, wondering vaguely how I came to be there, when a hand smote my shoulder and a familiar voice spoke in my ear.

'Master Chapman! Roger? It is you, isn't it? I thought you'd gone home to Bristol.'

TWELVE

I turned quickly and found myself looking into a pair of bright hazel eyes beneath thinning brown hair and set in a roundish face whose smile exuded warmth and friendliness. The owner of both eyes and smile was a stocky individual, well past the first flush of youth but giving the impression of being somewhat younger than he actually was because of an irrepressible smile that lurked around the corners of his thin lips and an incongruous dimple that appeared in one cheek whenever he grinned. He wore an apothecary's apron splashed with various intriguing stains and was bareheaded, having just dashed out from his shop across the street as soon, so he informed me, as he had spotted me through his open doorway.

'Julian!' I exclaimed with pleasure. 'Julian Makepeace!'

He nodded and repeated, 'I thought you'd gone home to Bristol,' adding, 'weeks ago! Indeed,' he went on in a slightly injured tone, 'I'd swear that Clemency Godslove told me that you had.'

'Mistress Godslove was quite right,' I said. 'I did go home. And was summoned back again.'

'By the duke? Or the Lord Protector, as I suppose we should call him now? I know you stand on terms of friendship with him.'

I laughed. 'I don't think I'd put it quite like that. He commands and I obey. He's kind, considerate, but implacable whenever he needs my services. People of his rank never really make friends with folk like me, you know, and it's a great mistake to believe that they do. They give a good imitation of doing so, but that's all it is. An imitation.'

Julian clapped me on the back. 'You sound bitter, my friend, but I'm sure my lord of Gloucester regards you highly.' He jerked his head towards his shop. 'Come in and have a stoup of ale with me if you can spare the time. I don't suggest we go into the Voyager. You know how things are in there these days.'

St Brendan the Voyager had once belonged to Julian's elder brother, Reynold Makepeace, and a better run inn and sweeter ale could not have been found in the whole of London. But Reynold had been accidentally killed in a brawl between some Genoese sailors, since when the place had gone from bad to worse until nowadays it was little more than a drinking den for some of the roughest denizens in the area, and the ale was calculated to give you gut-rot.

I accepted Julian's invitation with alacrity, the warmth of the day having given me a thirst, but this was not my only consideration. I was looking forward to renewing my acquaintance with Naomi, the cosy young armful who was so plainly more than just his housekeeper. The situation intrigued me, for the apothecary could not be called a handsome man by any stretch of the imagination while she would have graced the arm of any youth in the city. But Naomi was obviously devoted to her middle-aged lover, ignoring, or perhaps more likely unaware of, the affectionate cynicism with which he regarded her. I think Julian was always conscious of the fact that one morning in the future, probably when he needed her the most, he would wake up and find that Naomi had gone.

She was as buxom as ever, tossing her head coquettishly and peeping at me from beneath her long lashes in a blatant way that made me start to sweat and Julian to grin appreciatively at my discomfort. He patted her buttocks and told her to bring some ale and two beakers to the parlour behind the shop, after which, he said, she could go and prepare some water parsnip seeds for old Master Wilson's medicine.

'They're very good taken in wine,' he informed me, 'for relieving the discomfort of a hernia. Also, according to Pliny, for getting rid of freckles on women and scales on horses, although I've never tried the latter.'

The little room behind the shop was cool and dim, lit by a faintly subaqueous light on account of some heavy green glass bottles lined up on a shelf against one wall. Julian waved me to a stool on one side of the table and seated himself opposite on the other. I made some desultory enquiries about the Godsloves which he answered in an equally half-hearted fashion, the pair of us just making small talk until Naomi had brought the ale and beakers and flounced out of the room again, obviously annoyed at being excluded from the conversation.

As soon as the parlour door had shut behind her, Julian paused in the act of pouring out the ale to demand, 'What's going on, Roger?'

Not quite certain of his meaning, I hedged. 'What do you mean, what's going on?'

He gave me a quizzical look as he handed me my beaker. 'Do you really not know? Or are you sworn to secrecy? The city's full of rumours that Duke Richard means to depose his nephew and take the crown for himself. I thought if anyone knows the truth, you might.'

I hedged some more. 'How ever do these stories get about?'

He smiled. 'From servants in the palaces and great houses who listen at doors, who pick up a word here and a word there from careless masters and mistresses who forget or overlook their presence, or, as often as not, treat them as a part of the furniture. There are whispers everywhere that the forthcoming coronation will be of King Richard III and not King Edward V. I can't believe that you of all people haven't heard the talk.'

'I only arrived in London last Friday.'

Julian heard the defensive note in my voice and grinned sardonically. 'You do know something. I thought you must as soon as you said you'd been brought back to London by the duke.'

'It wasn't for that reason . . .' I broke off, realizing that my denial had also been a tacit admission of the truth.

'Not for that reason,' Julian repeated. 'So there is some substance in the rumours.' He took a deep breath. 'The people won't like it, Roger. In fact they'll deeply resent it. They'll hate Gloucester for it. And on what grounds can he claim the crown? Not just because of the king's youth, surely! We've had child sovereigns before, two of them not all that long ago. Not one of their uncles ever proposed removing either the second Richard or the late King Henry because of their age.'

I hesitated, wondering if I was at liberty to disclose the

truth, anxious to come to Duke Richard's defence. After a moment's deliberation, I decided that Bishop Stillington's disclosure was bound to be become public knowledge before long.

I said, 'Those cases, and others before them, were different. They were true kings.' Julian raised his eyebrows in startled enquiry, but made no comment, continuing to sip his ale. I went on, 'You don't have to say who told you this, but the Bishop of Bath and Wells has informed my lord Gloucester that twenty years or more ago, he betrothed the late king to the Lady Eleanor Butler in a solemn, but secret, ceremony that he regarded as binding as a marriage. That, of course, was before Edward wed Elizabeth Woodville in an equally clandestine fashion. The bishop therefore regards this second marriage as bigamous and the children of it as illegitimate.'

My companion looked at me open-mouthed, unable for a few seconds to say anything at all. Finally, he got out, 'Dear sweet Virgin and all the angels!' His eyes narrowed suspiciously. 'Do you believe this story?'

I drank some ale. 'I can't see any good reason not to,' I said at last. 'If you're thinking that it's a conspiracy between church and state, let me tell you that Robert Stillington has never sat in Duke Richard's pocket, as the saying goes. I doubt if the duke could have identified him with any ease until these past few days. My lord has lived in the north as much as possible, coming south only rarely, while the bishop's diocese is in the heart of my own west country. Indeed, I was born and brought up in Wells. No, it was the Duke of Clarence Stillington was so friendly with.'

'Clarence?' Julian lowered his beaker and waited for me to continue.

I nodded. 'Their names were linked on more than one occasion. About seven years ago, I witnessed one of their meetings at Farleigh Castle near Bath. The duke was in residence there for a day or two, and the bishop had ridden over to see him. Nothing sinister in that you might think. A courtesy visit to acknowledge Clarence's presence in the neighbourhood. But . . .'

'But?' Julian prompted.

I shrugged. 'It's difficult to describe exactly, but there was something conspiratorial in their dealings with one another that struck me as decidedly odd. And then, at the time of Clarence's execution two years later, Bishop Stillington was incarcerated in the Tower. Oh, he wasn't imprisoned for long because he paid a hefty fine to the king for his release. But nevertheless, you could regard it as significant.'

Julian poured us both more ale.

'You think that this Stillington had told Duke George the same story? You think that this was why the king suddenly decided to rid himself of Clarence?'

I was pleased with his ready understanding. 'I feel sure it must have been. After all, Edward had put up with his brother's fits and starts, his disloyalty, his treachery and disobedience for years. He'd forgiven him time and time again in spite, I've no doubt, of the queen and her family all clamouring for the duke to be got rid of. But then, I think, George suddenly – and very stupidly, he was a very stupid man – threatened the king with what he knew. Threatened to make it public.'

'So the king had him executed.' Julian nodded slowly. 'It's a good theory, Roger, and I feel you may well be right. But surely such a claim should be referred to Rome so that a papal court could give its verdict. It shouldn't just be acted upon as if it were the inviolable truth. Is a betrothal as sacred in the eyes of the Church as a marriage?'

'I don't know. I'm no theologian. Stillington seems to think so.'

There was silence for a moment or two. From the shop, we could hear Naomi's voice upraised in a popular ballad of the day, singing decidedly off-key.

The apothecary grinned apologetically. 'She's no ear for music, I'm afraid.'

'Neither have I,' I assured him. 'I couldn't hold a tune to save my life.'

We listened painfully to another refrain before Julian asked, 'Do you think, then, that the Lord Protector will claim the crown on the basis of young Edward's bastardy? And, of course, that of his brother and sisters? But why doesn't he wait and do it legally through the papal courts?'

I drank some more ale and gazed steadily at him across the rim of my beaker. 'Can't you work it out?'

After a second or two, he laughed softly. 'The courts might find in favour of the king?'

'I think it more than possible. No one wants to dispossess a child. And no doubt for a substantial bribe, the pope would be willing to declare the original vows between King Edward and the lady Eleanor Butler null and void.'

'Is she still alive?'

'I don't think so.'

Julian sucked his teeth thoughtfully. 'Is it your opinion,' he asked, 'that the duke has been planning this . . . this coup for a long time?'

I was annoyed by the question. 'Sweet Jesus, no! King Edward was ailing, it's true, but I don't think anyone expected him to die. It came as a terrible shock to everyone, including Duke Richard. No, no! I feel certain, knowing him as I do, that such a thought had never crossed his mind.'

I was lying, of course. I knew, no one better, that it was not the bastardy of his nephew, but of his eldest brother that had been preoccupying the duke. But that was another story, and not one I was prepared to discuss with Julian Makepeace. Or with anyone else for that matter.

I got to my feet, a little unsteadily it must be admitted. The apothecary's ale was potent stuff and I had drunk three beakers of it.

'I mustn't trespass on your hospitality any longer,' I said. 'You must have work to do.'

'Nothing that can't wait,' he protested. 'Sit down again. You haven't told me yet why you were recalled to London.'

'Neither have I.' I resumed my seat but refused his offer of more ale.

He gave an understanding smile. 'So?' he urged. 'Why have you returned?'

I knew very well that I wasn't supposed to discuss the disappearance of Gideon Fitzalan and the murder of Gregory Machin with anyone not already in the know, but I badly needed to talk the matter over with someone not personally involved, and I trusted Julian Makepeace. He was a good man and, moreover, had an intelligent mind that might be able to offer a solution which I had overlooked.

But when I had finished relating the events at Baynard's Castle, his only comment, accompanied by a mystified shake of his head, was, 'A strange business. A very strange business! I don't envy you, my friend. A murder in a locked room, that smacks of witchcraft. Are you completely satisfied that this Gregory Machin's room was indeed locked, or that there was no possible second way for the murderer to have entered?'

I smiled wearily. 'Completely satisfied on both counts.' I couldn't help adding, with a touch of bitterness, 'What an incompetent fool you must judge me to be.'

He stretched out a hand across the table. 'Forgive me! I spoke without thinking. Of course I don't judge you to be either incompetent or a fool. But what, then, is the answer? Apart from supernatural means? And I gather – from your manner rather than anything you've said – that you don't favour that solution. Am I correct?'

I nodded. 'But don't ask me why because I couldn't tell you.' I could, of course, but I didn't want to bring my personal relationship with God into the discussion. I felt it might be misunderstood by outsiders. 'I just have this . . . this hunch that I'm dealing with human wickedness and not with demons and devils.'

Julian looked unconvinced, but didn't try to persuade me otherwise. He merely shrugged and murmured, 'It's a puzzle.'

I sighed and got to my feet. 'But one I have to try to solve,' I said glumly. 'And I shan't do that by sitting here and drinking your excellent ale.' I held out my hand. 'I'm glad to have fallen in with you again, Julian. Since Philip Lamprey left London after his wife died, I've had no real friend in the city. It's reassuring to think that I may have found one in you.'

The apothecary clasped my hand warmly in both of his. 'You have indeed found one,' he affirmed. 'Your warm regard for my poor brother would always be a recommendation to me, even if I didn't like you for yourself. But I do. Like you, I mean. Whenever you are forced to come to London, think of my home as your own. If you ever need a bed for the night, there is an attic – extremely small, it's true, but you wouldn't mind that I feel certain – where a makeshift cot can be made up for you. Or if you simply need to come and talk, you are welcome to do that also. If I'm busy with customers, you won't, I'm sure, object to waiting until I've finished.'

I returned my heartfelt thanks for this generous invitation, took a last swig of ale in order to empty my beaker, and went out into the afternoon sunshine.

On leaving the shop, I turned to my right, heading towards Wallbrook, and was just passing the ramshackle tenement on the corner, known as the Old Barge, when I heard the patter of feet behind me, and my name being called. I turned to see Mistress Naomi running after me, her cheeks pink with exertion and strands of hair escaping from beneath her cap. She came to a breathless standstill in front of me.

'Master says will you please come back,' she gasped. 'He's remembered something.'

'Remembered something?' I repeated stupidly.

She nodded vigorously. 'He says it's important, and . . . and that he's vexed with himself for not thinking of it just now.' She took another deep breath, flaunting two well-rounded breasts and giving me a sly, sidelong glance as she did so. I tried valiantly to keep my eyes fixed on her face, but failed. And it was then that I noticed the little sprig of birch leaves pinned to her gown, just above her heart.

As I began walking back with her, retracing my steps to Julian's shop, I commented on it and asked if it had any particular significance.

She smiled proudly. 'It means that next Monday, Midsummer Eve, I'm to be crowned Midsummer Queen of the Dowgate Ward. Every ward has its own queen, you know, and this year Dowgate's chosen me. It's a great honour, so the master says.' She grimaced. 'Well, I knew that without him telling me.' She gave a little giggle. 'He thinks I'm stupid, you know.'

I considered that she might be right about Julian's assessment of her, and thought to myself that the apothecary was probably mistaken. Mistress Naomi appeared on the surface

to be nothing much more than a cuddly, silly young girl, but
I got the impression that there was an altogether shrewder,
sharper side to her nature than was immediately apparent.

Julian was waiting for us at the shop door, obviously in
a state of suppressed excitement. He grasped my arm and
fairly pulled me inside, saying, 'I'm sorry to bring you back,
Roger, but it's too important to leave for another time. What
an idiot I am! Why on earth didn't I remember it sooner?'

'What? What is it you've remembered?' I asked urgently
as he led me once again towards the parlour.

We were interrupted by a customer who pointedly waited
to be served until Naomi and I had closed the door into the
shop. My companion giggled.

'Poor man! He comes in every week for a supply of
powdered mandrake root. It's for . . . well . . . you know.' She
broke off, blushing a little.

I nodded. Mandrake root was thought to be beneficial in
cases of impotence, although in this case, if the gentleman
came in every week, it didn't seem to be having the desired
effect. While we waited for Julian, and to curb my own impatience, I quizzed her some more about the Midsummer's Eve
festival.

She was nothing loath to talk about it. It appeared that
each London ward crowned its own Midsummer Queen with
a wreath of young birch leaves, and the selected maiden was
then carried, shoulder-high, in a chair also decked with
branches of birch, around her domain-for-a-night to accept
the greetings and adulation of her 'subjects'. Her path was
strewn with the herbs that people had been out in the
surrounding fields to gather, usually before dawn: St John's
wort, mugwort, plantain, corn marigold, elder, yarrow, vervain
and any other herb that was thought to ward off the possible
evil of 'Witches' Night' as Midsummer Eve was also known.

'And after that,' she went on, her eyes glowing with anticipation, 'everyone goes to St Paul's churchyard to see the
mustering of the great Marching Watch. Do you have a
Marching Watch in Bristol, Master Chapman?'

I denied any knowledge of such an event and learned that
in London all the main guilds, preceded by the twelve great
livery companies, processed down Lud Gate Hill and along

Cheapside, accompanied by musicians on trumpet, pipe and drum, everywhere illumined by torches and cressets and fire baskets, and the houses decorated with garlands of flowers and tapestries hung from balconies and windows.

'Oh, it's lovely,' my informant breathed ecstatically. 'And all the Midsummer Queens are given pride of place to watch the procession and to walk alongside it in front of the crowds.'

At that moment, the door into the shop opened and Julian rejoined us, raising exasperated eyebrows. 'I'm sorry, Roger. I couldn't get away sooner. That man regards me as his father confessor and unburdens himself of all his troubles.'

I grinned. 'And I gather from Mistress Naomi here that he has one in particular. Not,' I added hastily, 'that it's anything to make fun of. It could afflict us all one day. In any case, don't worry. I've been very well entertained. I've been hearing about Midsummer's Eve and the Marching Watch. It sounds to be an event worth the seeing. Moreover, you'll have the privilege of accompanying a queen this year.'

Somewhat to my surprise, Julian pulled down the corners of his mouth. 'Naomi will certainly try to persuade me,' he said, 'but Midsummer Eve festivities are something I normally avoid. I don't like the idea of celebrating what was originally, and in some respects still is, a pagan rite. Centuries ago, it was a time of bloodshed and sacrifice, with great fires lit on hilltops to appease the gods.'

I saw that Mistress Naomi was looking surly. She plainly had no patience with such antiquated notions and was about to fly into one of her tantrums, so I asked quickly (and also because I was impatient to know), 'What is it you have to tell me, Master Makepeace?'

He motioned me to sit down again at the table, saying, 'For pity's sake, call me by my given name. We've agreed we're friends.' He pulled up the other stool, suddenly all eagerness, his previous excitement returning in full force. And for once, he didn't bother to send Naomi away. It was almost, for the moment, as if he had forgotten she was there.

'Listen, Roger!' He clasped his hands together on the tabletop, the knuckles of his thin fingers showing white against the polished wood. 'You know the Old Barge at the end of the street?' I nodded. 'You know what it's like. It was once a gentleman's house, but now it's let out by the room to all the scaff and raff of London. The shrieks and screams that issue from that place at night are enough to make your blood run cold.'

'Yes, yes!' I said, wondering when he would get to the point.

'Well, one day last winter, I was walking past the place on my way home, when a fellow staggered down the steps and bumped straight into me, nearly knocking me over. He apologized in a very slurred sort of way, so I naturally assumed he was drunk. Then, to my disgust, he took hold of my arm and staggered along beside me. Said he wasn't feeling too well which, in view of my assumption, didn't surprise me in the least. But I supported him as far as the shop, where, of course, I disengaged myself and said that I must go inside. This was where I lived.'

'And?' I queried impatiently as Julian paused.

'And then,' he answered slowly, impressively, 'he gave a strange little sigh and dropped down dead.'

'Dead?'

'Yes. But not from any natural cause. He'd been stabbed in the back, just like this Gregory Machin you've been telling me about.'

I stared at him uncomprehendingly for a second or two. 'You're saying . . .?'

'I'm saying that this man had been fatally stabbed by another of the Old Barge's inmates – a man was later hanged for his murder – but between the blow that killed him and the moment he dropped dead, he had walked the length of Bucklersbury, unaware that there was anything wrong with him. True, he wasn't quite himself; his speech, as I said, was slurred, he was weak and disorientated, but he didn't realize that he was dying.'

'Is such a thing possible?' I asked.

Julian nodded eagerly. 'Apparently it's not as uncommon a phenomenon as you might suppose. I consulted a physician friend of mine who lives in Old Jewry, and he assured me that it can occur from time to time. It had happened to a man he knew of who complained that someone had thumped him. A minute or two later, the man fell dead of a stab wound in the chest. It depends, I should imagine, on the weapon. If the blade is long and thin, there is no immediate blood-letting. What bleeding there is, is internal and takes longer to bring about death.' He leaned forward excitedly, gripping both my wrists. 'Don't you see what I'm saying? Your man could have been knifed without his realizing it. He may then have been able to walk into his room and bolt the door before he collapsed and died.'

I took a deep breath. 'You're sure about this?'

'I saw it happen with my own eyes.'

'Then . . . then that explains it.' I went on slowly, picking a careful path through my teeming thoughts. 'Tutor Machin's room wasn't far from the head of the stairs he and young Gideon Fitzalan were last seen climbing. The staircase curves, so the two of them were out of sight of the person following behind them for perhaps a minute or so. Long enough, probably, for someone waiting at the top to stab Gregory in the back as he passed and seize the boy. Whoever it was must have been amazed to see Gregory blunder on into his room instead of immediately falling dead at his feet. And even more amazed if he heard the bolt being shot home. He may even have been terrified that the tutor wasn't dead, only wounded, and would be able to identify him later.'

Julian frowned. 'You assume the murderer was a man?'

'Don't you? Knives and daggers are not normally a woman's weapons. Although I have to admit that I have known them to be so, so maybe it's not the most convincing of arguments.' I got to my feet, freeing myself from the apothecary's clutching hands and stretched out one of my own. 'Julian, I owe you a debt I can never repay. Even if I can't prove that this is exactly what happened, we both know you're right. If you eliminate the forces of evil, this has to be the only explanation.'

'I hope so,' Julian agreed, warmly returning my clasp. 'I can't imagine why I didn't think of it at once.' He smiled. 'I'm delighted to have been of some use. Let me wish you all good fortune in solving this mystery, Roger. If any one can do so, you're the man. Look at how you resolved the one surrounding the Godsloves.'

I made a deprecating gesture (which I don't suppose fooled

him for an instant) and politely refused his offer of further refreshment. I wanted to be on my own. In the light of this new knowledge, I needed to reassess everything I knew about this case so far.

THIRTEEN

I walked back to Baynard's Castle like a man in a trance, completely unaware of the jostling crowds around me. I remember bumping into one or two people and being cursed for not looking where I was going, but for the most part, I might have been all alone in that bustling throng.

I had no doubt that Julian Makepeace's solution to the mystery of the locked room was correct, and meant that almost anyone could have been lying in wait at the top of the stairs, knife in hand, for Gregory Machin and his charge But the solving of one riddle led only to the next. Why would anyone want to kill the tutor? Why was it necessary that he should die?

The obvious answer was that the boy had to be snatched and spirited away with the minimum of fuss and outcry. In a place like Baynard's Castle there was always somebody somewhere within earshot, and it would surely have been inevitable that that somebody – or, indeed, several some-bodies – would have come running to see what the noise was about. At the same time, it bothered me that there must have been subtler methods of getting possession of young Gideon. A story perhaps that one of his uncles wished to speak to him, or one of his brothers, or Dame Copley . . . On second thoughts, not the nurse: he had but just come from her room if Amphillis Hill was to be believed, and I could see no reason at present to doubt her word.

But if the murderer had been a stranger to Gregory, he might well have demurred or insisted on accompanying his charge. At best, there could have been an argument, at worst, a struggle. No, taken all in all, it had probably been wiser to dispose of the tutor altogether, because when it was discovered that Gideon had disappeared there was no one to bear witness to, or give a description of, the person who had taken him.

Which brought me, of course, to the thorny questions of

why the boy had been taken in the first place and where he was being held captive. Or was he, like his unfortunate tutor, also dead? But somehow I doubted he had been killed. Someone had gone to great trouble to snatch him from his guardians, and I could not bring myself to believe that it had simply been to murder him in his turn. It didn't make sense, so my guess was that he was being held a prisoner somewhere. Once again, however, I was faced with the problems of where and why?

I suddenly found myself, without knowing quite how I got there, back at the Thames Street entrance to the castle. The sentries manning the gate passed me through easily enough, having got used to my presence in the past few days and recognizing me from my exceptional height. (I stood six foot in my stockinged feet, nearly as tall as the late King Edward, a fact which – unfortunately on occasions – made me extremely visible among my fellow men whose average height was at least six or seven inches shorter.)

Once inside, it was my intention to seek out a member of the Fitzalan family, but my purpose was delayed by the sounding of the trumpet for supper. I was not to be balked of my victuals, having eaten nothing since ten o'clock dinner, so I made my way to the servants' hall with the rest of the hungry crowd. I joined in the general groan of disgust at the sight of the inevitable pottage, warmed up from the previous meal, and added my voice to the loud condemnation of Duchess Cicely's parsimony where the lower orders were concerned. Not that that stopped any of us falling to our bowls like ravening wolves in the hope of being the first to finish and so being able to claim a second bowlful. And I'm proud to record that I won the race on my table, having learned a trick or two worth the knowing while a novice at Glastonbury Abbey.

'Feeding your face again, Roger?' enquired a mocking voice behind me.

I swivelled round on the bench. 'Piers! Do you know if any of the Fitzalans are still in the castle?'

He was carrying a beaker of small beer and sipped it with a moue of distaste before answering. 'Sir Pomfret and his lady must still be here, but I think Godfrey and Lewis have gone to Crosby's Place to wait upon the duke. And Bevis and Blaise set out an hour or more ago for the Tower to be with the king.' He cocked a knowing eyebrow. 'I suppose we may still call him that, may we?'

So the rumours were circulating even here! I thought the conversation in the hall had been more than usually subdued, with heads bent close together and hands cupped over whispering mouths.

I avoided the question, pretending I hadn't heard.

'I don't want to bother Sir Pomfret or Lady Fitzalan,' I said, 'but perhaps you can tell me, lad. Do you happen to know if a ransom demand for Gideon's return has been received by anyone?'

Piers hesitated, then shook his head. 'Not that I know of, and I feel sure I should have heard something if one had been sent.'

I bit my thumbnail thoughtfully. 'And it's now – what? – eleven days since Gideon disappeared, and still nothing has been seen or heard of him. Or from his captor or captors. I think, therefore, it's safe to presume that he wasn't taken for money.'

Piers grimaced. 'Why, then?'

I continued biting my thumbnail, a childish habit that my mother had sought in vain to cure and which seemed to have manifested itself again of late. I would be thirty-one at the beginning of October. Maybe I was reverting to a second childhood.

'I don't know,' I admitted. 'That's what I have to find out.'

'You'd better hurry in that case,' Piers advised callously. 'Time may be getting short.'

I finished the remains of my small beer, swung my legs over the bench, accidentally kicking my neighbour as I did so (but we were all used to that) and stood upright.

'Will you lend me your aid?' I asked.

Piers looked startled. 'How?'

'I want to search this building from top to bottom, look in all the unused rooms, cupboards hidden away under stairs, that sort of thing. There's a chance, a remote one I agree, that Gideon might be being held somewhere in the castle.'

My companion, who was also in the act of finishing his beer, choked. When he could speak again, he demanded, 'Do you have any idea how many rooms there are in a place like this?'

'A fair notion, and I daresay I'd never discover all of them. But I feel I must try.' I gave him a wheedling smile. 'Will you help me?'

He thought for a moment before nodding. 'But not tonight. I'm promised to some fellows for a game of cards this evening. Tomorrow, however, after breakfast, we'll try this madcap scheme of yours. Not that I'm expecting anything to come of it, but I've nothing better to do with my time since Gideon vanished.' Piers replaced his empty beaker on the table to be cleared away by the servers. 'Meanwhile, shouldn't you be concentrating your energies on finding out how Master Machin was killed inside a locked room?'

'Oh, I know that,' I answered grandly – and walked away, leaving him staring.

Piers didn't wait until after breakfast the following morning to seek me out, but came knocking at my chamber door as soon after sun-up as was reasonable. His curiosity was such that he would have followed me the previous evening had his fellow card players not claimed him at almost the same instant as I left. I was tempted to feign sleep for a while, but relented and let him in.

'Well?' he asked, his voice trembling with excitement. 'How was it done? I've hardly been able to sleep, trying to puzzle it out. And I lost at cards last night, thanks to you. I couldn't concentrate.'

I indicated he should sit on the bed while I finished dressing, and then kept him waiting even longer while I found my willow bark and cleaned my teeth. But, finally, I took pity on him, described my meeting with Julian Makepeace and recounted the story he had told me.

When I had finished, Piers sat quietly for several minutes, obviously turning it all over in his mind, occasionally making little grunting sounds and nodding.

'My friend assured me that such a thing could happen,' I said at last, to break the silence. 'He had taken the trouble to consult with a doctor acquaintance of his, who confirmed that it was possible.'

'Oh, I wouldn't doubt the word of Julian Makepeace,' Piers agreed. 'He has the reputation of being a thoroughly honest man. A learned man.'

It was my turn to stare in surprise. 'You know him?' I asked. 'But according to you, you only arrived from Minster Lovell less than two weeks ago.'

'Oh!' He flushed slightly. 'Let's just say that I've met the buxom Naomi.' He added defensively, 'She's friendly with one of the pantry boys in the bakery. She's Apothecary Makepeace's . . . er . . . housekeeper, I believe.' He slid off the bed, grinning. 'Seems quite fond of the old fellow.'

I felt my hackles rise. I certainly wasn't inclined to discuss Julian's domestic arrangements with young Master Cock-up-spotty. (Not that Piers was at all spotty. As I have said before, he had an extremely smooth complexion.)

'Let's go down to breakfast,' I said. 'I'll shave afterwards. I see you've already done so.'

Piers and I spent a frustrating morning, both before and after dinner – pottage again, need you ask? – getting filthier and filthier as we explored parts of Baynard's Castle that I don't think even the duchess or her steward knew were there. (On second thoughts, I don't suppose the duchess would have known. I don't imagine she ever left the royal apartments.) Some of the rooms we investigated were occupied and we got very short shrift from the tenants. Twice I got hit on the head by a boot – and once by a pair of boots – while Piers got an elbow jammed in his ribs and, on another occasion, was helped through a doorway by an oversized foot. We then descended to the cellars, which might once have been used as dungeons but were now innocent of anything other than cockroaches, mould and damp, hardly surprising as they were below the river's waterline. We next ascended to the attics, tiny, claustrophobic cells stuffed with the detritus of years, one or two even inhabited by the lowest of the low; chamber-pot emptiers, stool-cloth washers and the like. I even insisted on a thorough search being made of the sewing room, leaving Piers to charm the head seamstress while, to the great amusement and caustic comments of the girls, I peered under trestles and poked my nose into cupboards that obviously couldn't conceal a fly. (Well, all right, they probably could have concealed a fly, but I'm growing too old and crotchety to split hairs with you.) For once, the head seamstress was all compliance, the alterations to the duchess's coronation robe having been completed before time.

But of Gideon Fitzalan we found not a single trace.

'I'm sick of this!' Piers announced wrathfully as the sun strode up the cloudless sky and threatened us all with sunstroke. 'I'm tired, I'm hot and I'm filthy dirty. I've had enough, Roger, and if you're sufficiently stupid to go on searching for someone we're both reasonably sure isn't hidden here, then you can do it by yourself.'

'You're right,' I sighed. 'Mind you, I wouldn't go so far as to be certain that the boy isn't here somewhere. There are still places we haven't looked and quite a few, I imagine, whose existence we're unaware of. Mind you, I never really had much hope of finding him. I always felt it was a fool's errand, but—'

'You mean to say—' my companion began indignantly.

'But,' I went on inexorably, 'it was something I felt had to be done.' I slapped him on the back. 'You've earned a drink, lad. Let's go to the buttery and see if we can cajole Master Butler into giving us some ale.'

This the butler, a jolly, fat man as befitted his calling, was prepared to do, so Piers and I took our beakers out into the sunshine and sat on the water-steps, watching the play of light on the bustling Thames while we drank.

'Why Gideon?' I asked. 'If it wasn't for ransom, why was he taken?'

Piers shrugged. 'Perhaps he was just unlucky. Perhaps any boy would have done.'

I shook my head. 'No, I don't think so. If that was the case, why bother to snatch a lad who seems to have been so well guarded? Why go to the length of murdering one of those guardians in order to lay hands on him?' I sipped my ale thoughtfully. 'Which forces me to the conclusion that there's something special about Gideon Fitzalan that I'm missing. I shall have to talk to members of his family again to discover if any one of them can shed light on the riddle.'

'I told you, only Sir Pomfret and his lady remain here, and you said you had no wish to disturb them. And I think you're quite right,' Piers added sententiously. 'As bereaved parents, they ought to command your compassion.'

I gave him a look that should have withered him on the spot had he not been occupied with waving to someone in a twopenny rowing boat going upstream.

'In that case,' I said, scrambling to my feet, 'I must pay a visit to Crosby's Place and speak to Gideon's uncles. But first, I'll have another word with Dame Copley.'

However, when I tried to run the nurse to earth, I was informed that she was still in attendance on Lady Fitzalan and had moved permanently into the rooms put at Sir Pomfret's disposal by Duchess Cicely. I discovered this to be only too correct. The chamber she had previously occupied, close to the landing-stage, was bare of any trace of her. All that remained was the furniture normally to be found there.

This was not quite true, however. On top of the clothes-chest, someone had placed a small stone pitcher of birch twigs, wilting now in the midsummer heat, the leaves turning brown as the water dried up, depriving them of nourishment. I stood staring for a minute or two before opening my pouch and taking out the little twig I had picked up in the upstairs passageway a few days earlier. I recollected similar birch twigs worn by the seamstress Maria Johnson and by Julian Makepeace's Naomi; adornments, according to the latter, closely associated with the rites of Midsummer Eve. I recalled, also, Julian's distaste for a festival founded, so he claimed, on the blood sacrifices of the old religion that had preceded Christianity in this island. And suddenly, I was back amongst the stone henges of Avebury, thinking about the ancient legend of the Daughters of Albion, of Wayland the Smith, and of the white horse carved into the hillside at Uffington . . .

'What are you doing in here?' demanded Piers's voice. 'I thought you'd gone to find old mother Copley.'

'She's not here any more. She's with Lady Fitzalan.'

'I could have told you that if you'd asked me.'

'Then why didn't you?'

'You went off so suddenly I didn't have time to mention it. Besides, I thought you must have known.'

'I don't see why you should have thought that,' I snapped tetchily, then changed the subject as I realized that this exchange of words was descending to the level of a childish quarrel. I nodded towards the pot of birch twigs. 'Do you know what the association of birch is with Midsummer Eve?'

'The crown and the bough?' Piers shrugged. 'Not really. Only that its leaves and branches are used to crown the Midsummer Eve queens. I believe the tree has an association with virginity or some such nonsense.'

'Virginity?'

'Nowadays.' Another shrug. 'I think that in the past it may have been more to do with celibacy. I believe it was an emblem for women who wanted to live a chaste life but had been forced into marriage by their families.'

'Like St Etheldreda you mean?'

Piers turned his head sharply to look at me. 'Yes. You know about her? She's not one of the more celebrated saints.'

'You forget that I was once a novice. Brother Hilarion, our Novice Master, made certain that his charges were well versed in the lives of all the saints. But,' I went on, 'I might say the same about you. You also seem familiar with Etheldreda's life.'

'Oh . . . well, there's nothing remarkable in that,' he said, stumbling a little over his words. 'I learned about her from Mother Copley. The lady's a favourite of hers.'

I raised my eyebrows. 'For any particular reason?'

Piers looked uncomfortable. 'As to that – I suppose there's no harm in my telling you: it's not exactly a secret, though Rosina doesn't talk about it very much – she was married once, forced into it against her will by her father when she was very young. She felt she'd had the call to become a nun, but the old bully wouldn't hear of it.'

'What happened?'

'Oh . . . fortunately, the husband died after a year or two. Her father died, too, so she was finally free to do as she pleased.'

'But she didn't become a nun?'

'You're mighty curious about Mother Copley all of a sudden,' Piers objected. 'Why?'

'Curiosity's my business,' I answered mildly. 'If I don't ask questions, I don't learn anything. And if I don't learn anything, how am I to find answers to these mysteries that God keeps sending to plague my life?'

'I suppose there is that,' Piers admitted grudgingly. 'No, Rosina didn't pursue her vocation after all. Don't ask me why not. I've never enquired and she's never told me. Some noblewoman took her on as nurse to her children and that's what she's done ever since, in one household or another. I suppose she'll soon be looking for a new employer now that Master Gideon is . . .' He broke off as though uncertain what to say, then finished lamely, 'Now that Master Gideon is growing up.'

'Or dead? That's what you're thinking, isn't it?' I accused him. 'Not if I can help it, lad!'

'You don't think he's dead?'

'To be honest, I don't know any more than you do. But I think it possible that he may not be – yet! He was taken for a purpose, that's obvious. But what? And why him? I have a feeling that if only I could answer the second question, it would shed light on the first. I was hoping Dame Copley might be able to help me.'

Piers pursed his lips. 'Let me see what I can do. As a member of the household, I can slip in and out of Sir Pomfret's and Lady Fitzalan's chambers without occasioning remark. Maybe I can approach Rosina without disturbing anyone else or intruding on parental grief. Wait here and I'll be back as soon as I can.'

So I sat down on the edge of the bed while Piers sped off on his mission. I can't say that I had much hope of his succeeding, but I felt it was worth allowing him to try. I was sure that Rosina Copley didn't like me very much; indeed, that she had little time for any of my sex, a feeling amply borne out by Piers's account of her history. I was as certain as I could be that she would refuse to speak to me, taking refuge behind Lady Fitzalan's skirts.

I was wrong, however. I don't know how long it was before

Piers made his reappearance, but it was sooner than I expected.

'She'll speak to you,' he said, 'although she insists it's a waste of effort. I told her why you wanted to see her – it seemed best – and she's positive that she knows nothing that could be of any use to you. However, if you wait in the little ante-room of the Fitzalan chambers, she'll come out to you, but you'll have to be brief. She doesn't want to leave Lady Fitzalan alone for long. Can you remember the way?'

'You're not coming?'

Piers shook his head. 'There's no point. I've other things to do. Besides, it must be nearly supper time.'

I cursed myself for having forgotten this vital fact – I must have swallowed so much dust in the course of the day's explorations that it had blunted my normally keen appetite – and decided to keep my interview with the nurse as short as possible. Like herself, I suspected that it would prove to be a fruitless waste of time.

But when I presented myself at the suite of chambers put at the Fitzalan's disposal, to my astonishment I found the ante-room occupied not by Rosina Copley, but by Lady Fitzalan, seated on a small, uncomfortable-looking chair that was the major item of the room's sparse furnishings. Her red-rimmed eyes and puffy cheeks told their own tale, as did the whiteness of her knuckles as she gripped the arms of the chair, but she otherwise had her emotions under control. She looked up and gave me a hostile glance as I entered.

'I-I-forgive me,' I stammered. 'I was expecting to see Dame Copley.'

'I know you were.' The tone was curt. 'I've sent her out to get some air. Since this terrible business happened, she's hardly slept, poor soul. I've sent her to visit her sister, in Dowgate.'

'Her-her sister? In Dowgate?'

The lady raised haughty eyebrows. 'Why should you find that strange?'

'I thought . . . that is, I presumed that Dame Copley came from Yorkshire, like . . . like the rest of you.'

The eyebrows went up even further. 'Sir Pomfret and his brothers certainly hail from Yorkshire. The family is an old established one there, and has been ever since the Conquest. But I am a Godwin and was born and bred on my father's estate near Chichester, where at least three of my sons were also born, including Gideon.' She added, unbending a little, 'He was a seven months' child and took us all by surprise. The services of Rosina Copley were recommended to me by a friend, my former nurse having unfortunately died.' She stopped short, as though feeling that such explanations were more than my due.

'Dame Copley is also, then, a native of Chichester?'

'No,' was the terse reply. 'She was born here, in London. You seem surprised.'

'It's just that I thought she . . . that she spoke in the north country way.'

Lady Fitzalan gave a bark of laughter. 'Oh, we all pick it up in time. It's insidious.'

She spoke with that slight contempt of the southerner for the barbarous north. I hoped she never employed such a tone with my lord of Gloucester. He was a northerner to his backbone and loved every last blade of grass of its wild and rolling hills and dales.

It had come as a shock to me – although I wasn't quite sure why – to discover that Rosina Copley was a Londoner and had family, a sister at least, in the capital. I tried to marshal my thoughts.

'My lady,' I said at last, 'the reason I sought this interview with Dame Copley was to ask her if she had any idea – any idea at all – why your son has been abducted.'

'Yes, I know. I walked in while that nephew of hers was explaining why you wished to see her, and—'

I interrupted ruthlessly. 'Piers Daubenay is Dame Copley's nephew?'

Once more the eyebrows came into play. 'You didn't know?' She shrugged. 'Oh well, why should you? The tie of affection between them doesn't appear to be great.' Lady Fitzalan took a deep breath. 'As I was saying, I thought Rosina seemed a little overwrought at the prospect of being questioned by you. She-she blames herself beyond all reason for Gideon's –' her voice became suspended for a moment on a sob, but then she continued valiantly – 'for Gideon's disappearance. And she knows no reason, any more than I do, than anyone does, why he has been abducted. We naturally thought, Sir Pomfret and I, when we first heard the dreadful news, that we should soon receive a demand for money for his safe return. Such things . . . such things are common.' She was becoming upset again. I could hear the hysteria behind her words, saw her eyes suddenly fill with tears. 'But, as you know, no demand of that sort has been made.' Her voice rose sharply and she pressed her hands together. 'Where is he? Where is he? What's become of my baby?'

I was growing nervous. The last thing I wanted was a hysterical woman on my hands, or for a furious Sir Pomfret to burst in, accusing me of being the cause of his wife's distress. I edged towards the door, but on the threshold I paused.

'My lady,' I urged, 'you're sure that you can think of no reason why Gideon should have been taken in this way? Is there anything in his history that might set him apart from your other children? From any child?'

She shook her head, no longer able to speak coherently, and I realized that to a woman of her temperament, the effort needed to indulge in any sort of rational conversation had been immense. I thanked her and hurriedly took my leave.

I went down to the servants' hall where supper was almost over. Only a few people remained, most having finished their meal some time ago, and now sat over their pots of small beer, idly chatting. There was no sign of Piers.

I toyed with the idea of going in search of him, but then decided that what I had to say could wait. It was more important that I go to Crosby's Place to talk to Godfrey and Lewis Fitzalan. I would set out as soon as I had eaten.

But the thought of a bowl of leftovers was not attractive. I had money. I would treat myself and eat at one of the many inns with which the city abounded. But first I must clean myself up. I climbed the tortuous flights of stairs to my room where I poured the contents of a pitcher of water into a basin, washed and changed into one of my decent suits of clothes.

Refreshed, I was ready to set out.

FOURTEEN

Where I should eat my supper was a problem, not because of a lack of inns and alehouses, but because London boasted too many of them. Of the former, to name but a few, I could have my pick of The Bull and The King's Head in Fish Street, The Paul's Cross in Crooked Lane, The Boar's Head and The Greyhound in East Cheap, or The Saracen's Head near the Ald Gate, while the less salubrious drinking-dens, tucked away in side streets and alleyways were too numerous to identify. In the end, I decided on the inn known familiarly as Blossom's, just off West Cheap; the inn of St Lawrence the Deacon, the painting of the saint's head being surrounded by a garland of flowers, hence the nickname.

My reason for choosing Blossom's was simple. It was the unloading point for carters, particularly those from the West Country. There, they dropped off their goods to await collection by the purchasers and refreshed themselves in the ale room until the arrival of these gentlemen and the receipt of their money. It was just possible, I told myself, but without much hope, that I might encounter someone I knew who could give me news of my family.

Imagine my joy and utter astonishment, therefore, when the first person I laid eyes on as I entered the inn courtyard was my old friend, Jack Nym.

'Jack!' I exclaimed in disbelief, clapping him heavily on one shoulder. 'You here again? What is it this time? Not more Bristol red cloth for the coronation?'

He jumped violently and spun round, fists bunched. 'Gawd!' he muttered feelingly when he realized who it was. 'Don't do that, Roger. I nearly died o' fright.' He eyed me satirically. 'Still here, are you, shirking your responsibilities an' leaving that poor wife o' yours to cope on her own as best she can.'

Annoyed, I clipped him around the ear. 'I'm not here by

my own choice, Jack! I'm here because I was sent for by
the Lord Protector. Adela knows that, if you don't.'

Jack propelled me towards the open door of the ale room.
'Come on, I want my supper. The lord who?'

We found seats at a table occupied by only three other
men, immersed in their own conversation.

'The Lord . . . the Duke of Gloucester,' I answered irritably. 'And I'm not shirking my responsibilities. I didn't ask
to be here.'

'All right! All right! Keep your codpiece on! I was only
teasing. You shouldn't have startled me like that. Stupid thing
to do.' He suspended the recriminations while we ordered
supper – bacon collops, sizzling hot and fried to a turn, fresh
oatcakes, dripping with butter and a large beaker of ale apiece
– before continuing, 'Yes, since you ask, it is another load
of Bristol red cloth I've just delivered for use at the coronation. But the point is, Roger –' and he swivelled round on
the bench so that he could see me more clearly – 'whose
coronation? The young king's or . . . or someone else's?'

I grimaced. 'So the rumours have reached Bristol already,
have they?'

'Already?' Jack was scathing. 'Rumours were rife long
before I left. Bristol's not the back of beyond, lad! Second
city in the kingdom! Besides, anyone who's been within ten
miles o' Wells this past month or more, will tell you that the
place is buzzing with all sorts of tales. It seems as if Bishop
Stillington's hurried departure for London almost as soon as
the old king was dead set tongues wagging with a vengeance.
Apparently, there have always been whispers around the town
that His Grace knew something he shouldn't. So what's the
story?'

'How should I know?'

He snorted. 'You know everything.' Our food and ale
arrived, and for a minute or so there was silence while we
both fell to with a will and stuffed our mouths full of bacon
and oatcakes. After a while, however, our appetites blunted,
Jack returned to the attack. 'Well? Are you going to tell me?'

In the face of his persistence, I gave in and repeated Bishop
Stillington's story of the late King Edward's contract with
Lady Eleanor Butler, at which he had presided, and his

contention that the king's subsequent marriage was therefore invalid.

'Which makes all the children of the union bastards,' I added.

I was interested to know what Jack's reaction would be. It wasn't long in coming.

'Sounds like a Friday tale to me. What's your opinion?'

I hesitated a second or so, then shook my head. 'No. I think it's most likely true.' Jack looked sceptical and I hurried on, 'For a start, it's exactly the same tactics King Edward employed to get his way with the present queen dowager; secret ceremony, secret vows. And in addition, the panic-stricken behaviour of the whole Woodville family since the late king's death makes me more or less certain that they knew what was coming. I tell you, Jack, that the Duke of Gloucester has been in jeopardy of his life from the moment his brother drew his last breath.'

Jack considered this while he chewed on a piece of bacon.

'Now that I might grant you,' he said at last 'By all accounts there's never been any love lost between him and Queen Elizabeth's family. But that don't make it right for him to depose his nephew and seize the crown for himself, that's what I say.'

The trouble was that it was going to be what a lot of people said unless the duke made public his other belief; the belief that King Edward himself had been a bastard, the progeny of his mother's long-ago affair with one of her Rouen archers, named Blaybourne. But that wasn't my secret to reveal to anyone unless and until my lord of Gloucester did so himself.

'You're entitled to your opinion,' I said lamely.

'We're all entitled to that,' was the cheerful response as Jack called for more ale. 'Well, now that we've met up, Roger, lad, we might as well make a night of it and I'll tell you all the news from home.'

So much for my decision to go to Crosby's Place that evening to speak to Godfrey and Lewis Fitzalan! The visit would now have to wait until the following morning. By the time Jack and I eventually parted company, he to his bed in

Blossom's Inn, I to return to mine at Baynard's Castle, we were both pleasantly drunk. I don't say we were legless, far from it, but we were most definitely friends with all the world. I had learned that my family were missing me, but getting along without me, thanks to my wife's excellent management and good sense. I wasn't quite so happy with the news that Richard Manifold had been seen in Small Street on more than one occasion, but, I told myself stoutly, I could trust Adela. (The sheriff's officer was a former admirer of hers from bygone days, but it was me she had chosen to marry.) My former mother-in-law from my first marriage, Margaret Walker, was also busy doing what she did best; keeping an eye on, and poking her nose into, everything that was going on in Bristol, ably abetted by her two faithful henchwomen, Bess Simnel and Maria Watkins. So nothing much had changed, except for the state of nervous apprehension that seemed to have the city in thrall. Jack didn't put it quite like that, but I knew what he meant. It was the same sense of unease that I was encountering everywhere in London.

The streets were quieter now. It was beginning to get dark, the sun disappearing behind clouds streaked with amethyst and gold, long streamers of red and orange fading to a weak and watery rose. The curfew bell had sounded half an hour since and the great gates were shut, but people still moved about within the walls as freely as in the daytime. The ancient Norman imperative of 'couvre feu!' no longer meant that people had to stay indoors, provided that they made no attempt to leave the city.

It was growing dusk when I arrived at Baynard's Castle, but once again, I had no difficulty in being passed by the sentries. One of them even gave me a courteous, 'goodnight'. The other winked knowingly and made the universal gesture to indicate that I had been out with a woman, guffawing heartily when I shook my head. As I made my way indoors and started to mount the stairs to my room, I reflected that such growing familiarity could only mean I had been here too long. I was becoming a recognizable part of the place. It was high time I solved this mystery and went home to my family. The trouble was, of course, that I was still not a whit the wiser as to Gideon Fitzalan's whereabouts or why he had been taken than I had been when I arrived. I had learned something, but not enough.

There was still a certain amount of noise, the subdued hum of conversation from behind closed doors or from the bowels of the castle, where some unfortunates continued hard at work, stoking the great furnaces, setting the dough to rise for tomorrow's bread or fetching and carrying at their masters' beck and call. But in general, the staircases that led to my room were silent and deserted. I passed a couple of weary-looking pages earlier on, nearer ground level, but as I rose higher, I saw no one. Once or twice, I heard a voice in the distance, otherwise I seemed to have that part of the castle to myself . . .

I don't know what suddenly alerted me to danger, some sixth animal sense, perhaps, that never leaves us. Suffice it to say that I was within sight of the door of my room when the hairs on the nape of my neck began to lift and a shiver ran the length of my spine. I swung round just in time to see the cloaked and hooded figure emerging from the shadows at the top of that particular flight of stairs and coming straight for me, one arm raised. And I caught the glint of metal . . . Whoever it was had a knife and was intent on plunging it between my shoulder blades.

I didn't wait to exchange pleasantries. I grabbed the upraised arm with my left hand whilst hitting out with my right fist. It was not as much of a blow as I could have wished, but I had been taken by surprise and had been unable to put my full strength behind it. It was nevertheless of suffi-cient force to make my assailant drop the knife and to cause the hood to fall back from his head. To my disgust, however, he was wearing one of those animal masks used in plays and mummings, a cockerel's head with feathers sticking out at the side, but before I could make a grab at it, he had wrenched his wrist out of my hold and was running down the stairs as though the Devil himself were at his heels. The knife lay where he had dropped it on the ground.

Of course I ran after him, but by the time I reached the bottom of the second flight, he was nowhere to be seen. Somehow, he had given me the slip, but I was in no mood to pursue him further. The ale that I had drunk with Jack was making my head swim and my limbs feel like lead. Only fear and shock had caused me to act with the promptitude that I had done, and now the immediate danger was past I could no longer force myself to that extra effort. All I wanted was to lie down and sleep. I would consider the situation in the morning. I climbed back to my room, bolted the door and fell on my bed fully clothed. In spite of everything, within two minutes I was asleep.

It was the first rays of morning sun, filtering between the slats of my shutters, that woke me.

My throat felt parched and my tongue seemed several sizes too large for my mouth. My breath smelled foul, my good clothes were horribly creased, and for several moments I had difficulty in remembering where I was. But gradually recognition returned. The events of the previous evening came flooding back and caused me to sit up in a hurry. This was a mistake. I groaned and clutched my head, feeling awful and convinced that I was about to throw up at any moment. After a while, however, the nausea passed and I was able to stagger to the window where I threw open the shutters and stuck my head outside. A few bracing gulps of air – one could hardly call it fresh on this particular stretch of the Thames – were enough to bring me completely to my senses.

I sat down again on the edge of the bed and considered what had happened. Someone had tried to kill me. The question was who and why? Strictly speaking, of course, that was two questions, but I felt they were really one. Discover who and I might know why. Discover why and I might know who. It did suggest to me, however, that perhaps I knew more than I thought I did, but the idea did little to cheer me, because for the life of me I had no notion what it was that I knew. There was one thing, though. Whoever had attacked me was going to have a very nasty bruise on his face. Those masks were flimsy, made of little more than stiffened paper and paint, not sufficient protection against the sort of punch that I had landed.

After a while, feeling a little more like my old self, I slid off the bed and reached up to the shelf just inside the door where the candle and tinderbox were kept. Here I had placed the weapon my assailant had dropped before he fled, but close examination of it in daylight revealed nothing more than had the darkness of the night before. It was an ordinary black-handled, long-bladed knife of the sort to be found in any kitchen. No doubt there were scores of them in Baynard's Castle; far too many, at any rate, for it to be noticed if one went missing. Frustrated, I replaced it on the shelf.

I stripped to hose and a shirt and descended to the courtyard to take my turn at the pumps, before proceeding to one of the sculleries to collect a jug of hot shaving water. Returning to my room – by which time, of course, the water was rapidly cooling – I scraped the stubble from my chin with a knife that was badly in need of sharpening, cleaned my teeth after a fashion, combed my hair and struggled into my other suit of decent clothes before going in search of breakfast.

I looked for Piers amongst those already gnawing away on yesterday's stale oatmeal biscuits and grumbling about the thinness of the gruel, but there was no sign of him. I wanted his opinion on the events of last night, but although I hung around for as long as I could, I eventually had to cede my place at one of the tables to the importuning of latecomers, the hall being by now packed to capacity. I did ask a number of people if they knew of his whereabouts, but his name was unknown to most of them. The one or two that did recognize it merely shrugged, saying they hadn't seen him; and remembering Piers's dislike of sleeping anywhere near his fellow men, this was hardly surprising. Foiled, I at last set out for Crosby's Place to fulfil my mission of the previous evening; to speak to Godfrey and Lewis Fitzalan.

This was easier said than done. Crosby's Place was a hive of activity, busier than I, at least, had ever known it.

Even as I approached the main gate, I was thrust unceremoniously back against the wall by a man-at-arms in the Gloucester livery, to allow a horseman, similarly attired, to gallop off in the opposite direction. I recognized him – the horseman, that is – as Sir Richard Ratcliffe, one of my lord

Gloucester's innermost circle of friends, a Yorkshire man to his fingertips and therefore trusted by the duke.

The next obstacle to be surmounted was the gatekeeper who eyed me suspiciously and refused to accept the statement of my business as a reason to let me pass.

'Where's your authority? How do I know you're who you say you are? You might be any pisspot trying to get in. And who are these men you say you want to see? I don't know of any Fitzwhatsits. Mind you,' he added fair-mindedly, 'that don't mean they ain't here. Never seen such a crowd in all me born days. The comings, the goings, the to-ings and fro-ings, it's driving me mad, I can tell you. So you just hop it, my lad, and come back again when you've a warrant.'

'Look—' I was beginning angrily when, by the greatest of good fortune, Timothy Plummer bustled up to the gate to enquire if Sir Richard Ratcliffe had already left. Upon being told that he had, the spymaster swore fluently and turned to go back the way he had come, whereupon I shouted as loudly as I could in order to attract his attention.

He stopped in mid-stride and glanced over his shoulder. 'Roger? What are you doing here?'

I explained that I wanted to speak to Godfrey and Lewis Fitzalan. 'But this fool –' I indicated the gatekeeper – 'won't let me in.'

The man began to defend his actions with a wealth of angry gesticulation, but Timothy cut him short.

'That's all right. I can vouch for this man.' He motioned me inside and led me in the direction of the house, sending a harassed pageboy to discover the twins' whereabouts and to bring them to me as soon as possible.

'And don't take "no" for an answer,' was his parting shot as the boy scuttled away. 'Tell 'em Master Chapman's here on the duke's business.' He waved me to a cushioned window seat in one of the ante-rooms, then sank down wearily beside me. 'I don't know if I'm on my head or my heels, Roger. I don't think any of us do. So much is happening all at once.' He dropped his voice to a whisper, even though there was no one to overhear us. 'Hastings will be executed tomorrow, Friday. Oh, don't look so disapproving: he's been given a fair trial and a chance to speak in his own defence. But he admits there was a plot to overthrow the Protector. Jane Shore will have to do penance for her part in the proceedings. But that's about it. In my opinion – and in the opinion of a lot of other people, I might tell you – the duke's been far too lenient with the other conspirators.'

'Oh?' I said curiously. 'In what way? What's happened to them?'

'Nothing. Well, not much. Archbishop Rotheram's been imprisoned, but it's my guess that he won't be incarcerated for long. The duke has too much respect for the Church. That bastard Stanley has been handed over to his wife, who's to stand surety for his future good behaviour—'

'But she's Henry Tudor's mother!' I objected incredulously.

Timothy nodded grimly 'Quite so. But that's Duke Richard all over. As ruthless as an avenging angel one minute and soft as duck down the next, completely oblivious to his own self-interest. He hasn't even ordered the execution of that snake-in-the-grass, John Morton, simply given him into the safe keeping of the Duke of Buckingham, who's packed him off to his castle at Brecknock. That's in Wales,' he added condescendingly.

'I know where fucking Brecknock is,' I snapped, but hurried on before a wrangle could develop. 'Is the duke mad, allowing those three to walk free like this? Perhaps not free, but compared with his old comrade-in-arms, Hastings, as good as.'

'I've told you, he ain't predictable.' Timothy lowered his voice even further, although the room was still empty. 'While you were waiting at the gate, did you see a man ride out of here?'

'Yes. Sir Richard Ratcliffe. Why?'

'He's bound for the north with orders for Rivers, Grey and Vaughan to be tried and executed. They're all to be taken to Pontefract to be beheaded.'

There was a protracted silence. Then I asked again, 'Why? Surely they present no further threat to His Highness? That plot failed with the upset at Northampton. Their teeth have been drawn.'

My companion drew a deep breath. His voice now was the merest whisper. 'Myself, I think it's revenge for Clarence's

death. My lord has always been convinced that the Woodvilles
persuaded the late king to sign the death warrant; that without
their intervention, Edward would have pardoned his brother.
And this revelation of Bishop Stillington has confirmed his
conviction. I tell you, Roger, Duke Richard is a wonderful
master and the most faithful of friends, but my advice is,
whatever you do, don't make an enemy of him. He can be
a dangerous man.'

I vaguely recalled the Duke of Albany once saying something similar which, at the time, I had dismissed as spite.
But maybe the Scot had known his cousin better than I had
thought.

Before I was able to make any rejoinder, however, the
door to the ante-room opened and the page ushered in Godfrey
and Lewis Fitzalan. Neither appeared to be in a very good
humour.

'What's all this about?' the former demanded truculently,
addressing me and ignoring Timothy. 'Lewis and I have told
you everything we know concerning our nephew's disappearance, chapman.' I noticed wryly that I was no longer
worthy of the courtesy of 'Master'. 'The Protector has work
for us to do. We can ill be spared at this present.'

His twin nodded in agreement.

Timothy rose majestically to his feet. In spite of his lack
of inches, he could impose his presence on a room when he
was so minded.

'I think you'll find, sirs,' he said, 'that His Grace regards
your nephew's abduction as a serious matter, and one which
he is very anxious to have resolved. He'll be extremely
displeased, take it from me, if you fail to give Master
Chapman –' was there the faintest emphasis on my title? –
'all the help he needs.'

Godfrey flushed angrily and Lewis looked resentful, but they
nevertheless stood aside respectfully for the spymaster to leave
the room, which he did with magnificent aplomb. Fortunately,
neither noticed the wink he gave as he passed me.

'Well, master,' Godfrey asked impatiently as the door
closed behind Timothy, 'what do you want to know?'

'I want to ask if either one of you can think of anything
– anything at all, however trivial – that might account for

Gideon having been taken? Ransom is clearly not the reason, therefore why him? Whoever snatched him was prepared to go to the length of killing the person he was with in order to make certain of his abduction.'

The brothers seemed somewhat taken aback by this request, but after a moment or two, when I thought they were going to laugh it to scorn, they relented and gave it their serious consideration. In other words, they hummed and hawed a lot and screwed up their faces to give the impression that they were doing a deal of thinking, but all without any result. I don't really know that I had expected any, but there had always been a faint chance that one of them might dredge up something, some little known, half-forgotten fact, from the depths of memory.

It was a forlorn hope.

'The truth is that neither of us had much to do with Gideon,' Lewis admitted at last.

'Better acquainted with his brothers,' Godfrey added.

'Although not much,' his twin amended. 'Oddly enough, we've no children of our own, but our five brothers more than make up for our lack. We've a whole flock of nephews, Master Chapman –' he was careful to address me formally, but there was a derisive gleam in his eyes – 'and keeping track of them all is difficult.'

Godfrey nodded his agreement. 'You'd do much better to talk to Bevis or young Blaise. They're the two of Pomfret's brood nearest to Gideon in age.'

'Unfortunately,' I said, 'they are no longer at Baynard's Castle. They've gone to attend upon the king in the royal apartments at the Tower.'

'Surely there's no problem with that,' Lewis protested. 'You seem to have the ear of the duke, or at least of that pompous little spymaster of his. I've no doubt you could obtain the necessary authorization to speak to the boys if you wanted to.'

This had already occurred to me, and as it was obvious that I should get nothing from the twins of any value – indeed, it had been plain from the start that they knew of nothing that could help me – I let them go and went to seek out Timothy. He, however, had vanished to attend to business of his own,

and my request to other ducal officials for a word with the
Lord Protector was treated with scorn. It was the lawyer,
William Catesby, last seen by me (although he did not know
it) in a house in Old Dean's Lane, who came to my rescue.
Overhearing yet another of my pleas to an over-officious
lackey, he took me in charge.

'Come with me, Master Chapman. I know who you are
and I know that His Grace will wish to see you.'

I was unaware of it at the time, but I later learned that
this unassuming man had just been made Chancellor of the
Earldom of March, but I should never have guessed it from
his demeanour. His quiet friendliness was in stark contrast
to the brusque treatment I had suffered at the hands of infe-
riors. Within a very short space of time, I was being ushered
once again into the duke's presence.

He came forward to greet me, hand outstretched, and
as I knelt to kiss it, I was conscious of an air of suppressed
excitement about him. Looking up into his face, I noticed a
glitter in his eyes that I could not remember ever having
seen before. He had lost his usual pallor and seemed
suddenly taller. In spite of his lack of height, he dominated
the room.

'Roger! Have you solved this mystery for me? Do you
know what has happened to young Gideon Fitzalan?'

'Not yet, my lord. But,' I added, thankful to be able to report
some progress, 'I do know how Gregory Machin's body came
to be found in a locked room.'

He waved me to a chair and sat down himself, listening
attentively while I explained the details to him. He always
had the ability to concentrate on one thing at a time, no
matter how many others were vying for his attention. When
I had finished, he took a deep breath and nodded.

'Now you put me in mind of it, I believe I have heard of
such cases. Death is not instantaneous even though the wound
is fatal. Well, that would appear to be one part of the mystery
solved. But where is Gideon Fitzalan? His uncles tell me
that no ransom has been demanded of his father.'

'No, my lord. Why he has been taken is as great a riddle
as where he is being held. Which is why I am asking for
your authority to question his brothers. They are at present

at the Tower, in attendance upon the . . . the . . .' For some reason, I was totally unable to pronounce the word 'king'.

'The lord Edward,' he finished for me.

My gaze jerked up to meet his. The eyes glittered more than ever and the thin lips curved into a triumphant smile. And yet it was the same sweet smile that I had always known. I realized then that he truly believed himself to be the rightful king. And in my heart, I agreed with him.

But I knew that there were hundreds who wouldn't.

FIFTEEN

had never before seen the Tower at close quarters, although it dominated much of the London skyline. As, of course, it was meant to. Like everything that was built on the orders of William of Normandy it stressed Norman domination over the conquered Saxon. Throughout the kingdom, these great castles and fortresses were intended to let us know who was the master and who the serf, and woe betide anyone who ever forgot it. I had said to Etheldreda Simpkins that surely after five hundred years we were all one people, and she had scoffed at this idea. And she was right. The divide, however subtle, was always there, and maybe always would be.

Armed with Duke Richard's authorization, written at his dictation by his secretary, John Kendall, I obtained easy access to the royal apartments, passed from one guard-post to the next without so much as a raised eyebrow, and was finally left kicking my heels in a small, barely furnished room while an usher went in search of Bevis and Blaise Fitzalan. Staring out of the window at a stretch of sun-washed greensward and a magnificent beech tree in full leaf, I thought back to my recent interview with Duke Richard and realized that events were gathering momentum. It could not be long now until he made his intentions public and claimed the crown. Twelve weeks had elapsed since the death of the late King Edward and the acclamation of his young son as Edward the fifth, and now the lad's reign seemed to be drawing to a close. What would happen to him and his siblings? In particular to him and his younger brother, the Duke of York? Or should one even call the boy by that title any longer? 'May you live in exciting times,' was generally held to be a curse. I was beginning to think that it was true . . .

The usher returned to conduct me to another, more comfortably furnished chamber where the two Fitzalan brothers awaited me, curious to know why I wished to see them, but

at the same time a little resentful at having been dragged
away from whatever it was they had been doing.

'I hope this isn't going to take long, Master Chapman,'
Bevis said in a fair imitation of his uncle Godfrey. 'We're
in attendance upon the king this morning, and it's very nearly
dinner time.'

I could have told him that by the rumblings in my belly.

I explained my mission as briefly as possible and begged
them both to think as hard as they could of everything they
knew about Gideon. Was there something, however slight,
that might set him apart from other boys? Anything at all
that would explain his abduction?

The brothers seemed astonished by the request.

'He's always been a miserable little fart, if that's what you
mean,' Bevis said, not mincing matters.

'Always got something wrong with him,' Blaise con-
tributed. 'Always running to old Mother Copley with a
headache or a bellyache or earache or some such ache.'

'And she doses him up with physic and tells the rest of
us off for not being more sympathetic towards our dear little
brother.' Bevis made a gagging sound. 'It makes us all puke.'

'All of us being?'

'Well, us –' he waved a hand at Blaise – 'and our other
brothers, Thomas and Peter and Maurice and Cornelius. We
all call him a whinging little toad.'

I sighed and urged them to think of Gideon with something other than a healthy young man's contempt for an ailing
younger brother. It was quite possible that, as the runt of the
litter, the boy was genuinely delicate. Was there something
different about him that distinguished him from the rest of
the family?

But this appeared to confuse Bevis and Blaise more than
ever. They didn't understand what I meant – which led me,
of course, to the reluctant conclusion that there was nothing
either peculiar or extraordinary about Gideon Fitzalan which
might explain why he had been taken, or, indeed, what he
had been taken for.

I was about to return to the attack for one last time, in the
vain hope of eliciting some fragment of information, when
the door to the room burst open and a young man came in,

a petulant grimace on his pretty lips. Although I had only set eyes on him once before – some weeks earlier, riding into his capital between his uncles of Gloucester and Buckingham – I recognized him immediately. It was the king.

Or then again, perhaps not.

For the moment, however, I had no choice but to treat him as the former. Following Bevis's and Blaise's example, I sank to one knee and bowed my head.

'What's going on?' he demanded querulously. 'I thought we were playing cards.' He caught sight of me and gave me an imperious stare. 'Who's this?'

Bevis saved me the trouble of replying. 'Roger Chapman, Sire. He's enquiring into the mysterious disappearance of our brother, Gideon, at the request of your uncle, the Protector.'

Something very like a scowl marred the delicate features. 'I don't like my uncle Gloucester,' was the petulant reply, but there was also something akin to fear lurking in the blue eyes that were so much like his mother's. 'I want my uncle Rivers.'

An icy hand squeezed my bowels. In a very few days his uncle Rivers would be executed at Pontefract along with Edward's half-brother, Sir Richard Grey, and his cousin, Sir Thomas Vaughan. I stared hard at the floor, watching the royal fleas hopping in and out among the sweet-smelling rushes.

'And have you found out what's happened to Gideon Fitzalan?' asked that small, cold voice which had none of the warmth and bonhomie of the late King Edward's.

I raised my eyes to that sour little face, then realized with a jolt of compassion that one side of the boy's jaw was badly swollen and that it was obviously giving him pain. He kept rubbing it with one beringed hand and screwing up the eye above it.

'Not yet, Sire,' I said gently. 'I came to see if either of Master Gideon's brothers knows anything that could assist me. That's why I'm here.'

The fair head turned sharply in the direction of Blaise and Bevis. 'And do you?' Edward asked abruptly. When they shrugged and looked blank, he gave a high-pitched crow of laughter. 'I didn't think you would.'

The door opened once again and the nine-years-old Duke of York – it was difficult as yet to think of him as anything else – entered the room. There was no doubt that he was Edward's brother; indeed, except for a marked disparity in height, they could have been twins. They were both fair-haired, blue-eyed and displayed the handsome Woodville features of their maternal family. But there the similarity ended. Whereas the elder boy was all gloom and acidity, the younger was sweetness and light.

He grinned at me and gave me a friendly nod before turning to his brother. 'Ned, it's almost dinner time and we haven't finished our game.' He smiled mischievously. 'Or don't you want to finish because you're losing?'

The other turned on him, the pale face suddenly crimson. 'Don't you dare speak to me like that!' he screamed. 'I am your king and don't you forget it!'

I think we were all shocked and the younger boy flinched. Bastard or not, there was no doubt that Edward had the Plantagenet temper. Wasn't the whole race reputed to be descended from a daughter of the Devil?

'Sire,' Bevis said hastily, 'His Grace didn't mean . . . He's only little . . .'

'He's nine! Old enough to know how to address his sovereign.' Edward glared at his frightened sibling for a moment, then put up a hand to rub his cheek 'My jaw's hurting again. Where's Doctor Argentine? Why is he never around when he's needed?' He waved a hand at Blaise and Bevis. 'One of you go and find him and tell him I want him. Now!'

Bevis gave me a speaking look and scuttled off, muttering out of the corner of his mouth as he passed me, 'I'd come with me if I were you.'

I took his advice. There was, after all, nothing to stay for. I had obtained as much from the Fitzalan brothers as I was likely to get and any further questioning would obviously be nothing but a waste of time. So while Edward's attention was focused on the other two – young Richard of York plainly offering an olive branch and trying to make friends again – I made a deep bow and edged towards the door. I had barely stepped across the threshold, however, when a voice arrested me.

'Tell my Uncle Gloucester not to send his lackeys bothering my people again! And you haven't taken proper leave of me! I am your king!'

There was a note of desperation in the last sentence that moved me in spite of myself. The same wave of compassion washed over me as it had done earlier. I went back, knelt and kissed the little hand held out to me. It was stone cold against my lips; almost, I thought, like the touch of dead flesh.

Once outside in the fresh air, I took a deep breath and leant against one of the massive walls, looking at, but not seeing, the archery butts set up on the green, where the boys had been shooting some time during the morning if the abandoned bows and arrows were anything to judge by. My emotions were in a tangle. I didn't like young Edward and yet I felt deeply sorry for him. He was frightened and in pain, suddenly deprived of all the people he knew best, on whom he had always depended, and surrounded by strangers. Even his brother he did not know well.

I heaved myself away from the wall and gave myself a mental shake. It was no use standing there, worrying about things which I could not alter and over which I had no control. In any case, my loyalty had always been to my lord of Gloucester. I liked him as a man and knew him for a faithful friend so long as one returned that faithfulness. But I suspected he could be an implacable enemy to those who betrayed his trust.

It was nearly dinner time. I could feel it in my belly even if I couldn't guess it by the way in which the out-of-door workers were flocking inside to the sound of braying trumpets and the banging of gongs. Once again, I had to decide where to eat, and this time settled on the Boar's Head in East Cheap. It was not a hostelry I was acquainted with at all well, so was unlikely to meet anyone there whom I knew or who might recognize me. I therefore left the Tower by the Postern Gate and directed my footsteps in a westerly direction.

The traffic, both four-wheeled and two-legged, was dense

at that time in the morning and the June day was beginning to heat up. The ranks of the innumerable street-vendors had been augmented by strawberry sellers coming in from the country, anxious to dispose of their wares as quickly as possible before they became overripe and mushy. The season was, in any case, short for these luscious fruits, so one was accosted on all sides by men, women and even occasionally children pushing their trays right up under people's noses, thus making progress even more difficult than usual.

It was while I was repelling a particularly persistent man, with black stumps of teeth and a body odour to make the eyes water, that I saw, some little way ahead, her back towards me, a woman I was sure was Amphillis Hill. She, too, was staving off the importunities of a strawberry seller, who was trying to force a sample berry between her teeth.

I raised my voice and hollered her name and, in spite of the din all around us, I thought for a moment that she had heard me. She half-turned her head and gave a quick glance over her shoulder, so I shouted again, but this time with no effect. She elbowed the strawberry seller aside with a strength surprising in so small a woman and vanished among the crowds ahead of her. It had been my intention to offer to buy her dinner, but now resigned myself to a solitary meal.

Of course, it was inevitable that the moment I entered the Boar's Head in East Cheap the first person I clapped eyes on was Amphillis. But she was not alone. She was sitting – huddled one might almost have said by their postures and the closeness of their heads – with two other women at one of the smaller tables beside an open window, whose shutters had been flung wide in a vain attempt to allow some air into the ale room. So engrossed were the three of them in their conversation that they failed to notice my entrance, despite the fact that my height drew the usual curious stares from some of the other customers.

I hastened to sit down, choosing a seat in a shadowed corner where I could observe without being seen. As I edged on to a rickety stool that had seen better days – and had probably been there since King Henry V's misspent youth, the inn having been one of his and his cronies' favourite haunts if all the stories about him were to be believed – I realized that one of the other women with Amphillis was Rosina Copley. I had not thought them to be such good friends. And then, with a start of amazement, I recognized the third member of the group as Etheldreda Simpkins. But a greater shock was to follow. It was when Dame Copley turned her head to stare in disapproval at a noisy group of young men seated at a neighbouring table, and who had already consumed too much of the tavern's good ale, that I saw a marked likeness between her and Etheldreda. I recalled Lady Fitzalan saying that the nurse had a sister who lived in Dowgate.

A potboy came to take my order and my attention was momentarily distracted. By the time I was at liberty to look again, the three had been joined by yet a fourth woman, and another stool was being dragged across from the large table in the centre of the ale room and accommodated at their own. I knew at once that the newcomer was the woman I had twice before seen in Amphillis's company and whose back view I had been so certain that I recognized. And yet, now that I saw her face, I was unable to place her. Nevertheless, the sense of familiarity persisted.

Once more, the heads were bent towards one another and the earnest conversation resumed. That it was earnest was apparent by the set expression of their features. This was no idle gossip between friends. There was no giggling, no head thrown back in laughter, no hand extended to press another's arm or shoulder, no purchase produced for the approval of the rest. Whatever the four of them were discussing, it was a serious matter.

My food, a rabbit stew with sage and onion dumplings, arrived to claim my attention, together with a beaker of the inn's best ale. For quite a few moments I had no thought for anything but filling my belly and slaking my thirst, and when I had time to look around me again, the women had gone. I stared in consternation at the table where they had been sitting, but this was now occupied by three men, carpenters judging by the tools jutting from the pockets of their leather aprons. I half-rose from my seat, then sank back again to finish my meal. There was no point in wasting such excellent fare.

And in any case, why did I want to go after the women? Why did it matter where they had gone? Yet something nagged at me, something I could not quite put my finger on. It was not simply that I could not place the fourth woman, even now that I had seen her face, nor the fact that I felt certain of having met her somewhere before. No, there was something else, some small thing that irritated me like a fly buzzing around my head that would not go away.

In the end, I gave up thinking about it. I knew from long experience that it was the only course. The more I tried to remember, the less my brain was amenable to divulging its secrets. I called for bread and cheese to round off my meal.

'Stuffing your belly again, Roger?'

I recognized Piers's voice, and I wondered briefly when the more respectful 'Master Chapman' had been replaced, not just by the familiarity of my Christian name, but also by a certain mocking intonation whenever it was pronounced.

I glanced up to find the lad standing by my table, but the slight protest I had been about to make died on my lips. The left-hand side of Piers's face was marred by a bruise that spread upwards from his cheekbone to encircle his eye.

'Wh-what happened to you?' I stuttered.

'What happened? Oh!' Piers put up a hand to touch the discolouration. 'You mean this? Careless of me, wasn't it? I wasn't looking where I was going and walked straight into the edge of a door.'

'When was this?'

He waved a vague hand. 'Yesterday evening sometime.' He winked. 'I'd had a drop too much to drink.'

'Was there someone with you when it happened?'

He frowned. 'Does it matter? Why do you want to know?'

'Because someone attacked me with a knife last night, just as I was returning to my room. I managed to hit whoever it was a good right-hander on the left-hand side of his face and he ran away.'

The smile was wiped from Piers's lips and he stared at me in horror. 'Roger, that's terrible.' He gave a little gasp and his eyes widened. 'Sweet Virgin and all the saints! You don't – you can't – think it was me?' When I didn't answer, he went on, 'Roger! I swear to you that I really did walk into the edge of a door. It's true! If you don't believe me, ask Dame Copley. As a matter of fact, it was partly her fault that it happened. Some of the other lads and I had just returned to the castle by boat – we'd been across to Southwark, to the Tabard – and had gone in by that landing-stage door not far from her room. As I said, we were a bit drunk. More than a bit if the truth be told, and we were kicking up quite a din. We disturbed her and she flung open her door just at the very minute I was passing. I walked straight into it. Caught myself the devil of a crack as you can see. Not that I got any sympathy from her, I can tell you! She said it served me right and gave us all a great scold, just as if we were children.'

'Dame Copley's gone back to that room then, has she? I thought she'd moved permanently into the guest apartments so that she could be a comfort to Lady Fitzalan. When you and I looked into her old room yesterday, it was empty.'

For a moment, he seemed utterly taken aback. Then he shrugged. 'I'd forgotten that,' he said. 'So it was. Of course! I arranged for you to see her in the guest apartments, didn't I? I must be losing my wits. But it did happen as I've told you. All I can think of is that she must have returned there for something. The pot of birch twigs, perhaps.'

'Why in heaven's name would she want them? The leaves were all brown and wilting.'

Piers gave me a sharp look. 'Why are you so suspicious? I swear to you that what I'm saying is the truth. Ask Mother Copley if you think I'm lying. I promise you she'll bear me out.'

'Why didn't you tell me that you're Dame Copley's nephew?'

He blinked. 'I-I never thought about it. I-I didn't realize you didn't know. It's not important, anyway. We're not that close.' The mockery had vanished and he appeared genuinely perturbed. 'Roger!' he pleaded. 'You can't really believe that I would try to murder you! Why? Why should I wish to? You're my friend.'

I sighed and got to my feet. 'It was just the bruise,' I said apologetically.

'I've explained that.'

'I know. I'm sorry. But you must see that it looks suspicious. Here,' I added, 'take my seat. If you're going to eat, I recommend the rabbit stew.'

He slid on to my vacated stool with a nod of thanks. 'You do believe me, don't you?' He sounded anxious. I nodded and he continued, 'You mustn't walk about by yourself at night. There's a killer somewhere amongst us, and if he's now after you, you're in serious danger. Make sure someone always goes with you.'

I laughed. 'Anyone determined to kill me could do it just as well by day. Baynard's Castle is a veritable rabbit warren of passageways and staircases, as you well know. But I shall be careful.'

He nodded. 'Do be.'

'By the way,' I said, as I handed over some coins to an anxious potboy who thought I was about to abscond without paying my shot, 'Dame Copley was in here not very long ago, together with Amphillis Hill and two other women, one of whom I'm sure must be her sister because of a certain family resemblance between them. Her name's Etheldreda Simpkins.'

Piers looked startled, staring at me as though he didn't quite know what to say. 'You . . . you know Aunt Etheldreda?' he managed at last.

Of course! If he were Rosina's nephew, then he would also be her sister's.

'We've met,' I said, and explained, in part, the circumstances of that encounter. What I didn't say was that when I stumbled across St Etheldreda's Church, I had been following Amphillis Hill. I let him think it had been by chance, but offered no explanation of why I had been in the Dowgate Ward. Fortunately, he displayed no curiosity on that head.

'And . . . and Aunt Etheldreda actually showed you the crypt?' he asked.

'She fetched me a lantern from her house so that I could see my way down the steps,' I told him cheerfully. 'What she didn't tell me, but which I discovered for myself quite by accident, is that there's another chamber below that one whose foundations look to me to be very ancient. They may well be those of the Roman Temple of Mithras that stood, so I understand, close to that site, and might indeed have actually stood on it.'

'Well!' Piers looked, for once, lost for words. 'Did . . . did you tell Aunt Ethel about this second chamber you found?'

'No. I thought it best not to. She seemed such a game old lady that I thought it wisest not to. She would probably have decided to explore it for herself and might have slipped and broken a limb, if nothing worse.'

'Quite right,' Piers said. 'There's no doubt she would have.' He still seemed a little dazed by my revelation. 'I must go and investigate it for myself one of these days.'

A potboy finally came to take his order and, with a parting admonition to have the rabbit stew, I seized the opportunity to take my leave.

I made my way westwards along East Cheap into Candlewick Street and suddenly realized that I was only yards from the place where Etheldreda Simpkins had her dwelling; the little bow-shaped alleyway that linked Candlewick Street to Dowgate Hill and bypassed the junction of both with Wallbrook. On impulse, I decided to pay another visit to the church and its crypt, for no better reason than that I could think of nothing else to do and didn't want to own to myself that, in the matter of Gideon Fitzalan's disappearance, my thinking had reached a standstill. I had no idea why he had vanished, where he was being held or who was holding him. It was time for prayer and a word with God in private.

'You're not very gallant,' said a reproachful voice, and a hand caught hold of my arm. I turned to see Naomi, obviously on her way home to Bucklersbury with a covered basket in one hand. 'I saw you come out of the Boar's Head,' she went on, 'and I called to you, but you took no notice.'

'I didn't hear you,' I protested.

She ignored this. 'I've been buying meat for the master's supper tonight and dinner tomorrow. All the best butchers are in East Cheap, just as all the best drapers are here, in Candlewick Street.' She smiled happily, withdrawing her hand from my arm and raising it to finger the birch twig pinned to her bodice. 'The master's treating me to some new material for my Midsummer Eve Queen's dress. I'm off now to choose it.' And planting a light kiss on my right cheek, she darted away across the road to a stall whose proud owner was shouting something about newly arrived 'silks from the Orient'.

Of course, I thought, that was it! That was what I had been trying to remember. All four women in the Boar's Head had been wearing little sprays of birch twigs pinned to their gowns. Did the fact have any particular significance, or was it something many women did at this time of year? I recalled the two boys I had met on the downs at home, not far from the great gorge, and how they had been denuding a birch tree of its twigs and tender young branches. The Crown and the Bough. The birch leaf wreaths that encircled the Midsummer Eve Queens' heads. I sighed. It seemed like common practice after all.

I had paused for my moment's contemplation, leaning against the nearby wall of a house, letting the tide of humanity flow by me. Now, as I heaved myself upright once more, I glanced idly to my right – and saw a flicker of movement as if someone had suddenly ducked down out of sight. Was I being followed? But by whom and why? I stood still, staring, oblivious to the opprobrium of people trying to push past me, but knowing full well that I was being foolish. In those sort of crowds, how could one distinguish one kind of movement from another? After last night's attack, I was becoming unnecessarily jumpy.

A few more steps brought me to the mouth of the alleyway and I turned into its cobbled silence with a feeling of relief. The racket and bustle of Candlewick Street was making my head ache, especially as it had not really recovered from my drinking session with Jack the evening before.

The door of the church was still unlocked and I pushed my way inside, then waited a few seconds to allow my eyes to adjust to the gloom. I easily found the cupboard where candles, their holders and the tinderbox were stored and, having provided myself with light, proceeded to the back of the altar. Within minutes, I was descending the stairs into the crypt, its unpleasant smell rising to meet me. I spent a few minutes looking around, but nothing seemed to have altered since my last visit three days earlier until I noticed that the planks, previously propped against the second door, had been removed. For a moment, I hesitated, then telling myself not to be a fool, I opened the door and went down the second flight of steps into the fetid atmosphere of the lower chamber.

There was something different about it, but before I had time to work out what that difference was, something caught me a swingeing blow on the back of the head.

I descended into blackness.

SIXTEEN

I knew that for my past sins I was going down to Hell. The only thing that surprised me was that it should be so wet. Fire and brimstone I would have expected, but who could have supposed that the road to the nether world would be by water?

My head was throbbing and I had not yet dared to open my eyes. Lights – very bright lights – flashed across the inside of my lids, and there was a humming in my ears that sounded louder than a swarm of bees. But I could also hear people shouting, distant cries which I presumed came from other unfortunates like myself who were on their way to the realm of Old Nick. I reproached myself bitterly for not having lived a more blameless life. The shades of Juliette Gerrish and Eloise Gray haunted me, together with all the other women I had lusted after . . .

I was sinking lower. Water closed over my head and I swallowed a mouthful of something that smelled disgustingly of public latrines or the night-soil carts that rumbled about the city in the early morning. At the same time, a voice echoed somewhere in the depths of my mind, 'I know who you'm talking about. I've seed her once or twice lately. Don't know who she is . . .' I wanted to protest that this statement was untrue; that I had just seen the speaker, Etheldreda Simpkins, and Amphillis Hill talking together in the Boar's Head in East Cheap as though they were old friends. I took another mouthful of water. An oar smacked me smartly on one ear – and suddenly I was fully conscious, horribly aware that I was struggling for my life in the River Thames.

I trod water as hard as I could while trying to get my bearings. A swift glance over my shoulder just before I went under again, informed me that I was not far from the bank, but I knew from experience that many of the boats and barges rowed dangerously close to the shore. Moreover, I had briefly recognized the great bastion of the steelyard where the

Hanseatic merchants plied their trade; where vessels containing cargoes of timber and oil and pitch tied up ready to be unloaded, before being reloaded again with bales of the broadcloth that the Germans exported to all the markets of eastern Europe. And to the west of the steelyard was Three Cranes Wharf belonging to the vintners of the city, where ships from Bordeaux berthed.

My brain still wasn't functioning properly, but the instinct for danger is one of the strongest we have and I knew that I was in trouble. How I came to be in the Thames and why my head hurt so much were problems that would have to wait for a solution at a later time. For the moment, all my energy was concentrated on keeping myself afloat and trying desperately to avoid the water traffic all around me. I tried shouting, but in the general din my voice was lost. I tried waving, but no one noticed me (hardly surprising I suppose as half the time I was being sucked under by the wake of whatever was passing closest to me). I tried catching at oars as they flashed by me, but my strength was ebbing rapidly and I wasn't quick enough. Only sheer desperation and the determination to survive preserved me from simply giving up and letting the water take me. Heaven knew, I was tired enough for it to begin to seem like an attractive proposition. My mind was starting to cloud over again and reality and fantasy were becoming one. Sometimes I was at home with Adela and the children, at others in some church with steps leading down into a crypt. But whether it was St Giles in Bristol or somewhere in London, I really couldn't tell. And what was more, I really didn't care . . .

'Fer the sweet Lord's sake, grab 'old of the bloody oar,' screamed a voice from above me.

I must have obeyed this injunction because the next thing I knew I was sprawled anyhow in the bottom of a rowing boat while a vaguely familiar face hovered between me and the sky.

'God save us! I thought it were you, lad,' said a voice from the past. 'What you up to now, then, eh? Poking yer nose into other people's business, I daresay. Lie still or you'll upset the fuckin' boat. I'll take you 'ome to Southwark and get you dry.'

Bertha Mendip! I recognized the West Country burr which, in spite of all her years in the capital, she had never quite lost. I had first met her twelve years earlier during my very first visit to London when I was enquiring into the disappearance of Clement Weaver, and then again some six years or so later. She had her home amongst the beggars and criminals of the Southwark stews, making a living by dragging dead bodies out of the Thames and selling the corpses' clothes, plus any other trinkets they might have had about their persons.

From what I could see, she looked much the same; a woman who had appeared old before she was thirty, but who seemed to have aged very little since, although the unkempt hair which straggled about her skinny shoulders had, when I first knew her, been a dark chestnut-brown. Now it was completely grey and, in places, turning white. But her eyes were just the same, a brilliant blue and still full of eagerness and life.

I smiled at her foolishly, too tired even to make the effort to speak, but I think I must have mouthed the word, 'Bertha,' because she nodded and gave a gap-toothed grin.

'Tha's right, lad. Jus' lie still and don' try talkin'. I'll soon 'ave you right as rain again when I get you back to Angel Wharf.'

At least, I presume that's what she said because the last part of the sentence was lost as I either fell asleep or fainted.

Now I knew I really was in Hell. I could feel the heat of the fire as it warmed and dried out my shivering body. But it wasn't unpleasant; indeed, quite the opposite. Perhaps the nether world wasn't as bad as it was painted . . .

'Comin' round then, are we?' There was a cackle of laughter.

I was suddenly fully conscious and in command of all my faculties. I remembered everything that had happened to me: St Etheldreda's Church, the crypt, the lower chamber, being hit over the head and, finally, my rescue by Bertha Mendip. I opened my eyes and immediately recognized her hut on Angel Wharf with its smell of drying clothes which had been too long immersed in water and in contact with decaying flesh. They hung from poles at one end of the single room, while smoke from the fire disappeared through a blackened hole in the roof. My own decent hose and tunic were being held in front of the blaze by Bertha herself and a scrap of a girl who looked no more than about ten years of age, but who, I guessed, was probably some years older than that. I realized also that I was naked – who had undressed me didn't bear thinking about – and that I was wrapped in a filthy old blanket which was almost certainly verminous.

'Where's your son?' I croaked, saying the first thing that entered my head.

There was another cackle. 'Lord love you, 'e's long gone. 'Opped it the moment 'e were old enough t' do without me. Got in with a gang o' cutpurses working' the city. Never seen 'im from that day t' this. Thirsty?'

I was suddenly conscious of a raging thirst, but Bertha didn't wait for my answer. She put down my tunic and vanished outside the hut, returning after a while with a beaker of ale which at first I sipped cautiously. But to my great surprise it tasted wonderful. Bertha picked up my tunic again and resumed her station by the fire.

'This is good stuff, this is,' she remarked over her shoulder. 'Gen'leman's stuff. 'Ow d'you come by it?'

'It was a present,' I answered shortly.

There was an explosion of mirth. 'From a woman, I'll be bound!' I didn't disillusion her. She went on, 'So what 'appened? 'Ow you come t' be in the water?'

'Someone hit me over the back of the head. But not hard enough, I fancy. I suspect I'm supposed to be dead by now. But how I came to be in the river is more than I can fathom.'

Bertha half-turned and looked at me thoughtfully. 'There's a drain thereabouts,' she said, 'what empties into the Thames. Years gone, when I first come to Lunnon, someone told me it were a stream what had been built over, but stills runs underground.'

The Wallbrook! I had a sudden vision of the semicircular aperture I had noticed on my first visit to the chamber below St Etheldreda's crypt. It must be a secondary pipe which connected to the main culvert . . .

Bertha was speaking. 'I found a few bodies there at

different times. Tha's why I goes there. It's a good spot fer pickins.'

'Do you . . .? Do you think these bodies come out of the drain?'

'Lord, I never thought about it! Maybe they does, maybe they doesn't. But I s'pose it's possible. Not my place t' question what the good God sends me. I just fishes out the corpses and am thankful for what I gets.'

'And I might have been another of them,' I mused. 'I feel certain I was intended to be.'

'G'arn with you! Nobody ain't goin' t' kill you that easy.' Bertha was dismissive. Nevertheless, she added, 'What you up to, then? Pryin' and pokin' about I guess, like the first time I met you?'

'I suppose so,' I admitted sheepishly, not feeling up to telling her the whole story. I changed the subject abruptly. 'Will those clothes ever be any good again?'

She was indignant. ''Course they will! Think I don' know me own business? I bin restorin' clothes what've bin in the river fer years. And most of 'em've bin soaked a lot longer than what yours 'ave. But it won't be done in a trice. You may 'ave t' stay 'ere the rest o' today an' t'night. You can't run through the streets as naked as the day you was born, now can you?'

I was appalled at the prospect, but I could also see that I had no alternative. My tunic and hose would take some time to dry before they could be worked on to bring them back to anything like their former glory. And I suddenly remembered my hat with the fake jewel pinned to the upturned brim. Had I been wearing it? If so, it was probably gone for ever. Moreover, I wasn't certain that I could move, even if I were prepared to expose my manly body to the interested of Southwark. A great lassitude was stealing over me, and the heat from the fire was making me feel stupid.

'Wha-what did you put in that ale?' I asked sleepily. I remember that I wasn't at all perturbed by the realization.

'Lettuce juice,' Bertha answered, her voice coming from a long way off. 'You needs the rest. Don' worry. I ain't goin' t' rob you. You'm a friend. You comes from the same part o' the world as what I do . . .'

Her voice grew fainter, dwindling to a mere thread of sound before it ceased altogether. I sank deeper into the velvety darkness . . .

I was standing in the great solar in Baynard's Castle between Sir Pomfret and Lady Fitzalan. There seemed to be no one else present except the Dowager Duchess of York, facing us and tapping on the floor with her silver-handled cane.

'Where are the rest of you?' she was demanding of Sir Pomfret. 'I was told that all your brothers would be present.' Sir Pomfret made no reply and the duchess tapped even harder, adding an impatient foot to the beat. 'Well, man? Speak up! Ah!' This exclamation followed the opening of the solar door as Godfrey and Lewis appeared. 'Here at least are two more.' The twins bowed and went to stand behind their brother, jostling me out of the way as they did so, while the duchess continued glaring at us all. Her voice rose to a screech. 'But some are still missing. Where are the others? Where are Henry and Warren and Raisley and George?'

'No, no!' protested Bevis and Blaise, getting up from the window embrasure where they had been sitting (although I felt sure that they hadn't been there earlier). 'Your Grace means Thomas and Peter and Maurice and Cornelius. Young Gideon can't be with us because he's disappeared.'

Duchess Cicely had turned towards them as they spoke, but now she swung slowly back to point an accusing finger at me.

'Haven't you found him yet, Master Chapman?' she demanded. 'The king told you to do so and before his coronation. The king, my son . . . The king, my son . . . The king, my son . . .'

I noticed the expression of horror caused by her words on all the other faces, mouths opening and shutting as though they were trying to protest. They reminded me of the fish that used to be netted from the abbot's carp pond at Glastonbury and how ridiculous the poor creatures looked once they were landed. I started to laugh, loudly, stupidly, and found myself shouting, 'You fools! You fools! You never thought Edward was going to be king, did you? Did you? Did you . . . ?'

The cry died on my lips and I sat up with a start, aching in every joint and limb. Opposite me, seated beside the fire on a rickety three-legged stool and watching me fixedly, was Bertha Mendip. We were alone – there was no sign of the young girl – and early morning sunlight was streaming in through the open doorway of the hut.

'What . . . What day is it?' I mumbled, struggling to get my bearings.

'Friday,' she said. 'Freya's day – the mother o' the gods. You'm slept all night through, but not easy. You'm bin tossin' and turnin' and mutterin' in yer sleep somethin' terrible, so you 'ave.'

Friday. Today, Lord Hastings would be beheaded on Tower Green, quietly and without fuss. Indeed, so little attention would be drawn to the proceedings that, in after years, many people would continue, mistakenly, to assert that that he had been executed out of hand the preceding week.

'Yer boots aren't quite dry yet,' Bertha said, 'but the rest of yer gear's ready.' And she indicated my hose, shirt and tunic lying beside me. 'There's a hat, too,' she added, 'what I fished out the water. Gawd! You in a gen'leman's hat! Velvet!' She rocked to and fro, convulsed by a paroxysm of laughter.

I couldn't have taken umbrage even had I wished to. It had been no vain boast when she said that she knew her business: all the garments had been restored, if not quite to their former glory, then to a condition that would deceive most eyes.

'You're a marvel, Bertha,' I breathed, picking them up and examining them one by one.

The next moment, I was hurriedly pulling the blanket I was wrapped in up around my shoulders as I realized that by sitting up I had rendered myself half-naked.

My companion gave another of her cackling laughs. 'No need fer modesty, lad. I seen better nor you in me time. Still, if you'd rather get dressed on yer own, I'll get meself to the Rattlebones and get you summat to eat and drink. Big fellow like you needs 'is victuals.'

'Wait!' I said. 'Bertha, I can't pay you. I've no money.'

She grinned. 'Oh, yes you 'ave.' She picked up my belt

with the money purse still firmly attached to it and shook it in my face. 'Whoever 'it you on the 'ead weren't after robbin' you. This 'ere was still strapped round yer waist when I pulled you out the water.'

I breathed a sigh of relief, opening the purse to check the contents. All my money seemed to be there and I handed a couple of coins to Bertha. For her part, she continued to regard me curiously.

'Who did 'it you over the 'ead,' she asked, 'and whereabouts were you? From what you said yesterday, seemed like you reck'ned you'd been pushed down that drain what empties the Wallbrook inta the river. What you got yerself mixed up in, lad? You've nearly got yerself killed, you knows that, don't you? If it 'adn't bin fer me, you'd likely be fish meat by now.'

I nodded humbly. 'I know that, Bertha, and I'm grateful, believe me. Is it really Friday? I must have been asleep for hours and hours and hours. If I remember rightly, I hadn't long had my dinner when . . . when . . .'

'You 'ave bin asleep fer hours and hours and hours,' my companion acknowledged, 'but that were the lettuce juice. I got some from 'pothec'ry when I went fer the ale. Sleep's the only cure fer a shock like you'd 'ad. But it weren't easy sleep, like I told you. An' afore you woke up jus' now, you was in a right sweat. Callin' out a lot o' men's names, you were. An' summat about a sun an' a king.' She eyed me sternly. 'You goin' t' tell me what 'appened or not?' She sat down again on her stool. ''Cause I ain't goin' fer yer breakfast until you do.'

I could see she was in earnest and I owed her my life. So I arranged the blanket more modestly about me, to the great irritation of the fleas settled within its folds, and proceeded to tell her as much as I knew (but making no mention of my lord of Gloucester or his intentions regarding the crown). Bertha heard me out without comment and when I had finished, she got to her feet once more.

'I'm off t' Rattlebones now,' she said, 't' get yer breakfast.' She hesitated as though she would add something, then, obviously deciding against it, left the hut without further remark.

During her absence, I got dressed, although it cost me a greater effort than I had anticipated. I felt as weak as a kitten. I was getting too old, I decided, for these sort of adventures.

I wandered across to the doorway and looked out at the busy scene as Southwark stirred into early morning life. A part of London and yet outside the city's jurisdiction, it was a place of contrasts; a warren of noisome alleyways, an absolute haven for criminals, cheek by jowl with the splendid houses of various abbots and bishops. St Thomas's Hospital and the church of St Mary Overy were two of its more imposing buildings. The Tabard and the Walnut Tree were respectable enough taverns, but others, like the Rattlebones, were of a more dubious nature, patronized by thieves and whores and others not anxious to be noticed by officers of the law. Overhead, the sky was a clear, cloudless blue. It was going to be another warm day.

After a while, I went back inside. The heat of the fire and the stench of the drying clothes suddenly turned my stomach, and I began to retch. My own clothes, too, seemed to have a smell about them previously unnoticed, and they felt stiff and uncomfortable. I wondered irritably where Bertha was and what was keeping her. She seemed to have been gone an unconscionable time, and I was longing to be off. My head ached, and I was no nearer finding out what had become of Gideon Fitzalan, or why he had been taken, than I had been a week ago.

I knew that my dream had been telling me something, but what it was I had no notion. God was speaking to me, but I was too stupid to understand. I remembered what Bertha had said, that I was shouting out names – the names, obviously, of the Fitzalan tribe. I could recall the events and circumstances of the dream quite clearly. It was interpreting them that presented a problem.

The nausea was beginning to pass, but my legs still felt too fragile to support me, so I pulled Bertha's abandoned stool well clear of the fire and sat down near the door, trying to marshal my thoughts. I had been in the chamber below St Etheldreda's crypt when I had been assaulted. Someone had either followed me with such stealth that I had been unaware of pursuit, or else somebody had already been down

there and had concealed him – or herself before I had time
to descend the steps. Of the two, I favoured the latter theory.

I also recalled that, just before I was struck, I had thought
there was something different about my surroundings; that there
was something there I had not noticed on my previous visit.
I closed my eyes tightly, trying to picture the scene, but
try as I might, I could recollect nothing, only the blow to
the back of my head which had sent me plunging into
oblivion.

So what had happened next? Someone – more than one
person? – had dragged me across the floor and bundled me
bodily into the drain which connected with the Wallbrook
culvert. Judging by the bruises with which my body was
covered, it had been a tight squeeze, although wide enough
to prevent me from becoming stuck, and I must have been
helped on my way by a good shove from above. (I concluded
that the drain itself was fairly short in length and had been
made to stop the underground chamber from being flooded
when the Thames was in spate.) But I was a big man and a
heavy weight. It must surely have taken more than one person
to shift me.

Bertha entered the hut, nearly falling over the stool in the
process, carrying a covered dish in one hand and a jug of
ale in the other. The first smelled deliciously of hot bacon
collops and the other made me realize that I had a raging
thirst which, until that moment, I had been too preoccupied
to notice.

When she had finished cursing me for getting in the way,
Bertha handed me the dish and placed the jug on the floor
where I could reach it, along with the beaker she had brought
yesterday from the Rattlebones. This she wiped out with a
handful of straw picked up from the floor. I decided to drink
from the jug.

'Gettin' nice all of a sudden, ain't we?' she jeered, throwing
more sticks on the fire and pulling one of the racks of drying
clothes nearer to the blaze. Then she sat down on the floor,
arms locked around her knees. I offered her the stool, but
she shook her head. 'You finish yer breakfast. But you'll
'ave t' give it up in a minute. I've invited someone in t' see
you.'

'What do you mean? Who?'

She shook her head. 'Jus' eat and don' ask so many questions.'

With this I had to be content as she plainly intended to say nothing further. The sunlight coming through the open doorway had strengthened and it was now full daylight, while the sounds from without had steadily increased. The denizens of Angel Wharf were up and busy. I thought again of Lord Hastings in the Tower watching the dawn of his last day on earth and wondered what it must feel like to know the hour of one's death; to hear the birds and feel the warmth of the sun on one's face and accept that in a while it would all be gone. I thought, too, of Earl Rivers, young Sir Richard Grey and old Sir Thomas Vaughan as yet, probably, unaware of their fate, but soon to learn that they also must die. Twelve short weeks ago, when King Edward had breathed his last, how could they possibly have known how soon they would be following him into the grave?

'Cheer up,' Bertha said. 'You've got a face as dismal as a week o' Fridays. Which reminds me, I s'pose, bein' Freya's day I oughta brought you fish, but you don' look to me like one what takes fastin' very serious.'

'Not when my wife isn't here to keep me up to it,' I admitted, which made her give yet another cackle of laughter.

'Like that is it? Well, I can't say you looks too bad on married life. I reck'n you'm one o' the lucky ones.'

A shadow fell across the door, blocking out the sunlight. Bertha got to her feet and went to welcome her visitor.

'Come in, me dear an' this gert lump 'ere'll give you the stool t' sit on.' I lumbered awkwardly to my feet, trying to prevent my head from hitting the hut's roof and provoking my hostess to even further mirth. 'I told you 'e were a big un.' (Her chosen calling had never dimmed her sense of humour.) She turned to me. 'This,' she said, 'is Audrey Owlgrave.'

I found myself facing a small, sharp-featured woman of indeterminate age – she could have been anywhere between thirty and fifty – but who, I suspected, appeared older than she probably was. Her weather-beaten skin was seamed with lines and her lips were the thinnest I have ever seen, almost non-existent. She was poorly dressed – I could see at least

two darns in the skirt of her homespun gown – but everything about her was clean and neat and, astonishingly for
Angel Wharf, sweet-smelling. Her eyes were a very dark
brown and dominated her little pinched face.

'Mistress Owlgrave.' I made her a bow and indicated the
stool. 'Please, sit down.'

She thanked me, and the most surprising thing of all about
her was her voice. She spoke with a quiet, ladylike accent
that would have done credit to the Duchess of York herself.

'Mistress Mendip has been telling me of your adventure,'
she said. 'I trust you are feeling better?'

'A little,' I acknowledged.

She smiled gently. 'I understand that when you were
so cruelly assaulted, you were in St Etheldreda's Church
in Dowgate?'

'Not in the church itself, but in a chamber beneath the
crypt, which I think might be Roman, perhaps a part of the
Temple of Mithras, which originally stood on that site.'

She nodded in concurrence. I had obviously told her
nothing that she did not know already.

'The cult of Mithras was not itself a sacrificial one,' she
said, 'although some of its followers did interpret it as
such because of the cutting of the bull's throat by the god.
In the Christian faith, it is, of course, God Himself who
is the sacrifice.'

I had sat down again on the floor, my back propped against
one of the doorposts, and I stirred uneasily at the mention
of the word 'sacrifice'. Something continued to nag uneasily
at the edges of my mind.

Mistress Owlgrave went on, 'But in fact we are not
concerned with Mithras or his worship. The fact that the
church of St Etheldreda stands on, or very near, the Roman
site, is neither here nor there. What I am about to say to you
has to do with the saint herself. Do you know her story?'

I nodded. 'I was a novice at Glastonbury Abbey before I
renounced my calling and took to the roads.'

I didn't know how much Bertha had told our visitor of
my life history, but she seemed to accept my explanation
without demur.

'Very well then. You know about Etheldreda's dislike of

the carnal dealings between men and women.' She shifted slightly on the stool so that she was looking directly at me. 'But have you ever heard,' she asked with great emphasis, 'of the thirty-three Daughters of Albion?'

SEVENTEEN

'I-I know the legend,' I stammered. 'But . . . but what . . .?'
Audrey Owlgrave nodded briskly. 'Very well,' she said.
'But what you probably don't know is that there's a secret sisterhood in this country called the Daughters of Albion. A secret society of women.'

'A woman's secret society?' I queried stupidly.

She gave me a pitying look. 'You think women aren't capable of such a thing? No,' she went on scornfully, 'I suppose, like most men, you think it impossible that women would, on the one hand be able to organize something without male guidance, and on the other, that they would be able to keep anything secret.'

'Well, they haven't managed to keep it a secret if you know about it,' I retorted, nettled by her assumption that all men were crass fools in their dealings with women and under-rated their intelligence. No man who had been married to a woman like Adela for as long as I had would make such a mistake.

Bertha, an interested and, for the moment, slightly puzzled listener, gave another of her laughs. ''E's got you there, Audrey my old acker,' she remarked, using the ancient West Country word for 'friend'. It provoked in me such an over-whelming feeling of homesickness that, for a second or two, I was afraid I really was going to be physically ill.

Mistress Owlgrave glanced contemptuously from one to the other of us. 'I was once a Daughter of Albion, myself,' she said. 'Which is why you may assume that I know what I'm talking about.'

Bertha nodded slowly. 'I always suspicioned you was mixed up in summat you shouldn't've bin. There's always bin summat secretive about you, my lady, which is why I come to you now. When Roger 'ere told me 'is tale, I thought to meself that maybe you jus' might be able to shed some light on what's goin' on. 'Course, you might not 'ave, but in that case, no 'arm's bin done. Anyway, who are these Daughters of Whatnot?'

While Audrey Owlgrave made Bertha free of the legend, I was absorbed in my own thoughts. I realized now that God had been with me, guiding my steps, from the very beginning of this adventure. He it was who had prompted my memory of the story – long forgotten by me – as I stood among the prehistoric stone circles at Avebury. And He was still trying to guide me, except that I was too stupid to see what it was He was saying.

Mistress Owlgrave had by now finished her recounting of the tale, but judging by Bertha's demeanour it had found little favour in her eyes.

'I never 'eard so much faradiddle in all me born days,' she snorted indignantly. 'Matin' with demons, indeed! What next? And 'ow d'you come t' know such stuff, me young master?' she demanded fiercely, turning on me.

I explained how I came by my knowledge, something which afforded her enormous amusement and completely did away with her ill humour.

'I allus wondered what went on in them religious places,' she said, rocking herself backwards and forwards in a paroxysm of enjoyment that put all previous ones in the shade. 'And now I knows.'

Her unrelenting ability to find amusement in every situation was beginning to pall, and I turned back to Mistress Owlgrave. 'Tell me more, if you please, about this society. Who belongs to it? Women, obviously, from what you say, but what is it for? And why are you no longer one of its members?'

Our guest shifted her stool slightly so that one shoulder was towards her still convulsed hostess. From then on, she addressed me exclusively.

'It's a society, as perhaps you could guess, for women who dislike men.' She hesitated, then corrected herself. 'Not who dislike men for themselves, but who dislike the . . . the carnal relationship that follows marriage. They are women who have either refused to marry, who have suffered at their families' hands for such refusals, or women who have been forced into marriages that were distasteful to them. They are

dedicated to the cult of St Etheldreda, whose Feast Day is
Midsummer Eve. And they call themselves the Daughters of
Albion for obvious reasons.'

I wasn't sure that it was so obvious considering what was
supposed to have happened after Albia and her thirty-two
sisters landed on these shores. But I let my objection go.
They had, after all, freed themselves from their husbands,
even if the means had been somewhat drastic.

'How many women belong to this society?' I asked. 'Does
it exist only here, in London?'

Mistress Owlgrave shook her head. 'Oh no! There are
sisters all over the country.'

'All over the country?' I repeated. 'But how do you keep
in touch?'

She shrugged. 'How does anyone keep in touch? Some of
us can read and write, and letters are sent by carriers or
carters or itinerant friars. In the summer, travelling parties
of clowns and acrobats and jongleurs will be willing messen-
gers. Each group of women, whether in city or town, village
or hamlet, has its own head, preferably someone who is
literate. You must know as well as I do that almost anyone
will take anything anywhere provided the fee makes it worth
the trouble. But in any case –' she shrugged again – 'members
of the Sisterhood don't need to communicate all that often.
Once or twice a year perhaps, or when someone has something particular to say.'

I sat silent for a minute or two, digesting Audrey
Owlgrave's information. I had heard of the Brotherhood
many years earlier, around the time of Picquigny when there
had been an attempt to assassinate the Duke of Gloucester,
but that, as I had understood it, was an organization that
spread beyond the shores of this country and was not above
dabbling in the affairs of the great. This so-called Sisterhood,
on the other hand, appeared to be a society dedicated to a
single idea: women's dislike of the carnal side of marriage
and, presumably, support for those who had either resisted
its bonds or been forced into them against their will.

I wondered which of the two had been Mistress Owlgrave's
fate.

Almost as if she had read my thoughts, our visitor said,

'I come of good yeoman stock, Master Chapman, and was my father's only child. In the natural course of events I should have become mistress of a sizeable holding in Lincolnshire had I agreed to marry the man of my father's choice. Or, indeed, had I agreed to marry at all, for he was not an un-reasonable man and would have welcomed as a son-in-law anyone of sufficiently gentle birth who took my fancy. The trouble arose when I refused to marry anybody and so perpet-uate the Owlgrave line. My father wanted, above all else, to have grandchildren, even if they did not bear his name. They would have his blood and that was all that mattered to him.'

'What happened?' I asked.

'I was cast out of my home with only the clothes I stood up in. I have never seen my parents from that day to this, nor have they made the slightest attempt to find me. When I reached London, I wrote a letter and, with my last few remaining coins, sent it to them by a carter from Lincoln, who knew them and where to find them. When the man returned, he sought me out and told me that my father had destroyed the letter unopened. From that moment onwards, I knew that I was on my own for as long as the good God should grant me time upon this earth. I would have starved had it not been for the people of Southwark who took me in and gave me a home. One of the first women who befriended me belonged to the Daughters of Albion and, once she knew my story, arranged for me to enter the society's ranks. I was a member for many, many years and in those days we did a great deal of good work among the whores and fallen women of this district.'

I couldn't help wondering what the 'Winchester geese'– so named after the owner of the Southwark brothels, the Bishop of Winchester – had thought about this well-meant interference. In general, they were a noisy, merry bunch, unashamed of their calling, but doubtless there had been some among them – perhaps many – who had been grateful for a helping hand.

It was time to ask the question that had been bothering me since almost the beginning of Audrey Owlgrave's life story.

'From what you have said, Mistress, I assume that you

are no longer a member of the Sisterhood. No longer a Daughter of Albion.'

She moved her stool away from the heat of a fire to which Bertha had just added another handful of sticks. Moreover, the sun was now beating in relentlessly through the open doorway.

After a moment's hesitation, she inclined her head.

'That is so,' she admitted.

'Why not?' I demanded bluntly.

She passed her tongue over her mouth before replying. 'During the last ten years or so, a different element has crept into the Sisterhood and is gradually gaining ascendancy over the rest.' Again there was a pause and again she licked her lips. 'An element that wishes to revive the old pagan associations with Midsummer Eve.'

There was a silence this time that you could cut with a knife. Audrey seemed reluctant to continue, so at last I asked, 'You mean . . . blood sacrifice?'

Bertha gave a scream and dropped the pair of men's hose she was holding to the flames.

I thought for a moment that the other woman wasn't going to answer. But then she drew a deep breath and said quietly, 'Yes.'

The monosyllable was so quietly spoken that I had to strain my ears to catch it, and even then I wasn't certain that I had heard aright. I repeated my question.

Her answer this time was unequivocal and spoken with firmness and clarity.

'Yes. Blood sacrifice is what I mean.'

'Ye're joking,' Bertha accused her, picking up the dropped garment with hands that were not quite steady and holding them once more to the blaze.

Mistress Owlgrave shook her head and looked me straight in the eye. 'In pagan times, at Midsummer, the Beltane fires were lit on the hillsides and people danced around them, offering up sacrifices to the god Baal; Baal Zeboub, or Beelzebub as he came to be called, Lord of the Flies.'

Beelzebub! I wondered suddenly who had named the brute at Minster Lovell. I had naturally presumed that it was either William Blancheflower or even Francis Lovell himself. But supposing it had been the now dead Eleanor? Was it possible that she had been one of the Sisterhood? Had she been unhappily married, or married against her will? If that were indeed so, the events of that night just over a week ago might have a significance that I had so far overlooked.

I told Audrey Owlgrave the story and asked her opinion. Bertha listened open-mouthed.

Our visitor shook her head. 'I can't give you an opinion – not a definite opinion that is – one way or the other, Master Chapman. What happened may well have been simply an unfortunate accident in which you played an unwitting part. But then again, it might not. Perhaps when you saw Mistress Blancheflower in the inner courtyard, she meant, somehow, to let the animal in to attack her husband while he was sleeping. When she saw you, she hid by slipping out through the postern gate to wait until you had returned to bed. Unfortunately for her, you noticed the drawn bolts and locked her out. Her presence out of doors in the middle of the night is certainly suspicious, but offers no proof of fell intent. What makes you suddenly suspect her of being a member of the Sisterhood?'

'It's only . . .' I paused, looking back and trying to conjure up the scene when Piers had first informed Dame Copley of Nell Blancheflower's death.

Audrey Owlgrave raised her eyebrows and waited. Bertha cursed as a stray spark from the fire threatened to burn a hole in the gentleman's hose she was drying.

I continued, struggling to get my thoughts in order, 'It's only that when one of Mistress Blancheflower's friends was first informed of her death, she – the friend, that is – at first refused to believe it, insisting there must be some mistake. I distinctly remember her saying, "It can't be Nell! You mean it was William." It didn't strike me at the time, but now it seems almost as if the friend had been expecting to hear of the husband's death. At one point, I thought Dame Copley was going to faint, she seemed so grief-stricken, but it could have been from shock.'

Mistress Owlgrave frowned. 'Are you saying that you think this friend is also a member of the Sisterhood?'

It was my turn to suffer a shock: I hadn't really stopped

to consider the implications of what I was saying. So did
I believe that Dame Copley was a Daughter of Albion? I
received another jolt when I realized that the not improb-
able answer was: yes. And the more I thought about it, the
more it began to make some sort of sense. Piers had told me
that Rosina had been forced into an unwanted marriage by
her father when all she had wished to do was embrace the
religious life. And yesterday – was it only yesterday? It
seemed like a lifetime ago – I had witnessed her with my
own eyes huddled together with Amphillis Hill and the
unknown woman in the Boar's Head in East Cheap. Until
that moment, I would not have said that she and Amphillis
were anything other than the merest acquaintances. Indeed,
by all accounts they had not known each other long, only
since Rosina's arrival at Baynard's Castle two weeks previously. And, within my hearing at least, the nurse had always
spoken slightingly of the younger woman.

I turned again to Mistress Owlgrave. 'Do you think,' I
asked in a voice that quavered a little, 'that young Gideon
Fitzalan has been taken for . . .' I could not bring myself to
say the words and finished lamely, '. . . for a particular
purpose?'

There was a moment's hesitation before Audrey nodded.
'I should think it possible, yes.'

'But why him in particular? His captors were prepared to
murder his tutor in order to secure his person.'

'That I don't know, but I feel there must be a reason.
Victims are rarely selected at random.'

'But where could they be holding him? It's not in the
chamber below St Etheldreda's crypt.' And suddenly, as I
uttered the words, I knew what had been different about that
chamber when I had seen it the day before. The statue of
the saint had been removed from the church and brought
down to stand on a natural ledge of rock running almost the
length of one wall of the underground room. Why? Did it
have any significance? I put the question to Mistress
Owlgrave.

'Not that I know of,' she answered quietly. 'Nor, I'm afraid,
can I suggest any place where the boy might be held. You've
searched Baynard's Castle?'

'As much as it's possible to do so. A friend helped me, but we found nothing. However, that's not to say he isn't there somewhere. A place like that has a score of hidden corners where anything or anyone could be concealed.' I climbed somewhat groggily to my feet. 'I must go back at once and inform Sir Pomfret and Lady Fitzalan of my suspicions.'

I experienced a strong sense of revulsion. If what I now suspected were indeed the truth, what an evil woman the nurse truly was! What an accomplished liar, with her protestations of grief, her sympathy and endless tears for her mistress's loss, her lamentations over Gregory Machin's death!

Audrey Owlgrave, who had also risen, put a steadying hand on my arm. 'You mustn't do that,' she said quickly. 'That would be dangerous.'

I stared blankly at her. 'What do you mean?'

'Sir Pomfret would be bound to question this Dame Copley immediately. Moreover, he would take the tale to Lord Lovell or even possibly to His Grace of Gloucester himself, since you tell me of his interest in the matter.'

'So?'

She gave my arm an impatient shake. 'Don't you see? Dame Copley would deny all complicity in the abduction. So would this Mistress Hill you mention. Where's your proof? You have none. Only suspicions based on what I've told you. And don't expect me to come forward to back you up. In Southwark, most of us steer clear of any contact with Authority. Finally, I warn you that you would never see the Fitzalan boy alive again, nor ever find out what had become of him. He would be killed at once and his body disposed of.'

I looked at her despairingly. 'What am I to do, then?'

Audrey grimaced. 'As far as I can see, your only hope is to trace the boy's whereabouts and rescue him before any harm befalls him. It's a slim chance, a very slim chance I agree. But take it from me, you have no other choice.'

While she was speaking, her features had grown blurred, as though a hand had smudged them, and her voice had grown fainter. Suddenly my legs collapsed beneath me, so

that I found myself once again sitting on the floor. I heard
Bertha curse, and the next moment two pairs of female hands
were pushing my head down between my knees. Gradually,
the yellow mist that had been clouding my vision dispersed
and I began to feel a little better. Cautiously, I lifted my
head.

'What . . . what happened?'

'You was nigh on swoonin' that's what 'appened,' Bertha
said severely. 'You'm not well, which ain't surprisin' after
all you'm bin through. That were a nasty blow to the back
o' your 'ead, not to mention nearly drownin'. Before you do
anythin' else me lad, you needs rest.'

'I don't have time,' I protested.

Mistress Owlgrave added her voice to the argument.
'That's foolish, talk,' she reproved me. 'If you don't give
your body time to recover, you won't be fit enough to do
anything at all. Besides, I would advise you to lie low for
the remainder of today and tomorrow for another reason.
Let your attacker – or attackers – think, for a while at
least, that they've succeeded in their object; that they've
successfully disposed of you. It might make them less
careful in laying their plans which inevitably will be for
Monday, Midsummer Eve. And the shock of seeing you
when you do eventually turn up, may disrupt those plans
even further.'

There was a great deal of sense in what she said, and I
couldn't deny that the thought of sleeping solidly in a comfortable bed for several hours was most attractive. But where
could I go? Baynard's Castle was out of the question. Even
the sentries would recognize me there, and the news of my
return would circulate within minutes. On the other hand,
the thought of another prolonged stay in Bertha's hut, with
nothing but the floor for a bed, was an uninviting prospect.

I became aware of the women's voices.

'A room at the Rattlebones,' Audrey Owlgrave was saying.
'Does he have money?'

'Enough.' Bertha answered shortly. Then she added, 'Ye're
right. 'E'll be safe there. No questions asked and none
answered if anyone comes pokin' around. Which ain't likely.
But still, you never knows. If ye're goin' 'ome now, I'll

come with you and make arrangements with the landlord. 'E knows me.'

'He knows me equally well,' Audrey said a little stiffly. She glanced down at me, where I still sat ignominiously on the floor. 'However, I suppose Master Chapman is your responsibility. I'll wish you good-day then, Bertha.'

She made for the door, while Bertha assisted me as best she could to rise. As I felt the stool wobble insecurely beneath me, Mistress Owlgrave paused, then turned and came back into the hut.

'These Fitzalans,' she said thoughtfully. 'From something Bertha mentioned when she was telling me your story, I gather that there seem to be a lot of them. Brothers, uncles. All men, in fact. Can you tell me exactly how many? Start with the missing boy. Would you be able to name his brothers?'

'Is it important?' My head was splitting and growing worse in the heat from Bertha's fire.

My interrogator nodded. 'I think it might be. But if it's a feat beyond your powers, don't fret yourself. Perhaps it doesn't matter.' And once again, she turned to go.

'No, wait.' I smiled weakly. 'If there's one gift God gave me above all others, it's a good memory. Gideon, I think, has six brothers. I've met two of them, Bevis and Blaise, and heard the other four mentioned.' I wiped the sweat from my brow with my sleeve. 'Let me see . . . Thomas . . . Maurice . . . and Henry, is it? No, Henry's one of the uncles. Thomas, Maurice . . . Peter. Yes, Peter! And . . . and Cornelius,' I finished triumphantly.

Mistress Owlgrave gave a grunt of satisfaction. 'And the father and uncles?'

'Sir Pomfret is his sire.' I chewed on a fingernail, while Bertha, her mission to the Rattlebones temporarily forgotten, regarded us both, saucer-eyed. 'Then there are the twins, Lewis and Godfrey and . . . and . . .' Suddenly my dream came back to me. I could hear the Duchess of York's voice ringing clearly in my ears. I finished with perfect confidence, 'And Warren, Henry, Raisley, George.'

Audrey Owlgrave stared at me long and hard. 'You're sure of this?'

'Yes. Perfectly sure. I tell you, my memory—'

She interrupted ruthlessly. 'And this Sir Pomfret, the father, do you happen to know if he is the youngest of his brothers?'

'I believe so.' I was still baffled.

'Ah! Then the mystery is solved.' Audrey flung out her hands. 'Gideon Fitzalan is that comparatively rare being, the seventh son of a seventh son. A child possessed of special powers, and therefore . . .'

'And therefore what?'

The fire suddenly hissed and spat, making me jump. I felt ill again. The hut was starting to spin once more and I was finding it difficult to breathe. I was conscious of something evil reaching for me out of a darkness that threatened to engulf my very soul. I was terrified as I had never been terrified before.

''Ere, drink this.'

I realized that Bertha had an arm about my shoulders, pressing me to her unsavoury bosom, while with her right hand she was attempting to force a fiery-tasting liquid down my throat. I recognized the taste and I hated it. It was some disgusting stuff that the Scots drank. The Water of Life they call it (they would!), but it had never done anything for me but make me sick. Spluttering, I pushed the leather bottle away from my lips.

'Where's . . . where's Mistress Owlgrave?' I asked unsteadily, freeing myself from Bertha's determined embrace.

'Gone 'ome.' Bertha stoppered the mouth of the bottle with a grimy rag. 'Don' you like this? Sometimes, when boats do come down from Scotland, the sailors'll part with a drop or two if I speaks 'em fair.' She smacked her lips. 'It makes you forget yer troubles. Well, I'm off now to the Rattlebones. You just sit there quiet, my lad, until I gets back.' She shook her fist at me. 'I've taken some money out yer purse, enough t' pay yer shot fer a night. But you'd best leave the rest with me until you goes back over the river. The Bones ain't no place to be carrying money on you.'

With that, she disappeared out of the door, leaving me, my head still swimming, to think over what Audrey Owlgrave had told me. I knew now that whatever I was up against was entirely evil and that both Dame Copley and Amphillis Hill were probably mixed up in it; also, quite possibly – indeed, more than likely – the nurse's sister, Etheldreda Simpkins. I also knew that Gideon Fitzalan was in mortal danger and that I had to find him. But where he was, or how to start looking for him, I had no idea. I was so tired that my mind refused to function. All I wanted to do was sleep.

Bertha came back almost before I realized she had gone, helping me up off the stool and pulling my clothes into shape.

'I've fixed you a room,' she said. 'Small back one, out the way o' pryin' eyes. But the bed's comfortable. You c'n 'ave yer meals there, too if you wants to.' She seemed pleased with herself, as well she might be. 'Ain't cost you much, either.' She winked lasciviously. 'Landlord owes me a favour.'

I preferred not to dwell too much on the implications of this remark and followed her meekly out of the hut and across the quay. I guessed it was probably getting close to dinner time, but for once the thought of food made me feel queasy, and the smell of cooking that emanated from many of the houses as we passed turned my stomach.

I knew the Rattlebones by sight but had never been inside. To my relief, it seemed a lot more salubrious within than it looked without, and the landlord himself, a jolly-faced, curly-haired fellow, wore a fresh shirt and apron. Also his nails were reasonably clean. Nevertheless, there was a furtive atmosphere about the place. I doubted if anyone who was not a friend of, or at least known to, mine host would penetrate very far beyond the door and not meet opposition of some sort or another. Happily, he was obviously on good terms with Bertha.

More money – my money – changed hands and Bertha clapped me on the arm.

'I've paid fer two nights, so's you c'n stay till Sunday if you wishes. Otherwise you knows where I be. Come 'n get yer stuff –' she nudged me meaningfully – 'before you leaves.' And then she was gone.

The landlord led me up two flights of stairs to a small chamber at the back of the house. It was not home from home, but there was a bed that looked inviting and proved to have a goose feather mattress and down-filled pillows. So I pulled off my boots, flung my hat on the floor, shut my eyes against the whirling ceiling and was soundly and deeply asleep in less than two minutes.

EIGHTEEN

I awoke with a great start and sat up abruptly, unable for the moment to get my bearings.

I had been dreaming, not for the first time during this past week, of Eloise Gray. It had been an unusually vivid dream, but on this occasion she had been dressed as a boy, the guise in which I had originally known her. The clothes had not deceived me and I had been fully aware of her sex, in spite of the fact that I had addressed her on several occasions as 'Davy'.

The dream faded as I stared about me, tense and anxious, trying to remember where I was, then slowly relaxing as the evnts of the past two days began to take shape in my mind. I was in a small, back chamber of the Rattlebones tavern, in Southwark, and I had been asleep since early that same morning.

I reckoned it was now late afternoon or early evening. There was a subtle difference in the light filtering between the cracks of the closed shutters, and a different rhythm to the sounds that ascended from the bowels of the inn. Moreover, I was feeling ravenous, hardly surprising as I must have slept throughout dinner and, possibly, even supper time – although in such a place food was probably to be had at any hour of the day or night.

Carefully, I swung my legs to the floor and stood up, flexing my arms. There was still some stiffness in my limbs and the various bruises decorating my person protested slightly, reminding me that my body had been seriously knocked about during my passage down the drain into the Thames. But the dizziness and nausea had passed, leaving me feeling considerably fitter than I had done, despite the dull ache that still nagged at the back of my head. Whoever had dealt me the blow, had used a force that had surely been intended to kill, or at least to render me unconscious long enough for the river to complete the job.

Which brought me to the question of who my assailant had been. Now that I knew about the Sisterhood, the so-called Daughters of Albion, and now that Rosina Copley was most likely one of them, it could have been her or indeed any of her three companions from the Boar's Head. The four women had left the inn well in advance of me. They had failed to notice my presence, and so my sudden intrusion into the underground chamber of St Etheldreda's Church must have come as a nasty shock for whoever was down there making preparations for . . . For what? My mind balked at the answer and I found that I was shivering violently.

I sat down again on the edge of the bed, my arms wrapped around my body, and waited for the fit to pass. I had not recovered from my ordeal as well as I had thought and must therefore take things carefully. My first priority was food and ale, although I decided that I could also do with a wash: the rancid smell of Bertha's hut still clung about me. My other desperate need was to relieve myself, but that was easily dealt with. I simply threw back the shutters, knelt up on a chest that stood beneath the window and peed into the courtyard below, a long, steady, golden stream that sparkled in the evening sunlight.

There was an indignant cry. Hastily adjusting my clothes, I leant out of the casement and found myself looking down into a pretty, dimpled face, at present marred by a furious scowl. The girl wore an apron over a grey homespun gown, and her abundant brown curls were partially covered by a triangle of white cloth, indicating her status as a serving-maid at the inn.

'Just give a warning before you do that again,' she hissed up at me. 'I might've been drenched. As it is, you've splashed my skirt.'

I apologized profusely. It wouldn't be too much to say I grovelled, and was rewarded beyond my deserts by the gradual lightening of her features into an impish grin.

'You're forgiven,' she said after a while. 'You're that man who's been asleep all day. Aren't you hungry?'

'Starving,' I agreed. I hesitated, then asked, 'If I come down to the ale room, is there a secluded corner where I can hide away, without being noticed too much by the other drinkers?'

She laughed. 'Like that, is it? Oh well, you'll be in good company. More'n half the people who come to the Bones don' want t' be noticed. Folk with prying noses aren't encouraged round here. But if you like, I'll bring victuals up to your room.'

I thanked her, but I was already heartily sick of the featureless little chamber and felt the need of company to banish the hideous images floating around in my brain.

'I'll be down immediately,' I said, 'if you'll serve me.'

She gave me a provocative, upwards glance from beneath drooping lashes and swung her hips.

'I daresay that can be managed,' she said.

A few minutes later, having made myself as presentable as possible, I descended the stairs to find her waiting for me.

She jerked her head in the direction of the ale room. 'Follow me. I know just the place where you won't be seen.'

The place was crowded, but not a single head was lifted, nor one curious glance turned in my direction as I followed in the girl's wake to a seat in one corner of the room. Nevertheless, I felt sure that my presence had been noted and was under discussion by everyone there, although I was unable to justify the feeling. The subdued laughter, the conversation might have related to any topic under the sun, but I was certain that they related to me. The air was charged with a suspicion deliberately masked and the atmosphere crackled with resentment. Then the landlord himself approached, according me a discreet bow, and the sensation immediately vanished. I had been accepted and was no longer seen as a threat.

The bench to which the girl had shown me was a high-backed settle placed along one wall and sheltered from the general view by just such another settle at right angles to it, the seat facing away from mine into the room at large and its back acting as a protective screen.

'This secluded enough for you?' my guide asked with a grin, and when I nodded, returning smile for smile, she again swung her hips invitingly. 'The mutton's good tonight,' she offered. 'It'll put beef into you.' She giggled self-consciously in the manner of one making a feeble joke.

I laughed dutifully and said I'd have the mutton and dumplings as well, if they had any. But most of all, I needed a mazer of ale.

'And none of your small beer,' I added. 'The real stuff.'

She flounced a little at that and said the Bones never served anything else. While she went to fetch my order, I moved further into a corner of the settle and closed my eyes, still suffering from the effects of my recent ordeal. Not without some difficulty, I worked out that it must be late Saturday afternoon, and realized with a shock that the day after tomorrow would be Midsummer Eve, the feast of St Etheldreda. I had two days left in which to find Gideon Fitzalan and prevent the fate which I was beginning to feel certain lay in store for him. The seventh son of a seventh son, he was to be a sacrifice to the old pagan gods of tree and stone and stream and the hollow places of the earth.

It seemed ridiculous to think that such things could go on in the fifteenth century, under the very nose of the Church, but the old religion died hard and found its worshippers not just in the lost byways of the countryside, but also among dwellers of the city streets. I felt the panic begin to rise, but had enough sense to accept that I must wait a little longer until I was fully fit again, before forcing myself to confront the problem. Tomorrow, however, Sunday, I must leave the Rattlebones and make a present of my suspicions to someone in authority. The problem was, would I be believed?

The girl returned with a steaming bowl of mutton and dumplings and, even more welcome, my mazer of ale. But instead of going away once she had served me, she sat down beside me on the settle.

'My name's Bess,' she announced. (It always is, unless it's Jenny. The girls in these places never give you their real names. Sometimes I think they've forgotten them, themselves.) 'I sleep in the attic and I'm alone up there at the moment. Apart from me, it's all pot-boys here and they sleep down in the kitchens or the cellars.' She tilted her head to one side and regarded me between lowered lashes. 'If you fancy a tumble later, to help you sleep, there's a stair just to the left of your doorway that'll bring you straight up.'

Taken aback, I stumbled over my reply. 'Th-thank you, my dear, b-but I . . . I . . .'

She laughed softly. 'It's all right. I ain't forcing you. I'm just letting you know that if you come up, you won't be turned away. It's not an offer I make to everybody, so there won't be any competition.'

With that she rose, treated me to a broad, salacious wink, wriggled her hips yet again and departed to attend to the needs of other customers.

As much shaken as amused by the invitation – and, if the truth be told, more than a little flattered – I addressed myself to the mutton and dumplings, which was indeed extremely good, and swallowed my ale. After that, my stomach comfortably distended, I leant my head back against the settle and allowed the warmth of the June evening to enfold me in its embrace. Gradually, the hum of conversation all around receded, fading away altogether as sleep intervened.

Once again, I awoke with a start and felt the same sense of disorientation as I had experienced earlier in the day. I realized that my neck was hurting because of my upright posture against the settle-back, and slowly stretched my arms and legs to help them regain some feeling. Once more the light had altered. It was now dusk and candles had been lit, but the ale room was as full as ever. No curfew obtained on the Southwark side of the river, and no one seemed in any hurry to seek the shelter of his own hearth.

I peered into my mazer, but it was empty. I was just debating the advisability of calling for a further pot when the settle at right angles to mine shook slightly as it was occupied. Almost at once, two female voices, raised to make themselves heard above the general hubbub, assailed my ears.

'I'm glad you could come. Until the chapman mentioned your name, I had no idea you were in London. It's good to see you again after all this time. Was it difficult to get away?'

The speaker was Audrey Owlgrave.

My thirst forgotten, I leant closer to the back of the other settle, pressing one ear to a gap between two of its boards.

'Not at all,' Rosina Copley answered. 'I told her ladyship

that I was going to visit my sister in Dowgate, and that I needed some air. I said the message you sent had come from Etheldreda. So why do you want to see me? You've left the Sisterhood!' The accusation was flung like a knife.

I sat as though turned to stone, surprised that neither woman could hear my heart thumping against the wood.

'I've not regretted it, if that's what you're hoping.' Mistress Owlgrave was taken with a fit of coughing, but then resumed, 'I don't agree with . . . with certain things you do. Indeed, I deplore them. You've always known that. But I still feel loyalty towards the Sisterhood and I shouldn't want any of you to suffer the full penalty of the law for what you believe in . . . for what you are about to do this Midsummer Eve.'

'What do you mean?' The nurse's voice was sharp with fear. 'Who knows?'

'The chapman I mentioned just now. I gather the Duke of Gloucester called him in to investigate the murder and the boy's disappearance. Where is the boy, by the way?'

Rosina snorted. 'Never you mind. We have him safe. But tell me more about the chapman. He's dangerous. He solved the problem of how Gregory Machin got into his room and bolted the door after he'd been stabbed. How do you know him?'

Audrey Owlgrave explained briefly the circumstances under which we'd met; an explanation that was met with a vicious curse, followed by a few minutes reflective silence.

'Amphillis must have done that,' Rosina muttered eventually. 'I know she was going down to the chamber, after we all left the Boar's Head, to make certain everything was ready for Monday night. Master Snooper must have surprised her and she hit him with something. But in Beelzebub's name, why didn't she make certain he was dead before she put him in the drain? A pity she didn't have her scissors with her. She would have made as short work of him as she did of Gregory.' There was another pause. 'Where is he now, do you know?'

I thought for a moment that the other woman wasn't going to answer, but then her newly revived loyalty to the Sisterhood forced a reply.

'Here, in this inn. He's not well. The near-drowning has

left him in a weakened state. But I know he doesn't intend staying here beyond the one night. Of that I feel certain.'

'Where's he sleeping?'

'I don't know. But the landlord's a friend of mine. If I ask him, he'll tell me.'

'Good!'

'What are you going to do?'

Rosina chuckled and my blood ran cold. 'What you don't know, Audrey my dear, can't hurt you. But this time, when he goes in the river, he'll stay there.' Another lengthy silence ensued before the nurse suddenly demanded, 'Why are you doing this? When you left the Sisterhood, you were adamant that you wanted no more to do with us.'

'I told you. I don't like the thought of you falling into the hands of the law. There'll be no mercy for any of you. You'll be burnt for witchcraft and murder. I've seen people burnt. It's a terrible, agonizing death.'

Rosina appeared to consider this, but finally said, 'No, there's something more.'

The noise had reached fever pitch in the ale room as people made the most of the short time before, inevitably, the weary landlord came to drive them all out. I strained my ears to catch Mistress Owlgrave's reply, should she give one.

She did.

'Many years ago,' she said, 'I had a very dear friend, Eleanor Cobbolde. She was forced into a distasteful marriage by her parents with a man called William Blancheflower. He was chief kennel man to the Lovell family and took Nell away to live at their place near Oxford—'

'You knew Nell?' Rosina broke in excitedly. 'So did I! After I went to live at Minster Lovell, when Gideon entered Sir Francis's household, we became friends. Close friends. She confided in me all about her marriage and how she secretly hated that brute of a husband of hers. It was I,' the nurse added proudly, 'who told her how she could get rid of him and make it look like an accident. It would seem that after we left, to come to London, she took my advice, but somehow it all went wrong. I couldn't understand it. I was heartbroken when I heard what had happened.'

Audrey Owlgrave snorted. 'It was all the fault of that

interfering chapman.' And she gave her companion a brief
version of the events which led to Mistress Blancheflower's
untimely death, adding, 'The chapman told me all this
himself, so I know it for the truth.'

I heard Rosina Copley draw in her breath, and when she
spoke her tone was vicious. 'Yet another reason to be rid of
him then. I shall tell Amphillis to enjoy her work tonight. I
must return to Baynard's Castle at once. But first, go and
ask the landlord where that bastard's sleeping.'

I sat there wondering what to do. I had no hope of leaving
the ale room unobserved: my height alone drew all eyes.
Then I realized that it didn't matter if the women saw me
as long as I pretended to be unaware of them, and just as
long as they didn't realize that I had been close enough to
overhear their conversation. So I stood up quietly and pushed
my way between the benches and stools around that side of
the room so that when I passed the two women on their
settle, I appeared to be coming from an entirely different
direction. I refrained, with the greatest difficulty, from
glancing their way, and managed to stumble a little,
suggesting I might be slightly drunk or still had a weakness
in my limbs. I climbed the stairs to my chamber and turned
to bolt the door.

There wasn't one. Nor a lock nor a key. Horrified, I sat
down on the edge of the bed to think.

I could, of course, simply lie in wait for my assassin. I
should have no difficulty in overpowering Amphillis Hill if
I hid myself behind the door. But the last thing I wanted was
to alert the Sisterhood to the fact they were in danger of
immediate discovery. Then, as Audrey had predicted, Gideon,
wherever he was, would be murdered and his body disposed
of without anyone being the wiser as to his fate. As for
Amphillis herself, even if I handed her over to the authori-
ties, she would no doubt wriggle out of any accusation I
brought against her. Who would believe that this sweet little
thing was a murderer? I could hardly believe it myself. She
could so easily claim that I had lured her to my room with
rape in mind, and it would be my word against hers. And
the landlord of the Rattlebones would never come to my aid
with a story of two women wanting to know where I was

sleeping. Whatever happened at his inn, he was always going to be looking the other way.

There was only one thing to do and that was to return to Bertha's, to let Amphillis find the room empty and the bird flown. But I jibbed at the thought of involving my old friend further in my affairs. Besides, I was bone weary and still not restored to full health and strength. I needed a soft bed for the night, not the hard floor of Bertha's unsavoury hut. Then, suddenly, like a gift from heaven, I remembered Bess's generous offer. No doubt she had something other than sleeping in mind, but I couldn't help that.

I stood up and arranged one of the pillows as best I could in a humped shape beneath the bedclothes. I couldn't really believe that it would fool anybody, but in the dark, and if Amphillis brought no light with her, it might just serve its purpose. I should know in the morning. Then I closed the shutters tightly, picked up my hat, tiptoed out of the room, carefully latching the door behind me, and mounted the stairs to the attics.

I opened my eyes to the early morning light and Bess's face staring indignantly down into mine.

'You went to sleep,' she accused me. 'You got into my bed and you went to sleep!'

'I-I'm sorry,' I apologized feebly. 'I-I was tired.'

There was a furious silence. Then she burst out laughing. 'So why did you come up here?' she asked at last.

'If I told you, you wouldn't believe me.'

'I could try.'

I made no reply. I had suddenly realized to my horror that I was as naked as she was.

'D-did I undress?' I stuttered.

'No,' she admitted. 'I did it for you. I hoped it might wake you up, but you were like one dead.' She grimaced. 'I've known a few men in my life, but never one like you.'

'I'm sorry,' I said again.

I made to rise, but was forcefully pushed down again by two small, but determined hands.

'Oh no!' Bess said. 'You don't get away as easily as that!'

'I'm a married man,' I pleaded feebly as she knelt astride me, still pinning me to the mattress.

'You all are,' she retorted. 'Or, at least, you all say you are.'

'I really am,' I told her desperately, but she just laughed and, leaning forward, kissed me full on the mouth.

It was a lingering, sensual kiss, and after such an invitation, I felt I should be a brute to disappoint her.

Well, what else could I have done?

Later – quite a while later in fact – noises of the household stirring and the landlord's voice shouting up the stairs, 'Bess! Bess! Where are you, you lazy whore?' alerted us both to the fact that it was now some time since sun-up. We scrambled out of bed and into our clothes.

'Come back tonight,' she whispered, giving me a parting kiss.

I made no answer, but she was in too much of a hurry to notice my lack of reply.

When Bess had gone, I finished dressing in a more leisurely fashion, then, my heart thumping in anticipation, I descended the attic stairs to my own room, wondering uneasily what I should find.

The door was still closed. Cautiously, I unlatched and pushed it open, waiting for any tell-tale sound from within, but all was quiet. I stepped inside. The room was empty and there was hardly anywhere for anyone to hide. Even so, such was the irritation of my nerves, that I peered under the bed, behind its dust-laden and much torn curtains, and, finally, lifted the lid of the chest beneath the window. There was of course no one there. Had anyone come at all? Was it possible that Amphillis liked me sufficiently to have refused this murderous assignment?

Then I opened the shutters and turned my attention to the bedclothes and all such vainglorious thoughts went flying. The pillow had been pulled free of the blankets and ripped open from end to end (there were feathers everywhere, some beginning to stir again in the draught from the open casement). And lying beside it, just in case I failed to get the message, was a black-handled knife and a sprig of birch leaves.

I suddenly remembered Bertha and wondered if Amphillis, finding me missing, as she thought, from the Rattlebones, had gone to search for me there. I hadn't actually heard Mistress Owlgrave mention Bertha's name to Rosina Copley, but then I hadn't by any means been privy to all their conversation, and it would be strange if Audrey had not explained how and where she met me.

The thought had no sooner entered my head than I was down the stairs and out of the inn, running for Bertha's hut on Angel Wharf as though the Devil and all his cohorts were at my heels, bursting in on her and shouting her name. Just for one heart-stopping moment, I thought she wasn't there; then what looked like a heap of old clothes, drying beside the dying embers of her fire, stirred and sat up.

Bertha regarded me indignantly.

'Sweet Jesus, what's the matter with you, lad? Frightened me out o' my wits, you did! Come fer yer money, 'ave you? Yer purse is over in that corner, under them pile o' rags.' She dragged herself to her feet and, still grumbling, went to fetch it for me. As I attached it to my belt again, she inspected me grimly. 'I can't say 'as 'ow ye're lookin' much better fer yer night's rest. Pale, an' dark shadows under yer eyes. What you bin up to?'

So I told her, not about Bess, of course, but all the rest and warned her to be on her guard for a day or two, in case anyone thought she might be hiding me. She cursed herself roundly for confiding in Audrey Owlgrave and then cursed Audrey with a variety of colourful oaths, some of which were new even to me. Finally, she gave me a hug, a smacking kiss on one cheek and begged me to be careful.

I promised, adding, 'Beware of Mistress Owlgrave, Bertha. I don't think she's ready to return to the Sisterhood quite yet, but it may be only a matter of time.'

An expression flitted across Bertha's face that I had never seen before and she gave a little, secret smile.

'Don' you worry any more about 'er, my dear,' she said. 'I knows 'ow t' deal with 'er. Where you goin' now? Not back t' Baynard's Castle, I 'ope.'

I shook my head. 'Not for the moment. I'm going first to Crosby's Place to try to see the duke.'

'Don' forget it's Sunday,' she reminded me. ''E'll no doubt
be getting ready fer church.'

I had completely forgotten it was Sunday! So much had
happened that the days of the week were getting muddled
up in my mind

'Then I must find Timothy Plummer,' I said.

'You any nearer discoverin' where the boy is?' Bertha
asked, and yet again I shook my head.

'No, but I'm hoping God will guide me.' I gave her back
hug for hug and told her once more to take care. And once
more she gave me that secretive smile and said not to bother
my head about it.

An hour or so later, having crossed the river and with the
church bells clamouring in my ears, I strode up Bishop's
Gate Street Within and forced my way into Crosby's Place.
But neither the duke nor Timothy nor anyone of note was
to be found.

'Everyone's gone to Paul's Cross,' a page informed me.
'His Grace of Buckingham as well. A great procession it
was, right through the city.'

'Paul's Cross? Why?' I demanded.

The lad shrugged. 'Someone said it's because the mayor's
brother, Friar Shaa, is preaching a very important sermon
there this morning.'

More than that he didn't seem to know.

I swore silently. I had no option, however, but to follow.

NINETEEN

The crowds gathered in the vicinity of Paul's Cross were so dense, it was almost impossible to get closer than halfway along West Cheap, and I doubt if I should have got much further had not my elbow been suddenly grasped.

'Tryin' to get to the Cross, are you?' enquired a solicitous voice, and I glanced round to see a small, sandy-haired figure, wearing the Gloucester livery, standing just behind me. 'Simon Finglass,' the man reminded me. 'Met you with Timothy Plummer some days back. Day of the arrests at the Tower.'

'I remember,' I said. 'Do you know what Friar Shaa's sermon is about?'

My companion shrugged. 'Something's in the wind. Don't know quite what. But it's important. The duke's there an' most o' the lords with him.' He looked up into my face. 'Want to get nearer, do you? Then follow me.' He tapped the man ahead of us on the shoulder and shouted, 'Make way for the Lord Protector's messenger!'

I must confess I wasn't expecting much result from this, but his livery acted like a charm and the crowds parted before us like the Red Sea before the Israelites. In a surprisingly short space of time, I found myself at the very front of the press, somewhat to one side, it's true, but within sight and hearing of the tall, ascetic figure of the mayor's brother in his flowing Franciscan habit. Immediately in front of him were ranged my lord of Gloucester, the Duke of Buckingham, the Archbishop of Canterbury and what I guessed to be more than half the nobility, both lay and clerical.

All around me, I could feel the tense expectancy of the mob. At last, something was about to happen. The quivering uncertainty of the past weeks since King Edward's death was about to be resolved. Anticipation hung in the air like a tangible force, but whether the resolution would be what people wanted was another matter.

The friar stepped forward and began to speak. The text for his sermon, he announced, was, 'Bastard slips shall not take root'.

The crowd gasped and there was a ripple of movement like wind through corn. Someone, a woman, cried out, then there was a profound silence broken only by Ralph Shaa's throbbing tones.

I forget now all that he said, but I know he reminded us that of the late Duke of York's four sons, the Duke of Gloucester was the only one who had been born in England and was therefore the most truly English. Next, he lauded Richard's character and bravery in battle from a tender age. Indeed, it was only last year that he had won back Berwick-on-Tweed from Scotland's clutches. And for decades, he had tamed the unruly north with his good laws and sense of justice. Was this not a man worthy to be our king? Was Richard of Gloucester not entitled to wear the crown?

Before either of these rhetorical questions could be answered by a crowd now shifting uneasily and murmuring among itself, the friar continued that, by the grace of God, it had recently been discovered that the late King Edward's marriage to the Lady Elizabeth Grey had been bigamous, the king being at the time solemnly contracted to the Lady Eleanor Butler (who was then still alive) and therefore not free to marry. Consequently, all children of the union were illegitimate and barred from accession to the throne. The Duke of Clarence's son, the young Earl of Warwick, was similarly barred by reason of his father's attainder. Ergo, the friar ended triumphantly, the Duke of Gloucester was the rightful king of England!

I don't know if he expected there to be wild acclamation from his audience, but if so, he was disappointed. Certainly, the nobles raised a cheer – although I thought that some of them, including, surprisingly, the Duke of Buckingham, looked a little sour – but the crowds, once they found that it was the end of the sermon, simply shuffled away for their Sunday dinners. There was a good deal of muttering and low-voiced conversation, but whether people were discussing the momentous news they had just received, or simply debating if it was wise to dish up the remains of Thursday's pig's cheek for a second time in three days, no one could be certain. I did, however, get the impression of a sense of relief, as if a boil that had been suppurating had suddenly burst, leaving a wound that might – or might not – heal cleanly.

My lord of Gloucester was preparing to move, the other lords falling back before him as though he were already king – nothing but a matter of time now, of course – and I looked frantically among his retinue for any sign of Timothy Plummer. He wasn't there, and I turned anxiously to Simon Finglass.

'Where's Master Plummer?'

The man spat and wiped his mouth on the back of his hand. 'Dunno. In view of what we've just heard, off on His Grace's business I should reckon.'

I cursed. 'I must see him.'

My new friend was unable to help. It was dinner time and he was off to Baynard's Castle to make sure that he got his fair share. It was as he moved away that I saw Amphillis Hill and the unknown woman deep in conversation beside one of the graves in the churchyard. For a moment or two, knowing now what I did about the former, I could not drag my eyes away from the delicate girlish face and wide, innocent eyes. Was she, could she possibly be, a ruthless killer? I recalled some words of Master Chaucer in one of those amusing tales of his. 'The smiler with the knife under the cloak.' Even so . . .

I switched my attention to her companion whose features I could not place, and was struck by how many times God had brought this woman to my attention: at Westminster, at the Boar's Head and now here at St Paul's. He was trying to tell me something and, as usual, I was too stupid to understand what it was. Worse, it came to me that, so far, I had not really tried to solve the riddle of her identity. I had simply put the problem to one side as something to be thought about later. Now, suddenly, I realized that the answer might well be of the greatest importance.

She was going, moving towards the Lud Gate, saying

something over her shoulder to Amphillis who nodded and walked off in the opposite direction without, fortunately, once glancing my way. The crowds had thinned to almost nothing and I was highly visible. I turned quickly to find a place of shelter, tripped and was caught by someone's steadying hands.

Piers Daubenay and I stared at one another.

'Roger?' he queried uncertainly. 'Wh-where have you been? I haven't had sight nor sound of you for nearly three days. Not since you left the Boar's Head.'

He was very pale, and the bruising down the left-hand side of his face, although it was beginning to fade, was still prominent, making him look as if he were wearing a half-mask. I remembered the cockerel's mask of my assailant and once again knew a niggle of doubt. Whether or not Piers saw it, I don't know, but he suddenly embraced me, saying with genuine warmth, 'It's so good to see you again. But, I repeat, where have you been?'

I didn't answer, instead asking abruptly, 'Where's your aunt?'

'Rosina?' He grimaced. 'I don't know. Still with Sir Pomfret and Lady Fitzalan I presume. Why?'

Once more, I avoided the question and countered with one of my own. 'Do you recollect once saying to Master Plummer and me that you reckoned she was a witch? Were you serious?'

He stared at me for a long moment before bursting out laughing. 'I don't know,' he said at last. 'There's always been something a bit odd about her . . .' His voice tailed away and the laughter faded. He regarded me doubtfully. 'What's wrong, Roger? Something's happened. What is it? Perhaps I can help with what's troubling you.'

But I wasn't really listening; at least only with half an ear. Enlightenment had suddenly dawned, breaking over me in a great, crashing wave. I seized Piers by the shoulders, opening and shutting my mouth like a stranded fish. He stared at me as though I had taken leave of my senses, and who could blame him.

He pushed my hands away and backed against the nearest wall. 'Roger, what's the matter? Are you ill? Shall I fetch help? There must be a physician hereabouts.'

'No, no!' I managed to get out. 'I'm quite all right. It's just . . . It's just that suddenly I know who that woman is, where I've seen her before. I know where Gideon is being held! Sweet lord! What a fool I've been!'

I dragged Piers with me to Crosby's Place, but there was no getting in to see the duke. He had other, far more important matters to concern him now than the fate of one young boy. Moreover, the place was crammed as sycophants and time-servers flocked to swear their allegiance to the future king. For who could any longer doubt that it would be Richard III, not Edward V who would go to his coronation in Westminster Abbey before many more weeks had passed?

I was unable to find either William Catesby or Francis Lovell, either of whom might have taken a message for me to His Grace. I didn't doubt but that they were there somewhere, but all my requests for someone to convey a message to them fell on deaf ears. I was equally frustrated in my attempts to locate Timothy Plummer. No one knew where he was or what he was about, only that he couldn't be found and that no one could be persuaded to seek him out.

'Take yourself off, you great oaf,' one of the stewards snapped. 'Can't you see that you and your petty concerns are of no importance here?'

'This is a child's life I'm talking about,' I yelled, losing my temper, but the man had already gone, bustling away through the press of bodies in answer to a summons demanding his immediate attention.

Piers grabbed my arm and pulled me outside into the equal chaos of Bishop's Gate Street Within. All the world and his wife seemed to be congregated in the roadway, and, finally, in desperation, I allowed him to steer me free of the crowds into the comparative Sabbath calm of the Poultry, where he forced me to sit down on the edge of a water trough.

'Now,' he begged, 'for God's sake, will you tell me what this is all about? Because not another step do I stir until you do! You've already dragged me halfway across London, running me off my feet till I'm so out of breath that my heart feels near to bursting, and with nothing more than a few garbled words and phrases I can't make head nor tail of.'

I stood up, pushing aside his restraining hands. 'Where can we hire a couple of horses?'

He choked with exasperation. 'Will you answer? Oh, never mind! We don't need to hire horses, you fool! Our own – the ones we came to London on – are in the stables at Baynard's Castle. Eating their heads off most likely.'

Of course! Dolt that I was, I had forgotten them. My brain simply wasn't functioning properly, so filled was it with my momentous discovery. For it was as though God had suddenly taken pity on me and, tired of trying to jog my memory, had hit me over the head with a truncheon.

Amphillis Hill's companion was none other than the woman I had encountered at the homestead west of London, on my way home to Bristol all those weeks ago; the woman with the young daughter and the unprepossessing husband. And the vicious dog so like the dead Beelzebub. Was she a member of the Sisterhood? I had no proof, but I was willing to wager a considerable sum of money that she was. I was also willing to wager that the homestead was where Gideon Fitzalan was being held prisoner.

I had hoped to convince Timothy of my reasoning and persuade him to raise a posse to go with me to the farm-house, but more momentous events had intervened. I should have to go alone unless Piers would accompany me. But first I should have to tell him all that I had discovered, and time was running short. Tomorrow was Midsummer Eve and if what I feared were true, Gideon would have to be moved to the capital before nightfall. I could hardly ask Piers for his help on so dangerous a mission without putting him in full possession of the facts.

I sat down again on the edge of the water trough and indicated that Piers should do the same.

When he had done so, his face alight with curiosity, I patted his hand and said, 'What I'm going to tell you, lad, you will probably find hard to believe. Indeed, you may refuse to believe it as both your aunts are involved.' I hesitated for a second or two, then went on, 'The reason you haven't seen me for the past three days is because someone tried to murder me.' He gasped and half rose from his seat, but I pulled him down again. 'We don't have a lot of time, so just sit still and listen. And however much you want to, don't interrupt me until I've finished.'

It was growing dusk before we finally sighted the homestead in its sheltering dell. For this, several factors were responsible. Firstly, Piers, understandably, but infuriatingly, had required a great deal of convincing that I wasn't making the whole thing up; that I hadn't accidentally fallen into the river after drinking too much ale at the Boar's Head on Thursday, and that my mind hadn't suffered as a consequence. Secondly, by the time he was at last persuaded of the truth, it was well past dinner time and he insisted on eating, declaring that no one could be expected to face danger on an empty belly. Thirdly, getting free of London was a nightmare, the normal traffic being engorged with troops of mounted men who suddenly seemed to have sprung from nowhere and who were themselves constantly hampered by groups of agitated and excited citizens discussing the morning's events in the middle of the roadway. And fourthly, it had taken me a considerable while to locate the house again, being unable to recall exactly where I had originally turned off the main track and taken to the bypaths. Moreover, the bright June day had grown overcast and the light had faded early.

And then, suddenly, just as I was desperately wondering if I should ever find the place again, there we were standing on the tree-lined ridge, looking down at its daub-and-wattle walls and roof of twigs and brushwood. This evening, there were no hens scratching for food in the courtyard, but I could hear the pig snorting and snuffling in its sty. I dismounted, indicating that Piers should do the same, and we tethered the horses to a tree a few yards further back and out of sight of the house.

As Piers strode forward to descend the slope, I flung out an arm to stop him. 'You fool!' I hissed. 'We can't just go marching up to the door. We have to think of some story to get us inside. And I've told you, there's a dog very like Beelzebub and just as vicious.'

Piers then proceeded to take my breath away by flinging off my restraining arm and saying loudly, 'I'm not afraid of a poxy dog even if you are, Roger!' and half-running, half-slithering down the bank into the courtyard.

I had, perforce, to follow, but I drew my knife as I went and was hardly surprised when the door of the homestead opened and the great beast I had encountered weeks earlier bounded out, fangs bared and its malicious little eyes gleaming evilly.

'Piers, beware!' I yelled at the top of my voice, and was preparing to launch myself forward in a valiant attempt to protect the mad fool when I was brought up short by the most amazing sight. Piers simply raised his right hand, the first finger extended upwards, then slowly lowered it, at the same time emitting a piercing whistle whose volume sank with the finger. As it did so, the dog crouched on the ground, slobbering out of the corners of its great jaws, and grovelled on its belly.

'How on earth . . .?' I was beginning when the woman, still in the decent Sunday clothes I had seen her wearing that morning, when she had been talking to Amphillis, appeared in the doorway. Then she started forward, her first look of angry suspicion turning rapidly to smiles.

'Pernelle, my dear, what on earth are you doing here? Nothing's amiss, is it? All's well for tomorrow night?'

Pernelle? *Pernelle?* And suddenly I remembered Rosina once addressing Piers as 'Perry'. I had thought the name a little strange, but had dismissed it as an affectionate diminutive. Which, of course, it had been, but of a female name! And in the flicker of an eye, certain facts began to resolve themselves. First of all, Piers's insistence on never sharing a bed or a room with other people started to make sense (twice during our journey we had stopped to relieve ourselves, and each time he had disappeared into the bushes with what I considered to be modesty taken to extremes). Secondly, those recurring dreams about Eloise Gray had been trying to tell me what, deep inside me, I had already known but failed to recognize: that Piers was a woman masquerading as a boy. And the third fact which stood out like a sore, pulsating thumb, was that she was one of them, one of the infamous Sisterhood, and that I had walked blindly into a trap from which I would be fortunate to escape with my life.

I turned to run. Immediately, at a word from Piers – Pernelle! – the dog was up and barring my way, saliva dripping from its bared teeth, its whole body quivering with hatred. I guessed that a command from either woman would be enough to set it at my throat.

'My dear,' I heard Piers – Pernelle – say, 'let's go inside. There's a great deal I have to tell you. But first, has the boy been safely got away?'

The other woman nodded. 'John took him to London in the cart late this afternoon.'

'Still drugged?'

'Still drugged and concealed under some sacking and a load of cabbages. I sent the girls as well. I thought an officious gatekeeper less likely to search the cart – and considering this morning's events, everyone in London is probably as jumpy as a cat – if they were with their father.' She glanced towards me. 'But who's this? I seem to recall his face from somewhere. Yes! Now I have it. He was here, snooping around, several weeks ago. John was suspicious of him to begin with, but then we decided he was harmless.' The hazel eyes narrowed. 'Can it be that we were wrong?'

'Very wrong,' was the grim reply. 'But let's go inside and I'll tell you all about it.'

Half an hour had gone by and I was sitting in the only chair the cottage afforded. This fact, however, had nothing to do with the women's concern for my comfort. It simply meant that my arms could be pulled around its back and my wrists lashed together with rope. A foot or two away, its wicked little eyes fixed almost unblinkingly on my face, lay the dog, ready to spring if I so much as moved a muscle.

Pernelle – for as such I was now forced to think of Piers – had finished her story and was easing her throat with some of our hostess's ale, regarding me mockingly as she did so, understanding how parched I must be. But I refused to beg a drink and tried to ignore my raging thirst.

Pernelle knew this, of course, and grinned at her companion, whom she addressed as Margaret.

'Roger's very stubborn. And he's nigh impossible to kill. I've tried twice already so I should know.' She shifted on her stool so that she could see me better. 'Oh yes, I'm the executioner, not Amphillis. Amphillis hasn't the stomach for it.

Whatever my aunt told this Owlgrave woman you mentioned, she was simply protecting me. After all, why would she trust someone who has left the Sisterhood and might decide, in the future, to betray us? I killed Gregory Machin.' She turned momentarily back to her friend. 'It frightened me half to death, I can tell you, when he walked away into his room and bolted the door, even though he did seem more than a little dazed and disorientated. Imagine my relief when I discovered that he was in fact dead!'

'Yes, indeed,' the other agreed with a shudder.

Pernelle turned again to me. 'I was the one who attacked you outside your chamber.' She touched the disfiguring bruise down the left-hand side of her face. Her voice hardened and she sneered. 'Fortunately, you were easy to fool. You believed me when I said I'd walked into a door. Just as when you thought I'd hurt my foot when you saw Margaret here going into the sewing room to speak to Amphillis.' The sneer became more pronounced. 'The bigger the body, the smaller the brain. You large men are so easy to dupe.'

'And the blow over the head in the room beneath St Etheldreda's crypt?' I asked.

Pernelle grinned malevolently. Still in her boy's clothes, it was difficult to remember that she wasn't really Piers.

'No, unhappily I didn't have that pleasure. If you remember, you'd left me behind in the Boar's Head eating my dinner. That was Aunt Etheldreda, which is why you survived. Her arm doesn't have the force of mine. Had I hit you then, you wouldn't have survived the water. You'd have been dead before your body left the drain. But I did go to the Rattlebones.' Her expression sharpened. 'Incidentally, where exactly were you last night?'

It was my turn to curl my lip, but I said nothing.

This intransigence annoyed her and she half-rose from her stool, an ugly look on her face, but the other woman interrupted by asking, 'What are we going to do with him? Kill him? But I don't want the body disposed of here. From what you've told me, if he really is an agent of the Lord Protector, his disappearance will cause a stir and there's bound to be a hue and cry. The trail might well lead to us. John can look out for himself, but I've the girls to think of.'

Pernelle got to her feet. 'Oh, I'm in no hurry to get rid of him. He can wait. I'll think of something later. Meanwhile, we've tomorrow to concern us and there's still a lot to do to prepare for the ceremony. John knows to take the boy straight to St Etheldreda's Church?'

'Of course. Your aunt will be waiting for him?'

'Yes. He and the girls will stop the night with her. It's all arranged. Three of the Sisterhood will stay with the boy in the underground chamber, administering more of the drug if he seems like waking. You've had no trouble with him?'

'None. We did as we were told. If he stirred, we forced more of the potion down his throat before he had time to recover consciousness. That apothecary's assistant you recruited certainly knows how to concoct a potent brew.'

I caught my breath. Could it be Naomi they were talking of? I remembered the sprig of birch twigs pinned to her bodice, but that was commonplace at this time of year. I prayed for Julian Makepeace's sake that it wasn't true, but without much hope of having my prayer answered. Naomi was just the sort of giddy young woman to be easily influenced and convinced of her own importance. Moreover, she had access to all of Julian's drugs, and I wouldn't put it past her to have picked his brains without his realizing why she needed the information. And indeed, why would he suspect her of any nefarious dealing?

'So what do we do now?' the woman called Margaret went on anxiously. 'Are you leaving him with me?' She nodded in my direction.

'No. I need you in London. There are horses outside. If we ride hard, we may reach the gates before curfew. If not, there are ways in and out of the city if you know them.' Pernelle laughed suddenly and stretched her arms above her head. 'You know, Aunt Rosina couldn't believe her luck when Lady Fitzalan asked her to be nurse to young Gideon. The seventh son of a seventh son! She knew the time must come when we could make use of him. It's been a long and patient wait in the cold and gloomy north, but the gods have moved at last. If you believe in them and make them sacrifice, the Old Ones never fail you.'

Her friend ignored this. 'If I come to London with you, what happens to him?' she demanded.

Pernelle laughed again, a sound that increasingly made me break into a sweat. Why had I never noticed before that there was a hint of madness in it?

'He can stay here until we return the day after tomorrow. He can't escape. Even if he could manage to get his hands free, the dog won't let him move.' She smiled at me. 'He's a brother of Beelzebub. He's from the same litter.' The smile grew even more pronounced. 'Margaret is Nell Blancheflower's sister. I shall have something to tell her on our journey.' She turned to the dog, pointed a finger at me and uttered the one word, 'Guard!'

The vicious brute growled and bared his teeth. I shivered inwardly. I had seen what his brother was capable of and I didn't fancy my throat being torn apart.

Pernelle turned once more to her friend. 'Hurry,' she said. 'Get your cloak. We must be going. We'll see you again, Roger. The day after tomorrow!'

I must, in spite of my agonizing discomfort, have fallen into an uneasy, nightmarish doze, because the light now coming through the cottage window was rosy with the first feeble rays of the rising sun. For a moment or two, I stared around me, unable to get my bearings, before the pain in my legs, my wrists, my bladder brought me once more fully to my senses. My distress, after so many hours, was acute enough to convince me that another day and night of this torment would very likely kill me. Was this what Piers – Pernelle – had planned? Death by slow torture?

My throat was so parched that I could barely swallow, every joint screamed out in pain, cramp had both legs in its grip. My bowels, like my bladder, were full and would shortly humiliate me even further by emptying themselves. I should stink as badly as the room in general where the dog, un-hampered by any such inhibition, had fouled the rush-strewn floor throughout the night.

Once more, I made a desperate attempt to free my wrists. In a second the creature was up and baring its teeth, but so long as I remained still, I guessed it wouldn't attack me. I recalled my earlier assessment of its character; that it was a stupid animal who would slavishly obey orders, but whose enterprise and initiative had been eroded by cruelty and lack of affection. In that moment, I almost wished it would attack. I felt that death would be welcome. There was no hope of escape. The homestead was so isolated that nothing and no one ever seemed to pass that way. No sound disturbed the silence except the soughing of the wind in the trees . . .

It was with total astonishment therefore, that I saw the door of the cottage slowly opening. Seconds later, the daughter of the house, the young girl I had seen weeks before trying to escape the clutches of her mother, stepped across the threshold.

'Hello, who are you?' she asked, staring at me in astonishment.

TWENTY

'The dog!' I croaked in a voice I barely recognized as my own. 'Beware the dog!'

The brute had risen to its feet at the opening of the door and now stood facing the child, hackles raised and teeth bared in a way that made me tremble with fear. She, however, seemed entirely unperturbed.

'I'm not afraid of him!' was the scornful reply. Pointing one small, rosy finger at the animal, she yelled, 'Lie down and go to sleep!'

And to my utter amazement, the beast did just that. It stretched its full length among the rushes and closed its eyes. A moment later, it was snoring.

Meanwhile, the girl had advanced into the room and was studying my face intently. 'I know who you are,' she announced. 'You're that man who was here – oh! – a long time ago when my sister was ill. Why have you come back?' But she spoke without curiosity and evinced no further interest when I ignored the question.

'My hands are tied,' I whispered hoarsely. 'Can you find a knife and cut me free?'

Without another word, she fetched a large, wicked-looking blade from the cooking bench and hacked through the rope which bound me. I regret to say that I didn't even stop to thank her, but staggered outside to the lean-to privy which I had noticed yesterday at the back of the cottage and then, when I finally emerged, to the barrel of rainwater where I bathed my face and badly bruised wrists. Finally, as the sun lifted clear of the horizon and the dawn chorus sounded ever louder from the neighbouring trees, I stretched my limbs and filled my lungs with the cold, sweet morning air.

When I returned to the cottage, this remarkable child was calmly filling two beakers from a jug of her mother's home-brewed ale. She pushed one towards me and I swallowed the contents gratefully.

'Aren't you supposed to be in London?' I queried.

She nodded and shrugged her thin shoulders. 'I got bored sitting on that cart with my sister and a load of cabbages and that stupid boy who's been living here for the past two weeks. So, when my father wasn't watching I escaped. I knew he wouldn't come looking for me because he had to be in London by yesterday evening. I heard Mother tell him so and he mostly does as she says. I shall get whipped for it,' she added philosophically, 'but I'm used to that. I'm always escaping. I was escaping that day you were here. One day, when I'm a bit older, I'll escape for good.'

'What's your name?' I asked.

'Albia. What's yours?'

'Roger. Who was the boy who was here, do you know?'

'No. He was no fun.' Her tone was contemptuous. 'He did nothing but sleep, like I told you, or when he was awake he wouldn't eat and just grizzled and cried for someone called Rosina.'

My heart went out to Gideon. Little did the poor young devil know that the person he was crying for was not his friend and protector, but one of the people responsible for all the evil which had befallen him. I decided there and then that whatever punishment was coming to Rosina Copley – and it would not be pleasant – she deserved every second of it.

'I must be on my way,' I said, and again this strangely incurious child nodded her head.

But she was eminently practical, too. 'If you're hungry, there's bread and cheese.'

I realized that I was, very hungry. And I also realized that after all I had undergone in the past few days, my limbs were like lead and my head felt as if it were stuffed with old rags.

'Thank you,' I said.

While we ate, I asked Albia if she knew anything about the young woman who dressed as a boy.

'Oh, her!' My youthful companion was dismissive. 'She's only been here once or twice. Since the boy came, so I think she must be something to do with him. She's strange. She says she doesn't care for men, but she dresses like one. That's

stupid. But Mother liked her very much. Father was angry
about it, I don't know why.'

I didn't enlighten her and we finished our meal in silence.
Indeed, I had a job to stay awake, especially after another
two beakers of ale. Consequently the sun was rising in the
sky when I finally climbed out of the hollow to the ridge
above and set out on the long walk back to London. The
horses had been taken, of course, by Piers – Pernelle – and
the woman Margaret, and Albia had confirmed that the
carthorse was the only beast of burden that her father owned.
My hope must lie in some friendly carrier giving me a ride.

I awoke with a start to instant awareness and the horrified
realization that the light was fading. I knew at once what
had happened.

I had found the path leading to the main track with none
of the difficulty I had experienced going in the opposite
direction the previous day. The track itself was busy as
always, and there was no dearth of carts heading for the
capital. But the drivers were a singularly surly bunch and
not one of them was prepared to offer me a ride in spite of
my many appeals to their better natures. Two whom I physically attempted to halt by clutching at their horses' reins
were most abusive, and one even caught me a stinging blow
across the shoulders with his whip. A couple of others showed
me the two-fingered devil's horn and consigned me verbally
to the fires of Hell, while the rest simply ignored me or
pretended not to hear.

Shortly after noon, when the sun was directly overhead and
at its hottest, I stopped at a wayside cottage for a further drink
of ale which, on reflection, was probably a grave mistake. If
my limbs had felt like lead earlier on, they now rebelled altogether. My legs obstinately refused to obey my brain even
on the increasingly rare occasions when my brain was capable
of giving them orders. Three times I stumbled and nearly fell,
but the fourth time I measured my length on the ground and
my bruised and battered body insisted on staying there. I had
just enough energy and will-power remaining to haul myself
behind a large brake of gorse, out of sight of the highway,
before falling into a deep and dreamless sleep.

It was from this no doubt healing, but unfortunate, slumber that I had now awakened to discover that it was almost dusk. I had no idea how far I still was from London, but I knew that the hour was advanced and that it must be almost curfew. I scrambled to my feet and staggered back to the road which now boasted only a handful of people, late travellers like myself.

I caught one of them by the elbow. 'How far is it to London?' I asked, waiting with bated breath for his answer.

'About a mile, by my reckoning.' He turned and looked at me. 'I shouldn't try making it tonight,' he advised. 'There's a little inn I know of 'bout a furlong further on. I'm going t' rack up there for the night. If you've any sense, you'll do the same. If you don't mind my saying so, you don't look too good.'

A mile! I knew that normally my pace was roughly two miles an hour which, at the best of times, would mean another half-hour's walking, and even that might be too late. (Unlike Piers-Pernelle, I had no knowledge of where one might breach the walls after the gates were closed.) I stared at the speaker in dismay.

'I have to reach London tonight,' I said.

He shrugged. 'Well, you might get there before curfew, I suppose, if you hurry. But if you'll pardon me saying so, you don't look like you could hurry. If you want the truth, you look like a man who's none too steady on his feet. You'd far better come with me to this inn I told you of. I'll give you my arm.'

I shook my head. 'Thank you, but I must get to London.'

He gave another shrug and washed his hands of me. 'In that case, I'll be getting along. If you want to kill yourself . . .'

A minute later, he was just a speck in the distance and I was left alone on a highway that now seemed completely deserted.

'Look, God,' I said desperately, 'you'll have to do something – and something spectacular – if you want me to save this child. I know I've been stupid and obtuse, ignoring or not understanding the hints you've given me. But let's face it, that's nothing new. You must realize after all these centuries that you may have made us in your own image, but you didn't give us your mind or brain. So, if you could . . .'

I never finished the sentence. My silent prayer was interrupted by the sound of hoof beats, at first in the distance but then accompanied by the sight of a rider in the saddle of a great bay mare approaching at a shocking speed. Indeed, man and beast were almost upon me before I gathered my wits sufficiently to leap into their path, clutching at the animal's reins. With a shouted curse, the horseman swerved to avoid me and, convinced he was being attacked by footpads, would have ridden me down had he not, suddenly and by the grace of God, recognized me just at the very moment that I recognized him.

William Catesby!

'God's toenails!' he fumed as the horse came to a plunging halt not a yard from me. 'Do you want to get yourself killed, Master Chapman?' He uttered a few choice epithets before taking a closer look at me and stopping short. 'What's the matter, man? You look like death.'

'Take me up behind you,' I begged. 'I'll tell you as we go.'

We made it to the Lud Gate just as darkness fell and the gate was about to be closed.

'We'll go first to Baynard's Castle,' the lawyer said, 'and get reinforcements. We can't tackle these she-wolves on our own.' He hesitated before adding defiantly, 'King Richard has moved there to be with his mother. Queen Anne is staying for the moment at Crosby's Place.' The die was well and truly cast then. The duke's closest adherents were already referring to him as monarch. Catesby added, 'Hold on tightly. Let's go.'

But we were going nowhere. It was Midsummer Eve, the Eve of St John the Baptist. We had forgotten the Marching Watch.

Thousands of citizens had been assembling in St Paul's churchyard since mid-afternoon, and hundreds of shops all over the city had closed early so that masters and apprentices alike could take part in the spectacle. The procession, headed by members of the twelve great livery companies were just now moving off towards Cheapside followed by the guilds in all their glory of scarlet and gold. Everywhere was light as hundred upon hundreds of cressets illumined the scene. These iron baskets at the end of long poles, each containing burning wood and coals, were carried by poor men of the city especially chosen for the occasion. Every man was given a straw hat and a painted badge (proudly worn and then stored away to show his grandchildren at some future date) and beside him walked another poor man, similarly attired, carrying a bag of coals for refuelling.

The heat and light generated by these cressets was overwhelming, but as nothing to the noise that assaulted the ears from what sounded like thousands of trumpets, pipes and drums – but were probably less than a hundred in all. It was the enthusiasm of the players that created the din. Lines of armed men guarded the processional route and the flames of bonfires leapt and warmed the crowds at every crossroad. Earlier in the day, women and children had been out in the surrounding fields picking armfuls of flowers and greenery – green birch, fennel, St John's Wort and others – to make garlands and decorate the houses. Streamers and tapestries hung from every window of those folk who could afford them, while tables groaning with food and drink stood outside the houses of the rich, each man vying with his neighbours to outdo the rest. And in the midst of all this, the Midsummer Queens of each ward were carried shoulder-high, crowned with birch leaves.

Finally, just as it seemed that the splendour had reached its zenith, came the Mayor's Watch with Mayor Edmund Shaa mounted on a magnificent roan, his armoured swordbearer riding before him, two mounted attendants behind and torch-bearers on either side. The crowds exploded with excitement.

Every street, alleyway and lane appeared to be blocked with a solid mass of people, moving more slowly than the procession itself because of other diversions.

Catesby said despairingly, 'We'll never get through these crowds, at least, not on horseback.' He signalled to me to dismount, then followed suit. The mare was already showing the whites of her eyes and shied nervously at a more than usually ear-splitting burst of sound. The lawyer went on, 'You'll have to try to get to Dowgate on foot. Meantime, I'll lead Dorcas round the long way to Baynard's Castle, south by Old Change and Lampard's Hill and then turn west along Thames Street. I'll be with you again as soon as I can. Don't do anything foolish.' And with that, he was gone, swallowed up by the crowds and leaving me fuming.

Don't do anything foolish, indeed! Easy enough to say, but I was always finding myself in desperate situations thanks to my involuntary involvement in the duke's affairs. No! Not the duke's any more. The king's!

I took a deep breath and began to shoulder a path through the press of hot and sweating bodies, their owners already high on the excitement of the occasion, but also starting to get high in another sense, on all the free wine and potent cuckoo-ale that was on offer. Women were becoming shrill, men raucous and both belligerent. My determined efforts to forge a way between them soon met with an aggression that threatened my safety long before I reached my destination. But there was one good thing; my anxiety for young Gideon Fitzalan seemed to have given me a renewed strength of which, an hour earlier, I would have deemed myself incapable. The result was that I was able, finally, to outstrip the crowds and turn into Bucklersbury, head south down Wallbrook and east into Candlewick Street much sooner than I had expected. And a very few moments after, the mouth of the alleyway connecting the street with Dowgate Hill yawned on my right.

I plunged along it, my heart hammering in my chest, but taking comfort from the fact that only the length of Thames Street, at the bottom of the hill, now separated me from Baynard's Castle. I prayed fervently that Catesby had managed to get there with even less hindrance than I had encountered.

As I approached the church, I noted that Etheldreda Simpkin's house was in complete darkness, the candle which most people put in their windows to guide travellers after dark unlit. Cautiously, I tried the handle of the church door.

It was locked.

I should have been prepared for this, but for some reason it took me by surprise. For what seemed like an eternity – in reality no more than three or four seconds – I stared at the iron ring in the palm of my hand and decided that that was it then. There was no more I could do. But suddenly, very faint and far off, I thought I heard a cry. A child's cry. A cry of fear and horror. Whether I really heard it or whether I imagined it I have never been quite sure, but it spurred me into action.

The door of St Etheldreda's was old, the wood splintering in places, in others already rotting. Exerting all my strength, I hurled my whole weight against it, once, twice, three times. And at the fourth attempt, one of the planks split from its neighbour, leaving a sufficient gap for me to squeeze through.

The church itself was deserted, but I had expected that. Whatever was happening, was taking place in the chamber below the crypt. I considered lighting a candle, but decided against it. I knew my way sufficiently by now to risk the comforting cloak of darkness, so I made my way behind the altar, felt for the rope and lifted the trapdoor which fell open with its usual thud.

I stood stock still, listening, my heart in my mouth, waiting to see if the noise was loud enough to have attracted attention. Nothing happened, so I proceeded to descend the stairs into the crypt. The sound of the Wallbrook gushing along its underground bed was loud in my ears and I shivered, recalling the coldness of its water as it emptied itself into the Thames.

Carefully, my eyes now well accustomed to the gloom, I picked my way between the accumulated rubbish of other people's lives to the door which led to the lower chamber; that chamber which had once, centuries ago and if local lore were to be believed, been the Roman Temple of Mithras. It flashed across my mind that it, too, might be locked, in which case there was nothing further I could do until help arrived. This sturdy door with its iron studs had been carefully maintained and repaired. It would need a battering ram to demolish it.

I found that the hand I had extended towards the latch was trembling, and that with half my mind I was desperately hoping that the door was locked, thus relieving me of all further responsibility. But then there came another scream, high pitched and full of terror, and there was no possibility this time of it being in my imagination. This was real. My blood seemed to freeze in my veins.

I pushed up the latch without even stopping to consider any personal danger and charged down the half-dozen steps into the room below.

It was like a scene from a nightmare, and even now, all these years on and myself an old man who has seen much evil in his life, it still haunts my dreams and wakes me in the night, sweating with fear. At first my eyes were dazzled by the light that came from a dozen or more candles all concentrated in one area of the room. Shadows flickered menacingly over the damp, moss-encrusted walls and plunged the corners of the chamber into darkness. For a moment or two I was blinded, coming as I had from the gloom of the crypt into this blaze of flame and smoke, but as my sight cleared, I saw with mounting horror that there was a makeshift altar set against the far wall and to this was bound the body of a young boy, no longer drugged into blessed unconsciousness but fully awake and aware of what was happening. And grouped about him were figures robed in white, each face hidden behind a hideous bird mask of the kind used at Christmas and Easter mummings, while the figure standing closest to the altar wore a cockerel's head. And in the cockerel's upraised hand was a wicked-looking, long-bladed knife.

Somebody shouted – and I realized a second later that it was me.

I threw myself forward, reaching desperately for that hand before it could plunge downwards into its victim's heart, but if I had recovered my powers of speech and motion, so had others. Robed figures suddenly hemmed me in on all sides and I could hear the sounds of their fury hissing behind the masks.

'Kill him!' came a muffled shout in a voice that, in spite of the distortion, I recognized as Rosina Copley's.

'Hold him!' someone else commanded, and the grip on both my arms tightened.

The figure at the altar – which I could now see was nothing more than a double row of planks from the crypt, piled on top of one another and lashed together with rope – advanced towards me, knife held high, the light from the candle-flames reflected in its steel and giving the eerie impression that it was already covered in blood. Exerting all my strength, fear and horror lending me the energy of ten, I tore free of my captors and looked around me for a weapon. For a heart-stopping moment I could see nothing.

'God!' I whispered feverishly. 'Help me!'

Almost at once, a flicker of light from an errant candle-flame, blowing sideways in a sudden draught of air, illumined the statue of St Etheldreda brought down from the church and placed on a ledge of rock close to the 'altar'; a good woman whose name, story and feast day had been appropriated by an evil sisterhood for their own bloodthirsty ends. I lunged and as I grabbed the statue, I realized with relief that not only was it made from heavy plaster but it was also weighted in the base (either to discourage theft or to prevent it being easily toppled). Grasping it by its head (a sacrilege for which I felt sure the saint would forgive me) I lashed out, catching my nearest assailant a stunning blow to the side of her chin. She fell like a stone, taking the woman directly behind her with her and pinning her temporarily to the ground.

Immediately all was uproar. The rest of the women, mad with fury, struggled to reach me where I stood with my back to the wall, lashing out with my improvised club. But it was the one with the knife I had to watch, the one I was convinced was Pernelle; my old friend Piers whose swaggering and swearing had always seemed a little unnatural and which, together with my recurring dreams of Eloise Gray, should have apprised me of the truth much sooner. Her reach was longer than that of the other women, and twice I felt the blade nick my face before managing to hit it away. To add to the confusion and general nightmarish quality of the scene, the terrified child was screaming and trying to free himself from his bonds. Suddenly, one of the knots which bound his ankles came untied.

I saw it out of the corner of my eye as I swung again at one of the women – hitting off her mask whose strings had become loosened to reveal the plump, pretty features of Amphillis Hill – but so did Pernelle. With a cry of rage she turned away, leaving me to the frenzied attentions of the others and raised the knife.

I remember yelling 'No!' at the top of my voice, but in

the event my cry was lost as the chamber door burst open
and dozens of armed men in the Gloucester livery poured
down the steps, swords and daggers drawn ready, if needs
be, for use. After which I have only a hazy recollection of
what happened, largely due to the fact that I disgraced myself
by fainting yet again and did not recover consciousness until
I had been safely conveyed back to Baynard's Castle.

I came to to find the duke himself – no, the king himself
– bending solicitously over me. A cool hand was laid on my
brow.

'I understand I have to thank you once again, Roger, for
your services,' he said, smiling. 'You see, I was right to put
you in charge. You have never failed me yet, even when it
means putting your own life in danger. And this time you
have also saved the life of a young boy, a very precious
thing, and averted a very unpleasant scandal at the beginning of a new reign.' I noticed that he carefully avoided
saying whose reign. 'So how can I reward you?'

I was in no doubt about that. 'By just letting me go home,
Your Grace,' I said.

It wasn't as simple as that, of course. Nothing ever is.

As a reward, I was to be given a place, humble and obscure
maybe, but a place nevertheless in Westminster Abbey so
that I might witness Richard's coronation, and afterwards in
Westminster Hall for the coronation banquet. As both these
events were fixed for Sunday, the sixth of July, it meant that
I had to kick my heels in London for almost another two
weeks. This enforced delay, however, was alleviated by the
discovery that I was being treated like a hero, and that even
Timothy Plummer accorded me an uncharacteristic respect.

I did not enquire what was happening to those members
of the Sisterhood, those Daughters of Albion, who had been
arrested at the church. I'm a coward insomuch as while I
uphold the due process of law, I'm reluctant to contemplate
its workings, hideous as so many of its punishments are. I
did ask if anyone of the Daughters was named Naomi, and
when the reply was in the negative, I went so far as to visit
Julian Makepeace, making him free of all that had happened
and what I had learnt. He was appalled and I have reason

to think that he sent Naomi away into the distant countryside for her own safety. But I felt sure that whatever had
been between them was finished.

Three days after my ordeal I stood pressed against one
wall of the great hall of Baynard's Castle while a great
concourse of nobles, both spiritual and temporal, packed it
to capacity and listened to the Duke of Buckingham make
the case for offering Richard the crown. And when, finally,
the duke himself appeared at the head of the marble staircase, accompanied by his mother (who looked, I may say,
far more triumphant than he did) they went wild with enthusiasm, waving their hats in approval and falling to their knees
while their spokesmen – the Archbishop of Canterbury and
half-a-dozen others – begged my lord, with tears in their
eyes, to accept the throne.

He made a little show of reluctance for modesty's sake,
but he would have been a fool to carry it too far. The upshot
was that he descended the stairs, mounted his horse, White
Surrey, which had been led indoors, and rode off to
Westminster Hall where, so I was later informed, he seated
himself on the marble chair of the King's Bench and formally
laid claim to the crown as his father's rightful heir. Again,
the acclamation of the crowd was overwhelming. He then
sent for Sir John Fogge, a close relative of the Woodvilles
and one of his own deadliest enemies, gave him the hand of
friendship and appointed him Justice of the Peace for Kent,
a gesture of reconciliation which the crowd cheered to the
echo. (But over which those of us who knew my lord well
shook our heads despairingly. It was the same old story: he
was clever, but too often not wise, letting his heart rule his
head.) He then rode on to the abbey to make an offering at
the shrine of St Edward the Confessor.

On the eve of his coronation, I was among the cheering,
excited crowds who watched him ride from the royal apartments of the Tower to Westminster, dressed in blue cloth of
gold embroidered all over with golden pineapples and with
a purple velvet mantle trimmed with ermine. His seven pages
wore white cloth of gold and crimson satin. The overall effect
was magnificent. Two things bothered me, however. First,
Queen Anne was being carried in a litter, obviously too frail

to ride the distance on horseback. Second, the Duke of
Buckingham was also wearing blue, blazoned all over with
a design of golden cartwheels. There was a similarity between
his and the king's costume that I found vaguely disturbing.

The following day, I was squashed into a corner of the
abbey to watch the crowning. (Well 'watch' is an exagger-
ation. I didn't see much of the actual ceremony from where
I stood, but it was described to me by various people afterwards.) And then it was off to Westminster Hall where I,
along with hundreds of others, gorged ourselves on enough
food to have kept the entire population of Bristol in victuals
for a month. Probably longer. I have never, before or since,
seen so many varieties of soup, joints of meat, roasted birds,
pies, jellies, syllabubs, spiced fruits, nuts, fish – fried, boiled
and baked – all crowded together on one table at the same
time. As for the wines, I never knew the names of a quarter
of them. All I do know is that it took me two whole days
and nights to recover.

Then I went home.